UNSPOKEN
FEAR

Books by Hunter Morgan

THE OTHER TWIN

SHE'LL NEVER TELL

SHE'LL NEVER KNOW

SHE'LL NEVER LIVE

WHAT SHE CAN'T SEE

UNSPOKEN FEAR

UNSPOKEN FEAR

HUNTER MORGAN

ZEBRA BOOKS
KENSINGTON PUBLISHING CORP.

PROLOGUE

It was an ordinary night after an ordinary day. Dinner. TV. To bed after the evening news. Toothpaste. Toothbrush. The bathroom mirror. The same reflection.

The voice that seemed to come out of nowhere was completely unexpected. It had come before, but not for a very long time, and then only as a whisper.

"Azrael."

No! The toothbrush fell. Hands clenched the edge of the sink as the image in the mirror blurred. Suddenly, the single-bulb light fixture seemed to glow brighter. So bright, it was blinding.

Pain. Excruciating pain. Not up to the task.

"Azrael."

The voice was louder this time; it couldn't be ignored. "Azrael, it is time."

Azrael, the Archangel of Death.

"Azrael, my will must be done."

The voice was so loud that it boomed, reverberating off the walls. It could no longer be resisted, and Azrael fell under the attack. Knees hit the dull linoleum. Hands clenched the skull cavity, trying to block out the light and the pain.

There was no need for struggle any longer. Azrael could not defy the command. Could not ignore the voice any longer.

The voice of God.

CHAPTER 1

The chain-link fence seemed tall to Rachel, taller than the last time she was here, and the coiled barbed wire on top appeared even more menacing than she remembered. No one could scale that wall, could they? Not after five years. Not scale it and survive.

Her sweaty hands gripped the Volvo wagon's steering wheel, and she glanced through the chain links of the ominous fence to the old barn in the distance. It had once held dairy cows but now served as a workshop for inmates. A sign on the end door read FURNITURE BARN.

"Mama?"

Rachel glanced up at the guard in the cement block tower in the distance. Even from the highway, she could see the rifle in his hands as he paced.

"My hands *awe* sticky. Mama!"

Rachel blinked and reached up to adjust the rearview mirror to see her daughter in the backseat of the car.

"Mama, I need a wipe." Mallory waved her starfish hands. "Mattie wants a wipe."

Rachel absently reached for a container of baby wipes on

the seat beside her, popped open the blue lid, and grabbed a handful. "Help Mattie," she told her daughter as she handed them over the seat.

Movement on the far side of the fence caught Rachel's eye, and her hands found the steering wheel again. Her knuckles turned white as she clenched it tighter, watching him walk toward her. He wasn't dressed in a teal jumpsuit as he had been the last time she had seen him. He was wearing ordinary jeans, sneakers, a faded green T-shirt. He carried a blue gym bag.

She suddenly felt sick to her stomach. She glanced up at the guard in the tower and swallowed the sour bile that rose in her throat.

"*Aw* done. *Aw cwean*, Mama," Mallory sang from the backseat with the innocence only a four-year-old could possess. She was completely oblivious to what was going on, why they were here at the Sussex Correctional Institute, and Rachel wanted to keep it that way. Forever, if she could.

"Fine," Rachel whispered, unable to take her eyes off him. He was approaching the open gate, almost free of the fence. "Just throw them down on the floor. We'll pick them up when we get home."

"Mama, you said—"

"I know, Mallory," Rachel snapped. She made herself breathe before she spoke again. "It's OK. Just throw them on the floor, sweetheart. We'll clean up the trash when we get home."

He turned the corner, came around the fence, and walked straight toward them. Through the windshield, even in the glare of the late-day sun, Rachel could see his handsome face clearly, the arch of his eyebrows, the tiny knot on his nose from when he had broken it when he was nineteen, the crinkles at the corners of his eyes. But he kept his gaze cast downward, never looking up at her or back toward the guard tower.

Rachel was afraid she was going to be sick. The stench of

the cold french fries coming from the backseat was almost overwhelming, and for a moment, she seriously considered shifting the car into first and taking off, leaving him there beside the road.

But she didn't move, and a moment later she heard the click of the car door's handle.

Hands on the wheel, she stared straight ahead as he climbed in and closed the door.

"Noah," she heard herself murmur.

"Rachel."

There was a moment of silence that seemed to stretch to the point that it might break. A thousand memories flooded Rachel, the smells, the tastes, the sounds of the life she had once shared with this man.

An erratic pounding on the leather seat behind them shattered the silence. Mattie, belted in beside Mallory beat on the car seat with meaty fists, making guttural sounds.

Noah just sat there, gym bag on his lap, staring straight ahead.

Rachel glanced in the rearview mirror, shifted the car into first, and eased off the grass onto the right lane of the highway. "Yes, I know," she said, readjusting the rearview mirror so she could see the car behind them. "I know, Mattie. It's Noah. Noah is home, isn't he?"

"It's OK, Mattie," Mallory soothed. "It's OK."

Rachel could see her sweet, round face in the rearview mirror as her head popped up.

"Mama, put the CD on. Mattie *wikes* the Arthur CD."

It was on the tip of Rachel's tongue to refuse. It was May and she was sick to death of listening to Arthur the Aardvark's holiday music, which had been in the CD player since Thanksgiving, but Mattie was still beating the car seat with his fists, still crying out in that harsh, rasping voice that had never spoken a word, to her knowledge, in thirty-eight years. Anything to prevent having to speak to her husband in the passenger seat beside her.

Ex-husband.

She hit play on the CD player in the dash, and the Hanukkah song blared from the speakers. Mallory began to sing in her baby voice that was not so babylike anymore, and Mattie quieted instantly. In the rearview mirror, Rachel could see him begin to play the notes with his fingers on an imaginary keyboard.

They rode a good five miles and into the next song before Rachel dared to look at Noah. Dared speak. "You could say something to Mattie. You have no idea how much he's missed you."

Noah pressed his lips together. "Thank you for coming for me."

"What was I supposed to do?" She spoke before she thought, turning east, off Route 113. "Tell you to walk your sorry ass home from prison?"

He glanced out the window at the picturesque small town they were passing through. "Nice language for a priest's wife."

"Ex-wife."

"Ex-priest," he trumped.

They were quiet again through another song, but Rachel refused to allow her thoughts to wander. She concentrated on the road, taking the Georgetown Circle, continuing to head east, and sang along with Mallory, knowing the ridiculous lyrics by heart. "We three kings ate boiling tar . . ."

Noah just stared out the window.

Several times she stole a glance at him; she couldn't see his brown eyes, didn't know what he was thinking. But then, it had been a very long time since she had been able to fathom anything Noah Gibson was thinking.

Rachel followed Route 9 to just west of Lewes and took a left, heading north. The countryside changed at once from small neighborhoods and businesses on the busy road to the beach, to pine woods and a rutted paved road barely wide enough for two cars to pass. Singing "It's Baxter Day!" louder than Mallory in the backseat, she took the left fork just over the bridge and headed into town. They passed the wooden sign, hand carved by Buddy Peterson, who made a decent living carving duck decoys and selling them at the beach resort souvenir shops. The sign announced WELCOME TO STEPHEN KILL with a date beneath it, 1698.

She drove down Main Street, passing turn-of-the-century Victorian houses that lined both sides, the small diner that served the best breakfast in the county, a new convenience store, and the post office housed in the old train station before Noah finally spoke up.

"Where we going?"

She signaled, turned, and pulled up under a giant beech tree, easing the hood of the car toward the crumbling red brick fence that surrounded the churchyard of St. Paul's Episcopal Church. Here, they had both been baptized as infants, married, buried their baby boys. It was the church where Noah had served as parish priest before life as they had once known it had ended.

She cut the engine and let her hands fall to her sides on the soft leather of the seat. "I thought you might like to visit your parents' graves. I know . . ." Her voice faltered, but she found it again. "I know it's been five years, but you never saw the headstones. I thought you—"

"No."

He was so abrupt that he startled Mallory into silence midnote. In the rearview mirror Rachel saw her little girl's lower lip tremble, and her hackles went up at once.

"Don't speak to me like that, Noah," Rachel whispered harshly under her breath. "Don't you *dare* speak to me like that, not after . . ." She looked away, not knowing how to finish the sentence.

"I'm sorry." He lowered his gaze to somewhere around his knees, his arms tightening around the gym bag. "I'm sorry, but I just want to go home. Is that so terrible, Rache?"

For a moment she sat there staring at the brick wall,

thinking of the simple headstones on the other side, listening to Arthur the Aardvark continue to belt out another Christmas song. Such an ethereal moment. . . . She still missed Joanne and Mark so much; she knew Noah had to miss them too.

But who was she to tell him the proper way to mourn, a mother who did not visit her own children's graves?

She started the engine and backed up, and she didn't speak again until they turned into the long, white, crushed oyster shell driveway that led up to the farmhouse where she and Mallory lived, less than three miles outside of town.

It was on the tip of her tongue, as she followed the familiar winding drive, to tell Noah that the grapevines that flanked both sides of the road looked good this year. She wanted to tell him that the new hybrid would make that excellent pinot noir his parents had dreamed of but had never seen realized. But she couldn't bring herself to speak again, not when she knew the place would be going up for sale soon, knowing she would soon be forced to take a serious look at the responses piled on her desk, unopened, that she'd received from the vineyards in Pennsylvania and New York she'd contacted concerning a job.

Noah closed his eyes, gripping the gym bag on his lap, unable to bring himself to look at the long, graceful lines of new, budding grapevines. He'd been dreaming about these orderly rows for days, weeks, months in anticipation of his release, and now he couldn't look at them. Would not. He had no right, not to the pleasure of the sight, not to any pleasure, just as he had no right to set foot on the holy ground of the churchyard.

The sound of a barking dog made Noah open his eyes. He knew that bark. *Chester.* To his amazement, he smiled. "He's still alive," he murmured.

"Yup. Still alive." Rachel pulled up in front of the detached garage that stood just beyond the cream and blue Victorian farmhouse. "Minus one leg." She threw the station wagon into park.

"Minus one leg?"

"Got *twapped*," the little girl in the backseat offered. It was the first time she'd spoken since he'd snapped at Rachel. "Dr. Mawy cut it off."

Noah glanced over his shoulder at the little cherub face. She had Rachel's green eyes. Rachel's child, she had to be. But not his, because his children, his and Rachel's, were lying in the churchyard beside his mom and dad.

A lump rose in Noah's throat, surprising him. Just when he thought the last shard of emotion, of feeling, had gone from him forever, he found another. "What happened to Chester?" he asked Rachel, not allowing himself to contemplate who had fathered Mallory.

Rachel had climbed out of the car and gone around to the other side to open the back door and let the little girl out of her car seat.

"Got *twapped* in a *muskwat twap*," Mallory told him matter-of-factly as she lifted her arms above her head to allow her mother to release her from the harness that belted her into her booster seat. Noah noticed she was wearing a pair of jean shorts with a pink tutu over them and a pair of fuzzy purple slippers.

Noah looked at Rachel. "Old Man Tewes still setting those illegal traps of his?"

"Was." She lifted the harness over the little girl's head, and the child scooted under her mother's arm and escaped out the door. "Till Snowden put him in jail." She reached for Mattie's seat belt and released it. "Go ahead, Mattie. Go up to the house with Mallory," she urged gently.

"Snowden has enough pull to throw a Tewes in jail?"

"I'd say so." She looked at him over the tan leather seat. "He's chief of police now."

"Snowden Calloway, chief of police?" Noah said it as much to himself as to Rachel. "Never thought that day would come."

She shrugged one shoulder. "Who said affirmative action would never hit Stephen Kill?"

Snowden Calloway was actually half black, born illegitimately to Tillie Calloway, the town's librarian, and a black man never identified, an indiscretion still considered an unpardonable sin in some small towns in southern Delaware. The citizens of Stephen Kill were subtle enough with their prejudice against Tillie for sleeping with a black man and Snowden for being one, but when Noah had returned home after college in California, he had realized that kind of prejudice could cut far deeper than outright bigotry.

"What happened to Chief Mears?" Noah still looked at Rachel over the backseat of the car. Somehow it offered some protection to him, serving as a buffer between him and the woman he had once known intimately. Once loved.

"Had a coronary over a stack of hotcakes at DJ's, triple bypass. He and Margaret moved to Florida more than a year ago." She climbed out of the car, slamming the door.

So much for the buffer.

But Noah sat a moment longer inside the Volvo, listening to the dog bark and Rachel call to Mattie, watching the pigtailed girl mount the front steps. Obviously, he couldn't sit here forever; he just wasn't sure what to do once he stepped outside.

The idea of freedom after more than five years of imprisonment was still pretty remarkable and more than a little bit scary.

"You coming?" Rachel hollered from the wraparound porch.

Noah opened the door to find the old Chesapeake Bay Retriever that had been his father's, chuffing eagerly, headed straight for him. To his amazement, the old dog was still leaping and bounding, despite his age and the amputation of his right rear leg.

"Hey, boy." Noah reached out to pat his head, then scratched behind his ears. The dog panted with obvious delight, plopping down on Noah's sneakers the way he always had. "Good boy, good Chester."

Noah looked up to see Mattie standing on the porch, watching him, his big hands dangling at his sides. He wore the same thing he'd been wearing the last time Noah saw him, the same thing he'd been wearing for the last twenty years, spring through fall, temperature permitting: a men's white Hanes T-shirt, khaki-colored Dickies work pants, no-name athletic shoes, and a navy ball cap. Any ball cap would do as long as it was navy.

The look Mattie gave him broke Noah's heart. Mattie's face rarely showed emotion, but Noah knew Mattie was hurting, hurting because of him. "Mattie, it's good to see you."

For years, it had been debated just how much Mattie McConnell understood because he had been born mentally handicapped. But Noah knew from experience that Mattie comprehended far more than he let on or others gave him credit for. Diagnosed as an idiot savant and only two years Noah's junior, Noah had grown up with him and, in time, had become his caretaker of sorts after the death of Mattie's father in an accident at the church. Noah and Mattie had been through a lot together, and even though Mattie was mute, they had found ways over the years to communicate. Noah owed Mattie more than he was offering right now, he knew that; he just couldn't bring himself to give more, and the look on Mattie's face conveyed the man's understanding of that fact, at least on some level.

"I missed you, Mattie," Noah said simply, walking toward the front steps with Chester dancing along beside him.

Mattie just stared with big, puppy brown eyes. He looked much older than the last time Noah had seen him. His face was craggier, his brown hair was sprinkled with gray, not un-like Noah's own hair, and he'd put on weight. He'd always been a big man at six feet tall and stocky, but now he seemed massive . . . soft.

"Missed me too, didn't you?" Noah wanted to reach out and hug him, but he couldn't bring himself to do it.

The screen door squeaked open, startling Noah, and he glanced up to see Rachel coming out of the house, a glass in each hand. "Tea?" She raised both hands.

Noah nodded.

"Go on inside, Mattie," Rachel said. "Go see Mrs. Santori. She has cookies for you and Mallory." When he hesitated, seeming torn between the cookies and Noah, Rachel lifted her chin in the direction of the screen door that had just slapped shut. "Go on, before Mallory eats them all."

Noah watched Mattie shuffle by him. "So Consuelo and Mateo are still here?"

She brushed past him, headed for the big rockers around the corner of the porch. "Still here. You don't think I could have done this alone, do you?"

She didn't look at him, but he saw her square her shoulders inside the slim, peach-colored T-shirt. She was thinner than he remembered her and somehow seemed more delicate, but her face was still the same. With her shoulder-length honey blond hair and green eyes, she was just as beautiful now at forty as she had been at fourteen, the first time he had kissed her.

"I suppose." He followed her to the chairs, dropped his gym bag, and sat down on the edge of his father's rocker, mostly because he didn't know what else to do. He was as nervous right now as he could ever remember being. Funny what time and murder and a prison sentence would do to a man.

Rachel set one of the glasses on a wooden table between the two chairs and took a sip as she slid into his mother's rocker.

"She's very pretty, you know. Mallory." He took the glass she had left for him and sipped the sweet tea. It was his mother's recipe.

"More important, she's smart," she said.

She looked at him, her eyes filled with a mixture of pride and something else he couldn't recognize. What was it? Fear? Fear of him? He certainly hoped not.

He held the dimpled, amber-colored glass between his hands, savoring its coolness, and gazed out over the vegetable garden in the side yard. It was no longer planted in rows the way his mother had, and his grandmother before her, but had been turned into raised beds instead. There wasn't much planted yet, but one of the beds had a plastic hothouse cover and he could see green seedlings poking through the soil. "I didn't know you had a daughter, Rache."

She glanced in the direction of the garden, sliding back in the chair and setting it in motion. "Because I didn't want you to."

He stared at the porch's plank floor painted gunmetal gray, not knowing how to respond. He wanted to ask her whose child Mallory was, of course, but considering the circumstances, he knew he had no right. He glanced at her left hand—no wedding band. The one he had given her with the Celtic love knot was long gone, of course, but it hadn't been replaced by another.

He was quiet for a moment, wanting to press her further, but instead he changed the subject. "Mattie's here with you. Does he come often?"

"He lives here."

"Lives here?" He met her gaze, just for a second, then glanced away.

Mattie had lived in the basement of the church, first with his father, then alone. He had been the St. Paul congregation's responsibility for years, but the day-to-day care had fallen to Noah, so just as Noah had failed Rachel, he had failed Mattie as well.

"He was devastated after your arrest. Inconsolable." Her voice was flat and without emotion—his beloved Rachel, who had once been so full of life, so full of emotion. Of joy. And he would have to live the rest of his life knowing he had done this to her.

"No one knew what to do with him," Rachel continued. "The new priest couldn't be held responsible, so the state social welfare system was called in. They put him in a group home on the west side of the county, but it didn't work out."

"Why not?"

"He kept running away. They moved him to another facility up in Kent County after he'd taken off twice more, thinking that if he didn't recognize landmarks, he'd stay put. He was missing three days, and somehow he found his way back to Stephen Kill. We still don't know how he got here, but he was dirty and scared."

"And so you took him in?"

"The state didn't know what to do with him. They were talking about some kind of home in New Jersey that sounded too institutional to me. It wasn't a place he could play the organ, and you know how much he needs that, so I convinced the state to allow me to have guardianship of him."

"That was good of you, Rachel."

She frowned. "It wasn't that hard. I mean, it wasn't like anyone else wanted him." She was quiet for a moment, lost in her thoughts. "He settled well here after a few false starts. We tried a regular bedroom in the house, but he didn't like it. There wasn't enough room for his shelves of Bibles, so we fixed up a nice space in the barn cellar; it looks just like the church basement." Her mouth turned up in a half smile. "Added some walls, because you know how open spaces scare him, a bathroom, some more electrical outlets, and a bed. It might not seem like much, but for Mattie—"

"It's home," he finished for her.

Then, again, there was silence between them. Both sipped their tea.

"Are . . . did you remarry?" he asked after a while. His voice sounded strange in his head. Ethereal and far removed.

"Nope." She continued to rock, sipping her tea. "Not like I've had a lot of time for dating. You know how much work this place is to keep up, and I've been doing it myself, Noah. I've been doing it myself for a long time. If it wasn't for the Santoris—"

"I know," he interrupted. "Thank you." It was lame, but he didn't know what else to say. He'd been living like a man floating beneath ice for so long that he felt numb. He didn't know how to express himself any longer. He wasn't even sure he had anything inside him left to express, either feelings or opinions.

She set down her glass. "I felt it was the least I could do for Joanne and Mark. It didn't seem right to let the place run down, not after they worked so hard for almost forty years. You'll get a better price this way when you sell."

"I'm not selling." He was startled by the sense of determination he heard in his voice.

"Not selling?" She sprang out of the chair and turned to lean back against the painted porch rail, sliding her hands into her jeans pockets. "What do you mean you're not selling?"

It was his turn to shrug. "I'm not selling. I need a job, obviously, now that I'm no longer employed on the road-cleaning crew with DOC." It was a lame joke. "I thought I would keep the vineyard. Continue to grow the grapes, maybe even start making wine again rather than just selling our grapes."

After his parents' murder, he hadn't been able to bring himself to start the fall winemaking process and had sold the grapes to a vineyard in southern Pennsylvania. By then, their second son Isaac was already dead and his life had begun to spiral out of control.

"You can't make wine," she said, looking at him as if he'd grown another head. "You're an alcoholic."

"I'll get a taster."

She groaned, gripping the wooden rail with both slender hands, and looked away. "That's a bad plan, Noah. An alcoholic should not surround himself with alcohol . . . not one who means to stay sober, at least."

He sat back in the rocker, even more determined now that he'd said it out loud. "Pretty decent hair shirt, if you ask me."

She looked at him, her green eyes angry. "I'm not going to sit here and watch you do this to yourself. I'm leaving. I've got several offers."

"I'm sorry to hear that." He leaned forward on his bony knees, lacing his fingers together, almost as if in prayer. But not in prayer. Not ever in prayer again.

"So that's it?" Rachel crossed her arms over her chest, looking away, then directly at him. "It's not even up for discussion?"

"Think they're going to give me my old job back at the church?" He was quiet for a moment, watching her. "Didn't think so," he said when she didn't answer.

"I thought you said you were sober and you wanted to stay that way."

"I am. I do. I will. I've already got info on when AA meets. Noon three days a week at the Elks' lodge. Once a week at St. Paul's of course, but I'm not sure that would be appropriate. There's also a group that meets at the Grange twice a week."

"And your sponsor approved of this idea?"

"No, but he's not offering me a job, either."

"Noah, this is crazy." Her hands fell to her sides and she took a step toward him. "You have a master's degree—"

"In divinity," he interrupted. "Not a lot of job opportunities for priests who have murdered."

"Don't say that." She closed her eyes.

"Why not? It's true. It's one of the things they teach you in AA—you have to admit to the truths no matter how painful they might be."

"I should go check on Mallory."

She started past him, and Noah stood abruptly, almost knocking into her. He went to raise his hand, to catch hers. He wanted to tell her again how truly sorry he was for what he had done, but the words sounded so pathetic, so inadequate, that he let her pass.

CHAPTER 2

Supper seemed long and more than a little awkward. Noah was thankful when Rachel excused herself from the table under the pretense of getting Mallory's bath started, leaving Noah and Mattie alone in the large eat-in kitchen to clear the table and load the dishwasher. Mrs. Santori had served the meal of baked chicken, fresh asparagus, and new potatoes but then excused herself for the evening to eat with her husband, as had been her routine for years. She had given Noah the cold shoulder since he'd arrived, remaining polite but aloof, but he told himself that was to be expected. He knew the sixty-year-old Mrs. Santori blamed him for his parents' deaths no matter what anyone else said.

For a moment Noah just sat there staring at the French country, blue and white checked wallpaper and listened to Mallory chatter as her mother led her away. He didn't know what was stopping him from getting up except that it had been a long time since he'd had a meal in which he could excuse himself without the approval of an armed guard.

He rose slowly, testing the waters, still half expecting a dozen pairs of eyes to glance his way. "So Mattie, I saw the organ in the living room. You're still playing on Sunday mornings, aren't you?" He stacked his dirty plate on Rachel's. The food had smelled delicious, the best in . . . well, five years, three months and seventeen days, but it had tasted like sawdust in his mouth. Neither he nor Rachel had eaten much.

Mattie rose slowly like a mountain from one of the delicate antique ladder-back chairs Rachel had refinished, taking his time as he placed his fork and knife carefully on his plate. Mattie was slow to learn, but once he had mastered something, he could do it over and over again in exactly the same way, day after day, year after year. He nodded.

"Good. I'm glad, because you know I always thought you played so beautifully. Quite a bit better than Mrs. Long; she's not always on key, is she?" Not expecting any type of response, Noah carried the two stoneware plates to the sink, balancing the *Incredibles* plastic child's plate on top. Apparently, his release from prison had not affected Mallory's appetite, as her plate looked as if it had been licked clean by the Chesapeake Bay Retriever currently waiting on the back porch to be let in.

Noah stood at the sink, scraped the scraps into the little covered pail on the counter, and rinsed off the plates. Mattie walked in his slow, lumbering, foot-scuffing manner from the table, left his plate on the counter, and shuffled back to the table to retrieve the iced tea glasses.

"Look, Mattie, I want you to know how sorry I am about all this. About leaving you so suddenly, staying away so long." Noah exhaled, struggling for the right words as he gazed over the sink, out the open window. It was almost dark, and he could see light seeping from the small rectangular cellar windows of the barn where Mattie slept. "And I know . . . I know you probably don't understand all that's happened, but I . . ." He looked over his shoulder at Mattie, who stood halfway between the table and the sink, a glass in each hand, staring at the floor in front of him.

Mattie was listening.

"What I did, Mattie, was wrong. It . . . it was terrible. Unforgivable." Noah's voice caught in his throat, and he gave himself a moment to recompose. "But I can't change what happened, you have to understand that. All I can do is move on from here, and I know you're angry with me, and you have every right to be, but . . . but I hope we can be friends again." He glanced at the man who was said to have an IQ of no greater than fifty points. "Truth is, I need you, Mattie. I need a friend. Bad. So you think you can do that?" Noah took the dirty glasses from his hand, trying to make eye contact with him. "Can you find it in your heart to be my friend again?"

Mattie slowly lifted his heavy-lidded gaze. He didn't nod yes, but he didn't shake his head no either.

Noah managed a smile. "You think about it, OK, buddy?"

Mattie shuffled back to the table to retrieve Mallory's plastic tumbler that matched the plate with the masked, caped cartoon figures on it. Noah turned back to the sink feeling a slight lifting in the heaviness he carried in his chest, a heaviness he'd been carrying so long that he'd grown far too used to its burden.

Mallory, seated naked in half a bathtub of water, grabbed a rubber shark and held it under the water, shaking it violently as if the animal were in the throes of a kill. "Who's the man, Mama?"

Rachel drew back, raising her hands, trying unsuccessfully to keep from getting splashed. "I told you, his name is Noah and this is his vineyard and his house."

"I thought the *vineyawd* was Grandma and Grandpa Heaven's."

"It was," Rachel answered patiently. She'd given up a year ago trying to explain it was Grandma and Grandpa *in* heaven and that heaven was not their surname. "But now it's Noah's."

Her little girl raised the toy shark out of the water, looking up with quite a serious face for a preschooler. "Does he want my *bedwoom?*"

Rachel looked away, shaking her head. "No."

"Is he going to sleep in *youwrs?*"

Mallory's innocent words stung, and Rachel struggled not to react. She was determined not to allow Noah, or what a mess he had made of their lives, to affect her daughter. "No, Mallory. He's going to sleep downstairs in the spare bedroom."

Mallory pushed the shark under the water again, making it swim toward a floating Barbie doll whose hair had been shorn by a pair of blunt-nosed safety scissors guaranteed not to cut anything but paper. "*Thewre's* a lot of junk in the *spawre woom.*"

"*Room*, Mallory. *R*oom, and I'll clean it out, OK?" Rachel reached for the no-tears shampoo that smelled of pineapple and mango. Mallory's preschool teacher had suggested it was time the little girl begin seeing a speech therapist; Rachel wasn't ready to do that, not yet, but it was tense times like this when Mallory's lack of ability to pronounce Rs and Ls made her a little crazy. "Did you wash your hair?"

Mallory tried to ease the shark's jaws around the Barbie's head, but when it didn't fit, she grabbed the doll and popped its head inside the shark's mouth. "Is Noah gonna be my daddy?"

"No. No, of course not. What makes you say such a thing?" Rachel squirted some shampoo on top of the little, wet, blond head and began to work up the lather with her free hand.

"*Ma-wee-a* got a daddy when he got out of *pwison.*"

Rachel froze. Maria was Mrs. Santori's granddaughter, the daughter of her worthless youngest child, Connie. Connie lived with at least two different men a year, dragging her daughter from rundown mobile home to rundown mobile home with frequent stops at the old motel on the edge of town. Maria only made it to preschool half the time. "What are you talking about?" Rachel set down the shampoo bottle and picked up a plastic cup off the edge of the tub. "Tip your head back."

Mallory followed her mother's bidding. *"Ma-wee-a's* new daddy, *Shawntewl.* He come from the *pwison* where we picked up *Mistah* Noah."

Rachel dumped the water over Mallory's head. "How do you know?" She grimaced, scooping up another cup of water. "How did you even know that *was* the prison?"

"It *wooked wike* on *Shawshank Pension."*

"You watched *Shawshank Redemption?* "

"It's Mattie's *favowit."*

"I told Mrs. Santori she needed to keep a better eye on what the two of you are watching on TV."

"It wasn't on TV, it was a DBD," Mallory explained.

"Mallory," Rachel groaned. "A D*V*D is still TV, and it doesn't matter. That is not an appropriate movie for a four-year-old. Now stand up." She tossed the cup into the water and got to her feet, grabbing a folded towel off the toilet seat.

Mallory stood.

"Leave the shark."

The little girl let it fall with a big splash. "Bye, *shawk."*

"Out," Rachel ordered.

Mallory climbed out of the tub and allowed her mother to wrap her up in the big, green beach towel. "Mattie covers my eyes in the bad parts," she said softly, looking up at her mother. "He knows 'cause of the music."

Rachel met her daughter's big, green-eyed gaze, and her own eyes teared up unexpectedly.

"Got soap in your eyes?" Mallory grabbed the corner of the towel to reach up toward her mother's face.

Rachel laughed and scooped her slippery daughter into her arms. "So what are we reading tonight? A storybook or more *Harry Potter?"*

"Not *Hawwy,* not without Mattie. He loves *Hawwy Potta."*

Rachel's first impulse was to ask how on earth Mallory knew Mattie liked *Harry Potter*, or anything else for that matter. The man could barely communicate his basic needs, but the two of them had a strange, special relationship that had existed from the time she brought Mallory home from the hospital, and she'd given up long ago trying to figure it out.

"All right," she conceded, carrying the little girl down the hall toward her bedroom. "But if you want Mattie to come up for reading time, you have to get into your jammies and go downstairs to get him quickly. Mama's tired and she wants to put on her pj's and relax."

"The ones with sheep, Mama?"

"Mmm-hmm."

"Does Noah have pj's with sheep?"

"I don't know." Rachel turned into the bedroom doorway and lowered her squirming daughter to the floor. "And I don't care, now hurry up."

Noah stared into the mirror over the pedestal sink in the half bath off the kitchen and studied his sallow face. He'd shaved this morning in preparation for his homecoming, but his five o'clock shadow, more like a nine o'clock shadow, was beginning to creep across his face. It made him look like a pretty shady character with his hollow cheekbones and longish, poorly cut brown hair.

Of course, most people would consider him a shady character. Someone you might see standing in the supper line at the God's Solid Rock Holy Word Mission . . . just another damaged soul hoping for a hot meal and a dry place to sleep.

He flicked on the cold water faucet and dug his toothbrush and toothpaste out of the bottom of the blue gym bag that he'd left on the toilet seat. He wore a white T-shirt and his prison-issue blue boxers because it was all he had to sleep in. Tomorrow, when Rachel left the house, he would go upstairs to the storage room that, when the house was built a hundred years ago, had been designed to serve as a nursery. It was the room where their sons had slept for a very brief time.

There, according to Rachel, were some boxes marked with an N, and inside he would find his personal belongings, mostly clothes, he guessed. He'd been gone so long, the previous life he had lived with Rachel so dim in his mind, that he couldn't even think off the top of his head what else could be in there.

Still staring into his pained, dark eyes reflected in the mirror, he ran his toothbrush under the water and then drew a thin line of Crest over the bristles. Today hadn't gone too badly, all in all, he thought. Not as good as he had hoped, but certainly not as badly as he deserved. He stuck the toothbrush into his mouth and began to move it up and down, unable to take his eyes off his own reflection.

There hadn't been any real mirrors in the correctional facility, only small metal ones that produced an eerie, wavy reflection. He'd pretty much avoided them, maybe because he looked weird in them, but maybe because he just hadn't been able to face himself.

After five years, he barely recognized the man looking back at him. "Father Noah Gibson," he murmured, spitting into the sink, raising his head to see his reflection again.

As he lifted his head, he suddenly caught a scent on the air that made him stiffen in fear. A familiar scent. Unwanted.

Not again, was the only thought his mind had time to register before the darkness descended.

Azrael knew better than to argue, to fight any longer. Resistance was ineffective—worse, painful. The task had been laid out quite plainly, and there was no need for further argument or questions. Azrael understood what must be done, and even why, at least on some level. And what wasn't clear shouldn't be questioned. Who was an angel to question God?

Azrael drove up the narrow dirt driveway with the headlights off, using the moonlight as a guide. The road was rutted and in need of a wheelbarrow or two of fill dirt—better yet, a dump truck load of gravel—but Johnny Leager probably didn't have money to make improvements to his driveway, not working at the plant, even if he was a shift manager.

Parking the car in front of the house, the angel walked around toward the back, hands empty except for the note that would be left behind. God would provide the weapon.

Johnny grabbed a Bud hidden behind the orange sodas in the garage refrigerator and popped it open, enjoying the hiss it made. He'd promised Stacey he'd cut back on the beer if she cut back on the tacos, and she was doing good with her diet, so it was only right that he should curtail his Bud consumption. That didn't mean a man couldn't have a beer on a Friday night after his wife and kids went to bed, after a long day at work.

He flipped off the garage light and walked out into the backyard illuminated by a security lamp on the far corner of the single-story rancher. The place was starting to look decent. With the extra money he was making with his promotion at the plant, he'd been able to get a home equity loan to buy Stacey the new living room furniture and the exercise bike she wanted, and he'd been able to get the materials to build the new deck. Maybe next year, they'd even put in a hot tub. If Stacey kept losing weight the way she was, looking hot again, it might be fun to jump in with her after the kids went to bed. He might even be able to convince her to take her bathing suit off if he plied her with a piña colada or two first. The idea made him grin.

Sipping the cold beer, Johnny crossed the deck, breathing in the smell of the freshly cut, salt-treated wood. He sat down on the lawn chair facing the brick barbecue he was building and leaned back, stretching his feet out in front of him. By the light of the security lamp, he could see the base and the back wall he'd already completed. It was going to be nice when he finished it, and sturdy. Shoot, it would be big enough to roast a small pig on, if he wanted to, and certainly great for cooking burgers and ribs and polish sausage. Perfect for afternoon barbecues with Stacey's brother's family.

As he sipped his Bud, taking in his handiwork, he considered putting in a horseshoe pit. This summer, while the women sat on the deck in lounge chairs getting a tan and the kids played on the swings, the men could play horseshoes, share a couple beers and a few laughs.

He set down the beer can, staring at the outline of the swing set as a lump rose in his throat. It was hard to believe he'd almost been dumb enough to give all this up. To lose it. Good thing he'd come to his senses.

He grabbed the beer and drained the last of it, thinking he needed to get to bed. He wanted to get up early. Johnny Jr. had T-ball practice, and he'd promised Stacey he'd take him so she could go to the aerobics class at the church. She'd take Tiffany with her because free child care was offered for the Saturday morning sessions. St. Paul's was good about that kind of thing, providing for its parishioners.

It would be a fun Saturday. Johnny would take Junior out for their favorite breakfast of eggs, bacon, and hotcakes, then off to T-ball practice, then home to work on the barbecue. He had plenty of bricks to finish the job, but he'd have to pick up some more cement mix on his way out of town.

The flutter of something white on the edge of the brick barbecue caught Johnny's eye, and he stared at it, wondering what it was. Had he left a hardware store receipt out here? Stacey was keeping them all in case there was some way they could get a tax deduction. House improvements or something.

He got out of the chair, crushing the beer can in his hand as he crossed the deck. The circle of yellow light from the security lamp didn't quite reach the barbecue. He reached out and grabbed the paper, secured by a red brick. He didn't remember leaving a brick out, and it wasn't a receipt. He turned toward the light by the corner of the house, his back to the wall of the barbecue. It was a note, handwritten; he squinted to read it.

If a man commits adultery with another man's wife, both the man and the woman must be put to death.

"What the hell?" He let go of the paper like it had burned his fingers, and the beer can fell out of his other hand, rattling as it fell on the deck. He looked over his shoulder toward the pine trees beyond the swing set, suddenly feeling weird, like someone was watching him. Was this some kind of joke? Some kind of sick joke?

Suddenly his heart was pounding and his mouth was dry.

He never saw it coming until it was inches from his face. A brick. It hit him hard in the temple, and he stumbled back under the impact, pain exploding in his head. He would have fallen had it not been for the wall of the new barbecue. Before Johnny could look up to see who had thrown the damned thing, another brick hurled through the air and struck him square in the jaw. He grunted, flinging out both arms as another brick hit him and another and another.

One hit him right in the nose and he heard the sickening crunch of cartilage busting, and blood spewed from his nostrils. He tried to raise his hand to ward off the next blow, but it came too hard, too fast. His head hit the brick wall and his legs went out from under him. His jeans were wet, stained with dark splatters. Everything was spinning, and he felt like he was going to throw up as he slowly sank down, his back still against the wall. He couldn't get away, couldn't ward off the blows. Another brick hit him in the forehead, and blood spattered as white-hot pain shot through his head.

Blood ran into Johnny's eyes, stinging, and he squinted to see the figure standing on the deck still throwing bricks. He couldn't make out who it was, not with the quartz halogen light from the security lamp behind his attacker. In the dark, through a film of blood, with a circle of eerie yellow light around the figure, it almost looked like an angel.

CHAPTER 3

Noah woke to find himself lying beside Rachel's car on the cold cement floor of the garage, barefoot, in his underwear. Slowly he sat up, wiping his mouth with the back of his hand as if just waking from a good drunk. Only he hadn't had a drink in five years, three months, and seventeen days.

The driver's side door was open a crack, and the interior light cast shadows on the paint-splattered concrete floor. There was a steady ding, ding, ding coming from inside the car, alerting him that the key was still in the ignition. He pushed himself to a seated position, resting against the back door of the car, and hung his head.

Not another blackout, he thought miserably, still able to catch a slight hint of that weird, awful smell that came with them. It couldn't be. It had been more than four years since the last. He thought for sure they were gone for good.

But a man didn't poison his body the way he had without physical repercussions, he told himself. A man didn't destroy his family's lives and not pay.

He shifted his gaze to the driver's side door and wondered why it was open.

He got to his feet, slid in behind the steering wheel, and turned the key Rachel must have left in the ignition. The dinging stopped and the digital clock on the dash lit up: five after twelve. It had been around ten when he went to the bathroom to brush his teeth. More than two hours had passed. Had he been going somewhere? Gone somewhere?

Noah closed his eyes, gripping the steering wheel. He didn't have a driver's license, couldn't even begin to apply for one before he paid fines that had been levied and he attended a weekly class the state set up for violators like himself. It would be at least a year, probably longer.

He turned the key to the off position, got out of the car, and closed the door, contemplating whether or not he would lay his hand on the hood to tell if the car had been running.

Some things were better to not know.

He waited for his eyes to adjust to the darkness and then walked around behind the car, crossed the space where his pickup had once been parked, and exited the side door.

Outside, one of the many security lights on the property illuminated the path up to the front porch. The crushed white oyster shells hurt the bottoms of Noah's feet, and he hurried for the steps. Chester, asleep on the porch near the door, lifted his head and looked curiously at the barefoot man in his boxers.

Chester had been in the house when Noah had walked to the bathroom to brush his teeth; he remembered distinctly seeing the dog lying in the hallway.

Noah took the painted wooden steps slowly, as if he were an old man. So, during his blackout, he had let the dog out and gone to the garage. Why, he didn't know. And of course, he didn't remember a thing, just as he didn't remember anything from that night beyond the argument he had with Rachel on the front porch here, then getting into his truck and heading down the lane.

Chester rose and trotted in his awkward gait to Noah.

When Noah didn't immediately pat him on the head, the old dog pushed his muzzle into his hand.

"OK," Noah whispered. "So someone still loves me around here." He gave the dog a pat, then scratched behind his ears. With one last glance at the garage, he walked into the house, the dog trotting behind him. In the kitchen, he locked the door and went down the hallway to the spare room, not bothering to turn on the lights. For the last five years he had walked these floorboards at night in his mind; he didn't need any light.

Noah woke to the familiar sounds of breakfast in the Gibson household and for a moment, half asleep, he imagined life was as it had once been. He and Rachel in love with their whole lives before them. He could smell Mrs. Santori's strong coffee mingling with the heavenly scent of frying scrapple. Saturday and Sunday mornings Mrs. Santori had always made a big breakfast and scrapple was Noah's favorite.

By the time he threw his legs over the side of the bed, waking Chester, who slept near the door, reality had begun to set in. As he looked around at the stacked boxes, his mother's old sewing machine and ironing board still piled with "mending," a broken chair, a ladder, and cases of mason jars, he listened to the sound of Rachel's voice as she spoke to Mallory, and the little girl responded in that cute voice of hers.

Without anything else to put on, Noah stepped into the jeans he'd worn the previous day and replaced the white T-shirt with the green one again. He slid his bare feet into the black Converse low-tops that had been prison issue and opened the door, setting Chester free.

After a quick stop in the bathroom, where he found his toothbrush lying in the sink, his gym bag still on the toilet lid, he hesitantly entered the sunny kitchen.

"*Buenos,* Señora Santori." Noah walked around the table to let Chester out the door.

"*Buenos,*" she answered, tight lipped. "Your breakfast, Señor." Consuelo Santori had lived in the United States for the last forty years of her life; she spoke perfect Queen's English, but when she was angry, her speech became heavily accented. She dropped a plate on the table for him, already loaded down with scrambled eggs, rye toast, and scrapple.

Noah's mouth watered as he slid into his designated chair. Sometimes scrapple was served at the prison when they got it cheaply from a local company, but it was never cooked the way he liked it, crisp the way Mrs. Santori made it. And rye toast . . . He had forgotten how good freshly toasted and buttered rye toast smelled and tasted.

He put his napkin on his lap and glanced up at Rachel, Mattie, and Mallory, who had been served ahead of him. "Did we say grace?" he asked. Funny thing was, he hadn't said grace in five years; it was just something ingrained in him from the time he was younger than the little girl seated across from him.

"We don't say *gwace,*" Mallory piped up, sucking on the straw of a juice box. This morning she was wearing a red felt cowboy hat and a pink nightgown. "Only if somebody comes *fow dinnew.*"

Rachel glanced up, blushing.

Noah surprised them all, including himself, by tipping back his head and laughing. The sound of his voice startled Mattie, who dropped his fork.

Rachel half smiled. "What's so funny?" She dumped sugar straight from the sugar bowl into her coffee.

Mrs. Santori brought Noah his coffee, and he nodded his thanks. "I don't know," he said. "I guess her honesty." He glanced up at the little girl, her blond hair pulled into a little ponytail over each of her ears, sticking out from under the cowboy hat. "It's not like I'm anyone to judge who should and shouldn't be saying grace."

Rachel rose, coffee mug in hand, her plate untouched. "Hurry up, lovebug, or we're going to be late for your riding lesson. You still have to get dressed."

"I am *dwessed.*"

"I told you, no pj's in the barn." She turned back to Noah. "I'm taking Mallory to riding, leaving Mattie off at the church to practice for morning service, then I have a few errands to do in town." She didn't turn around as she headed for the door, but Noah knew she was now speaking to him. "We'll be back by lunch, and we can take a walk around the place, if you want. I'll show you what we've been doing."

He nodded. "I'd like that."

The screen door slammed shut behind her as she stepped onto the porch.

Mallory scrambled down from the blue plastic booster seat in her chair, a piece of scrapple in each hand. "Wait for me. Wait, Mama," she called as she clip-clopped across the hardwood floor in red cowboy boots. "I'm coming. I have to change my pj's. *Huwwy* up, Mattie," she threw over her shoulder.

Mattie moved as quickly as Mattie ever moved, methodically wiping his plate with half a slice of toasted white bread and stuffing it in his mouth as he rose from the table. He pushed in his chair and stiffly carried his plate to the sink, nodding to Mrs. Santori, his baby-fine sandy-brown hair falling into his eyes.

"*De nada,*" she told him with a smile as he lumbered out the door.

Feeling awkward, alone in the kitchen with Mrs. Santori, Noah sipped his coffee. As he buttered his toast, he realized that he was the only one at the table with rye bread. She had remembered. . . .

That realization made him feel good and sad at the same time. "*Gracias,* Señora Santori," he said, raising a piece of buttered toast. "For the rye and . . . and taking care of Rachel."

She walked around to the opposite side of the table from

him and placed her small, brown hands on the back of Mallory's chair. "I miss them, Señor and Señora Gibson."

He nodded, glancing down at his plate. "I miss them too."

She stood there for another minute looking directly at him, then picked up Mallory's plate and utensils and carried them to the sink.

Noah took a bite of the scrapple and closed his eyes in sheer pleasure at the taste of it, the taste of home. "Is there something you'd like me to do for you today, Consuelo?" he asked. "Something that needs fixing, maybe?"

"Faucet leaks." She nodded in the direction of the kitchen sink. "I ask my husband for two years to fix it." She gave a wave of her hand. "He tells me *si* every day. He doesn't fix it."

Noah smiled to himself. Consuelo and Mateo were an interesting couple. She was at least ten years older than he was, and they argued constantly, yet they were utterly devoted to each other and would not stand to listen to someone else criticize the other. In their family, Consuelo gave the orders, and for the most part, Mateo ignored them. Noah's parents had hired them when Noah was still in high school—Consuelo to care for the house and help with the cooking, and Mateo to work in the vineyard alongside his parents. The Santoris had been as devoted to his parents as they were to each other.

When Noah had finished his breakfast and accepted a second cup of coffee from Consuelo, he joined Chester on the front porch. He was just easing down to sit on the top step and enjoy his coffee when he heard a vehicle approaching up the driveway. Despite the years that had passed, he recognized the old black truck and the bearded man leaning with his arm out the open window as he pulled into the yard.

Joshua Troyer nodded, lifting his sweat-stained straw hat as his truck sputtered to a halt. "Eeh-ya," he greeted.

Noah nodded back. "Morning, Joshua." He got to his feet, offering his hand to the man in his early sixties. Though Joshua was Mennonite and had been for as long as Noah had known him, he still looked as if he were Amish, dressed as if he were Amish, spoke as if he were Amish. The only give-away to his "leaving the church" to marry Miss Trudy Haan, a Mennonite, was the black '77 Ford pickup he drove. Even the "modern" Amish in Delaware still didn't drive cars, not for personal use at least.

"Good to have you home," Joshua said solemnly.

"Can't tell you how good it is to be home." Noah was touched that Joshua would come to welcome him home. "Can I get you a cup of coffee?"

Joshua shook his head. "Not thirsty. Just wanted to stop. Got to go to the mill." He stroked his brown beard, streaked with gray. "Outta chicken feed."

Noah nodded.

Joshua nodded. Spat on the ground. Glanced off in the distance. He was a man of few words. "Eeh-ya . . ."

Noah could tell the man had something to say, but there was no need to rush him. Joshua, like Mattie, wasn't a man to be rushed. He'd come out with it when he was good and ready.

"You heard the news from town?" Joshua said finally.

Noah took a sip of his coffee. "I've been out of touch with Stephen Kill for some time, Josh."

He nodded, running his thumbs beneath his dirty sus-penders. "Eeh-ya . . . figured you might." He rocked back. "Last night's news."

"What's that?"

"Man been stoned."

"Stoned?" Noah stared at him, his meaning not register-ing. Where he'd been living, stoned meant something differ-ent than what Joshua Troyer probably meant by it. "I don't understand."

"Kilt. Stoned to death." Joshua continued to gaze out on the fields beyond the house.

Noah took a step back, sitting down hard on the second step. "You're kidding," he breathed, glancing up. "Who?"

"Johnny Leager from off Old Mill Road."

Noah closed his eyes for a moment, tenting his hands. He didn't pray, but old habits died slowly. Johnny Leager had been one of his parishioners at St. Paul's. He knew him well, knew his whole family. Johnny and Stacey had hit a rough place in their marriage at one point, and Johnny had come in for counseling.

"Nobody sayin' fer sure what happened." Joshua eyed him shrewdly. "But I heard he was kilt with the bricks from his own house. Head bashed in."

Noah didn't know what to say. A murder in Stephen Kill? It had been at least thirty years since someone was murdered in the sleepy little town, and that had involved a land dispute and two drunks with shotguns. They'd only had a police force for fifty years, and it mostly issued parking and speed-ing tickets and dealt with trespassing and hunting on private property. A murder so vicious . . . Noah couldn't imagine who could do such a thing. Certainly not anyone among them; it had to be a stranger from outside.

"Was it a robbery?" he asked. He couldn't imagine how it would be, though; the Leagers barely lived above the poverty line in a modular home built thirty years ago on a sandy piece of property outside of town. What could they possibly have to steal?

"Don't know that anybody knows yet why." Joshua gave the front tire of his old truck a kick and spat. "Eeh-ya." He stood another moment and then opened the door. "Wanted to greet ya, neighbor."

"Well, thank you." Noah rose from the step. "I appreciate that."

"Know it's gotta be hard comin' back." Joshua climbed into the truck and slammed the door, resting a suntanned arm through the open window. "Don't know where you'll be goin' to church, wanted to extend the invitation. We're all sinners in God's eyes, son."

Noah stared at his feet. He had no intention of attending

Stephen Kill Mennonite Church, or any other church, but he wasn't going to insult Joshua. He was a good man with a good heart. "I'll keep that in mind."

"Eeh-ya." The older man cranked on the ignition and it fired. He threw the old truck into reverse, backed into the spot in front of the open garage, and pulled away, oyster shells flying, tipping his straw hat as he went.

Noah lifted his hand and watched the truck disappear. "Eeh-ya," he muttered, mimicking the Mennonite.

Chester whined and trotted awkwardly down the front porch steps, wagging his tail. As Noah leaned over to pat the dog's head, he heard car tires on the driveway again. He doubted it was Joshua coming back; it just wasn't like him. He came to say what he had to say and then he was gone.

A moment later a blue sedan appeared, crawling slowly up the driveway. Behind the wheel was gray-haired Cora Watkins, the woman who had been the church secretary at St. Paul's for the last forty-some years and had served as Noah's secretary when he'd been the parish priest there. He wasn't surprised to see her. Maybe surprised she hadn't turned up sooner. She and her sister and their neighbor were the unofficial welcome wagon of Stephen Kill. Not only did they welcome newcomers to town, but they made an appearance at every death, illness, or crisis, being the first to inquire and collect the gritty particulars of any occasion.

Cora Watkins steered her late-model Pontiac into the parking space in front of the garage, fished something off the floor on the passenger's side and got out, making her way toward him with surprising vigor for a woman of her age and girth. Like most of the single or widowed middle-aged women in town, she was short, slightly plump, and wore a sensible helmet of white hair, which she had done every Friday afternoon at the Fantasy Hair Salon across from the post office in town.

Noah wasn't certain he was ready to face his old secretary from the church, but it didn't matter because here she came. "Miss Cora." He stood his ground at the base of the porch steps, stiffening his spine, and Chester slumped into the grass beside him in a show of solidarity.

"Father Gibson—"

"Noah will do."

She drew a plump palm to her cheek, flustered. "I brought this banana nut bread over." She offered the foiled-wrapped loaf, neatly marked "Banana Nut" in black Sharpie.

The bread was cold in his hand. Frozen. He imagined she and her sister had hundreds of loaves in their freezer for just such occasions as welcoming their ex-priest home after a stint in county prison. "Thank you." He raised the loaf and let his hand fall, not knowing what else to say. It didn't matter; he knew Cora would do all the talking for him.

"Just wanted to welcome you home." She smoothed her navy polyester shirt over her slightly protruding abdomen. "Clara and Alice send a warm welcome. They were sorry they couldn't come by this morning, but it's folding day at the thrift shop. We thought about coming this afternoon, but I thought it wouldn't be right, waiting that long."

He nodded.

"We just wanted to see if you were getting settled." She glanced around the farmyard. "Are you getting settled? Rachel, she isn't home?"

He shook his head.

"No, I don't suppose she would be. Saturday. Mallory has a horseback-riding class this morning, and Mattie's off to the sanctuary to rehearse for tomorrow morning, isn't he?" She clucked sympathetically. "One of God's angels. And Rachel a guardian angel for taking him in when nobody else would. Don't you think?" She didn't even wait for a response this time. "I see, well, I just wanted to see if you were getting settled, bring you the bread." She nodded in the direction of the frozen loaf he held at his side. "It's good. Fresh from this week.

Alice made it, was her turn. Alice's banana bread. Special. She gives nobody that recipe. Not even me." She smiled, obviously feeling awkward but seeming to be in no hurry to go. "So are you?" she asked. "Settling in?" She paused.

He figured he was going to be forced to answer this time. "Yes, thank you. And thank you for the bread." He raised the loaf a couple of inches and let his hand fall at his side again.

"I should be going. I know you must have heard. A terrible tragedy at the Leagers'." Her gray-blue eyes lit up with a macabre excitement. "Clara and Alice and I thought we would wait until this afternoon, until after the police have gone, and then go to pay our respects to the widow and children. She'll be needing plenty of loaves of bread, don't you think? Terrible tragedy, just terrible. What with family coming and all for the funeral." She looked at him, his cue for another response.

"Yeah," he agreed, sliding his free hand into his jeans pocket. "It probably would be a good idea to wait, maybe even a day or two."

"Well, must be off." She raised her hand as she trotted for her car. "Enjoy your bread, Father."

"I will." He held up the frozen loaf that suddenly seemed immensely heavy to him. "Thank you, Miss Cora."

"Oh." She turned back. "Clara told me to mention to you that the bell choir still meets on Wednesday nights if you'd care to join us. There'll be brownies afterwards, of course." She gave a little giggle as she got into her car.

As Cora drove away, Mateo strolled across the yard toward him, his face shadowed by the large, dog-eared, straw cowboy hat he always wore.

"Miss Cora, my old secretary," Noah explained. "Banana nut bread."

"If I had pigs," Mateo said with a slight Hispanic accent, his tanned brown face devoid of emotion, "I would feed the bread to the pigs. Bad cooks. Not like my Consuelo." He grimaced and then shrugged. "Come. Posts to be planted." He walked past Noah, taking the foil-wrapped loaf from his hand and setting it on the porch rail. "Hard work. Sweat. It will be good for you."

Noah and the dog followed.

Snowden stood in the stone tile vestibule of St. Paul's Episcopal Church, his feet planted firmly, his thumbs tucked in his wide, black leather gun belt, trying not to fidget. His partner today—a Miss Delilah Swift, barely five feet tall, blond and cute as a button—stood beside him, her attempts far less successful. The handcuffs on the back of her belt jingled as she seemed to dance, reminding him of a busy bee. Ordinarily, he didn't get the chance to do much real police work anymore, but she was still in training and he didn't want her working alone yet.

"I still can't believe someone would kill a man that way, Chief, can you?" she asked in her sweet southern drawl, not giving him time to answer before she went on. She continued to shuffle through the leaflets on a table near the entrance from the street. "I mean, you know this kind of thing happens, you read it in the magazines at the doctors' offices and the like, but you just don't think it can happen to you, do you? Not a nice town like this, not nice people like the Leagers."

Snowden slid his hand into his gray uniform pocket, checking again to be sure the photocopy of the note was still there, even though he knew very well it was. He was a detail man. A man who didn't lose things and didn't make mistakes. A man better than most because he had to be.

The original note left at the scene of the crime was already sealed and placed in the evidence box back at the station. He didn't know what to make of it, that was why he was here, but he had a bad feeling in his gut. Aching bad.

A door clicked somewhere, echoing in the high ceiling overhead, and Snowden instinctively gazed upward to the vaulted ceiling with its intricately carved, arched beams and the old chandelier that had once held candles but been altered for electricity at some point in time. It was one of the church's finest antiquities, he had learned from reading the brochure on the table behind him.

Father Hailey appeared, dressed in jeans, an oxford shirt, and shiny white Rockport sneakers. He was an ordinary man, late fifties with a slight paunch and a bald head except for the characteristic ring of white hair he wore like the crown of olive leaves on the saint's head in the stained-glass window behind them. He offered his hand, pumping Snowden's. "Chief Calloway."

"Thank you for seeing me, Father. This is Sergeant Swift."

"Pleased to meet you, Father," she said in her southern drawl, shaking his hand.

"I'm only sorry it's not under better circumstances. Let's go to my office." He gestured, showing them the way. "I understand you're new with our fine police force, Sergeant."

"Yes, sir. Transferred from a little town west of Atlanta. Needed a change of scenery after I had to lock up my boyfriend for assaulting an officer of the law." She smiled sweetly.

Snowden smiled inside. He liked Delilah, and had from the first fax he received from her applying for the job.

Of course there had been nothing but talk since he hired her. A black man, hiring a twenty-eight-year-old white woman instead of the fifty-year-old ex-marine everyone said should have had Snowden's job to begin with. To his disappointment but not total surprise, the talk had turned foul within days of her arrival, once everyone got a look at her and found out she was attractive and single. Twice in the first month she'd been on the force, he'd had to place an order with the public works department to have inappropriate graffiti referring to their relationship removed from city facilities, once on the brick wall in front of the junior/senior high and then on one of the dugouts at the Little League park. Whichever little pecker-head had done it hadn't even gotten the anatomy quite right, though he'd been a stickler for skin color.

"I'm not certain that I can be of much help," Father Hailey said, leading them down a short flight of steps, then a hall-way lined with preschoolers' drawings of lambs and rocks. "I've already been out to see Mrs. Leager. A doctor had to be called in to sedate her, so I thought I'd return this evening. She has family flying in this afternoon."

"What I have to show you, Father, must be kept in the strictest of confidence. The state police recommended that we not reveal to anyone that a note was left. It's a way of fil-tering out false leads."

"I understand, of course. Confidentiality is in the job de-scription." He flashed a wane smile over his shoulder as he passed the secretary's empty desk and led them through a doorway into his office. He indicated they should sit in one of the chairs in front of his desk as he walked around to the other side and sat in the executive chair.

Snowden chose to stand, and when Delilah realized he wasn't sitting, she popped off the end of the chair, her hand-cuffs jingling. It almost would have been comical, had it not been for the circumstances.

As Father Hailey settled behind his desk, Snowden took the opportunity to study the bookshelves that lined one wall of the cramped, musty-smelling office. Books could reveal a great deal about a person, he had discovered over the years. The priest had the usual various translations of the Bible, biblical commentaries, and concordances. Then there were hardback and paperback books on the Gospels and an as-sortment of annotations on Old Testament books. On the far end, toward the bottom beside a child's sculpture of what was either a Christ figure or a penguin, was Father Hailey's small, personal collection: a daily devotions workbook; a small, worn Bible; some Christian men's magazines; and a book on freshwater angling. Snowden found that last book

interesting because southern Delaware was far from any angling river he knew of.

"Chief Calloway, could . . . could I see it?" Father Hailey
asked, putting on a pair of large wire-framed reading glasses.
Suddenly he seemed a little nervous.

"Of course." Snowden turned from the bookshelf and
slipped the photocopy from his pocket. He leaned over the
desk to hand it to the priest. "The original has to be kept for
evidence," he explained. "We were just wondering what your
initial impression of it was, you being a man of the cloth. I
intend to visit Father Clyde at Our Lady of Lourdes as well."

Father Hailey glanced at the copy quickly and then
peered over the rims of his glasses. "The verse is from the
Old Testament, of course."

"Yes, Leviticus." Snowden watched him carefully, interested in his change in demeanor. Why was his forehead
sweaty all of a sudden?

"You know your Bible, Chief. Leviticus is a book most of
us like to avoid if at all possible."

"Grandson of a Southern Baptist, sir. The more hellfire
and damnation, the better we like it." His gaze strayed to the
cross-stitched sign on the opposite wall from the bookshelf.
It was poorly done, in bad color combinations.

"My wife made that for me years ago when I was first or-
dained," Father Hailey explained, smiling.

"Mr. Leager was murdered, Father, in a very personal
way." Snowden's gaze returned to the bookshelves. "Nothing
was stolen. Nothing inside the house was disturbed. There is
not even any indication that an intruder entered the house.
This note, which we assume was written and left by the
killer, would suggest Mr. Leager had committed adultery,
don't you think?" He glanced at the man behind the desk.

"I wouldn't be at liberty to say, of course . . . if he had,"
Father Hailey answered, fiddling with the piece of paper. "I
mean if I knew he had."

Delilah looked at Snowden. She thought it was a strange

response to the question, too. Snowden hadn't asked the father if Johnny Leager was cheating on his wife. "We just wanted to confirm our interpretation. And you of course don't recognize the handwriting."

The priest gazed over the rims of his glasses. "Certainly not."

Snowden stuck his hand out across the messy desk. "I appreciate you seeing us on a Saturday, especially a holiday weekend."

"I don't know that I was any help." He handed off the photocopy, rising.

"We'll see ourselves out."

Snowden and Delilah were silent until they reached the vestibule, and then she halted, glancing down the steps in the direction they'd come. "Strange duck," she murmured in her charming southern drawl. "Quack."

Rachel had no idea what made her toss her bag from the drugstore into the car the following Wednesday morning and then walk up the street to the police station. She hadn't been there in ages. Not since she and Snowden stopped seeing each other. Maybe that was why she wanted to see him . . . just to be sure she'd made the right decision.

Since Noah's arrival home, she found herself questioning many of her decisions, having a lot of conflicting feelings.

When Rachel walked into the reception area, the young woman behind the glass wall asked her to wait while she checked to see if Chief Calloway was available.

Rachel had barely taken a seat in one of the hard plastic chairs when Snowden himself appeared at the door to the inner offices. "Rachel." He smiled. "Come on in." He held the automatically locking door open for her until she passed in front of him, and then he walked past her, leading her down the hallway to his office.

"Nice," she said, having a look around as he took a seat in

a black leather executive's chair behind a massive cherry desk. The last time she had been here to see him he hadn't been promoted to the chief of police yet and they'd chatted in a room set aside for questioning suspects. Here, the walls were painted an eggshell color and the drapes were in neutral tones, classy but subdued . . . much like Snowden. The only things hanging on the walls were a large-dial institutional clock, his college diploma, and the certificates of commendation he had earned over the years, first as a Delaware state policeman, then a member of Stephen Kill's local force.

"Everything OK?" Snowden asked. "With Noah? I know he's staying at the house."

"Yes, of course. Everything's fine." She walked up behind one of the two black leather chairs in front of his desk and placed her hands on the back. "I just came by . . ." She laughed at herself. "I don't know why I came by, Snowden. I didn't mean to intrude. I guess I was just thinking about you." She glanced up at him; he was as handsome as ever. "This thing with Johnny Leager is just awful. I know what this job means to you."

He offered a meager smile. "I'm fine, Rachel, but it's nice to think that you would care."

"Of course I care." She wandered away from the chair to the far right wall to study one of his commendations.

"Hey, Chief. We got the handwriting preliminary analysis back on the note left at the Leager crime scene," a voice said from the doorway.

Rachel couldn't see who was standing there, and he couldn't see her because she was near the far wall, the door between them.

"It's definitely not a match to the widow's, like you said, though the lab said there's something weird about the way the word *adultery* was written. Doesn't quite match the rest of the handwriting or something. The tech told me it was a pretty fascinating specimen. Doesn't follow any of the rules."

Snowden had placed his hands on his desk and risen when the police officer started to speak. Obviously the conversation hadn't been intended for her to overhear, but by the time Snowden got his mouth open, it was too late.

She turned to Snowden. The newspapers hadn't said anything about a note being left behind or that the murder had something to do with adultery. Neither had the local news.

The officer on the other side of the door, still unaware Rachel was there, made a sound in his throat. "Um, you want this now, Chief, or you want it added to the file?"

"Just put it in the file."

"You got it."

"And close my door, will you, Lopez?"

Rachel didn't move until the door was shut, and then she glanced over at Snowden. "Sorry about that," she said a little sheepishly. "I guess he didn't realize I was here."

"No. I'm sorry. We're all a little rattled around here." Snowden sat down again. "Obviously you can't share that information with anyone, Rachel. When investigating a case like this, the police don't always release all the details to the public."

"I understand. Of course." She started to move toward the door, definitely feeling as if she was intruding now. "I won't say anything." She rested her hand on the doorknob. "Well, glad you're doing OK. Good luck with the case."

He rose from his desk. "Want me to walk you out?"

"No, no, I know my way. Thanks." She slipped out the door, closing it behind her, and hurried down the corridor.

The killer had left a note accusing Johnny Leager of adultery? How could that be? Her heart beat a little faster. She thought it had been a secret no one had known.

Which made her wonder what other secrets had been told in this town . . . and to whom.

CHAPTER 4

Noah sat in his father's rocking chair on the porch, listening to the sound of Mattie playing the organ in the living room and of Mrs. Santori making dinner—pot lids rattling, her muttering in Spanish good-naturedly at Chester, who was apparently underfoot. He could hear the hiss of a steaming pot and smell the fragrant scent of tomatoes and fresh oregano. He found the familiar household sounds comforting, from this perspective on the porch at least. Once she called everyone for dinner and he was forced to go inside and face them, it would be another matter. That's when he would begin to wish he had a glass of wine or maybe a beer. Just a small one. Just enough to take off the edge.

He wouldn't have it, of course. He'd take his own life before he ever drank again, but it didn't make the desire any less keen.

It was difficult for him to sit at the table with Rachel and Mattie and the little girl, all of them looking at him, or worse, trying not to. No one knew what to say to him or each other when he was around. What was there *to* say?

It had been almost a week since he'd been released, and if

nothing, there was more tension in the household than the afternoon he'd arrived. He felt as if he and Rachel were tip-toeing around each other on dark ice. He knew she was angry that he had decided to keep the vineyard, but she refused to talk about it. When they were married, she had been the talker and he the grunter, but now it seemed as if their roles were reversed. Twice this week he'd tried to discuss the matter with her, to try to explain to her why he had to stay, why he had no choice, but she wouldn't even remain in the room long enough to hear him out.

The screen door slapped and Noah heard small footsteps. A moment later, Mallory appeared, peeking around the corner of the house at him.

"*He-wo*," she said shyly.

It was impossible for him not to smile at the angelic face. The little girl fascinated him and scared the hell out of him at the same time. "Hello," he answered, enunciating carefully. He had noticed that there was some tension between her and her mother over her mispronunciation of words, but he wasn't certain that Rachel was going about it in the best way. He was certainly no expert in speech impediments, or children, but he wondered if there wasn't a less stressful way for both of them than Rachel constantly correcting her.

"Whatcha doin'?" she asked, slowly coming around the corner, dragging her fingers along the wall, testing the waters between them.

She was wearing a pink polka-dotted skirt, a plaid sleeve-less shirt, and a pink fuzzy boa tied around her head. In the last couple of days, Noah had found himself waiting in anticipation to see what new outfit she would come out of the house in.

"I'm sitting in my daddy's rocking chair watching that chicken in the garden." He pointed to the hen scratching at the potato peels Mrs. Santori had thrown into the yard half an hour ago.

Mallory lowered her hands to her hips, studying the hen

rather seriously. "Mama *tewls Senawa* not to *frow scwaps* in the *yawd*. Not *san-tawy*. But she does it anyway."

He looked away so she wouldn't see him grin. "I think the senora and her people in Mexico have been *throwing scraps* in the *yard* for the last thousand years or so. Hard habit to break."

Mallory crossed in front of him and hopped up into the other rocker, setting it in motion. Her dusty bare feet dangled as she rocked. Her toenails were painted blue. "Can I ask you a question, *Mistah* Noah?"

"Sure, Mallory."

"Why was you in *pwison*?"

He felt as if he'd been punched in the stomach. He never saw it coming, not from a four-year-old. He cleared his throat, his gaze settling on the red hen again. "I think you need to ask your mother that."

"You said I *couwd* ask you a question."

"Maybe one a little less personal."

She thought for a moment. "What kind of ice cream do you *wike?*"

He was amazed by her comprehension of language and the words she knew. "Hmmmm." This one was definitely a lot easier to handle. "Butter pecan."

"I *wike chocowate*."

"I would have guessed that." He glanced sideways in her direction. She was still rocking, throwing her little body forward and back to keep up the motion of the big chair. "Now my turn for a question."

"OK."

"Why don't you have any Rs?"

She scrunched up her cute, freckled nose. "What?"

"Rs. When you talk, you don't have any Rs. Ls either, but let's worry about the Rs today. I think you dropped them, maybe in the yard, and then that little hen picked them up. You asked me why I'd been in *pwison*."

She scowled, ceasing her rocking motion. "Rs *awe hawd*

to say when *you 'we fouw*," she defended, crossing her arms over her chest.

Obviously it was a touchy subject.

"They sure are."

She looked at him suspiciously. "You think so?"

He nodded. "When I was four, I couldn't say Rs very well, either. I was supposed to be named Robert, but I called myself Wobert, so my parents had to change my name to Noah so I could say my own name."

She giggled and then looked at him seriously. "You say Rs now."

"Most of the time."

"How did you *wearn?*"

He shrugged. "I practiced moving my mouth right, I guess." He pressed his finger to his lips lightly making an R sound. "Like that."

She rose on her knees, studying his mouth carefully as she balanced herself on the arm of the rocking chair. "Do it again," she ordered as she drew her own finger to her mouth.

He made the sound again, leaning closer to her. "Robert, red, raccoon," he said.

She tried to make the sound with her own mouth, and when it didn't come out right, she stuck her little hand out to press her fingertips to his lips.

Her touch took him completely by surprise, like being struck by a lightning bolt . . . but just a tiny one. Her baby hand was so small, and she smelled so good, like shampoo and grass and grape juice. It was as if when she reached out to touch him, she didn't just touch his mouth, but his heart. One brush of her slightly sticky hand and he could feel his heart melting, a strange, protective sensation coming over him that he had never experienced in his life.

"Like this," he said, laying his hand over hers and opening his mouth slightly. "You have to do this with your tongue."

She squinted, peering into his mouth, and then tried to imitate him. "WWwraccoon."

"That's right!" Noah grabbed her shoulders. "Raccoon. Say it again. Raccoon. Rabbit. Roller-skate."

"Wwracoon . . . Wrabbit . . . Wwrollewskate!"

"That's it, Mallory! That's right. What a smart girl."

She sat back in the rocker, her hand still on her mouth. "W . . . red. W . . . rabbit. W . . . run. I can do it!" She laughed.

"I knew you could. It just takes practice." Noah pursed his lips. "Try this. Robert *r*an a*r*ound the *r*acet*r*ack."

"W . . . Robert W . . . ran around the racetrack!"

He clapped, and she clapped and leapt out of the chair, throwing herself into his arms. Before he had time to think, he wrapped his arms around her and held her tight. She felt so good. It had been so long since he'd had another human being touch him. Too long.

The screen door slapped. "Mallory!" Rachel called.

Noah let go of the little girl, sensing Rachel wouldn't want him so near her daughter. Nothing had been said between them; Rachel hadn't said to leave her alone, but he could feel it, could see it in her eyes.

"I'm very proud of you, Mallory," he whispered.

"Mallory?" Rachel came around the corner.

"Mama! W . . . Robert W . . . ran over the rabbit!"

Rachel laughed and reached out to scoop up her daughter in her arms. "Oh my goodness! That's very good," she said as she looked from Mallory to Noah and back to Mallory again. There was a slight tension in her voice. "What have the two of you been doing out here?"

"*Mistah* Noah has been teaching me. *Wisten.*" Mallory rested her hand on her mouth. "W . . . red robin. Run. Runny. Rubber band."

"Speech lessons?" Rachel asked, looking down at Noah, disapproval in her tone now.

Noah rose from the rocking chair with a shrug. "We were just talking about how hard certain letters were to pronounce."

"Mr. Noah used to be Mr. W . . . Robert but he couldn't say it so now he's Mr. Noah."

"Is that right?" Rachel raised an eyebrow.

Mallory bobbed her head excitedly.

"Well, I'm so proud of you." Rachel kissed her daughter on the forehead, then each cheek, then the tip of her nose. "I really am," she murmured.

Noah felt a lump rise in his throat. It had once been his dream that he and Rachel would have a child together, that they would share the love he saw in her eyes now for a child. Their child.

Mallory giggled and tried to push her away.

"OK, go get washed up for supper, giggle puss." Rachel lowered her to the porch. "And get Mattie. He's still playing the organ."

"Yes, Mama." Her bare feet hit the floorboards and she took off, racing around the corner and out of sight, the pink boa around her head, fluttering behind her.

Rachel and Noah stood there for a moment, watching her go. The little girl was so beautiful, so perfect, that she made his heart ache for what he knew he had lost, what he had given up for a bottle. The lump in his throat dissolved slowly. He had to ask . . . he just had to. "Rachel," he murmured, his voice sounding strange in his ears, "whose daughter is she?"

"She's mine," she answered, surprising him, her voice suddenly so full of emotion. They were standing only a foot apart, and she raised her hand as if she was going to take his hand.

Not once since he returned had she touched him, not a kiss on the cheek, not a hug, not even a handshake, and he felt himself tremble all over.

But her hand fell before it met his, and he didn't have the balls to reach out to her.

"You know what I mean," he said, his voice still a whisper. "Who's her father?"

"Why do you care?"

He was taken aback by the sudden change in her tone. One instant there had obviously been some connection from the past between them and the next it was gone. Now she was angry.

He glanced at the painted floorboards, then back up at her again. For the briefest moment there, when she had reached for his hand, he felt different than he had in a long time. Lighter, somehow. But the heaviness was weighing in again, falling across his shoulders, bringing him down. "I . . . I don't know. Of course, it's not any of my business, I just—"

"You're right, it's not." Rachel turned away, sounding tired when she spoke again. "Supper will be ready in five minutes. Mattie's still playing; I can hear him." She sighed. "Can you get him? Have him wash his hands."

She walked away without giving him a chance to respond on either subject.

Rachel drew a pink gingham sheet over Mallory's bare foot sticking out over the edge of the bed. She always kept her feet covered at night for fear the monsters might nibble at her toes. Rachel had given up trying to convince the four-year-old that there were no monsters under a little girl's bed in Stephen Kill, Delaware; it was easier just to stock up on sheets when they were on sale at the outlets.

Pushing back a lock of blond hair off her sleeping daughter's temple, her smile nearly turned into a sob before she was able to staunch it. Rachel turned out the light on the nightstand, dissolving the room into darkness.

For a moment she just stood there, her arms wrapped around her waist. She and Mallory had made the lamp themselves to go with the medieval theme of the bedroom; the lampshade looked like a damsel's cone-shaped hat, complete with pink veil. On the pink and lavender walls, they had painted a mural of a castle with a moat, and her bookcases looked like big, white, castle turrets . . . at least to a four-year-old.

Slipping out of the dark room, closing the door behind

her, Rachel slowly made her way down the hall to her room, the familiar night sounds of the old house settling seeming to surround her.

She heard ice fall from the automatic icemaker into the tray, Chester roll over in the downstairs hallway, and the rattle of the loose gutter near the front door. Then an unfamiliar sound . . . footsteps . . . Noah's footsteps.

Rachel had to cover her mouth to stifle the sob that rose in her throat and threatened to bubble up. She darted into her bedroom, closed the door and leaned against it, burying herself in the curtain of old flannel bathrobes and cotton pajamas that hung on the hooks on the back of the door. Tears streaming down her face, she slowly sank to the floor, her chest heaving as she tried to hold back the floodgate of tears, a floodgate she felt she'd been holding back for so long that if she opened it now, she might not ever be able to close it.

"Noah . . ." she whispered, her lower jaw trembling so that she stammered. "N-Noah, I-I'm s-so sorry. But I d-don't know what to do," she sobbed, shaking uncontrollably. "I don't know what to say to you."

She drew her knees up, hugging them against her, and began to rock back and forth, her head striking the door each time she leaned back. She felt as if her heart was breaking all over again.

It hurt so much.

But how? How could it hurt so much after all these years? After he'd been gone so long? After they'd all been gone and dead so long?

But if it was possible, the pain seemed even worse. Every time she saw Noah's haunted shadow of a face, every time he spoke, every time he looked at Mallory . . . she remembered what they'd had, what they had lost.

Abraham.

Isaac.

Joanne and Mark.

The Marcuses.

Noah.

Ghosts flying around the house, around her bedroom. Around inside her head.

So many innocents. It was so unfair. So damned unfair.

Another violent sob wracked her body. All gone. All dead. Noah's life as good as gone. Noah as good as dead. *And it was all her fault.*

Noah had just started up the engine to the John Deere lawn tractor when Mallory bounced down the porch steps, dressed for preschool, her green *Shrek II* backpack dangling off one shoulder. This morning she had settled for a shirt and shorts that matched, to please her mother no doubt. "Where you goin'?" she shouted above the rumble of the engine.

"Town to get some things at the hardware store for Mateo." He cut the engine so he could hear her better. The way everyone else in the house except for Mateo avoided him, she was his best buddy right now, after Chester, and he didn't want to miss a word she said.

"Because you was bad and went to p-*r*ison and you can't drive Mama's car?" she said.

He nodded, chuckling. "Something like that."

She swayed side to side, her hands tucked behind her back. Today she wore her blond hair in a ponytail with a flowered bucket hat pulled over her head. "Mama says you *wook siwwy*, a *g-rown* man *d-riving* in town on a *wawn-mower.*"

He adjusted his ball cap, resisting a grin. "Does she now? What else does she say about me?"

She tucked her hands behind her back and turned one way and then the other, rather coquettishly for a preschooler. "She said she thought you was cute."

This time he couldn't resist the grin. "And what brought that up?"

"I thought you was cute." She looked at him curiously,

pointing at the lawn tractor. "Think I *couwld* have a w . . . ride?"

"To school?"

She nodded.

"I don't believe your mama would go for it. You know, me already looking silly driving down Main Street on a lawn mower."

She slowly pushed her lower lip out into a pout. "But I don't think you *wook siwwy*, Mr. Noah."

"We're working on your Ls next week." He poked his finger into her soft belly.

She giggled and stepped back. "*Pwease?*"

"How about a ride around the yard and to your mama's car, hmm?"

She hesitated, then held up fingers. "Two times *awound* the *yard*?"

"You drive a hard bargain." He slid back on the tractor seat and offered his hand. "Madame, your chariot awaits."

She hopped up into his lap and he started the mower, blades off. They were just finishing their second turn around the front yard, ducking under a silver maple tree branch, when Rachel walked down the porch steps.

"Uh-oh," Mallory called.

"Uh-oh," Noah echoed, steering toward the garage. He stopped near the door and cut the engine. Mallory hopped off without having to be told.

Rachel passed him without saying a word.

"I'm going into town to get some wire and a couple of other things Mateo needs; you need anything?" he asked Rachel.

"Washing machine is acting up again. You think you could bring back one of those from the appliance store balanced in your lap?" She opened the car door and then halted, leaning on the roof to look at him. To his surprise, she was smiling, though her tone was a little dry for eight-thirty in the morning.

"I understand that some people think I look silly driving this thing around town."

"You should get a bicycle," she told him.

"Can't cut 'cross country on a bike."

"You could on a mountain bike."

"Can't hitch the utility wagon to a mountain bike."

She laughed and shook her head. "I'm taking Mallory to school and then I'll be back."

"What about Mattie?" he asked.

"He'll be fine. He's in the house helping Mrs. Santori with the laundry. She saves the socks for days for him. Sometimes it takes him hours to match them up, but he likes doing it." She lifted one shoulder in a shrug.

Noah glanced away, then back. "I feel like I haven't been spending much time with him, but I can barely catch him. He plays that organ by the hour. If I didn't know better, I'd think he was avoiding me."

"Yeah, well, you were gone five years. My guess is that he thought you were avoiding him somewhat."

He thought for a moment and then couldn't resist a lopsided grin. He adjusted the brim of his battered Orioles ball cap that he'd found in a box in his room with stuff marked "yard sale." "I get your point. So what do you suggest I do?"

"Just give him time. Keep approaching, but don't push it. You know he doesn't respond well to pushy."

She gave him a smile, a hesitant smile that made him smile back. It was a smile he remembered from a very long time ago.

"Got it. Thanks." He slid his hand into his pocket. "Well, guess I'll see you after awhile. You'll probably beat me back here." He crossed the lawn and got onto the seat of the lawn tractor, surprised that he was still smiling when he headed across the blossoming apple orchard.

* * *

In town, Noah stopped at Burton's Hardware and Appliances and paid for a new washer, a front loader, and arranged to have it delivered in the afternoon. He felt completely inadequate in Rachel's presence, and so guilty about leaving her with so many responsibilities for so long while he was in prison, that if he could help her out in any small way, even by buying her a washing machine that ran, he was happy to do it.

He was just crossing the street from the hardware store when he spotted Snowden Calloway striding down the brick steps of the police station. Noah meant to just tip his hat, but when Snowden started in his direction, he felt like he needed to meet him halfway on the sidewalk.

"Noah."

"Snowden." Noah nodded. He remembered almost nothing of the night of the accident except that Snowden had been the first responding officer on the scene. He remembered the blood on Snowden's large hands. He remembered the anger in the man's voice as he handcuffed him and put him in the back of the black and white, which actually was black and white. Noah felt his face grow warm with shame as Snowden put out his hand, and Noah accepted it.

They shook and Noah stepped back.

"So how you doing?"

Noah shrugged. "You know."

"A little hard."

Noah was surprised by the tone of his voice. There was no accusation. No anger. He looked up into Snowden's eyes. He was a tall man, six four at least, with café-latte-colored skin and the most intriguing pale blue eyes, eyes that really penetrated you, eyes that seemed to see you for who you were, not who you wanted people to think you were.

"Yeah, a little hard," Noah agreed, glancing away, then back at Snowden as he eased his hands into his jeans pockets. "And a little weird, you know."

"I can imagine." He chuckled, touching the brim of his uniform hat as some elderly ladies crossed the street half a block away. "I've sort of always felt like I belonged more on the island of misfit toys than in Stephen Kill."

Noah chuckled. "Right. Guess you have."

Snowden nodded in the direction of the John Deere parked in front of the hardware store. "I see you've figured out a way to get around. You making your AA meetings?"

"I sure am. Todd Corkland's my sponsor. You know him— Roland's father, retired from the state forestry service."

"Yeah, I know him. Fishes a lot out of Bowers Beach."

"That's him." Noah glanced up at Snowden, hesitant to say what was on his mind, but feeling like he couldn't help himself. "Hey, listen, I know everyone's probably been bugging you about the Johnny Leager thing, but I keep thinking about it. I knew him pretty well." He looked away, watching a clerk struggle with a Welcome flag that fluttered in the spring breeze as she tried to slide the wooden pole into its bracket on the wall outside the shop door. "I keep going over it and over it in my mind, you know. How he died. I was just wondering if you've got any leads. I just can't imagine who would have done something like this. Johnny was a good man. Worked hard. Loved his family."

"You think you know anything that might be helpful?" Snowden shifted his weight, standing a little taller.

He was watching Noah more carefully now, more carefully than Noah cared to be watched; suddenly, he felt uncomfortable.

"No, no, obviously I haven't seen him in years, I just . . ." Noah slipped his hands out of his pockets and rubbed them together. He didn't even know now what had made him bring up Johnny. Maybe because he had laid in bed last night thinking about him?

Or was it because he had woken up on the floor of the garage the night Johnny Leager had been murdered and he didn't know where he'd been or what he'd done?

It was a ridiculous thought. One that lasted only a moment before he dismissed it.

"He *was* one of your parishioners, wasn't he?" Snowden said.

"Yes, he was."

"Did you counsel him?"

"I counseled many parishioners in the years I was at St. Paul's."

"That wasn't an answer, Noah."

Snowden's directness took Noah by surprise. Noah turned to watch the young policewoman who'd just left the diner try to balance the cardboard tray of coffee and foil-wrapped sandwiches with a newspaper under her arm. "I hate even days," she called out to Snowden. "People always making smart-aleck comments about me fetchin' your darned coffee. Don't they notice odd days when we ride together you get the coffee? Even days I get it? No, they do not." She crossed the street, walking up to the two men.

"Sergeant Swift, Noah Gibson," Snowden introduced.

"Pleased to meet you," she said, setting the cardboard tray on the hood of the black and white cruiser.

"Noah was the priest at St. Paul's before Father Hailey."

She nodded. One look and Noah knew she knew the whole story.

"So back to my question," Snowden said. "Did you counsel him?"

Noah felt a smile tug at his mouth. "Back to my answer, Chief. I counseled many men and women in this town. I had certain responsibilities as to privacy as the spiritual advisor to these citizens, and despite my fall from grace, as it was, I'm guessing I still have that responsibility." He looked up. "Why do you ask? Something going on with your investigation that the Watkins sisters and I don't know about?"

CHAPTER 5

"That son of a gun, he knows something." Snowden reached for his cup of coffee as he watched Noah from the passenger's side of the black and white cruiser.

Noah walked slowly down the sidewalk, his hands stuffed in his pockets, his head down, his Orioles ball cap shadowing his face.

Delilah studied him from behind the wheel. Even days were her days to get the coffee and breakfast when she trained with the chief, which also meant she got to drive. Despite the teasing from some of her fellow officers, she didn't mind her training days. In fact, she found she liked them. Chief Calloway had a lot to offer; he was a good cop. Not half bad to look at either.

"Don't get your boxers in a twist, Chief. He was just saying he can't be tellin' you everything Johnny Leager told him in confession, else he'd be violating some kind of priest vow he took or something."

Snowden removed the lid from his Styrofoam coffee cup and slurped off the top of the steaming coffee. "Episcopalians don't go to confession, Delilah. That's the Catholics."

She raised both her hands as if to surrender to him, hands tiny and delicate, easily half the size of his. "How am I supposed to know? My family's been Baptist since John lost his head." She reached for her egg, scrapple, and cheese biscuit, home cooked at the diner. So far, fast food hadn't found its way to Stephen Kill, although she heard there was talk that Taco Bell or Pizza Hut was looking to buy land.

"No." Snowden took another sip of his black coffee, still watching Noah. "He was looking guilty from the minute he brought Johnny Leager's name up. It was as if he didn't want to mention it, but felt compelled to do so."

"If he had something to do with the man's murder, you think he would have walked up to you and started the conversation?" She frowned. "That kind of reasoning just doesn't fly with this gal, Chief." When he didn't respond, she went on. " Come on, Cora Watkins has asked me four times this week if we've got any leads. You think that means *she* killed Johnny Leager?" She shook her head. "Naw. From what you say, any guilt Noah Gibson's carrying around could come from a hundred things. Wouldn't you feel guilty if you were him?"

Snowden stared out the windshield. "So are we going to see Johnny Leager's shift boss this morning or aren't we?"

"We are." She made no move to start the car. "But not until I have my breakfast. It's not safe to eat and drive. Besides, I thought we'd sit here a few minutes and see where else Mr. Gibson goes. Who else he speaks to, since he's so curious about Johnny Leager and what we know about his murder."

"I thought you didn't think he looked guilty." Snowden grabbed his breakfast sandwich from the cardboard tray between them and began to unwrap the foil.

"You know me, Chief. Everyone looks guilty to me." She gave a nod in the direction of the woman Noah had stopped to speak to on the steps of the post office. "Even the nuns."

*   *   *

"Noah, it's good to see you." Sister Julie came down the old red brick steps, an armful of manila envelopes in her hand. "How are you?" She smiled, offering a one-armed hug, her pleasure seeming genuine.

He accepted the hug, figuring he could use all the hugs he could get these days. "I'm doing OK."

"You going to AA regularly?"

"You're the second person to ask me that in the last five minutes."

"Good." She grinned, tucking her mail under her arm.

Sister Julie Anne Thompson didn't look much like a Catholic nun to him or anyone else. She didn't wear a habit or any form thereof, and she in no way resembled the little old ladies who came to mind when a person envisioned a holy sister of the Catholic Church. She was easily five foot nine, with a long mane of rich chestnut hair she wore in a ponytail, and though she was probably pushing forty, she could have easily passed for thirty with a little makeup. Still, she was pretty, and nothing about her appearance gave her away as a nun, not the blue jeans and white sneakers or the blue Nike T-shirt. The only possible telltale sign was the simple gold crucifix she wore around her neck.

"I hope someone reminds you at least once a day to go to AA," she told him, poking him in the center of his chest with her finger. "It's got to be hard when you first get out. Probably hard the rest of your life."

He wanted to look away, at least squirm in his sneakers, but Sister Julie wasn't the kind of woman who would let you get away with that kind of thing, so he just nodded. "So," he said, "how's the place doing?"

Sister Julie and several women from her order and a host of volunteers ran a home for unwed mothers at the edge of town. It was one of those places that had lost favor in most small towns in the United States years ago, with most teenage unwed mothers now collecting their food stamps, WIC, or other social services, flaunting their big bellies in public schools, proud of their reproductive accomplishments. But there still seemed to be at least a small need in the country for the kind of place Sister Julie and the nuns ran, where girls who chose not to have abortions or keep their babies could have some privacy for a few months once their conditions became noticeable. Young girls came and went, staying a few months, being homeschooled by the nuns until they gave birth. The babies were usually given up for adoption through Catholic social services, and then the teenagers quietly returned to their lives in Boise or Dallas to finish out high school or college, their pregnancy often unbeknownst to most family and friends. Occasionally, word drifted down Main Street that a young woman had decided to keep her baby, and she returned home with the nuns' blessings and her bundle wrapped in a pink or a blue blanket, but that didn't happen often. Sister Julie offered a sanctuary for young women to rest a few months until they could pick up their lives where they'd left off, a little older, a little sadder, and hopefully a little wiser.

Noah had always admired what Julie and those women did, because they didn't just talk about their beliefs, they stood behind them. They didn't just tell young women they had solutions beyond the obvious, they offered solutions with kind words and actions to back them up.

"We're good. Seven girls staying with us right now, two about to deliver." Julie brightened at once as she always did when anyone asked about Maria's Place. "Short of funding, as always, of course, but we're making ends meet. We're having a fund-raiser later in the month, a picnic and auction. You should come and bring Rachel and Mallory and Mattie."

He grimaced. "We'll see about that; we're not exactly one big happy family right now, if you know what I mean."

Sister Julie studied him for a moment, still standing a step above him on the stairs, so that she looked him straight in the eye. "You know, Noah, what you've been through, what you did, was terrible, it was just plain damned awful."

He blinked. Nuns that cursed. It pleased him for some reason to think that there was still something in the world to take him by surprise. Gave him a weird sense of optimism. He studied the dirty toes of his sneakers.

"So the way I see it is that now that you're out of prison, now that you've paid your so-called debt to society, you've got two choices." She waited for him to respond.

When the silence got unbearable, he finally met her gaze. "And what two choices might those be, Sister?" he asked, unable to hold back just a hint of sarcasm. All he could think of was that there was no way she could have any idea what he was feeling inside right now. What it was like—every day of his life—to know that he had killed two other human beings. It was pretty easy to tell people to pull themselves up by their bootstraps when you didn't know what it was like or how far down it was when they fell.

"Well, Noah, I'm going to tell you. You can let your past sins drag you down and you can let them ruin your life and ruin the lives of those around you, those who love you: Rachel, Mattie, that cute little Mallory. Or, you can do what the good book says—you can accept atonement for your sins, you can accept the forgiveness that's been offered, stop feeling so damned sorry for yourself, and get on with the rest of your life. Get on to the living part." She waved an envelope in emphasis. "Because there're a lot of people out here who still need you. A lot of good still left to be done on this earth before you're called home. Obviously God's still got work for you, otherwise you'd have died in that car accident with the Marcuses." She finished her discourse with a firm nod of her square chin. "Well, I'd better be going." She smiled as she passed him, as if they had just shared the most pleasant of conversations concerning no more than the amount of rainfall they could expect or the Orioles' winning record. "Have a great day. Say hi to Rachel for me, and do think about coming to the auction." She took the last two steps backward. "We're still accepting donations if you'd like to make one. Gift certificates are always nice. A nice gift basket with a bottle of wine, some cheese, some wine glasses, maybe?"

She turned away, then back again. "And by the way. What you were thinking about a minute ago. You're wrong. I *do* know how you feel. I know *exactly* how you feel. Why the hell do you think I do this every day?" She turned and walked away.

Noah was so stunned that he stood on the post office steps for a full minute trying to remember why he was there, and when he couldn't, he gave up, turned back around, and headed for his John Deere.

By the time Noah arrived back at the house with the #3 gauge wire, the staples, and the clamps Mateo needed, he had a splitting headache. He went into the house to grab a couple of aspirin out of the bottle that still sat on the window-sill in the kitchen, where it had been since he was a kid. When he came back out of the kitchen onto the porch, Mattie was on the step, just sitting there, big hands in his lap. He was dressed as he always was this time of year, of course—white T-shirt, Dickies work pants, white sneakers, and the ever-present ball cap, which hid the fact, as Noah noticed at break-fast the other day, that his hair was thinning.

Noah's first impulse was to say hi and go on by. Mateo needed him out in the lower west field where he was mend-ing some fencing that kept the deer out of the grapes. The easiest thing to do right now would be to keep on walking. Later, Noah could tell himself, maybe even Rachel if he had the opportunity, that he had attempted to connect with Mattie and that Mattie was still being uncooperative.

Of course, the *easiest* thing to do would be to go back into the house and pour himself a glass of wine, maybe a shot of vodka. He wasn't naïve enough to think that Rachel hadn't rid the house of all the nice cabernets and shirazes before she picked him up at the DOC last week, but even a hit of cough syrup would have gone down nicely right now. His chats with Snowden and Sister Julie weren't sitting too well on his stomach.

"Hey, Mattie." Noah sat down on the upper step beside him.

Mattie stared straight ahead, his meaty hands pressed to his double-enforced knees.

"I saw you helped Mrs. Santori with the laundry this morning. That was nice of you."

Mattie made no response.

"Nothing like having socks that match." Noah stuck his feet out and tugged on the pant legs of his jeans to show off his white athletic socks. They'd come out of one of the cardboard boxes in the storage room that he'd had the guts to actually open. Once he found a few things he needed, he'd closed it up and not gone back upstairs since.

Still no response from Mattie.

Noah sighed and gazed out over the driveway, across the lawn. Rachel was back. He could see her, far in the distance, walking along a row of grapevines in a pink T-shirt. He'd always liked her in pink. He glanced back at Mattie, studying his face and the way his jowl sagged slightly.

Mattie was a hard man to read, always had been, even when they were kids. He never showed much emotion, but Noah had the feeling something wasn't right. Something was troubling him. "Hey, Mattie," he said softly. "Something up, buddy?"

Mattie looked at his hands resting on his knees.

"Something someone said, something that happened maybe that upset you?" Noah hesitated. "Maybe it's me that's upsetting you. Me being back?"

Mattie rose suddenly, startling Noah. He just stood there

stiffly for a second, staring straight ahead, his hands at his sides. Then he glanced over his shoulder in Noah's direction, not exactly making eye contact, and lumbered off in the direction of the barn.

"You want me to follow you?" Noah asked, walking after him. "Sure. Sure, I'll come."

Mattie didn't protest so Noah guessed it was what he wanted. He didn't say anything else as their sneakers crunched on the drive. He heard a vehicle approaching from the road and saw a panel truck; it was probably the washing machine, but Mrs. Santori was in the house; she would take care of the delivery. Noah followed Mattie into the barn, carefully closing the door behind him. Mattie was a stickler about doors, always had been. They went through another door and down the cement block steps into the cellar.

As Rachel had told him, the area was neatly divided by six-foot-high Sheetrock walls that had been patched and painted nicely, giving an appearance very similar to the rooms in the church cellar where Mattie had lived with his father, until Jack had died in an accident at the church. Mattie had then lived there alone until Noah had gone to prison. Beyond the wall dividers he imagined were the same items that had been stored here for years: old wine casks and bottles, broken and outdated equipment, the usual things stored in barn cellars.

"This is nice," Noah said, turning in the center of the room as he took a look around. It was cool in the cellar, and even with the two small rectangular windows and the overhead fluorescent lamps that had been wired by an electrician, the lighting was dim.

Mattie's single bed was neatly made with a navy blue bedspread and a stuffed green Shrek doll proudly displayed on the pillow, a gift from a little pigtailed girl, Noah suspected. Beside the bed was a nightstand with a lamp, a bottle of water, and a Bible. Mattie had never been able to learn to read, but he had always found comfort in the mere physical presence of a Bible. It was something his father, a deeply religious man, had impressed upon him.

Noah glanced in Mattie's direction. "So you wanted to show me your room? It's very nice down here, Mattie. It feels good. It feels very safe."

Then he spotted Mattie's latest creation. "Goodness," he said, taking a step back, genuinely shocked. "Your collection has really grown, hasn't it?"

Mattie had been collecting Bibles since he was a kid. The church gave them to him when they became damaged and unusable. People sometimes gave him an extra Bible they had lying around the house or one they no longer wanted. Sometimes, when folks from town went on vacation, they even brought a Bible back as a souvenir from Orlando or St. Thomas or the Grand Canyon. When he was little, Mattie had stacked the Bibles up under his bed and showed them off to anyone daring enough to follow him to the curtained-off room he shared with his father in the church basement. When he was older, he and his father had built bookshelves for them, and he had prided himself on the beautiful rows of Bibles on those bookshelves. But Mattie's books were no longer on the shelves. The Bibles were stacked on the floor waist-high. He appeared to be building something.

The sight of the Bibles on the floor made the hair rise on the back of Noah's neck, a sudden chill seeming to fall over him. It was the weirdest feeling.

"Whatcha doing here with your Bibles, Mattie?" Noah asked, feeling completely uneasy and not liking it one bit. He had no need for Bibles. No need for God. At least God had no need for him. But there was something specific about the Bibles on the floor that made him ill at ease.

"Do you want some help arranging them? Putting them back on the shelves?" Noah picked one up and started to carry it toward one of the empty shelves, but Mattie made a guttural sound in his throat and snatched it out of his hand.

Noah watched as Mattie carefully placed it back on one of the waist-high stacks.

"OK," Noah said. "That's fine. It won't hurt them to sit on the floor." He studied the stacks, nonchalantly backing up from them a step or two. "Where'd you get so many? You must have hundreds now."

Mattie went down on both knees in his faded work pants and began to neaten up the stacks of Bibles that were already as neat as library stacks.

Noah, now closer to the door, stood another moment longer. Mattie didn't seem now to want anything from him. Noah guessed he had just wanted him to see the Bibles. "I really like them, Mattie," he said, and then he headed up the steps and out of the barn, relieved to be back in the sunshine, out of the chill of the cellar.

CHAPTER 6

Noah sat on the edge of the bed in the little room still stacked with junk, staring at the hole in his white sock and the way his toe stuck out if he wiggled it just right. He needed to buy new socks. He had just two pairs, the pair he wore out of DCI and this pair, and nothing would please him more than to throw the prison-issue socks in the trash, but a man had to be practical. A man needed more than two pairs of socks.

He could get a pack at the old-fashioned Five and Dime in town, or at the grocery store, but it seemed silly to buy more when he knew there to be at least a dozen pairs upstairs in the boxes in the storage room. The thing was to find them; he'd have to dig through the boxes. And finding the socks would involve having to look at things in the boxes, touch things, stir up memories he just didn't know that he wanted to stir up.

He wiggled his toe again.

He knew there were just *things* in those boxes. It wasn't like he was a man who saved a lot of mementos. He didn't even know what was up there; he could be making a big deal

out of nothing. He could guess what was in the box ...
things he noticed missing around the house. There might be
nothing more innocuous there than a photo of him and
Rachel in California, barely looking old enough to be allowed out of the house without their parents, and an old
Dodgers ball cap. But there were other things there, he knew.
A lump rose in his throat. Things that had to be there ...

He wiggled his toe.

Debated.

It was nearly midnight; he should have been tired. Tired?
He should have been near to exhaustion. He'd worked hard
today. After his visit in the barn cellar with Mattie he'd been
driven by some kind of unnamed demon, pushing himself
and Mateo until well after dark and past suppertime. After
they had finished repairing the trellises and Mateo had gone
to see to some vine-tying, Noah had started sinking holes for
posts for a new row of trellises. No gas-powered auger for
him, not when he had a shovel. It wasn't like he didn't have
the time. He had nothing but time.

His arms, his legs, his back, his entire body ached from
the abuse of the day. If he'd lay down, he'd probably go right
to sleep. He could leave the boxes for another day.

But he knew he wouldn't go right to sleep. He'd lay there
and think. He'd think about how badly he wanted a drink
right now. He'd think about the blackout he had in the field
today. He'd been out only a few minutes, but he'd woken up
sitting under a tree fifty or sixty feet from where he'd been
working, and had no recollection of how he'd gotten there. If
he tried to sleep, he'd think about Johnny Leager, beaten to
death with bricks.

Noah pressed the heel of his hand against his forehead.

If he lay down right now, he would think about the
Marcus family and wonder how their little girl was, living in
South Carolina now without her mother and father because
he had murdered them.

Noah lifted his head. "So what do you say, Chester? Do we find ourselves some socks?"

The dream started out pleasantly enough. Rachel felt as if she were drifting through a sunny Sunday afternoon. Even though she was alone in the dream, she could feel others around her. She could smell Mrs. Santori's fried chicken cooking in the kitchen, and she sensed Noah was somewhere around the house, puttering before supper. She was sitting on the front porch, rocking on the porch swing.

A baby appeared in her lap. A baby boy. She didn't know if it was Isaac or Abraham. It didn't matter.

Dreams were like that.

In her dream, it was just her baby boy, the one she had desperately wanted. A baby who was alive in this fantasy world of her brain.

She rocked the infant, cooed to him, one bare foot tucked beneath her. In the house, she heard a sound. At first she didn't know what it was. She was too busy cooing at the baby, sipping a nice glass of her own pinot, listening to the ball game Noah had tuned to on his father's old radio on the porch.

But the sound grew louder. A mechanical sound, and she realized it was the washing machine. The new washing machine Eddie had delivered today. The time line made no sense. The dream took place sometime long in the past, before Noah had gone to prison, when there had at least been the possibility of a baby boy. When life had been full of possibilities. This washing machine she knew was a brand-new Neptune front loader. But dreams never made sense.

Rachel rose, the sleeping baby snuggled in her arms. She padded barefoot into the house. There was no sign of Mrs. Santori, but Rachel could still smell the chicken frying; she could hear it sizzling. She felt the cool boards of the old farmhouse's wood floor on her bare feet as she walked through the kitchen toward the laundry room.

The new washing machine was making a terrible sound as if something was stuck inside it, setting the drum off balance. "Noah!" she called.

As she stepped into the brightly wallpapered yellow laundry room, a chill settled over her, and she instinctively tightened her grip on the baby in her arms. Something was wrong. Something was terribly wrong.

Someone was watching her.

She looked over her shoulder. There was no one there, no one she could see, but still, she was uneasy. She turned back toward the new, white washing machine. It still had the yellow sticker on the front that explained the energy-saving benefits of the latest model.

The washing machine shook. It growled.

Rachel felt the hair rise on the back of her neck, and she lifted the baby onto her shoulder to draw him closer. A part of her wanted to run. There was something bad here in the sunny laundry room. Something inherently evil. But she couldn't run. You never could run away from things in your dreams.

She took a step closer. She could see the water inside the machine, see clothes tumbling, but there was something else inside . . .

She took another step closer. There was something inside the machine that didn't belong there.

That's when she realized the water was red.

She reached out to jerk the washer door open, holding the baby with one hand, and he vanished, leaving her nothing but the little flannel blanket and the scent of him.

Rachel cried out in anguish as the washing machine door swung open and water poured out. Only it wasn't just water. It was bloody water.

Clothes poured out.

Dead bodies poured out.

The pale white bodies of her baby boys.

The Marcuses.

She tried to scream but found herself mute.

The water washed over her legs and the bodies bumped into her. Thumped against the wall behind her.

They just kept tumbling out in the gush of bloody water. Legs. Arms. Wet hair. Noah's parents. Johnny Leager.

She drew the baby blanket over her face and screamed into it.

Rachel sat straight up in bed, yanking the blanket off her face and throwing it aside. Panting hard, she looked around the room. She knew no one was there, and yet she thought she had felt someone there in the room just as she was waking. Felt *something*.

"Just a dream," she whispered, shaking, seeing nothing but the familiar but not sure she believed her own eyes. "Just a dream."

She threw her legs over the side of the single, antique iron-post bed and stood, finding relief in the coolness of the floorboards on her bare feet. She pushed down her rumpled gray T-shirt over the waistband of the blue polka-dotted pajama pants that were so old they were nearly transparent.

She had to get out of the bedroom. Just for a second. She'd go downstairs and get a drink of water from the fridge. Once she was fully awake, she'd realize it was just a bad dream. There was no one in her bedroom or in the laundry room. There was nothing inherently evil possessing the washing machine Noah had bought today. It was really a nice washing machine. A nice thing for him to do.

Still feeling a little shaky, she opened the bedroom door and walked out into the hall. Her heart tripped in her chest at the sight of Noah seated on the floor at the top of the stairs. He was just sitting on the floor in his boxers and T-shirt and a pair of socks, his legs sprawled. Chester lay on the floor beside him.

"Were you just in my room?" Rachel snapped, wrapping her arms around her waist as if she needed to protect herself from him.

He looked up at her, seeming nearly as startled to see her as she was to see him. "N . . . no. Of course not."

She walked down the hall toward him, eyeing him suspiciously. "What the hell are you doing up here in the middle of the night?" She looked him up and down. "In your underwear." She looked toward Mallory's bedroom door suddenly, her heart giving a little trip. "You haven't been—"

"Sweet God, no, Rachel." He ran his hand through his hair. "What kind of monster do you think I am?" He looked up at her and then down again. "Never mind. Don't answer that." He gestured lamely at the stairwell across the hall from where he sat. "I couldn't sleep, so I came upstairs to get some more clothes out of the boxes. I just . . . I couldn't bring myself to . . ." He groaned aloud and grew quiet.

Rachel stared at him for a moment and then walked over to where he sat, leaned against the wall, and slowly sank to the floor until she sat beside him. They weren't touching, but her knee was only inches from his.

After a moment of silence, he glanced at her. "What are you doing up in the middle of the night?"

"Nightmare," she whispered. Then she chuckled, though she wasn't able to find much humor. She could still smell the scent of her baby boy on her hands, and she could still feel the presence of the evil that had been in that room in her dream. "Involving that fancy smancy new washing machine you had delivered today."

He tugged on the toe of his sock, which she noticed had a hole. "I've never heard of a nightmare with a washing machine in it."

She drew her knees up, wrapping her arms around them so that she could rest her chin on them. "This was really weird, Noah. Creepy weird." She turned her head to look at him. "This doesn't have anything to do with my dream, but did you know that the person who killed Johnny Leager knew something about him that other people didn't know?"

Noah looked at her.

Rachel had been avoiding contact with Noah since he came home. It made life easier . . . well, if not easier, at least bearable. She didn't look away when he met her gaze this time.

"What do you mean?"

"The police aren't saying anything to the general public, but there was a handwritten note left by the killer making an accusation."

"How do you know that?"

She caught her lower lip between her teeth. It wasn't Noah's business if she and Snowden had dated. It was long over, though they'd made a feeble attempt at rekindling the fires when Mallory was around two and a half, and they had eventually come to the conclusion that they were better friends than they would ever be lovers. "I just know," she said carefully.

"Snowden?"

She lifted one shoulder and looked down at her bare feet.

He was quiet for a minute. He had always been able to read her, better than she could read herself. He knew something had gone on between her and Snowden in his absence.

"I saw Snowden today," Noah said, "and he was a little weird with me. He specifically asked me if I had counseled Johnny. I'm guessing now it had to do with that note." He was quiet for a moment. "You didn't tell him about my sessions with Johnny, did you, Rache?"

She glanced up at him, a little hurt that he would even ask. "Of course not."

"Because anything my parishioners shared with me in the privacy of my office was in complete confidence. A man of the cloth has no right to speak of anything told to him in confidence, not even to his wife," he said gravely. "You must know that. "

"I would never betray the confidence we shared, Noah. Never," she whispered, her eyes filling with tears.

Then she felt his arm slide across her shoulder. She knew she should push him away. And she would.

In just a minute.

Azrael felt the presence even before the voice filled the dark bedroom. It woke Azrael from a deep sleep.

"No," Azrael muttered, rolling in the bed, pulling up the blanket to block out the voice, the very existence.

"You cannot turn away from me," the voice of God commanded. "You cannot hide, Azrael."

Go away, please.

"You cannot deny your obligation," God's voice boomed. "You cannot question my word. You do not question *The Word*!"

Azrael shook beneath the bedcovers. No, no, of course not. The Word is undeniable. It cannot be refuted. God and his demands cannot be denied.

"Come, Azrael, do not be afraid."

The voice was gentler when it spoke again. "I came only to say what a job well done you performed for me, for my kingdom.

Azrael eased the grip on the bedcovers slightly.

"I am very proud of you, Azrael. You must know that."

Azrael ceased shaking so violently in fright and lay perfectly still under the blankets.

"When I sought out a soldier, there were some who did not believe in you, but I believed in you, Azrael. I knew that you were up to the task. I knew that you had the strength to endure."

Azrael nodded.

Again, God was quiet for a moment.

"But there are others, Azrael. You know that, don't you?"

Quiet, and then the voice that could not be denied again.

"Others who have sinned, who must pay for the sins they

have committed—sins they may think are secret, but nothing is secret with me, is it, Azrael? Nothing is a secret with us."

No . . .

"I will come again. . . . Sleep now."

"I think he understands more than we realize," Noah remarked, gesturing with his coffee cup in the direction of the open window over the sink.

Rachel poured herself a cup from the stainless steel pot on the counter and came to stand beside him. Outside, Mattie was pulling Mallory in a red wagon, two barn kittens in her lap. She was laughing as he pulled her around and around in tight circles.

"Hmmm," Rachel said. She leaned against the counter, finding that she was thoroughly enjoying the early morning exchange with Noah. It was almost like old times, before his drinking, before his mom and dad had died, before everything. There was something about last night, sitting in the hallway there, that had changed things between them, and she didn't know what it was. For the first time since Noah's return he had had something to offer her, and she had welcomed it. It had only been the support of his arm and a few kind words, but it meant a great deal to her. It had been a glimpse of the Noah she had once known. The Noah she had loved.

"What makes you say so?" she asked.

"First off, for being uncommunicative, he seems to communicate just fine with us when he wants to. And his ability to play the organ these days is just amazing. I mean, I always knew he could play simple hymns, but he's playing stuff he's hearing on the radio, Rache. He seems to be writing his own pieces. How can you not—"

"I wasn't disagreeing with you." She sipped her coffee. "I was just asking what made you say so. As for uncommunicative, I'm not sure how true that is. Obviously he hears fine, he understands most of what we say, maybe everything." She hesitated. "Mallory says he talks to her."

"Mallory said he talks? You're kidding." Noah looked at her. "Like with words?"

She shrugged and took another sip of her coffee as she walked away from the sink, the heavenly scent of fried bacon luring her toward the table. "That's what she says. Of course, I can't tell you how reliable the source is. We're talking about a four-year-old, and this is the same young lady who insists that there are monsters under her bed that will nibble on her toes if we don't keep them properly covered at night."

He smiled, turning away from the window. "Who knows, maybe he can talk."

She took a piece of bacon off a plate Mrs. Santori had left on the table.

On Fridays, the housekeeper took half a day off. She came in early, started the coffee, made something for breakfast, and was usually out of the house by the time the automatic coffeemaker was spurting the aromatic brew into the stainless steel thermal pot. No one knew where she went on Fridays, but she'd been going for years.

As Rachel nibbled on her bacon she contemplated Mallory's revelation. "Don't you think if Mattie could talk, we'd have heard something? A word or two?" She reached under the paper-towel-covered plate for another piece of bacon.

"Maybe he's known us so long that he doesn't need to speak to us." Noah took a seat at the kitchen table, rocking back in the chair. "Maybe he talks to Mallory because he needed to, at least at first, in order to communicate to her. I notice he does move his lips. I just saw him out there in the yard doing it."

"But he's always done that," Rachel argued. She backed up against the chair next to Noah's, leaning her bottom against it, pointing her slice of crisp bacon at him. "Don't you remember how much trouble that Andy kid got into with

Mr. Johnson in Sunday School for making fun of Mattie for doing that?"

Noah snatched the bacon out of her hand and took a bite. "I do remember that. But he didn't make any sounds then, not any that sounded like words, at least. Of course, Mallory could be telling the truth. Anything is possible."

"That's true," she agreed. "God works in mysterious ways."

He glanced away, finishing off her bacon and taking a drink of his coffee.

The warmth Rachel had felt in the sunny kitchen had suddenly chilled noticeably. The moment between them had passed with her mention of God as if she had poured a glass of ice water over Noah's head.

She really had a way of putting her foot in the doggie doo.

She set down her coffee cup, acting cheerier than she felt. "Guess I better see if Mallory is going to stay with Mattie this morning while I meet with that guy to talk about distributing this wine you want to make."

"She isn't going to preschool this morning?" Noah asked, his voice sounding as if it stood at a distance from her.

He was standing at a distance now. A million miles away.

"Nope. School is Mondays through Thursdays." Next week is her last week. She started out the door and then turned back. "Hey, thanks again for the washing machine. It was nice of you. You didn't have to do that. I wasn't asking you to buy a washing machine yesterday when I complained about the old one."

He didn't turn around to look at her. "I know. I'm glad you like it. It's not a big deal, Rache."

"Well, it's a big deal to me. I love it. I swear, it holds twice as many clothes as the old clunker." She pushed open the screen door. "I just wanted you to know I appreciate it."

"So you don't want me to exchange it?"

She knitted her brows, confused. "Exchange it?"

"For one that's not possessed by evil spirits."

She laughed and let the screen door slap shut behind her. "Mallory! Where are you, lovebug?"

Delilah stepped out of the cruiser and adjusted her gun belt. Back before she was a cop, she had always thought the guys in the TV shows did that just to look cool, but now she knew they did it to keep from looking foolish in front of civilians. There was nothing to compare to the embarrassment one might experience when the weight of an automatic pistol and ammunition on the wide leather belt pulled one's trousers to one's ankles, showing one's tighty-whities . . . or one's white French-cut cotton Hanes, in her case.

"Be OK if I handle this interview?" she asked, walking up toward the Leager house, taking the lead in front of Snowden. "You know, Chief, me being a woman and all."

"You don't think I can handle the subject?"

She stopped and waited for him on the red brick sidewalk that Johnny had put down himself and never quite finished. She doubted it would ever get done now.

"I'm the one supposed to be training *you*, Sergeant Swift." Snowden loomed over her.

She barely came to his chin. She glanced up, not in the least bit intimidated. She had six brothers, every one of them every bit as tall as Snowden and a heck of a lot meaner. "I just think this needs to be handled delicately. We tried to get the information elsewhere and couldn't. It's bad enough we have to ask; I just think she might find it easier coming from me."

Snowden looked up at the house. Someone had pulled back a curtain and let it fall. A dog barked inside, and sounds came from behind the door. He glanced down at her. "Sure, you run the interview. You want me in the room or out?"

She pulled her notepad from her pocket and handed it to him. "You mind making me a quick sketch of the backyard?

I know we've got the photos, but sometimes a sketch is better when you're trying to figure out angles and stuff. I'm still not entirely convinced the killer didn't come out of the house. The wife found the front and back doors unlocked in the morning. If everyone in the house was asleep, how would they have known if the killer had taken a shortcut through the living room?"

Snowden took her notebook from her as the front door opened and a middle-aged woman in a flowered housecoat and blue scuff slippers stood waiting for them.

"Good morning," Delilah said, taking the steps. "I'm Sergeant Swift and this is Chief Calloway. I believe we've met before, ma'am. We have an appointment with Mrs. Leager this morning."

"She's in the dining room." The woman, Stacey Leager's mother, Delilah recalled, backed up to let them in.

The house was dim and smelled of coffee and cigarette smoke. There was a TV on in the living room. Cartoons. Delilah bumped a soccer ball with the toe of her shoe, and it rolled across the foyer and into the living room.

"Sorry 'bout that. Kids," the woman explained as if nothing more needed to be said. "Junior ain't ready to go back to school. I told Stacey ain't no need to send him, not yet, at least. He'll just have to make a fuss and then there'll be the gas money runnin' into town."

Delilah nodded as she walked into the dining room where Stacey Leager sat at the end of the table piled with an assortment of magazines, Wal-Mart bags, a shoebox, a sewing machine and fabric, and a pair of kids' sweatpants, among other things. Half of the bulbs were out in the cheap chandelier that hung over the table, so most of the light in the room came through the sliding glass doors that led out back.

Stacey Leager was wearing a men's old flannel bathrobe, her long blond hair unbrushed and looking as if it needed a touch-up at the roots. She was smoking a cigarette. Photographs around the house showed that she had once been a pretty woman, at least in her late teens, early twenties, but at thirty years old, she looked forty-five. Pregnancy, cigarettes, and weight gain and loss had not been good to her.

"Good morning, Mrs. Leager," Delilah said. "We appreciate you seeing us. If you don't mind, Chief Calloway is going to walk out into your backyard and have another look around. Make a quick sketch. I'll stay here and we can talk." She glanced at the mother hovering in the doorway.

The woman wandered into the kitchen, out of earshot.

"I guess there's no need to waste my breath or yours asking you how you are, ma'am. I can't even imagine how awful this must be for you." Out of the corner of her eye, she watched Snowden let himself out the sliding glass doors onto the patio where Johnny had been murdered. "Mind if I sit?" Delilah pointed to a chair with a blue bag on it.

"Just push the stuff off," Stacey Leager said, reaching for her coffee mug that said "World's Best Mom" on it as she pushed the cigarette between her lips. "I've been meaning to clean up, just haven't gotten the time. Johnny kept saying we ought to start eating here in the dining room instead of in front of the TV. You know, now that the kids are getting older." Her lower lip trembled and she took another drag on the cigarette, chasing it with a swallow of coffee.

Delilah picked up the bag full of craft supplies from the chair and added it to the pile on the table. She purposely did not take out a pad of paper to take notes. This kind of interview had to be personal, note-taking gave it the wrong feel. She faced Mrs. Leager, putting her hands together, leaning over.

"So, you have any idea who did this?" Stacey asked, setting the coffee cup back on the table. "You guys said you'd call me soon as you knew something." She grabbed a tissue from a box somewhere in the mess in front of her and wiped under her nose. "I kept thinking I would hear something from you by now."

Delilah looked down at her shiny size-six black shoes and

then up at her. "No, no, ma'am, we don't. Say, would it be all right if I called you Stacey?"

She shrugged. "Sure. 'Course. Mrs. Leager is Johnny's mom, far as I'm concerned." She gave a little snort. "Far as she's concerned, too, I guess."

"We got nothing from the tire tracks in your yard. No fingerprints anywhere. No one saw or heard anything, but of course your neighbors are far enough away that we wouldn't expect they would."

"And I never heard a thing," Stacey said quietly, gazing out the glass doors to where Snowden stood, his broad back to them. "Never even knew he didn't come to bed until morning."

"I know you know about the note. I know you saw it."

"Yeah, some Bible verse." She waved her hand, drawling a trail of cigarette smoke. "The Bible never made much sense to me. I go to church and all, but it's the priest who tells me what I'm supposed to do and not supposed to do. Now Father Gibson, he was a man who could give a sermon on a Sunday morning. This Father Hailey at St. Paul's now"—she shook her head, bringing the cigarette to her lips—"be honest with you, I don't know what he's talkin' about half the time. I mean he's nice enough, and I understand where Father Gibson can't be a priest no more, bein' what he did, but he sure could give a good Sunday morning sermon."

Delilah let her gaze drift to the children's photographs hung on the dining room wall. The daughter, four, was the spitting image of her mother; the son, nine, looked just like his dad, right down to the NASCAR shirt and crooked-toothed grin. She drew her gaze back to the woman in the robe.

"Well, Stacey, here's the thing. The only real evidence we have is that crazy note. Now I know it doesn't make sense to you and it certainly doesn't make sense to me, but it makes sense to the killer."

"Because he's crazy," Stacey said. "Have to be to kill a man that way, with bricks from his own barbecue."

"Stacey, I know this is kind of personal, and I wouldn't ask if I didn't need to, but how was your relationship, yours and Johnny's?"

She worked her jaw for a moment, took a last draw on the cigarette, and ground it out in an ashtray made from bottle caps. "What do you mean? Did I love Johnny? 'Course I loved him. I wouldn't have washed his underwear and put up with his snoring if I didn't love him." She smiled, her face softening as tears filled her eyes. "We were high school sweethearts, you know. He took me to the senior prom. We broke up for a while after high school. Johnny ran a little wild, but eventually he came back to me." She looked at Delilah. "I gave him two kids. Of course I loved him."

"And Johnny?" Delilah fought the urge to look away. She met Stacey's teary-eyed gaze woman to woman. "Was he happy in the marriage?"

The mother had been rattling around with dishes in the kitchen, but the noise had quieted. Delilah suspected she was listening to the conversation, but it was too late to back out now. Delilah had intended for it to be private, but she couldn't control people's nosy moms. Shoot, she couldn't even control her own nosy mother.

"Of course he was happy. He loved his kids, loved me," she said defensively. "Yeah, I gained a lot of weight with Tiffany, but I was on bed rest that last month. There wasn't anything else to do but eat and watch *Montel*."

"I understand. So you never sought marriage counseling or anything like that?"

Stacey sniffed, wiped her nose, balled up the tissue, and threw it. "I told you we were happily married. Comin' up on ten years. We were talking about taking a cruise or something, if we could get up the money." She reached for another cigarette from the generic pack on the table. "I haven't been working because Johnny wanted me here with the kids, but I used to be a checker at the drugstore when I was in high school. They're always hiring at the outlets." She flicked her disposable red lighter and lifted the flame to the cigarette dangling from her mouth.

"So as far as you know," Delilah pressed, "Johnny wasn't having an extramarital affair?"

"You mean was he cheating on me?" She raised her voice loud enough that it might have been heard over the SpongeBob cartoon on TV in the other room.

Delilah waited.

"No, *officer*. My husband was not cheating on me. I would know if he had been. Women know these kinds of things." She got out of the chair. "That all you wanted to know?"

"I'm sorry," Delilah said, rising. "I had to ask, because of the note left. You understand."

"What I understand is that there's some crazy bastard runnin' around out there who murdered my husband"—she gestured with her cigarette, leaving a trail of smoke—"and you're sitting here on your ass asking me if he was screwing some other woman." She started down the hall toward the back of the house. "Why don't you go do what you're sup-posed to be doing, huh? Catch this guy and leave us alone!"

Delilah glanced in the direction of the patio and through the doors she saw Snowden looking at her. He must have heard Stacey raise her voice. Delilah pointed and drew her finger around, signaling for him to meet her out front at the car.

She walked out of the dining room, past the living room where this time she saw the two Leager children in pajamas watching TV. At the front door, the mother came up behind her.

"You ought to be 'shamed of yourself," she hissed. "Asking a widow if her husband was cheatin' on her."

Delilah opened the front door to let herself out. "Just doing my job, ma'am."

CHAPTER 7

"You're late. Shoes." She pointed.

Snowden closed the door behind him and slid off his polished, black police-issue shoes, leaving them in the mudroom. No matter how old he got, how successful he was in his career, his mother could still make him feel like he was ten again. She could still make him feel guilty, even when there was no earthly reason for him to feel guilty. "Mom, I'm not late. I told you, eight o'clock. It's 7:55."

She was seated at the kitchen table, a chrome and red leatherette dinette set that had to be from the 1950s. But there wasn't a single tear on the seat covers or an inch of chrome that wasn't polished. The entire house, a tiny two-bedroom, white clapboard bungalow at the end of Holly Street, was like the dinette set. Time seemed to have ceased to pass here. As far as Snowden knew, nothing had changed in his grandparents' house since 1955.

His mother offered her cheek and he leaned over, kissing her. She was a petite woman with short brunette hair, still attractive for being in her mid-fifties. Not that it mattered. He had never known his mother to ever have a date. Not once.

The only proof she had ever known any man intimately was his existence.

"You work too much." She removed her reading glasses, allowing them to swing on the plastic jeweled cord around her neck, and folded her *Baltimore Sun* newspaper precisely on the folds before rising from her chair. "It's not good for a man to work so many hours a week. How's a man like that supposed to have time for a wife and children?"

Seeing that his place was already set at the table, with a laminated place mat, fork, knife, and paper napkin, he went to the refrigerator and removed a Tupperware pitcher of orange juice. "That's why I don't have a wife and children, Mom." He took a glass from a cabinet, one of those jewel-colored tin kind that were very retro now. Tillie's were original. He poured himself some orange juice.

She opened the white microwave he had bought her last Christmas, which still seemed out of place in the old kitchen, and loosened one corner of the plastic wrap before closing the door and punching the keypad to reheat his dinner. "How are you going to find a wife if you don't date? You can't date if you work until eight o'clock every night and never ask anyone out. Wife material doesn't just fall out of the sky into your lap, Snowden. You have to seek them out."

"Mom, we've had this discussion before. *Many* times before." He leaned back against the counter and took a drink from the glass. Meatloaf. He could smell his dinner reheating in the microwave. He hated meatloaf, particularly his mother's. "Not a lot of women in Stephen Kill suitable for me to date. How many fathers or brothers in this town do you think would approve of me as a suitor?"

"Because you're half African American?" she scoffed. "I'm tired of that excuse, Snowden. Where did you get that chip on that big shoulder of yours? Certainly not from me!"

He took another sip of juice. "Thanks for the dinner, Mom. I appreciate you saving me a plate. This Johnny Leager murder investigation is taking up every minute of my time. I'm not sleeping much. Certainly not eating much."

The microwave beeped, and she crossed the kitchen to retrieve his plate. She was wearing blue sweatpants, a sweatshirt, and scuff slippers, the only thing she ever wore around the house. He smiled to himself. If there was one thing Tillie Calloway was, it was predictable, which made his presence on earth all the more remarkable. At thirty-eight years old, Snowden still knew nothing of his father. Absolutely nothing except that he had been a black man. A product of an illicit affair Tillie's freshman year at the community college? A product of rape? He guessed he would never know, because his mother made it clear to him years ago that she intended to take that information with her to her grave.

"You should come every night for dinner," she told him, carrying the Corningware plate to the table. "It's foolish for you to cook for one and me to cook for one, living only a few blocks from each other."

"Mom, I'm a big boy. I can cook for myself. He pulled out his chair and set his juice glass on the table. He didn't have the heart, or the energy for that matter, to tell her that two or three dinners/lectures a week was all he could really stand right now.

"I know you can. I'm just saying there's no need for it. Sit. I'll start my tea and then sit with you while you eat. No need for your dinner to get cold waiting on me."

Snowden sat in the chair that had been his for as long as he could remember. He folded his hands, bowed his head, and silently gave thanks for the meatloaf in front of him. Before his amen, he prayed for Johnny Leager's family, prayed he'd find the killer. Prayed he was up to the task he'd spent his whole life working toward while others denied his ability and merit.

"Amen," Tillie finished for him as he lifted his head. She sat in the chair across from him and realigned the already straight newspaper in front of her. "So how's that sweet girl working out? The new one from down south?"

He rose to grab a bottle of ketchup from the refrigerator. He knew it would be the generic brand and taste like watered-down crap. It always was, always did, in Tillie's kitchen. "Sergeant Swift? She's working out well. Bright. Very conscientious. What she doesn't know, she seems willing to learn."

"I hear she's not married."

He let the ancient refrigerator door swing shut. She had to be the only person in Stephen Kill who still had the avocado-colored appliances. "No, I don't believe she is." He resisted a smile. Any encouragement and Tillie wouldn't let up on the subject.

"Never been married, Cora Watkins could tell me."

Snowden returned to his chair, flipped open the ketchup bottle, and squirted a healthy portion over the lump on his plate that had to be the meatloaf. "I wouldn't know, Mom. We don't talk much about personal things."

She fiddled with the edges of the newspaper. "Very attractive young woman. Smart, obviously has the same interests you do. You should ask her out."

"Mom, she works for me. I'm the chief of police. It would be inappropriate." He cut off a piece of meatloaf with his fork, tasted it, and dipped the rest in the runny ketchup.

The teakettle whistled and Tillie rose. "You don't think she's attractive?"

He stuffed some mashed potatoes into his mouth. "Whether I think she's attractive or not is a moot point. She works for me. I can't date Sergeant Swift." He frowned. The mashed potatoes were still cold in the middle and a little lumpy. He liked his mashed potatoes smooth, preferably with garlic and butter. Tillie Calloway didn't cook with garlic. "Besides, Mom, I'm ten years older than she is."

"Aha, so you *do* think she's attractive." She fished a tea

bag from a canister on the counter and dropped it into her teacup.

"Mom. Can we change the subject? Did you bring me any new books from the library?"

"Got the one on Genghis Khan. I read it. Fascinating how many ways the Mongols changed the face of Europe." She removed the teakettle from the gas burner, and the whistling ceased. "Of course I suppose I should have picked up a copy of *Dating for Dummies*. Do you more good."

Snowden pushed in another mouthful of meatloaf, vowing to pass on the next dinner invitation.

Pam walked down the hallway of the 1989 single-wide mobile home, hoping that was the last time she'd have to tell Amber to go to sleep. The four-year-old was having bad dreams and thought she ought to be allowed to sleep with her mother.

Ed was having no part of that, though, and Pam understood why; Amber wasn't his kid. He didn't want anyone thinking he was some kind of pervert or something. Pam just wished he'd be a little more understanding; Amber was only a little girl.

Of course, she wished Ed would be more understanding about a lot of things. He'd just moved in three months ago, and things had been pretty good at first, but she was beginning to wonder if she'd made a mistake. Even though he did help pay the rent and he bought a share of the groceries, he wasn't the easiest man to get along with. That wasn't to say he wasn't easier to get along with than Charlie, Amber's father, had been. Ed didn't get drunk and smack her around, she'd give him that. And he said he wanted to marry her, which was more than Charlie had ever offered. Pam thought several times about saying yes to Ed, but somewhere in the back of her mind she kept thinking she deserved better.

"I think she's asleep this time," Pam said, walking into the living room.

"I don't know why you don't just paddle her butt. That's what my mother would have done," Ed grumbled from the couch. The dark room flashed with light and shadows as he pushed the channel button on the remote control again and again.

Pam walked in front of the TV, around the coffee table, and Ed leaned one way and then the other so he could see around her. She plopped down on the end of the couch and dragged the laundry basket of clean clothes on the floor toward her. "Washer's not working again. I had to go to the Laundromat." She pulled a pair of his boxers from the basket.

"Think your dad can fix it again?" He didn't look at her.

"Maybe." She looked away, tearing up. She felt stupid, but she'd been like this for the last two weeks, ever since Johnny was killed. Crying over the stupidest things. She had really liked him, probably loved him. Certainly loved him more than she loved Ed. She just couldn't imagine why anyone would have killed Johnny. He was such a sweet guy. He was even nice to her after he quit coming over. She was upset when he said he couldn't cheat on his wife anymore and wreck his marriage, but a part of her had admired him for that. Shoot, she'd been in labor at the hospital with Amber, and Charlie had been off screwing some chick he met at a bar. Guys who did right by their women were few and far between, at least in this town.

Pam breathed deeply, glad the lights were out so Ed couldn't see that she was upset. He didn't know about her and Johnny, no one did, and she had no intention of telling him. That was the way Johnny had wanted it, and she had felt it was the least she could do. Especially now. "I was thinking maybe we could get a new washing machine," she said when she could find her voice.

"We don't have the money for a new damned washing

machine." Ed threw down the remote and got up. "Any beer in the fridge?"

She reached for another pair of boxers and folded them in her lap. "Not a *new* new one. One of those rebuilt ones they've got out back of Burton's."

She heard the refrigerator open and light from the kitchen spilled onto the stained carpet of the living room floor. He popped the top on his beer can. The light disappeared.

"You buy what you want, I'm not buying a damned washing machine."

She watched him walk back into the living room, cross in front of the TV, and drop back onto the opposite end of the couch. Beer in one hand, he reached for the remote.

She took one look at him sitting there with his beer and his TV remote, and she just couldn't stand it. Not a minute longer. She'd rather live alone than put up with this crap. "Fine!" She threw his boxers at him and got up off the couch. "So you wash your own friggin' underwear, and while you're on your way to the Laundromat, why don't you stop at the bank and get me that six hundred dollars you owe me?"

"I don't owe you six hundred dollars." He grabbed the boxers from his lap and threw them on the floor.

"Yes, you do. You borrowed the money two weeks before you moved in here. To fix your bike, remember?" She walked around the coffee table, putting herself between him and the *Comedy Hour* on the TV screen.

Ed craned his neck, but she didn't budge.

"We're together now, honey. We don't do *my* money and *your* money," he said. "It's all together now."

"All together when you want it to be!" She pushed a lock of brown hair behind her ear. "What about when you stopped for subs last night for dinner? First thing you did when you walked into this house was tell me how much I owed you for a six-inch meatball!"

"Jeez, do we have to do this right now?" He finally looked up at her.

Ed wasn't a bad-looking guy. His hair was thinning a little and his belly was pudging more than it used to, but he really wasn't bad looking and he wasn't a bad guy. She was just tired of his crap. "I'm tired of me doing all the work around here, Ed. I wash your clothes and I cook and I take care of Amber, and I'm still working and I'm trying to go to school." She rubbed at her eyes with the heel of her hand. "I could use a little help around here."

Ed slapped the remote down on the table and got up, moving toward her. For a minute she thought he was going to hit her. But if he did, God help him. She'd kill him. A long time ago, after Amber was born, after she'd called the police on Charlie for the third time and ended up in the ER with a broken nose, she'd decided no man would ever hit her again. No man would ever have that kind of power over her again.

Luckily, he just stomped by her. Lucky for him.

"I don't need this shit."

She turned around. "Where you going?"

"The hell away from here!" He jerked open the door and stepped onto the concrete block steps.

"Fine," she hollered after him. "Go! And you can stay gone for all I care!" She slammed the door so hard that a picture of Amber when she was a baby rattled against the paneling on the wall.

"I don't need this crap," she muttered as she walked over to the couch, sat down, and picked up the remote.

Outside she heard Ed start his Harley. There was still something wrong with the exhaust, and it was even louder than usual. "Be fine with me if you never came back," she said aloud. And with a satisfying click she changed the channel to something she wanted to watch, for once.

Ed sat on the barstool at The Pit just outside of town, beer in his hand, and laughed at his buddy's joke. Only he wasn't really listening. He was on his second beer, but it wasn't going down as smooth as they usually did.

Country music played through the scratchy speakers bolted to the ceiling over the bar. He thought about the Toby Keith song Pam liked. "It's all about you, you, you," she'd sing in the shower all the time. It was kind of cute, really, because she couldn't sing worth a damn.

He heard the clatter of balls hitting each other on one of the pool tables in the back as someone broke. Someone had asked him if he wanted to play, but he hadn't felt like it tonight. Just wasn't in the mood.

He felt bad about his fight with Pam. Felt bad he walked out on her. It was a stupid thing to do. He really liked her, maybe loved her. He didn't want to screw things up with her. She had been right about most of what she said, and he had acted like the asshole that he was.

He did tend to take advantage of her with money sometimes, and he certainly didn't do his share of work around the house. Pam, she worked like a dog at the plant, then she went to classes at the community college, and she still tried to be a good mother.

Wasn't any trying to it. She *was* a good mother, certainly better than his had been. She was so patient with Amber. She hardly ever lost her temper and hollered. And she was always teaching the little girl things like how to count and how to say her ABCs. Amber was smart, just like her mother.

Ed set his beer down on the bar. His buddy, Ham, was still talking, something about pulling one over on his old lady. Ed checked the mirrored Bud clock over the bar. It said eleven, but it ran slow so it was probably closer to eleven-thirty. He'd only been gone an hour, but Pam usually simmered down pretty fast.

He pulled his wallet on the chain out of his back pocket, left cash on the bar for his two beers, and walked out. Far as he could tell, Ham never saw him go. Probably wouldn't miss him until the next round.

He approached his Hog, thinking what a good-looking bike she was, but not as good looking as Pam. Not as important to him as Pam. Once, maybe, his bike had meant more to him than his woman, but he was getting older, maybe a little smarter. Things were different now. Pam was different than the other women.

Ed mounted his Harley, turned the key in the ignition, kicked her into gear, and headed home.

Azrael cut the headlights a hundred feet before the end of the driveway and eased the car off onto the shoulder.

"If a man commits adultery with another man's wife, both the man and the woman must be put to death," the Angel of Death murmured. "Thou shall not commit adultery. Thou shall not commit adultery."

Checking for the lighter, Azrael got out of the car and removed a gas can and a wooden baseball bat from the backseat. The angel did not know how the things had gotten in there, only the task that had to be performed, the order laid down by God that had to be carried out.

It was not Azrael's place to judge. Only God could judge.

The walk up the drive to the trailer was short, and though it was dark, moonlight guided the Angel of Death to the front door. Flickering light glowed behind the curtain in the window, and voices could be heard. Late-night TV.

Azrael set the gas can down on the ground, climbed the wobbly cinder block steps, and without hesitating, knocked on the door.

The knock at the door startled Pam; she sat up on the couch and ran her hand through her hair, pushing it out of her eyes. Had Ed forgotten his keys?

She didn't think she had locked the front door.

She hadn't heard the Harley pull into the driveway. She

knew she'd been dozing, but she must have been sleeping harder than she thought not to hear that racket.

The knock came again, and she rose off the couch. "I'm coming," she called, pleased he was back. So maybe there was some hope for the guy after all.

Pam opened the door and was surprised to find that it wasn't Ed at the door after all. "Hi," she said uneasily. It had to be close to midnight. She knew the visitor—must have been having car trouble or something. "Can . . . can I help you?" she asked, stepping down onto the first cinder block step as she reached up to push her hair out of her eyes again.

Out of the corner of her eye, she saw the baseball bat as it came around. She gave a little cry of fright, of confusion, and then her head felt as if it had exploded. Pain shot from her temple, through her eyes, and down her spine. She threw out one hand to catch herself as the bat came around again.

Pam felt herself lose her balance and begin to fall; there was no way to avoid the second strike. As the baseball bat made contact with her head and the side of her face, she heard bones shatter, making a sickening, crunching sound in her head. The pain was excruciating, yet the only thought that went through her mind as she tumbled off the steps to the ground was of Amber. "Please God, protect her," she prayed as she hit the dirt and her life dissolved into darkness.

Ed saw the flames as he came around the bend in the road, and his chest tightened in fear. "Holy shit," he muttered. Was the damned trailer on fire?

He hit the gas, and as he turned the corner off the black-top, he nearly spun out in the soft, sandy driveway. It wasn't the trailer on fire. Something was burning on the ground in front of it.

Sand and grass spewed upward as he slid to a stop, leaping off his bike. Whatever was burning smelled god-awful, like nothing he'd ever smelled before. "Pam!" he called, seeing the open door. "Pam, you all right?"

He halted near the bottom step that led up into the trailer. For a moment he couldn't figure out what the hell he was looking at; it was like he knew but what he saw wasn't registering in his brain. When he realized what was burning, bitter bile rose in his throat, and for a minute he thought he was going to upchuck.

"Oh, shit. Oh, God," he murmured, taking a step back.

It was a body, black and smoking, fabric melted to the skin, still flaming. Not some *thing* burning. *Someone.*

Ed covered his mouth with his hand as he stared into the flames where a piece of blue fabric fluttered, unburned. It took a moment for him to realize what the blue was. Whose it was.

"Pam!" he screamed, covering his head with his hands in horror. "Oh, God, no, oh, God." He knew she was dead already. She wasn't moving, not making a sound. No one could survive that.

How could she have done such a thing to herself? How was it even possible?

Then, suddenly, he thought of Amber. Amber and her blond curls, asleep in the house. God, let her still be asleep in the house. "Amber!" he cried, taking the steps two at a time.

He ran through the living room where the TV was still on, shadows and light flashing on the curtains behind the couch. His pounding footsteps echoed in his head as his boots hit the thin, stained carpet. The hallway was short, but it seemed like it took forever to get down to the end. He threw open the flimsy bedroom door, and even in the dark he could see Amber's still form.

He threw himself down on the bed, grabbing her up. He had to know if she was alive. She made a little sound and opened her eyes with surprise. Tears running down his face, he slid onto the edge of the bed, holding Amber tight against him, and rocked back and forth.

CHAPTER 8

Noah walked into the kitchen to find Mallory and Mattie eating stacks of Mrs. Santori's hotcakes. "Morning," he said, coming up behind Mattie and messing up his hair.

Mattie looked down at his hotcakes without smiling, but Noah could tell he was pleased by the attention.

"Hello, Mr. Noah." Mallory looked up at him with a grin, syrup dribbling from both sides of her mouth. "Did you *sweep* good?"

"I slept quite *well*, thank you," he answered, amused that she could behave so adultlike at times. "And you?"

"Quite wewll, thank you," she mimicked, and then stuffed another forkful of hotcakes into her mouth.

At the kitchen counter, he poured himself coffee in the mug left out for him. Mrs. Santori always left two mugs on the counter. Rachel was up; he'd heard the upstairs shower running more than an hour ago, but she was nowhere to be seen.

Mrs. Santori bustled out of the pantry. "Hotcakes on the table," she told him, a frozen chicken in her hands. "Fried chicken, asparagus, potato frittata for dinner."

"Thanks. Sounds good. I'll get myself some hotcakes in a minute." He sipped his steaming black coffee. "Mallory, where's your mama?"

"Outside in the garden," she said, her mouth full. "Burying something."

He frowned. "Burying something? Something die?"

She shrugged and stabbed at another piece of hotcake.

Noah nodded curiously. "I think maybe I'll go out and see what she's doing. After breakfast, I'm heading out to the Chancellor field to tighten some trellis wires. I might be able to use some help."

"*I'w* help!" Mallory declared, raising her fork. She looked at Mattie. "Mattie says *he'w hewlp* too."

"Oh, he says that, does he?" Noah lifted a brow, taking another sip of coffee. Everything the little girl said to him amazed him, amused him, or made him curious about her or her mother. He found her to be a bright light against the darkness inside him. "Funny, I didn't hear him say a word."

She made a face, wrinkling her freckled nose. "He said it."

Noah looked askance at her. "I've never heard Mattie say a word and I've known him my whole life."

She shrugged as she picked up her juice box. "Maybe you're just not *wistenin'*."

Not certain if she meant that literally or philosophically, Noah chuckled and walked out of the kitchen, onto the porch, and down the stairs. As he walked around the house, he noticed the automatic door on the shed next to the garage was open. Inside, he could see the lawn tractor parked crookedly. Last night when he'd put it away, he knew that wasn't how he'd left it. Pretty early in the morning for Rachel to be using the lawn tractor. . . .

He found her out in the garden, her coffee mug sitting on the edge of one of the raised-bed salt-treated frames. Dressed in a lavender T-shirt, a pair of calf-length pants that had apparently become the rage while he was in prison, and a pair of sneakers, she was busy raking a bed that was dark and moist with freshly turned soil. Her hair, pulled back in a high ponytail, appeared to still be damp from the shower.

A picture of her naked in the shower crossed his mind, surprising him. It had been a long time since those kinds of thoughts had wandered into his head. "Hey," he said lightly.

She glanced over her shoulder at him, then back at the bed she was dragging a light rake through. She'd built them the perfect size, four foot by eight foot and a foot off the ground, so that any plant could be reached without stepping into the bed. "Hey."

"You're at work early."

She shrugged and continued to rake. "Couldn't sleep."

"More bad dreams?"

"I took enough Benadryl last night to knock out a pony. Still didn't sleep well."

"What are you burying?" He indicated the freshly turned soil with a nod of his chin.

"What?" She set down the rake, turning to him.

He picked up her coffee cup and handed it to her, his fingers brushing hers. It was a simple gesture but somehow seemed intimate in the cool morning air. "Your daughter told me you were out here burying something."

She sipped her coffee. "I'd be smarter digging for something, buried treasure or China, maybe."

He half smiled, glancing away. It felt good to be here with her, alone in the early morning when there seemed to be more possibilities in the world than there had been last night. He'd made it through another day without drinking . . . or killing anyone. Had to be a good start on the day.

"You out mowing or something this morning?" He reached up to pluck a fallen leaf from between the branches of a dwarf apple tree on the edge of the garden area.

"No."

"The tractor." He hooked his thumb in the direction of the shed. "I saw you'd moved it."

She shook her head, looking at him oddly. "No, I didn't. I was going to ask you where you'd been."

"I haven't been anywhere. I parked it last night after supper. You saw me."

His tone sounded convincing even to himself, but as he spoke, the thought crossed his mind that maybe he *had* been somewhere last night. Maybe he'd had a blackout as he was dozing off and just couldn't remember.

"Hmm," she intoned as she lifted her stoneware mug to her mouth again. "Pretty bad parking job, bub."

He wanted to insist he hadn't left it parked that way, but his niggling doubts made him just change the subject. He didn't want Rachel to know he was still suffering from blackouts after five years of sobriety. "I told Mallory and Mattie that I was going out to the Chancellor field to tighten up some trellis wires. I thought they might like to tag along, if that's OK with you."

She hesitated for a moment, and he couldn't help wondering if she was considering whether it was safe to leave her child in his care. It made him feel small.

"Sure. That's fine, I guess. Just keep an eye on Mallory. She likes to wander away." She set down the mug and picked up the rake again.

He nodded, getting the distinct feeling he was being dismissed. Rachel had been that way all week, ever since the night they'd sat in the hallway on the floor in the dark. One minute it would seem to him that she was trying to reach out to him, the next minute she was definitely blowing him off.

He started to walk away, then turned back. "Hey, you need anything from town? I've got an AA meeting this afternoon."

She shook her head without turning to face him. "You want a ride in?"

"No. I've got my trusty tractor," he said, trying to make a joke of it.

She didn't laugh. "Whatever."

He walked away, wondering what was up with her this morning.

"Holy Mary, Mother of God," Delilah whispered, her voice ragged.

"Take deep breaths." Snowden spoke quietly, standing over the body. "Try to breathe through your mouth rather than your nose."

Delilah felt as if she was going to be sick, but she couldn't look away. She'd never smelled anything so horrendous, never seen anything so unspeakable. The young woman—charred black, posed gruesomely, her limbs drawn in to her torso in a fetal position—barely looked human any longer.

"Anyone move the body?" Snowden glanced at the EMT standing closest to him.

"No, Chief. On arrival, we checked for a pulse, but we didn't move her. No need to. She's been dead a couple of hours from what the boyfriend said."

Delilah took a step back, gritting her teeth, swallowing hard. "He inside?"

"Yes, ma'am." The EMT flashed a quick smile at her.

He was cute. Name was Jason, Jason Cline. She'd met him a couple of times before, but she wasn't in the mood for flirtation. Certainly not standing at the feet of the charred remains of a twenty-seven-year-old woman.

"I say we go talk to the son-of-a-bitch boyfriend," she murmured under her breath.

Snowden waited until she walked around the steps to mount them and then put out his hand to stop. "Sergeant," he said quietly.

She swallowed again, halting, staring at the cement blocks that were crumbling at the edges. Tears burned behind her eyelids, but she remained dry eyed.

"We need to remain objective," he reminded her, his voice surprisingly kind. Gentle.

"I know."

"We have no idea, at this point, what we're looking at."

"I know that," she intoned, fighting to get control of her emotions.

"We don't know that he did this. It could even be a suicide." His hand remained on her forearm.

She looked up at him, her temper taking over. "Then why the heck did he wait until six-thirty in the morning to call 911? Can you tell me that, Chief?"

"We're going to ask him." Snowden still remained calm and collected. "Now, are you ready for the initial interview or would you be more comfortable out here running this circus?"

She glanced up to see that the yard was teeming with commotion—cop cars, both state and local; EMT vehicles; an ambulance; and even a fire truck. There were police and emergency personnel everywhere, everyone talking at once, traipsing through her crime scene.

"I'm goin' with you, boss," she said, drawing out the last word with a thick Georgia accent.

He gave a nod, dropping his hand to his side. "That's fine, just let me lead."

She looked up at Snowden, about to ask why she couldn't interview him, when she realized what he was saying. Biker dude inside, tattoos and Harley in the yard and all. What was more intimidating, a five-foot-two blond police chick or a six-four black man? "Fine," she murmured.

Snowden led the way up the stairs, knocked on the doorway—the door was standing open—and walked in without waiting for an invitation. "Mr. Parson?"

"Here," Delilah heard a man say from the right.

The trailer was dim, but the moment she stepped foot inside, she saw a burly guy dressed in jeans, a T-shirt, and a black leather vest sitting at a cheap set of table and chairs in the kitchen. She noticed a tattoo of an eagle on one of his arms. The biker boyfriend, had to be. Across the table from him sat a little girl in her pajamas, slowly spooning Cheerios into her mouth.

"I'm Chief Calloway—"

"I know who you are. You ticketed me twice last year," the man grumbled.

"Sergeant Swift," Delilah announced, taking a look around.

The trailer was old and the furniture had seen better days, but the place was as neat as a pin. No dirty dishes in the sink like at her place. Nothing on the counters or the table except for the usual: salt and pepper shakers, flour and sugar canisters, a blue glass cookie jar that looked like Cookie Monster.

In the living room behind her was a worn plaid couch and a beat-up coffee table with a couple of accounting textbooks and a notebook on it. Across from the couch were a mismatched recliner and a large TV, by far the newest piece of furniture in the place. On the floor near the couch sat a laundry basket of neatly stacked clothes, and it immediately caught her eye. Most of the clothes were folded in the basket, except that there were a couple of pairs of boxer shorts and men's colored pocket T-shirts that looked as if they'd been balled up and thrown on top of the folded clothing. It appeared to her as if the woman had done laundry and the boyfriend had come by and thrown stuff on top. Had the boyfriend been doing some early morning laundry, she wondered, making a mental note to collect the clothes for trace evidence.

"Would you like to come into the living room?" Snowden glanced at the little girl.

The boyfriend seemed hesitant, but he nodded. "You sit tight and eat your Cheerios, Amber," he told the little girl.

She continued to chase the last of her cereal around in the bowl with her plastic spoon.

Snowden and Delilah entered the living room. The man walked past them, around the coffee table, and took a seat on the couch. He lowered his head for a moment, covering his face with his hands.

Delilah noted two empty beer cans beneath the couch.

Too much to drink? A fight that got out of hand? The guy seemed sober enough now, but they had no time of death on the victim yet. She could have been dead close to twelve hours for all they knew. Plenty of time to sober up.

"Could I have the full name of the decedent?" Snowden asked, taking a small notebook and black pen from his breast pocket.

"I don't even know if it's her," the boyfriend snapped. His voice changed, and for a moment he sounded as if he might cry. "But it's got to be. Her T-shirt—" He lifted his head. "Pamela Jean Rehak."

"And your name, sir?"

"Ed . . . Edward Parson."

"And your relationship to Miss Rehak?"

"I'm her old man. Her . . . boyfriend, I guess. I live here too."

"The little girl?" Snowden continued to jot in his notebook.

"Amber Marie Rehak. God." Ed dropped his face into his hands again. "She wants to know where her mommy is. What the hell am I supposed to tell her?"

"And Amber is not your child, Mr. Parson?"

He shook his head. "Nah, but her dad's long gone. Left the state when they started withholding part of his paycheck for child support."

"His name?"

Ed sighed and looked up again. "Charles Eikenberry, Eikenbury, somethin' like that."

"And you don't know his whereabouts?"

"State of Delaware can't find him. How the hell could Pam?"

The guy seemed touchy on a number of subjects. Didn't necessarily mean anything. Might.

Delilah glanced at Snowden and shifted her gaze to the photographs in cheap frames hanging on the walls. Most of them were of the little girl at different ages—a baby, then a toddler, maybe a preschool picture—but there was one of a thin young woman with brownish-blond hair, holding the same toddler. The young woman was sitting on a swing in someone's backyard, smiling at the camera as if she didn't have a care in the world.

Snowden looked up from his notebook. "Can you go over with me what happened last night?"

Ed threw himself back on the couch. "I already told the other cop. The first one here."

"I understand, but I'd like you to tell us," Snowden said patiently.

Delilah noticed he did not sit down across from the guy. By standing while the possible perpetrator was sitting, Snowden put himself psychologically in a position above Ed Parson. She admired Snowden, the way he always proceeded with any investigation. He never screwed anything up, and he always did things the best way they could be done.

Ed ran his hand over his face. "We were sittin' here watchin' TV together, and we got into a little argument. Nothing big, just the usual. She's naggin', I'm not listenin'."

"And what time was that?"

"I don't know. After ten, I guess. Amber kept hollerin' for Pam, wanting to get in our bed."

Snowden nodded. He was no longer taking notes, but listening attentively.

The biker boyfriend shrugged. "I got a little pissed and I left."

"And where did you go?"

"The Pit, you know, out on North Road."

Delilah knew the place, all right. A bit of a dive. They got called there at least once a month to break up a brawl. A lot of old bikers hung out there, people who'd had brushes with the law but weren't really criminals, the kind of misfits that lived on the fringes of Stephen Kill's little world.

"Had you been drinking before you went to The Pit, Mr. Parson?"

"No. I mean yes." He shook his head as if he was confused. "A beer or two."

Delilah eyed the beer cans under the couch, wondering how many more she would find once Snowden escorted the man out of his home.

"So you went to The Pit . . ."

"I went to The Pit. I can name ten people who saw me there," Ed Parson said quickly. "Including the bartender, Shorty. I had a beer or two—"

"How many?" Snowden questioned.

"Two. One," Ed Parson corrected, obviously beginning to become irritated. "I ordered a second, but I didn't finish it."

"And from The Pit, you drove directly back here?"

He nodded.

"And what time would that have been?"

"Hell, I don't know!" He rubbed his face again. "Before midnight, because I looked at the clock over the bar before I left and it said it was eleven, only the damned thing runs slow. Fifteen minutes back here, maybe."

"And when you arrived?"

"That's when I saw the friggin' fire!" He threw a meaty hand in the air. "At first, from the road, I thought it might be the trailer on fire, then when I got closer, I thought it was trash burnin'. You know, some jackass pullin' some kind of prank."

"When did you realize it wasn't trash burning in your yard, Mr. Parson?"

"When I saw her fu—" He cut himself off in mid-curse, looking down at the floor.

Delilah saw tears in his eyes. Tears of sorrow or tears of guilt, she couldn't tell.

Ed Parson took a couple of deep breaths and went on, "When I got off my bike, I saw the front door was standin' open. That's when I got scared. I thought something might be wrong. I ran over to the steps and that's when I saw her."

"And how did you know it was Miss Rehak, Mr. Parson?"
He wiped his eyes with his forearm, sniffing. "When I saw
her T-shirt. Blue. She was wearin' it when I left the house."

Snowden flipped the pages of his notebook. In the kitchen,
Delilah heard a chair scrape on the linoleum floor, followed
by a patter of small footsteps. Delilah glanced at Snowden.
There was no need for that little girl in the other room to
know any more than she had to about what had happened
outside her front door the previous night.

"I understand you were the one who called 911," Snowden
continued.

Ed Parson nodded.

"At six-thirty in the morning."

Ed Parson lowered his face into his hands again. "I know,
I know, it don't look good, but I'm tellin' you." He sniffed,
his face still hidden. "I didn't do this to Pam. I . . . I loved
her."

"Can you tell me why, if you came home close to midnight to find your girlfriend on fire, you didn't call 911 until
more than six hours later?"

The room was quiet for a moment except for the sound of
water being turned on at the kitchen sink.

"She was already dead, OK?" he said from behind his
hands. "I was just scared, that's all. I couldn't believe what
I'd seen, it was so awful." He let one hand fall. "I just sat
there in Amber's room, till morning. I swear to God."

The water cut off in the kitchen, and after a moment the
chair was dragged again. A moment later, the child entered
the living room.

"Go get dressed, Amber Bamber, OK?" Ed Parson said.
"I just called Aunt Ruthie, and you're gonna go over to her
house today."

"Is Mommy comin' home then?"

"Go do what I said."

The little girl looked at him and then obediently crossed
the living room floor and disappeared down the hall, still not

knowing her mother was lying on the ground outside, her body burned beyond recognition.

The innocence of childhood.

At that moment, Delilah wished she had a little of her own left.

"Did you hear, Father Gibson?" Cora Watkins asked from behind him in line.

Noah wondered if he didn't answer, if he pretended he hadn't heard her, might she just buy cold capsules or whatever it was she was buying in the drugstore and go on her way?

"I said, did you hear there's been another murder?"

Noah jerked around, his toothpaste, shaving cream, razor blades, and two coloring books—one for Mattie, one for Mallory—cradled in his arms. "What?"

She drew back, nodding authoritatively. "That's right, Father."

"He's not really a father anymore," said Alice Crupp from behind Cora in line, looking down at the row of candy bars in front of the cash register. "You shouldn't call him father anymore."

"Pam Rehak. You remember her, Father," Cora continued, ignoring Alice. "Young girl worked out at the plant, had that baby a couple of years ago, not married. Lived in a trailer, east of town."

Noah felt light-headed. "Last night?"

"I heard hours ago in Dr. Carson's office. Saturday morning hours, you know. I was sitting next to Mabel Ridgely when . . .

Cora Watkins continued to speak, but Noah barely heard a word she said. First Johnny Leager, then Pam Rehak?

It couldn't be a coincidence.

CHAPTER 9

It was all Noah could do that evening to choke down a couple of bites of Mrs. Santori's fried chicken and her famous potato frittata. He didn't even try to participate in the conversation between Rachel and her daughter concerning the worms in the bucket on the back step and whether or not they would make good house pets. He sat there as silent as Mattie, pushing his food around his plate with his fork, trying to make it look like he was eating.

As soon as supper was over, he excused himself to the side porch. He sat in his father's rocker in the fading June light and let his gaze drift over the backyard, the apple and pear trees Rachel had so lovingly planted when they had first moved back to Delaware, her vegetable beds and the freshly turned dark soil of the one she had planted zucchini plants in today. He watched a blue jay feather drift in the wind a foot off the grass.

He couldn't believe Pam Rehak was dead. Murdered, Cora Watkins had said. Burned to death, probably by her tattooed boyfriend. Noah didn't recognize the name of the boyfriend;

he'd only been in town a couple of years, according to the church secretary's boundless fountain of information.

Maybe the boyfriend did kill her. . . . Maybe it was just a coincidence, but he had a heavy feeling in the pit of his stomach that it wasn't. Question was, what did he do about it?

Boy, oh boy, did he want a drink right now. He wanted it so badly that his hands were trembling. He could taste the burn in his mouth.

The screen door squeaked open and slapped shut, and Noah sat back in the chair just as Rachel walked around the corner. She was carrying two glasses of sweet tea.

"I can't convince Mrs. Santori to use the decaf bags, so I'm warning you ahead of time," she said, putting a glass down for him on the table between the two rockers.

"Doesn't matter. I don't sleep that well, anyway." *Or so well that I don't know when I'm getting up and driving a lawn mower around in the yard,* he thought.

She was barefoot, and when she sat in his mother's chair, she tucked one foot under her. He had always liked her feet. Small, dainty. She used to wear pink nail polish on them, and she'd always been very ticklish. He remembered capturing her feet in their bed and tickling them until she begged for mercy. The memory made him want to smile and cry at the same time.

She sipped her tea.

He could tell she wanted to talk about something. She was a lot like his father that way. Though they were both very direct people, it always took them a while to come around to what was on their mind.

"That's really awful about Pam Rehak," she said, after a moment. She set her chair in motion. "Her little girl was in Mallory's preschool class at the church." She shook her head, taking another sip of her tea. "Guess it goes to show you, you better be careful who you sleep with."

It was the perfect opportunity for Noah to speak up about the coincidence. While he had told Rachel things he'd had no right to tell her, he'd never told her who Johnny Leager had the affair with. But he just couldn't bring himself to broach the subject. "Pretty awful" was all he could manage.

"Listen," Rachel said after another minute or two of silence. "I know you really don't want to talk about this, but I've got my résumé in order and . . ." She halted, then started again. "We need to start thinking about what we're going to do with Mattie."

"Do with him?"

Noah's thoughts were still on Johnny and Pam. Their affair had been typical, from his experience. A man with a certain amount of authority in a workplace who was lonely and not quite happy in his marriage, at the time. A younger, pretty woman who admired her superior and was willing to listen to him. They had pretty much fallen into bed together. Fortunately, Johnny had come to his senses before his wife found out. Before the damage was irrevocable.

"Yes, about Mattie," Rachel said, on the edge of her patience with him. "I can't remain his legal guardian if I move to California or Pennsylvania. If you're determined to keep the vineyard, to stay here, you need to file for legal guardianship."

Noah reached for his glass of iced tea, not so much because he wanted it, but because he needed a moment. "I . . . I guess I can do that."

"You need to go to Georgetown and file with the Court of Chancery."

He took another sip of tea. His hands were steady again.

"OK, Noah?" she pressed. "I need you to do this for Mattie . . . for me. I've got enough to worry about right now. I don't need to worry about whether or not Mattie will be cared for."

He looked at her, lowering his glass. "Of course I'll take care of him."

"I know you will. But you need to do this legally. Remember, he gets a social security check every month. You have to legally be allowed to deposit and withdraw from his account."

He set his glass back on the table. "You really are going to take a job in another state?"

He couldn't imagine life without Rachel. Even after she had divorced him, even when he was in prison, she had still been in his life in some way, still as much a part of him as his arm or his leg.

"There's only one other vineyard in Delaware, Noah, and they have a vintner. I have to go where there's work."

He felt numb, like in the days when he'd been drinking. No, this was worse than numb because he was feeling a hundred emotions all at once. "OK, sure. I'll take care of it."

"I can take you over."

"I said I'll take care of it, Rachel," he said, sharper than he intended.

"I just don't want you riding to Georgetown on that stupid—"

"I'll get someone to take me," he interrupted, rising from the chair. It was just too much to be here with her right now. He had too much on his mind. "I'll get Joshua. He said he'd take me anywhere I needed to go. I'll go next week when I check in with my parole officer." He walked past her. "Thanks for the tea."

Delilah poured herself a glass of her sweet tea; standing in her kitchen barefoot, in boxers and a T-shirt, she took a sip and frowned. It was good, but not as good as her grandmother's. She just didn't understand it. She followed the recipe exactly, measuring the sugar and the water. She even used her grandmother's brand of tea bags.

Shaking her head in disappointment, she walked back into the living room of her small but nice townhouse in the only townhouse community in town. Right now she was just renting, until she was sure she wanted to stay in Delaware, but she had the option to buy, and part of the rent she was paying would go toward the mortgage.

In the living room, she curled up in her favorite reading chair and picked up the cozy mystery she'd been trying to read. Usually, one of these books was just what she needed to decompress after a bad day at work. There was nothing like a case of a missing pearl necklace to work out the kinks in her neck, and the author was a good one. She came highly recommended from the librarian in town, where she'd gotten it. Snowden's mother seemed to have a knack for matching just the right book with the right reader.

But tonight Delilah couldn't concentrate on the cast of characters or clues in the book. She couldn't get the image of Pam Rehak's burned body out of her mind. The official identification wouldn't come until dental records were studied up at the morgue in Wilmington, but everyone pretty much agreed, unofficially, that it was Pam Rehak. She was wearing what was left of the shirt the boyfriend identified as the one she had on when he left the house, and the silver earrings found on the ground where they fell from her charred earlobes were also hers, according to Ed Parson.

After studying the scene and the fact that, upon closer examination, the skull was beaten in, she and Snowden had come to the quick conclusion that Pam Rehak had be murdered. That brought them to the next logical question, by whom?

The easy answer was that Ed Parson had done it. He'd gotten angry, he'd gone to the bar, that much they'd confirmed; then he went home, still angry, and shut up the nagging girlfriend. Shut her up permanently by bashing her head in with something heavy, then pouring gasoline on her and setting her body on fire.

But there were a few snags preventing them from arresting Ed Parson. There was no visible blood spatter on Ed or on any clothes in the house. The clothes he'd been wearing and the ones in the laundry basket had been sent to the lab in

Wilmington to look for trace evidence of blood, but she was afraid they weren't going to find any. And there was no evidence of any accelerant, gas or anything else, on the property. They'd found a gas can under the trailer skirt around back, next to an old lawn mower, but the can was empty and appeared to have been for some time. The lawn didn't look like it had been mowed in weeks. And there was no murder weapon on the property, at least that had been found, yet.

If Ed had killed her, he'd cleaned himself up pretty darned well and he'd disposed of the evidence. Of course, he'd had plenty of time, hadn't he?

But something about his behavior made her think he didn't do it. Back at the scene and then at the station house, he had seemed genuinely upset by Pam's death.

She glanced at the cordless phone on the table beside her. She'd talked to one of her brothers earlier tonight. A cop, too. They hadn't talked about the case really, just about dealing with a crappy day. He'd made her feel better about herself.

But she couldn't stop thinking about Pam and her responsibility to the dead woman, to that little girl she'd seen eating Cheerios this morning.

She felt like she needed to talk to Snowden.

She picked up the phone, but she didn't punch in his number. They didn't usually make personal phone calls back and forth. He probably would say it was unprofessional, but tonight she just needed to talk to him. She keyed in his number without having to look it up.

Snowden stood barefoot in running shorts and a T-shirt, watching the hot dogs boil in the pan of water. He'd gone for a long run, six miles, hoping to ease the tension in his neck, hoping to let the image of Pam Rehak's body recede in his mind, but it hadn't worked. Now he was tired and still haunted by the image of her burned body.

There was no sign of the murder weapon, a club of some sort he guessed. No sign of blood spatter on Ed Parson and no sign of an accelerant on the property. Snowden knew that Ed had plenty of time to hide the stuff, but they'd searched the woods within a half-mile radius and come up with nothing. The boyfriend just didn't act like he'd killed her. Sure, one could say he looked the part of a man who might lose his temper with his girlfriend and get drunk and kill her. He was a tattooed biker, an auto mechanic by trade, and had been arrested a few times in his twenties for petty stuff, the kind of man it was easy to conclude could have done such a thing. But Snowden's gut instinct told him he wasn't the murderer.

His gut instinct told him there was some awful truth hidden at that crime scene. In this town. And things were going to get worse before they got better.

Fighting a weird shiver, he turned to the counter across from the stove and grabbed a pack of hot dog rolls from the bread drawer. Untwisting the tie, he thought back on the scene, as it had appeared when they arrived. Was there something there that should have pointed him in a direction other than the boyfriend?

He and Delilah and two additional officers had been all over that yard, but maybe they'd missed something.

His phone rang, startling him. It hardly ever rang. Had to be the station. Johnson, the officer on duty tonight, must not have been able to find the coffee cups or something.

He removed the handset from its place on the wall near the door to the living room. "Chief Calloway," he said into the receiver.

There was silence on the other end.

"Chief Calloway," he repeated.

"Chief, it's Delilah."

He was stunned that she would call him at home and even more stunned by how glad he was to hear her voice. "What can I do for you, Delilah?" he asked, deciding it was probably okay to call her by her first name when they were both off duty. Besides, it was a private phone call. Who would know?

"I can't stop thinking about her," she said softly.

He liked her southern accent. He wouldn't admit it to his mother, of course, no more than he would admit he found her attractive, but there was something very feminine about her voice. He liked the idea that she could be as tough as he knew she could be, and yet still retain her femininity.

"I know." He walked back to the stove to turn off the burner. He left the hot dogs in the water and the rolls on the counter and wandered into the living room that mostly served as an office. He didn't even own a couch, and his TV was in his bedroom. When he read, his favorite pastime, he sat in a big recliner, feet up, with a good floor lamp positioned over his left shoulder.

He sat down in the executive chair behind his monstrous oak desk that had been his grandfather's. "The first time you see an incinerated body, it can spook you. My first was a vehicular accident. A bunch of high school boys from New Jersey at the beach for the weekend. I saw their bodies every time I closed my eyes for at least a month afterward." He didn't know why he'd told her that; he'd never told anyone.

"It's not just what she looked like," she said on the other end of the line, her voice full of emotion. "It's what she smelled like."

She was quiet for a second, and just when he was about to say something, she spoke again. "I don't think the boyfriend did it. I'm afraid we missed something at the scene."

He was quiet long enough for her to say, "Chief?"

"I'm listening. Thinking. What do you mean, missed something? Like what?"

She gave a little laugh. "I don't know what. How could I, if I missed it?"

He smiled.

"I just . . ." She paused and then started again, her voice

stronger now. "I have off tomorrow. I don't come in until Monday, but would it be all right if I go back to the scene?"

"I don't see why not. Place is still taped off. I haven't released the scene."

"I just thought I'd walk around, maybe early tomorrow morning. With the place cleared, I might see something we missed before."

He leaned back in his chair, propping his bare foot on one of the drawer handles of his desk. "We have the keys to the trailer at the station if you want to stop by and pick them up. Just sign them out."

"I might do that. The other thing, Chief . . ." She let her voice trail off into silence.

Snowden felt strange, holding onto the phone, waiting in anticipation for her next words. He found himself wishing she was here. Wishing they could sit here together and talk about this. "Yes?"

"I was looking over the file we started. I didn't take it home with me," she said quickly. "I followed procedure, making copies and logging in that copies had been made."

He smiled to himself. "That's fine, Delilah."

"This is going to sound crazy, and I'm sure one has nothing to do with the other, but did you see that even though she was working at the chicken plant now, she used to work at the cup factory?"

He felt the weird shiver again. "No, no, I didn't see that."

"It was on the next page. Easy to miss," she said.

"Did she work there while Johnny Leager was working there?"

"Had to have. He'd been there since he was twenty."

"Did they work together?" Snowden asked, sitting up in his chair.

"I don't know, but I can find out."

"Go pay a visit to the personnel office on Monday. I think you're riding with Lopez."

"Yeah, I saw that on the schedule," she said softly.

"I figured I better be in the station this week," he said, not knowing why he felt he had to justify that they would not be riding together. "Besides, I think we're just about through with your initial training. You're an excellent officer, Delilah."

"Thanks."

He could almost hear her smile, and it made him smile. "Let me know if you find anything tomorrow."

"Will do, Chief."

"Good night, Delilah."

"'Night, Snowden."

He hit the off button on the phone but just sat there holding it, wondering what the hell was going on with the case and what the hell was going on between him and Delilah.

Sunday morning, Noah found the kitchen a mass of confusion when he entered to grab his cup of coffee. Mrs. Santori was putting homemade waffles on the table and fussing about juice boxes all over the house. Mattie was standing smack in the middle of the kitchen between her and the table, slowly tying his tie, making the housekeeper go around him each time she went to the table with plates or syrup. And Mallory and her mother were going at it as only a mother and a four-year-old daughter could.

"Why can't I wear my w . . . red cowboy boots?" Mallory demanded, making a concerted effort to pronounce her Rs properly.

"Because they're old and they're dirty and they don't go with your pretty orange dress."

Mallory stood in the doorway that led into the living room, her red cowboy boots planted, feet apart, her arms crossed stubbornly over her chest. "They go with my dress."

"They don't." Rachel struggled to get an earring in her ear without the benefit of a mirror.

She looked nice this morning, dressed for church in a pair of tan capris, a robin's egg blue T-shirt, and sandals. She'd washed her hair and blow-dried it, leaving it to sweep loose over her shoulders.

"They don't match, and besides, they're too small, Mallory. They need to be donated to the church clothing closet." She finally got the earring in and let her hands fall. "Why don't you wear your nice, new white sandals we bought? You like those."

"I don't like them." Mallory uncrossed and recrossed her arms. "I like my boots."

"We do this every Sunday." Rachel threw her hands up in the air.

"Coffee?" he asked, making a concerted effort not to smile.

"Please," she groaned, turning back to Mallory. "In your chair. Breakfast is on the table, and Mattie's going to be late to play the organ for service if we don't hurry. You're going to be late to Sunday School."

Noah filled the two mugs Mrs. Santori had left on the counter and carried one to Rachel. Turning his back to the little girl climbing into her booster seat at the kitchen table, he murmured under his breath as he passed by Rachel, pushing a cup into her hand. "Personally, I think the red cowboy boots go nicely with the flowered orange and pink dress."

"You're not being helpful," she whispered back, cutting her eyes at him. Her tone was light, almost playful. "You know, I knew you'd be this way, I always said so. You just want to give the children anything they want."

Noah lifted the mug to his lips but didn't take a drink; his gaze met hers, her expression changing. She was referring to conversations they'd shared prior to Isaac's and Abraham's births.

The minute the words came out of her mouth, he could tell she hadn't meant to say it. At least not in that way.

For a moment, their gazes locked, they shared a ripple of

sorrow for the baby boys they had buried together in St. Paul's cemetery. He felt her pain, and he sensed she felt his.

She looked away, taking a swallow of coffee. "Mattie, stop fussing with your tie. You look fine. Sit down and eat."

Noah walked to the door to remove himself from the breakfast table and give himself a minute to recover. He had loved those baby boys so much. They both had. And he and Rachel had both felt guilty for bringing them into the world with a fatal genetic disease. The difference between them, though, was that she had been able to recover from their deaths. Obviously, he hadn't or he wouldn't have lost himself in a bottle.

She'd recovered, all right. Recovered well enough to try again. Of course, without him. With the disease tyrosinemia, a metabolic disease that affected the liver, both parents had to be carriers.

Which brought him back to the question of who Mallory's father was. Had Rachel fallen in love with a man but chose not to marry even though she carried his child? If so, where was he? Here in town?

Or had she simply had sex with another man just to have the child she so desperately wanted, the healthy child he couldn't give her?

Once, he would have gotten down on his knees and prayed to God to help him through these feelings of anger, of resentment, of jealousy. He wanted Mallory to be his child, his and Rachel's, so desperately that he lay awake in bed at night thinking about it. But he didn't pray. He had no prayers left inside him. No confidence left to believe anyone was listening.

The strange thing was, in his past, these feelings would have depressed him, making him feel hopeless. This morning, though, it just made him angry. Angry for what he had done. Angry that he wasn't taking advantage of the opportunities he had right here, right now.

He thought about what Sister Julie had said about accepting forgiveness, forgiving himself and moving on with his life, making the best of what he had. Making a difference in the world with the time he had left.

The day she had said it, the idea had seemed so far-fetched, so beyond possibility, that he hadn't really considered it. This morning, though, seeing Rachel and Mallory, having Mattie here at his table, made him *want* to make the best of whatever was left inside him.

It was an odd feeling, one he thought might take some getting used to. What was really strange was that he liked it.

CHAPTER 10

It was still cool early Sunday morning when Delilah arrived at Pam Rehak's place. She parked her red Toyota midsize pickup on the side of the road and walked up the dirt driveway, trying to open her mind to any evidence she might have missed the day before.

The lot was wooded, but not with the elegant oaks, elms, and other deciduous trees in many of the forests in the county. It was sandy here, and the trees that surrounded the beat-up trailer were mostly scraggly pine. Though it was late June, the underbrush of tangled briars and weeds was already thriving, pressing in, encroaching on the unmowed lot.

As she walked up the driveway, Delilah studied the mishmash of tire tracks in the soft sand. After all the vehicles that had been in and out of here the previous day, there was no way to distinguish one vehicle from another or tell how many times Ed Parson had been in and out on his Harley the night Pam had died. If he'd left to dispose of the evidence after he killed Pam, there was no way for them to know.

After entering the clearing where the trailer sat, underpinning sagging, its aluminum sides stained with streaks of rust, she halted and took in the scene. Pam's '86 Honda sedan sat parked catty-corner where she'd left it after arriving home from work Friday afternoon. The grass that was in desperate need of mowing had been crushed by all the vehicles and people on the scene the day before, but little tufts of weeds and crabgrass poked up here and there.

Delilah spotted a hint of color in the green grass . . . a kid's yellow bucket like the kind you took to the beach. She walked around the trailer to the backyard, where the grass was even higher. She could see paths where people had walked around yesterday, but no vehicles had been here.

She spotted a rusty metal barrel on top of cinder blocks. A trash barrel for burning. It was no longer a legal means for citizens to dispose of their garbage, but that didn't stop some people from burning anyway. It saved the cost of a trash service or the trip to the landfill. She walked over to the barrel and peered inside. A sample had been taken the day before to be analyzed to be certain no one had burned blood-spattered clothes in it, but the ashes removed had been caked and damp and probably there for some time. From the look of the pile of garbage bags around the cinder block back step, Ed was a little behind in his trash-burning chore.

She walked to the step to study the trash bags. They'd been searched, too. No sign of anything pertaining to the crime. She glanced up at the woods line, noticing a bunch of white papers, newspapers, and other assorted trash caught in the briars. Someone must not have re-tied one of the bags tightly. She plucked a pair of disposable gloves from the rear pocket of her jeans and slipped them on. She didn't know why she would care about the loose trash; the property was obviously not well kept. But the idea that law enforcement agents had created the mess made her feel responsible.

At the edge of the property, she leaned over, picking up sheets of white paper. There were pages of U.S. history notes. Pam had been a student at the community college; She must have tossed them when the semester ended. There were sheets of the local newspaper, hot dog roll wrappers, a chip bag. She balled up the paper and stuffed it into the chip bag. After picking up the last piece of notebook paper, she turned to walk back to the trash bags when a smaller piece of paper caught her eye. She'd almost missed it in the weeds.

She walked over, leaned down, and picked it up. As she lifted it, she recognized what it was, and the chip bag of trash fell from her hand. "Holy crap," she muttered.

How had they missed this?

It was a page torn from a Bible. A page from Leviticus with a verse underlined in ballpoint pen. She didn't have to read it to know what it said.

She studied the page for another second, thankful she had thought to put on her gloves, and then she reached into the back pocket of her jeans and pulled out her cell phone.

She didn't get Snowden, just his answering machine. He was probably at church, where she belonged, according to her mother. Delilah left a brief message for Snowden and then, grabbing the chip bag and depositing it in the burn barrel, she walked around front to sit on the steps and wait for him.

"There you are."

Noah looked up from where he knelt on the ground securing one of the anchor wires on an end trellis. Like most vineyards on the east coast, they used a two-wire trellis system with the trellises eighteen feet apart. In the Chancellor grape field, the rows were five hundred feet long and ten feet apart.

"Hey," he said, seeing Rachel hurrying toward him over the slight rise that was perfect terrain in the area for growing grapes. He got to his feet, brushing the dirt from his knees, sensing something was wrong. She was still dressed in her church clothes, traipsing through the field in her sandals. "What's up?"

"I don't mean to sound like a helpless woman," she said, exasperation plain in her voice, "but I need you." She halted at the end of the trellis row. "It's Mattie."

"What's wrong?" He picked up the tools he'd been using to tighten the trellises and carried them to the wagon hitched to the lawn tractor. "Is he all right?"

"He's fine." She ran her hand over her face. "No, I guess he isn't." She let her hands fall to her sides. "He won't get out of the car, and I don't know what's wrong."

Noah frowned. "Won't get out of the car?"

"We got home from church, and when Mallory and I got out, he didn't. I just left him, thinking he needed a minute. You know how he is about being rushed." She looked at Noah. "Mallory and I went in the house to make tuna salad— she wanted to bake cookies—and the next thing I knew, an hour had passed and still no Mattie."

"He was still in the car?"

"In the backseat, in the garage. Never moved. I tried talking to him. He won't even look at me. I put down the windows, because it's really hot in there, and then, when I tried to take his hand he—" She glanced away, not finishing her sentence.

Noah took a step toward her, now genuinely concerned. "He what, Rache?"

"He flinched." She met his gaze. "He acted almost as if . . . as if he was going to hit me."

"You're kidding. Mattie's never been violent in his life. Come on, let's get back to the house. Where's Mallory?"

"I thought it would be OK to leave her. I know he would never hurt her, and I didn't know where to look for you."

"It's OK, Rache," he said gently. "I know she's fine. Where is she?"

"In the house. I left her in front of the TV with cookies." She raised one slender shoulder. "I mean, he won't get out of the car, right?"

Noah climbed on the tractor and started the engine. "Come

on," he said, putting out one hand as he adjusted the throttle with the other.

She shook her head, raising her voice above the rumble of the engine. "I'll just walk."

"And ruin those pretty sandals?" He looked at her, offering half a smile. "Come on." He slid over on the seat and put out his hand again. "There's plenty of room."

She hesitated for a moment and then, glancing up, must have realized it was easily a five-minute walk back to the house and it was silly to walk if she could ride with him. Reluctantly, she climbed onto the tractor, squishing into the seat beside him.

Noah pushed the tractor into gear and followed the dirt road along the edge of the Chancellor grape field, past the hardy Pinot Noir field, and cut onto the main lane that ran east to west across the property and directly back to the house. As he drove the lawn tractor back toward the farmhouse, which they could already see in the distance, he tried not to think about the feel of Rachel pressed against him on the seat, or the scent of her shampoo that he could smell, even driving at the speed they were going.

She felt so good. Having her next to him, her body brushing his, made him feel stronger. More capable.

They passed the pressing shed and the fermenting barns, pulling into the yard, hitting the crushed oyster shells as they drove onto the driveway. The minute he hit the brakes, even before he cut the engine, she was off the tractor and running up to the house.

Noah set the parking brake on the tractor and headed for the garage. As he passed the house, he could hear the sound of the TV and Rachel's and Mallory's voices. Apparently Mallory was just fine. Noah knew she would be. He'd seen the little girl and Mattie together often enough to know Mattie adored her.

Noah found Mattie, just as Rachel had said, seated in the backseat of her Volvo station wagon. He walked around the back of the car and opened the rear door opposite where Mattie was sitting.

"Hey, buddy," he said, sliding onto the rear seat. Even with the windows rolled down, it was hot inside, and Mattie, still in his shirt and tie, was sweating profusely. "What are you doing in here?"

Mattie sat in the seat, his hands pressed against his knees, staring straight ahead.

"Mattie, you have to come out of the car," Noah said gently. "It's too hot to sit in here all afternoon." He waited.

Mattie just kept staring at the back of the seat in front of him.

"Was there somewhere else you wanted to go?" Noah asked after another minute of silence. "You wanted to stay at church or something?"

Still nothing.

Noah studied his face for a moment. Mattie was beginning to look older than his thirty-eight years. His hair was graying and thinning, and with the extra weight he had put on, his jowls were beginning to sag. He looked sad today.

"Come on, buddy, you have to help me out here." Noah glanced out the open door of the car, then back at Mattie. "Mallory tells me you can talk when you want to. You think you'd like to try it out on me, because you know, there's nothing I can think of that would make me happier than to hear what you have to say. To know for sure, for once, what you want. What you need."

Noah heard someone enter the garage, and he turned to see Mallory walking up along his side of the car, a plastic plate of cookies in her hands. Rachel followed her.

"No luck, huh?" Rachel asked.

Noah shook his head.

"Well, Mallory wants to give it a try. Mind?"

Noah shrugged, sliding out of the car to let Mallory in.

"*Howld* this," Mallory said, pushing the plate into his hands. "And no eating!"

Noah looked up at Rachel, grinning. "Yes, ma'am."

Mallory climbed into the car. "You have to go," she said rather sternly.

"We have to go?" Rachel looked at Noah.

"We have to *tawk*," Mallory explained. "Mattie and me."

"Mattie and I," Rachel corrected.

"That's what I said," Mallory declared indignantly.

Rachel met Noah's gaze, and without a word passing between them, he knew what she was asking.

"She'll be fine," he said gently. "Come on."

Rachel and Noah walked out of the garage and stood ten feet back, in the driveway. At once, they heard Mallory talking, but her voice was muffled inside the car so they couldn't hear what she was saying.

"What do you think she's telling him?" Rachel crossed her arms over her chest.

"Probably something profound like he doesn't get any cookies if he doesn't come out of the car." Noah flashed a grin at her.

Rachel chuckled. "It would work with me."

"You always were a slave to chocolate."

She smiled, and they both stood there watching the car. A minute later, the door opened on Mattie's side. Mallory popped out the other door. "Come on, we can go in your fort," she called in her sweet voice. "Come on, Mattie. Jump out, just *wike* me."

Mattie thrust one leg out the door, then the other.

Mallory came out of the garage. "He's coming now. We're going to go sit in his fort and eat cookies if that's *awright*, Mom. Mattie *wikes* to go to his fort when he's scared."

"How do you know he's scared?" Rachel asked.

"He *towld* me." The little blonde took a cookie off the plate Noah was still holding and bit a piece out of it.

"He told you this?" Rachel asked skeptically.

"Mmm-hmmm." Mallory munched on her cookie.

"What's he scared of, Mallory?" Noah decided there was no sense addressing the topic of Mattie's speech abilities again, even though they hadn't heard a word from Mattie inside the car. For all they knew, the four-year-old was making it all up.

"He doesn't know." Mallory stuck out her tongue to catch a smear of chocolate on the corner of her mouth. She walked around to the other side of the car. "Come on, Mattie. *Wet's* go eat our cookies in the fort. *I'w tewll* you a story so you won't be afraid." She looked at her mother over her shoulder, lowering her voice just as Mattie appeared from the car. "*I'w tewll* him about the prince who fights the dragons to save the princess, just *wike* you *tewll* me when I'm scared."

Mattie lumbered by them, not even glancing up. Mallory grabbed the plate of cookies and fell into step behind him, making a beeline for the barn.

"You think it's OK?" Rachel murmured, looking up at Noah. "I know he'd never hurt her. I'm sure he wasn't going to hit me. I just startled him, that's all. You know he's sensitive about being touched."

"I'm sure she'll be fine," Noah assured her. "I've got some things I can do around house though, some cleaning up so I can keep an eye on them. How about if you go inside and change and I'll hang out here?"

Rachel looked up, meeting his gaze, her green eyes warm with appreciation. "You like her, don't you?"

"Like her," he said softly. "I've known her less than a month and I love her like she's my own."

Rachel pressed her lips together, and for a moment he thought she might cry. She turned away from him. "I'll be back out in a few minutes. I'll work in the garden and keep you company." As she walked away, she grabbed his hand and squeezed it before she let it go.

Noah could feel his heart swell in his chest.

"So, what do you make of it?" Snowden asked. They were in his office, with the door open, of course, but the station house was quiet because it was a Sunday afternoon. Most of the officers on duty were on patrol, and the dispatcher worked in a soundproofed room that also served as the receiving desk to the general public when they entered the building.

"What do I make of it? What is there to make of it except the obvious?" Delilah said in her unmistakable southern drawl. "Johnny Leager was steppin' out on his wife, and with Pam Rehak, apparently."

Snowden pushed back in his comfortable executive's chair behind his desk, placing his hands behind his head as he thought. "Which brings us back to Mr. Parson as the prime suspect."

She perched on the arm of one of the two chairs in front of his desk. It was something Snowden had noticed about her. She was a percher rather than a sitter. Too much nervous energy to sit, he supposed.

"Or the grieving widow," Delilah offered. "Wife finds out about the affair, decides to end it permanently and cash in on the life insurance."

"It's only twenty thousand dollars." Snowden frowned. "By the time she pays the funeral expenses, she'll be lucky if she has ten left."

Delilah shrugged her petite shoulders. "You saw the house. Ten thousand dollars cash probably sounds like a lot of money to Stacey Leager. Especially when she gets rid of her no-good cheatin' husband in the deal."

"I don't know." Snowden let his hands fall to his lap as he shifted his weight forward in his chair. "The handwritten note left at the Leager scene didn't look like her handwriting according to our lab. We can send it off to a handwriting expert, but I'd guess it would come back not a match. Even I could tell that the writing was more masculine than the sample of the wife's that we kept with her written statement."

Delilah popped off the chair and began to pace behind it. "If I were goin' to kill my man and leave a note to throw off the police, I'd disguise my handwriting." She raised a finger. "In fact, I might get smart on the next one and rip the page right out of the Bible and just underline the verses."

"But why kill the woman two weeks later? We weren't even looking at Mrs. Leager as a suspect. And the notes suggest some kind of religious zealot. She attended church regularly at St. Paul's, but she didn't strike me as even particularly religious."

"Hard to say why people do the things they do, Chief. Maybe she killed him thinkin' it would make her feel better and it didn't." Another shrug. "Or maybe she enjoyed it and wanted to try it again."

"But these are such gruesome murders," Snowden said, thinking out loud. "I've been doing a little research from some files sent from the FBI in Quantico, and women don't usually kill this way. They don't like a mess."

"Always exceptions to every rule, I suppose. "

Snowden found himself meeting her gaze and he looked away, beginning to feel a little uncomfortable, alone with her like this on a Sunday when the station house was practically a tomb. He couldn't stand even a whiff of suggested impropriety. There were people on the city council who hadn't wanted to make him the chief to begin with, and he knew they were aching to fire him. Two unsolved murders were already two strikes against him. He certainly didn't need another.

"Well, listen, nothing else we can do today." Snowden reached for a file on his desk and flipped it open. "Go home, enjoy the rest of your day off, and we'll get on the case tomorrow. If Stacey Leager did this, she won't get away with it."

Delilah stepped into the doorway, one hand high on the doorjamb. She was dressed in jeans and a little pink T-shirt. It was perfectly respectable, covered her completely, but it was form fitting, making it quite obvious that, out of her uniform, Sergeant Swift had a mighty fine figure for such a small woman.

"I'll run over to the cup plant first thing in the morning, have a talk with personnel."

"You come into the station house first, hook up with Lopez."

She frowned. "I can do this myself, Chief. I don't need an escort."

"I said you were no longer in training. That doesn't mean you've been on the force long enough to ride on your own." He grabbed a pen out of the center drawer of his desk. "We go by the book here, Swift."

He didn't look up, but he knew she was making a face. She was very expressive when it came to her thoughts, especially when she disagreed.

But she didn't argue with him, and when he glanced up, she was on her way out the door. "See you tomorrow, Chief."

"Yup," Snowden called after her as she disappeared down the dark hall. And then, unable to resist, he added, "Good work, Delilah."

That night, Noah lay in his single bed, unable to sleep. A little afraid to sleep. He felt strange, anxious, as if something was going to happen, something bad, but he didn't know what.

Maybe he was just afraid of another blackout. They came without rhyme or reason, and there was no telling how long they would last. Sometimes it was just like a blink, just a moment of blackness, but even then, there was no denying it had happened. He came out of them feeling disoriented, confused, worried, never sure how long he'd been out or what he'd done. Where he'd gone.

When he first arrived in prison and sobered up, he'd lost whole days to the blackouts, but his roommate could relate to him things he had said or done during them. He would apparently go to the gym, to the mess hall, or to the library to work, without knowing he was doing it. It was just like the memory was gone from his mind. But that was why they called them blackouts, wasn't it?

Remembering those early days made him think of his roommate, lifer Clancy Jones. Clancy was there for killing his wife and his best friend with an axe after catching them in bed together when he was twenty-eight. He'd celebrated his sixty-ninth birthday a few months before Noah's release. The old man had been good to him, helped him adjust as well as anyone could to prison life, but Clancy had had his quirks.

Clancy Jones, a black man, had found God in prison and attended services held daily by various volunteers from the outside. In the five years that Noah had been in, the old man had never given up, asking each day if Noah wanted to attend service with him. No matter how many times Noah said he wasn't interested, Clancy would tell him that it didn't matter if Noah had given up on God because God hadn't given up on Noah.

Right now Noah almost wanted to believe it.

But what would make him believe a crazy man, and Clancy had certainly been crazy. It had been the old man's belief that Satan had entered his body the night he murdered his wife and friend, that Satan had killed them, using his human form, and that he was, actually, an innocent man.

Noah sighed, glancing at the digital clock beside the bed that said it was 2:04 A.M. Blaming Satan for the murders had always seemed like an easy out to him. Like him blaming hereditary alcoholism for what he had done.

In counseling while in prison, one of the things Noah had heard over and over again was that in order to recover, he had to take responsiblility for his own actions. He was responsible for drinking. He was responsible for killing the Marcuses. He was responsible for the divorce between he and Rachel. That little girl wasn't his because of things he had chosen to do.

However, he was not responsible for his parents' deaths. That was another part of recovery. They'd talked about it the other day at his AA meeting. The speaker said that recovering alcoholics sometimes became so enthusiastic in their willingness to meet their own failings head-on that they took on blame for things that weren't theirs to begin with. He was certainly guilty of that after his mom and dad were killed. It was part of the reason why he'd started drinking more.

Somehow, it had made sense in his alcohol-crazed mind. He'd given his parents the trip for their anniversary. It was something they had always wanted to do—a mission trip to Central America; it had sounded so perfect. It had been perfect until their Jeep caravan had been stopped by rebels with machine guns and his mom and dad had been murdered execution style.

Noah squeezed his eyes shut, a lump rising in his throat. He missed them so much.

He took a deep breath and opened his eyes, staring at the tiled ceiling, thinking he really did need to go to the churchyard and say good-bye. He wondered if Rachel would go with him. Maybe they could visit their boys' graves, too.

Well, maybe he wasn't ready for that yet, but he was definitely making progress. With a grim smile of satisfaction, he rolled onto his side and turned off the light. Rolling onto his back again, he closed his eyes and tried to let his mind drift toward more pleasant thoughts. He thought of the rows of grapevine trellises, the sunshine on his face, the smell of the grass that lay between the rows, freshly cut. And then, almost of their own accord, in his mind's eye he saw Rachel and Mallory, hand in hand, coming toward him, and they were smiling.

CHAPTER 11

Noah walked down the porch steps Monday morning to see Joshua Troyer coming up the driveway in his old pickup. Joshua took his time, window down, arm resting on the edge. As he turned around in front of the house, sending ground-up oyster shells skittering, he nodded in Noah's direction.

When Joshua pulled up in front of the porch, Noah opened the passenger's side door and climbed in. "I appreciate you doing this for me, Josh. Not a lot of people I feel like I can ask."

"Eeh-ya." He slipped the truck into gear and started back down the driveway. "Glad I can help you out. Know you'd help me out if I needed it."

"You're right, I would." Noah stared at the long rows of grapevine trellis running on both sides of the driveway. The vines were really beginning to leaf out and grow thicker and hardier as the days lengthened and the temperatures rose. He glanced back at the Mennonite man next to him on the bench seat. "But I still want you to know that I appreciate what you're doing for me and I appreciate your friendship."

Josh gave a nod. "Eeh-ya." He stopped at the end of the

drive, looked both ways, and then eased out onto the road. "Guess you heard the news from town. They say we made CNN."

"About Pam Rehak, yes. It's terrible. I can't imagine what's going to happen to her child."

"Took the man she was livin' with in for questionin'," Joshua said. He lifted his arm off the window's edge to stroke his wiry beard. "Think he did it?"

Noah stared out through the windshield. "I don't know."

"Weren't married." Joshua made a clicking sound between his teeth. "Bible says a man lives in sin pays the price."

The Bible said no such thing, that Noah could recall, but he didn't want to be rude and argue with the man willing to drive him to his parole officer. Besides, he'd learned a long time ago not to debate religion with Josh Troyer. The man was a fundamentalist who had never actually read the Bible himself, preferring to hear God's word in church services. He had some rather interesting takes on what it said, but Noah had learned a long time ago not to judge others by their interpretations of the Bible. Joshua was a good man who served as an elder in his church, was a leader in the Mennonite community, and had stood by his wife, despite the importance put on families and the fact that his Trudy couldn't have children.

"Bad thing to raise a child in an evil house like that," Josh continued. "Woman with a child should have known better."

Noah couldn't resist. "So what?" he said, turning to the older man. "Are you saying she deserved to die because she was living with a man who wasn't her husband?"

"God speaks against fornication." Josh gripped the steering wheel stubbornly.

"He also speaks of tolerance and not being judgmental."

"Not my place to judge."

"No, no, it's not." Noah turned to look out the window at the wildflowers growing along the road. There was something about Josh's words that made him uncomfortable. He felt so bad for Pam, who had never been one of his parishioners, but who he had seen in town on occasion. She'd been a pretty enough girl, but one who clearly seemed to be drifting through life, looking for something. Looking to be loved by someone. She had never come in for counseling with Johnny, but he had spoken of her several times, and he had obviously had feelings for her beyond sexual.

It had, of course, been Noah's job to insist that Johnny put an immediate end to the affair. Noah had talked a lot about Stacey, about Johnny's commitment he had made to her on his wedding day and his responsibility as a parent. That didn't mean Noah hadn't felt for the young woman, so desperate for love that she was willing to take another woman's husband to her bed.

His gaze drifted to the neat, white, turn-of-the-century houses that lined both sides of the road as they entered town. It looked so quaint, so peaceful. It was hard to believe two people could have been murdered so ruthlessly in such a short period of time.

Noah tried to block his next thought, but before he could control his line of reasoning, there it was again. *Was* it a coincidence that Johnny and his lover were dead? And if it wasn't, who had killed them? He knew it was none of his business, none of his affair.

So why did he, somehow, deep in his gut, feel it was?

Delilah hit the receive button on the cell phone mounted in a holder on the dash of the cruiser. "Sergeant Swift," she said, her voice transferring through the speakerphone. The department still relied on police radios for a great deal of communication, but cell phones for limited use had been added to the cars the previous year.

"It's Chief Calloway."

"Yes, sir." She stopped at the stop sign and then slowly pulled out onto Route 1, headed south toward Lewes, where the local hospital was located.

"I understand you left the station without a partner this morning," Snowden said.

She resisted a smile, afraid it might affect the tone of her voice. "Yes, sir. Lopez called in sick. Strep, I understand."

"So you took it upon yourself to leave without having him replaced?"

"Lieutenant gave me the go, sir. He asked me where I intended to go this morning, knowing I was working on the Rehak case. I told him. He asked if I required assistance for the interview, and when I told him I didn't, he gave me permission to go out alone."

She heard Snowden sigh on the other end, only it was a little closer to a groan. She'd followed procedure and he knew it. She couldn't be disciplined because her assigned partner came down with strep.

"You knew I didn't want you going out alone, Sergeant."

"Sir, we're trained on how to make decisions based on the information we have at hand. When information or situations change, we must be able to take the next step and adjust." She cruised in the left lane, going 65 miles per hour. Cars pulled into the right lane to let her go by even though she didn't have her siren and lights going. It was a power thing she loved about being a cop.

"So you adjusted?" Snowden said.

"Yes, sir."

To her surprise, he chuckled. She let herself smile.

"You're headed to the plant to see the personnel manager now?" he asked.

"Already been there, sir. Turns out Mr. Carpenter, the personnel manager, is in the hospital after having his appendix out Saturday night. I called him and he agreed to see me there."

"So you're headed to the hospital and then where?"

"Depends on what he tells me, sir. If there's any evidence that Mr. Leager and Miss Rehak were an item, I'm thinking I need to go have a chat with Mr. Parson again and then maybe Mrs. Leager."

"Listen to me, Swift, I want you to call in after you talk with the personnel manager. I don't want you conducting any interviews until I speak with you, do you understand?"

"I'm to call in after my interview." She made a left at Five Points and headed into Lewes. "Yes, sir."

"And there'll be no adjusting for circumstances this time, Delilah."

She heard the phone click and disconnect before she could respond. "Yes, sir," she said, grinning as she punched the end button on her phone.

Delilah walked down the wide hospital corridor, following the room numbers on the wall. She was surrounded by the usual sights of a hospital—nurses dressed in bright tops and white clogs hustling down the hall, techs pushing carts from room to room, doctors seated at nurses' stations filling out patients' records. She heard the squeak of cart wheels on the tile floor, the beep beep of IV pump alarms and the hushed murmurs of patients and employees. Reaching Mr. Carpenter's private room, she heard voices inside, and she halted near the door. A white curtain that fell from the ceiling to within eighteen inches of the floor was half-drawn, blocking her view so she couldn't see who was inside, but she guessed at once, by the chubby feet in sensible shoes. The Bread Ladies.

Every town had them. Gossips clothed in well-meaning neighbors' garb. She hadn't been in Stephen Kill two days when they were knocking on her door bearing a frozen lump of pumpkin bread and a grueling interview on the particulars of her life before she arrived in town.

"Just making our morning rounds, Mr. Carpenter. Glad to see you're on the mend."

Delilah recognized St. Paul's church secretary's voice. It was higher pitched than her sister's.

"It . . . it's very nice of you to stop by," a man said.

Had to be Mr. Carpenter.

"The banana nut bread is very thoughtful."

"Alice made it herself, didn't you, Alice?"

The room was quiet for a moment, and Delilah took the opportunity to knock on the open door. She knew, from experience, that this conversation could go on for hours, and she didn't have time to wait. "Mr. Carpenter, Sergeant Swift here."

"Come in," the male voice called.

Delilah walked in to what was a typical single-bed hospital room and stepped around the half-drawn curtain. A gentleman in his early to mid-sixties lay in the bed, his hair neatly combed. In three chairs, lined up against the far wall, sat The Bread Ladies.

And who said her powers of deduction weren't keen?

"Well, just don't sit there staring, Alice," Cora Watkins was saying. "What's the matter? Cat got your tongue?"

Delilah glanced at Alice Crupp, who lived next door to the Watkins sisters. She was sitting in the chair between the other two women, staring straight ahead. She didn't look like there was anything wrong with her to Delilah. Probably just bored out of her skull with the sisters' chattering.

"Miss Alice?" Delilah said, taking another step forward, her handcuffs on the back of her belt jingling. "Are you all right, ma'am?"

Alice blinked and looked up at Delilah. "H . . . hello, officer."

"Are you feeling all right, ma'am?" Delilah asked, although she could see that the woman was fine.

"Yes, yes, of course." She looked at Cora and then Clara. "But I suppose we should be going, shouldn't we? I don't think the hospital allows more than three guests at a time." She rose from her chair.

"Actually, I have some business with Mr. Carpenter," Delilah explained.

"Do you?" Alice Crupp's penciled-in eyebrows shot up.

"How do you do," Delilah said, crossing to the bed to extend her hand. "I'm Sergeant Swift, and I take it you're Mr. Carpenter?"

"Nice to meet you." The pleasant-looking gentleman in the bed shook her hand firmly. He shifted his gaze to the three women, two of whom were still planted in the chairs. "It was very nice of you ladies to stop by, and again, thank you for the banana nut bread." He smiled in Alice's direction, his gaze lingering on her. "It's my favorite."

Alice's cheeks pinkened as she took a side step toward the door. "Take care of yourself, Mr. Carpenter, and do enjoy the bread."

She reached the door before the other two women reluctantly rose from their seats. "Have a good day, Mr. Carpenter," Cora said. "Take care of yourself."

"Be sure to follow doctor's orders," Clara warned, waggling a finger.

Delilah gave a wave and waited until the women had disappeared down the corridor before she turned back to Mr. Carpenter.

"Please, have a seat, Sergeant." He directed her toward one of the chairs.

"Thanks, but no." She held up her hand. "I'll be brief. I apologize for even asking if I could come by the hospital, you just having had surgery—"

"No, no, it's fine. Gettin' out today, soon as that pesky doctor shows up and releases me."

Delilah smiled down at him and then let her smile fade, putting on the cop face she had practiced in front of the mirror as a rookie. "The reason I contacted you, sir, is that I'd like some information on two of your past employees."

"Johnny Leager and Pam Rehak. Soon as I heard 'bout Pam, I knew I'd be hearing from the police." He grimaced, sitting up a little farther in the bed. "Both good workers. Hard to believe they're dead. Hard to believe things like this can happen around here." He shook his head. "Terrible world we live in."

"Yes, sir, it is." She glanced at a homemade get well card tacked to a corkboard on the wall above the chairs. A child had drawn it, obviously. Had to be a grandchild. "Thing is, sir, what I need to ask you is a bit delicate. Not . . . not something I'd want you to share with others."

"Of course. I handle delicate matters with our employees all the time. Medical conditions. Child support issues. People on parole. What passes between us in this room, Sergeant Swift, is in strict confidence."

She nodded, looking down at the clean tile floor and then back up at him again. "What I need to know, sir, is, to your knowledge, what the relationship was between Mr. Leager and Miss Rehak when she worked at the cup plant."

"Relationship?" His broad brow furrowed.

"On what level they would have interacted." She gestured. "If they worked together directly or indirectly, that sort of thing."

He was still frowning. "They weren't even in the same departments."

"They weren't?"

He shook his head, thrusting out his lower lip in consternation. "He was in shipping. Pam worked the lid line."

"Same hours?"

"Sometimes, but Pam was doing shift work. Johnny only worked days. Then she left; went to the chicken plant, I heard." He stared at her. "You don't think their murders had anything to do with—"

"We try not to speculate, Mr. Carpenter." She rested her hand on her hip, trying to think. She'd come here anticipating that he would say they worked together, were in close contact on a regular basis. Now what?

She looked at him again. "So they had no regular contact at the plant when Pam worked there?"

"I'm not saying they never ran into each other, I just—" He halted, looking down at his feet as he thought for a moment. "Wait, they did work together once upon a time, though." He looked back at her. "But that's been years."

She could almost see a light going off inside her head. "They actually worked together?"

"Yeah, but like I said, that's been years ago."

She pulled her notepad from her pocket. "Do you know when?"

"I'd have to see my files for exact dates, but had to have been six, seven years ago. I been with the plant twenty-nine years come November, you know."

"I see." Delilah made a notation. "And can you recall . . ." She let the sentence die, trying to think of the best way to work her question. "Were there any rumors about the two of them?"

"You mean together?" He was frowning again. "Shoot, no, Sergeant. Now, I'm not sayin' we don't see a little monkey business at the plant now and then, but Johnny Leager, he was a good guy. He'd never have jeopardized his job to have a fling with another employee, especially him bein' a supervisor. We got strict policies against that."

"And there was never even a whisper about the two of them? Lunchroom gossip?"

"Not that I heard, and believe me, it all gets around. Everyone knows everybody's business at that plant, whether people like it or not."

She folded the cover down on her notebook, realizing it was silly to be disappointed. "Would it be possible, once you get back on your feet and back in your office, of course, that I could have the names and phone numbers of the other em-

ployees who worked the same shift they did? Saw them together?" She tucked the pad and pen back into her breast
pocket.

"Sure. No problem. I can go right in today when I leave
here and—"

She held up her hand. "Really, Mr. Carpenter, I'm sure
this isn't going anywhere. Just get it to me when you return
to work." She glanced at the card on the bulletin board again.
"Nice."

He looked at it and grinned. "Granddaughter. A joy to me
since my Mary passed on last year."

She smiled. "Quite the artist." She turned back to him, offering her hand. "Thank you again, sir, for seeing me. Again,
I apologize for barging in."

"No problem at all, Sergeant." He pumped her hand.
"Pretty young thing like you, don't mind helpin' out at all."

She turned for the door. "Take care, sir."

Delilah waited until she was in the hall and then muttered
under her breath, "Shoot, there goes that idea."

But just because no one at work knew anything about the
two of them having an affair, that didn't mean it hadn't happened, did it? After all, if they had any sense, they wouldn't
have let anyone know, would they? Not with him being married, both of them needing their jobs.

Delilah took the elevator down to the ground floor, her
mind racing. So, who would know? Who would he tell? Who
would she tell?

Best friend? Bartender? Minister?

Delilah barely had the door closed on the car before she
was dialing up Snowden. She didn't give him a chance to
speak. "Far as the personnel manager knew, no one at work
knew anything about an affair between Leager and Rehak.
Not even a whisper of impropriety. She wasn't even working
at the same plant at the time of their deaths," she told him,
starting the engine. "But they did work together a while back,
so here's what I'm going to do, Chief. I'm going to get a list

of people they came in contact with back then, especially friends, talk to them, and I'm going to talk to the bartenders in town, any ministers they might have come in contact with. People they might have confessed a dirty little secret to."

Snowden was quiet on the other end of the line, so quiet she wondered if they'd gotten disconnected. "Sir?"

"You think you still need to pursue this?"

She sat in the cruiser, her hands on the wheel. She knew he wasn't arguing with her, he just wanted her to see her thought process clearly. "Yes, I do. The Bible verses, Chief. No one knew about the first one except us and the family. Now a second? Can't be a coincidence."

"I agree. See the widow, talk with her and find out who his male friends were, especially back then. Then go have a chat with the boyfriend, do the same, and I'll see you back here at the station."

"Yes, sir. Anything else, sir?"

"Yeah. I need to officially put someone on this case, along with me, of course." A silence lingered between them for a moment. "If I cut your patrol hours, you interested?"

"Yes, sir." She was still grinning like a debutante who just received an invitation to her first cotillion when she ended the call.

It was close to one o'clock by the time Josh dropped Noah off at the end of the driveway. He offered to take him up the lane, but Noah felt like he needed a minute or two to himself before he reached the house and the fragile circumstances of his life there right now. With every passing day, passing hour, he found himself more attached to Mallory and the woman he had once vowed to love and protect for the rest of his life. He didn't want to walk into the barnyard carrying any of the shame he had felt in his parole officer's office, answering the questions, providing names and phone numbers if his PO chose to check up on him. He wanted to be able to offer Mattie and Mallory and Rachel more than that. They deserved more than that.

Giving a wave in Josh's direction as he pulled onto the road in his pickup, Noah started up the driveway. He'd gone to the courthouse, as Rachel had requested, and filled out the initial forms to begin the process of becoming Mattie's guardian again, but it had been all he'd been able to manage not to walk out.

It just didn't feel right, him taking over Mattie's care. He wasn't even sure he was equipped, not yet at least. But even worse than his self-doubts about his abilities was the tightness in his chest brought on by the idea of Rachel leaving the vineyard. Leaving him. Taking Mallory away from him.

Logically, Noah knew they were divorced. He knew Rachel didn't owe him a thing. He'd barely even seen her in the last five years because he'd been adamant that he didn't want visitors. He couldn't blame her a bit for wanting to get as far away from him as possible after what he did to their lives, to her life.

And Mallory, what right did he have to a single smile the little girl offered?

But somehow, in less than a month, they had become his world. They were his reason for getting up in the morning, his reason for not taking a drink, no matter how badly he ached for one. A crumpled leaf from Mallory's hand, a single glance or a smile from Rachel, was what he now lived for. Thrived on.

He kicked the ground in frustration, sending white oyster shells flying. He knew he had no right to happiness, but he was discovering that he wanted it, just the same. It was as if the shell he had been, the one he had existed inside for years, now was falling away. In a way it was frightening. In a way, it was easier to be that hollow nothing of a man. No one expected anything out of a washed-up priest, a divorced husband, a prison inmate. But a part of him was energized by the idea.

He was beginning to see possibilities in his life where there had been none before.

Still, he held back.

Sister Julie's words bounced around inside his head, as they did several times a day. She'd talked about forgiveness, forgiving himself. Didn't that mean allowing himself some happiness again?

The idea brought a cautious smile to his lips, and he walked a little faster. Mallory would be playing around the house. Mattie would probably be sitting on the porch, waiting for him to come home, the way he had been the last few days. Rachel would be there, too. They'd agreed to walk the Pinot field together this afternoon and assess the grape blossoms.

Noah hurried up the driveway, approaching the house, expecting to see Mattie, maybe even Rachel and Mallory waiting for him. Instead, he spotted two black-and-white police cruisers, and as he slowed to a walk again, an undeniable shiver of dread crept up his spine.

CHAPTER 12

"So how's your mom?" Rachel asked Snowden.

She lingered on the top step of the front porch. He stood on the brick sidewalk leading to the steps. Even standing on the ground with her on the steps, he seemed like a giant of a man to her. Of course, the police uniform with its crisp seaming and epaulettes only added to the appearance of his size. Even the tiny Sergeant Swift seemed formidable in a uniform.

"She's good." He nodded, seeming a little uncomfortable. He glanced in Sergeant Swift's direction.

Mallory had somehow managed to lure her away from the porch to the silver maple tree in the yard, where her tire swing hung. Apparently, there was a family of ants she was just dying to show the female police officer.

"Mom's slowing down a little, I think," Snowden continued. "Not wanting to admit it, of course."

Rachel smiled, her hands finding her waist as she wrapped them around her. Somehow this seemed awkward, talking to Snowden like this, now that Noah was home. She knew logically there was nothing wrong with it. They with two friends chatting in the yard for a moment, just like there had been nothing wrong with her stopping by his office a couple of weeks ago just to say hi.

So why did it feel so strange?

"Well, say hello to her for me." Rachel tucked a wisp of hair that had fallen from her ponytail back behind her ear. "I don't get much chance to get to the library this time of year, although Mallory has been driving me nuts wanting to get back and rent a new Wiggles DVD."

Snowden glanced out over the barnyard. She had the old pickup truck out that was tagged "Farm Use Only." The lawn tractor was out, too. She'd been hauling some new trellis posts to the Pinot field. Termites had done a number on several this spring, and she was just getting around to replacing them. At least Noah was.

"Place looks nice," he said, after an awkward moment of silence.

"Thanks. Always something to fix, though. You know how that is, right?" She chuckled, remembering going to his house once and helping him install a new ceiling fan. They had laughed and laughed as she had read the nonsensical directions aloud and he had tried to follow them. It had been fun. She'd always had a lot of fun with him when they were dating. When they drifted apart, it had been just that, a drift. No big blowup. No disagreement. They had both just sensed that, while they liked each other, they weren't right for each other romantically. He had actually suggested she still had a thing for her ex-husband, but she'd denied it, of course. Just like she was denying it now.

"Always something," Rachel said, glancing in Mallory's direction. Officer Swift had removed her hat and was stooping at the base of the tree to look at something the preschooler was showing her. "He should be back any time now, like I said." She glanced in the direction of the driveway, then back at Snowden. "Is this about the cases? The murders?"

"Just a couple of questions," Snowden said, avoiding making eye contact with her.

He had the most beautiful eyes Rachel thought she had ever seen on a man. So pale blue they were almost gray. Quite striking on a black man. He was already a handsome man, tall with broad shoulders and a finely chiseled face, but the eyes made him killer.

"You want to ask Noah about the cases?" She studied him, suddenly feeling a little off kilter, a little uncomfortable, and surprisingly enough, a little protective of her ex-husband. "Snowden—" She gave a dry chuckle. "He's been gone more than five years. I don't know what he could possibly—"

"Johnny Leager was one of his parishioners." Snowden shifted his gaze back to her. "We stopped by the church. Records from seven and a half years ago, according to Miss Watkins, show Mr. Leager saw Noah for counseling."

She let her hands fall to her sides. "So? So did a lot of people. It's part of a priest's job, to counsel his parishioners."

"I just have a few questions," Snowden repeated.

Rachel felt a flicker of annoyance with him. He'd been that way when they had dated. He wouldn't engage in give-and-take arguments; he would just repeat himself again and again. "You know very well whatever Noah and Johnny might have discussed, it's privileged information." The fact that *she knew* what they had discussed seemed beside the point. She had been Noah's wife then, and in many ways, *his* confessor. "I don't care what Noah's done, he still knows what his responsibilities are—*were,* to his parishioners."

"Don't get uppity with me," Snowden said with a half smile. "I'm just doing my job here."

There was something about the look on Snowden's face that suddenly worried her. "It's about the note that was left at Johnny's, isn't it?" Rachel came down one step, all at once, feeling heaviness in the pit of her stomach. Suddenly, the warm afternoon seemed cooler, and she shivered. "Was there a note left behind with Pam Rehak too?" She tried to keep her tone even. "I thought her boyfriend did it. Everyone said he got drunk, lost it, and murdered her. You don't think there's a connection to Pam's and Johnny's murders, do you?"

He leaned toward her, lowering his voice, probably so his officer couldn't hear him. "Rachel, you know I can't give you any details of our investigation. You shouldn't have known about that evidence. I shouldn't have allowed that information to be discussed in your vicinity."

A sick feeling washed over her, something akin to what she had felt after the dream about the washing machine. "There *was* a note with Pam, wasn't there?" Her eyes widened as she stared at his face, hoping to read something from it. "Oh, God, Snowden. The boyfriend didn't do it, did he?"

Noah spotted the cop cars first, then Chief Calloway standing at the bottom of the porch steps, deep in conversation with Rachel. She had come down the steps and he was leaning over her, their exchange seemingly intimate.

Noah stiffened. There was something about their body language that made him think they knew each other better than she had led him to believe. Something beyond being childhood aquaintances. He knew they knew each other and that Rachel had gone by the station a few days after Johnny died, but he just assumed . . . He didn't know what he assumed.

Snowden was single. Had they dated? He thought of Mallory, his mind flying in several directions at once. She was blond, but she wasn't fair like Rachel. Her skin was darker and she tanned easily. The gene pool was a funny thing. Just because she didn't appear to have any African American traits didn't mean—

Noah consciously ended his thoughts there. It was crazy, thinking like that. Wondering. He found himself doing it the other day when he was walking downtown, wondering who Rachel had dated since their divorce. Who she might have grown close enough to, to be willing to have his child.

"There he is now," Rachel said when she looked up and saw him cutting across the grass from the driveway.

"Chief Calloway." Noah felt his shoulders go back as he strode toward the larger man.

"He's here to see you," Rachel said, her voice sounding far off. "He and Sergeant Swift."

Rachel nodded, and Noah looked over his shoulder to see the female officer walking toward them, Mallory trailing behind her, chattering a mile a minute about ants.

"They have questions concerning their investigation," Rachel said. She lifted her lashes to meet Noah's gaze.

He instantly felt a strong connection with her. These last few days it was as if they were rebuilding their relationship, one tiny thread at a time, and when she looked up at him at that moment, he felt another silken thread draw him closer to her.

"How can I help you, Chief?" Noah asked Snowden, the expression on his face unwelcoming.

"We'll go inside." Rachel put out her hand to her daughter. "Come on, Mallory."

"I don't want to go inside." Mallory halted, crossing her arms over her chest.

"Well, you're going. Mattie is still watching his movie. *Fantasia*, I think. You can watch it with him for a few minutes."

"But I hate *Fantasia*! I don't want to—"

"Mallory," Noah interrupted, speaking sharply to the little girl for the first time since he had known her. "Please don't be disrespectful to your mother." He softened his tone. "Do as she asks."

Mallory took one look at Noah, dropped her little arms poised in her stubborn stance, and hurried up the steps after her mother.

Noah waited until the screen door slapped shut, and through the kitchen window, he heard Mallory and Rachel go into the living room. "Would you like to step out into the yard, officers?" Whatever they had to say, Noah didn't want it shared with those inside the house.

"Certainly." Chief Calloway followed Noah out into the driveway, close to where the two police cars were parked. "You know Sergeant Swift."

Noah acknowledged her presence with a nod in her direction.

"We'd like to ask you a few questions about Pamela Rehak," the chief of police said, dispensing with the pleasantries.

That was just fine with Noah. He didn't like Snowden Calloway. He didn't like the way he looked at Rachel. "I didn't know her personally."

"But you knew her?"

"I think I met her once at a graduation party or something like that. Eight, maybe nine years ago. I'm not sure we even spoke other than to say hello."

"Was she at this party with Johnny Leager?"

Noah frowned. He'd known why they were here the minute he saw the cars, and his feeling of dread increased even as he tried to fight it. "Of course not," he said, covering his uneasiness with impatience. "It was a family thing. A picnic or barbecue or something. One of the sons of one of my parishioners had graduated from high school."

"Do you recall if Johnny Leager was present?"

"No, I don't recall if he was present." Noah glanced over his shoulder at the house, then back at the police officers. "Look, just ask me what you want to ask me, OK?"

"To your knowledge," Sergeant Swift said, turning to him, "did Johnny Leager and Pam Rehak ever have an affair?"

"Why would you ask me that?"

In the last few days Noah had heard all sorts of tidbits

about the second murder in town, but everyone thought her biker boyfriend had done it. Everyone said he was a no-good bum, and they were all speculating on what had driven him over the edge. But no one had suggested her murder and Johnny Leager's might be connected. The cops knew something the general public didn't know. Noah knew things the general public didn't know about Johnny and Pam as well, but this was different. The cops knew something more.

"What makes you come here to my home and ask me these questions?" Noah demanded, surprised by the strength of his own voice.

"You know we can't divulge information concerning a case currently under—"

"Bullshit," Noah interrupted Chief Calloway.

His use of profanity startled them all. Noah had never used profanity in his previous life as a priest, for obvious reasons, but he had been surrounded, inundated by it in prison. He didn't know what overcame him at that moment, it just came out.

"This is bullshit," Noah said, lowering his voice but still remaining defiant. "And you know it. I already told you, anything someone revealed to me inside those church walls, anywhere for that matter, is not information I can share. Not ever, Calloway. Not ever," he repeated, emphasizing with a finger that prodded the air.

"We have evidence, Mr. Gibson, that forces us to ask questions we know are difficult," Sergeant Swift said in her sweet southern voice. "It's not our intention to make you or anyone uncomfortable, or force you to reveal information private between a man and his priest, but—"

"But you're asking anyway, aren't you?"

Officer Swift might have been a tiny slip of a thing, but the look on her face indicated she had no intentions of backing down.

She met his gaze head-on. "We're asking because two people in our town have been murdered, Mr. Gibson. We're asking because we believe you may be able to help us catch the murderer or murderers."

Noah glanced away for a moment, taking a deep breath. Thinking. He remembered the conversation he and Rachel had had about a note left at Johnny's. One with Biblical references. That information had never been released, not in the papers, not in the local or national news.

Had there been a similar note left at Pam Rehak's? Why else would the police be making a connection between the two and asking him if they'd had an affair? No one knew about their affair. Johnny had been clear on that. But the Biblical reference left behind at his place suggested otherwise, didn't it?

Noah stared at the oyster shells at his feet, not sure what to say next. He felt like he couldn't ask the police chief about the note because Rachel had told him about it, even though she shouldn't have. He wasn't going to put her in the middle of this.

"I can't tell you anything about Johnny Leager or Pam Rehak," Noah said calmly, looking up at the police officers.

Sergeant Swift and the chief of police exchanged glances. They knew they couldn't make him speak on this subject. They knew he had them.

Sergeant Swift folded back the cover on her little notebook and tucked it into her pocket.

Chief Calloway glanced over Noah's shoulder in the direction of Rachel's garden. "A murder like this, like these, is a terrible thing for our town, Noah."

"I agree."

"People are asking for answers. They are depending on us for answers. They need to know that there's not some crazy guy out there randomly killing people in our town."

"I completely agree," Noah said. "But I can't help you, Chief. I'm sorry. I truly am."

The chief stood a moment longer, staring into space. "Well, thank you for your time."

"You bet." Noah nodded. "Sergeant Swift."

"Thank you, Mr. Gibson."

Noah was standing near the porch steps watching the police cars slowly make their way down his driveway toward the road when he heard the screen door open behind him. The sound of the footsteps told him it was Rachel.

To his surprise, he felt her hand settle on his shoulder and remain there as she stood just behind him, watching the cars. "They don't know for sure about Johnny and Pam, do they?" she whispered.

He exhaled. "They have an idea, but I don't think they know for sure. Otherwise, why would they be asking me, knowing I shouldn't say?"

"Snowden doesn't know that I know about them," she said, her hand still on his shoulder.

Noah turned around to face her, and her hand slipped from his shoulder. "Did you go out with him?"

"That's not really any of your business, Noah."

He looked down at his sneakers, sliding his hands into his pockets. "I know it's not, but I'm asking anyway." He looked up.

"He's not Mallory's father, if that's what you're asking," she said softly.

He looked down again, unsure how to interpret the tone of her voice, her body posture. "I guess it was what I was asking."

She was quiet, but she didn't walk away from him. She just stood there for a minute, close, but not touching. He looked up again. "Listen, I apologize for snapping at Mallory a few minutes ago. It's not my place to—"

"No, it's fine. You were right. She shouldn't speak to me like that, and I shouldn't let her get away with it. It's just hard sometimes. I feel like I always have to be the bad guy with her." A little smile crossed her lips as she looked at him almost shyly. "It's kind of nice to let someone else take the heat with her."

He smiled back, reaching out to casually take her hand and lead her toward the porch. "What say we get Mallory and Mattie and get to work on these trellis posts? It's too nice a day to be inside watching *Fantasia*."

"Sounds good to me."

Her smile broadened and so did his world of possibilities.

Two days later, it was after six when Delilah knocked on Snowden's office door.

"Come in," he called.

She stepped into his office to find him buried in paperwork, his reading glasses perched on the end of his nose. She hadn't even realized he wore glasses. "Just checking in, Chief, before I go. Wanted to run a couple of things by you."

"All right." He removed his glasses and rocked back in his big, black leather chair. He looked tired. He looked as if he wasn't having any better luck sleeping at night than she was. "What have you got?"

She walked around to the chairs in front of his desk and perched on one of the arms. Growing up, her mother had constantly criticized her, deeming her manner of sitting unladylike, but Peggy Swift would just have to get over herself. Delilah didn't like settling into chairs, sinking down into upholstery. A person never knew when they might have to pop up out of a chair. They were too confining.

She flipped open her notebook, which was quickly filling up. She'd have to go to the old-fashioned Five and Dime on Main Street and get a new one soon. "Let's see, I've talked to every friend, relative, acquaintance I could track down of both Leager's and Rehak's. Talked to employees at both plants." She glanced up at him sitting patiently behind his desk. "If they had an affair, no one knew about it."

"At least no one is talking about it."

She made a face at him. "Chief, a town as small as this, everybody knows everyone's secrets. Don't you think if someone slept with someone else's husband last night, the Bread Ladies would have known about it by noon today? You know they would have." She looked down at her notes again. "Pam and Johnny really didn't have mutual acquaintances. She didn't have many friends at all. He hung around mostly with his wife's brother. They did family things together. Neither were barhoppers."

Snowden exhaled. "OK."

"And here's the biggie. If the two were murdered by the same person, which the two notes with the same Bible verse on them lead us to believe, it wasn't the widow or the biker. Parson has an alibi that checks out for the night Leager was killed. Witnesses out the ying-yang. And the night Pam Rehak died, Stacey Leager was on a bus on her way back from some amusement park with her son for a Cub Scout thing. The bus got a flat tire, so they didn't even get back to the school until 2 A.M."

"Past the time the coroner says Pam Rehak died."

"And the time the boyfriend says he found her on fire, strengthening the validity of the statement he gave us that morning. He really did just sit there all night with his girlfriend dead on the front stoop."

Snowden tucked his hands behind his back and stared out over Delilah's head. "So you don't think either of them was the killer, and they didn't do anything crazy like get together and kill them?"

"The biker would have no reason to be jealous of Johnny Leager. He didn't even know Pam then, and after Johnny, before Parson, she lived with another guy who was the father of the child."

"If he was going to be jealous of anyone, it would be that guy."

Delilah nibbled on her lower lip. "He just doesn't strike me as the jealous type. And honestly, I think he's really upset. He's staying with Pam's sister right now, talking about helping take care of the little kid. I don't think she'd let him stay there if she thought he was responsible for her sister's death."

Snowden closed his eyes for a moment and didn't say anything.

Delilah was quiet, knowing he liked time to think. He wasn't like she was, constantly chattering, speaking aloud every thought that popped into her head.

"So where do your conclusions take you, Sergeant Swift?" He opened his eyes and sat upright in his chair.

"It makes me think someone other than the biker or Johnny's wife did this."

"Who *would* do it?"

She shook her head. "I don't know, Chief. We're just guessing they had an affair. No one will even admit they were. My hunch is that if anyone knows about it, it's the ex-priest, and he's dug in. He's not going to verify our suspicions."

"But someone out there had to know about it to kill them," Snowden countered. "The notes suggest it was about sin. Payment for their sins. Who would want people to pay for their sins?"

"I don't know," she said, sliding her notebook slowly into her pocket. "A religious nut." She looked up at Snowden, a thought suddenly crossing her mind. "Or maybe an ex-priest who had to pay for his sins when someone else didn't."

CHAPTER THIRTEEN

Rachel sat upright in bed, her forehead beaded in sweat. She couldn't even remember what the nightmare was about, only that it was awful. That it was terrifying and left her feeling as if she were someone other than herself.

She glanced at the clock beside her bed. It was 4:55 A.M. She looked at the windows. The room-darkening shades were pulled down, but she could see the barest hint of light seeping around the edges. The sun would be up soon.

She threw her legs over the side of the bed with a groan, thinking she might as well get up and start her day. It wasn't like she was going to be able to sleep again. She turned on the lamp beside her bed, allowing it to cast a circle of soothing light over the bed and the floor at her feet. She crossed the room to an upholstered chair and grabbed a bra and a pair of jeans she'd left there the night before. Both could be worn again, but she'd tossed yesterday's T-shirt in the dirty clothes after Mallory had rubbed chocolate milk from her mouth all over Rachel. That was what mothers were for, right? A napkin.

Clothes in hand, she went to her dresser, a turn-of-the-century antique she and Noah had rescued from a yard sale a million years ago. She'd refinished it and the double bed they'd bought the same day. The bed now resided in the storage room along with Noah's boxes. She hadn't been able to bear to sleep in it after he went to jail, so she'd replaced it in the room they had once shared with the twin-size antique iron bed she slept in now. Once her grandmother's, it was one of the few possessions she owned belonging to her own family.

She'd been raised by her grandmother after her father was killed in the Vietnam War and her mother had taken off to be a hippie, abandoning her infant daughter.

Although Rachel saw her mother on and off over the years as she married, divorced, moved, married and divorced again, they had never been close. She hadn't even come to her and Noah's wedding, though what her excuse had been, Rachel couldn't even remember now. Not that she had cared that much. Her grandma, in her eyes, had been her mother, and she still missed her a great deal, even though she'd been dead eight years.

Rachel pulled a gray athletic T-shirt, a pair of panties, and a pair of socks from the dresser and stood as she dressed. Barefoot, socks in hand, she shut out the bedside light on her way out the door. At Mallory's door, she peeked in, saw her angelic daughter on her back, nightgown gathered around her waist to show a pair of pink butterfly panties, her limbs thrown out in abandon. With a smile, she closed the door and quietly retreated down the hall.

In the kitchen, Rachel turned on the light and started collecting the necessary items to start a pot of coffee. She used to let Chester out first thing when she came down every morning, but he had started sleeping in Noah's room and she certainly wasn't going in to get him.

As she measured out the coffee, she thought about Noah asleep in the other room. He was trying so hard. Doing so well. He was attending his AA meetings and hadn't had a single drink, to her knowledge, since his release. He worked from dawn to dusk on the property and seemed to be genuinely interested in the vineyard's day-to-day operations. And as much as she hated to admit it, even to herself, she was glad to have him around.

It was interesting that he was so much like the Noah she had once known, but different, too. Not necessarily a bad different. Just different. But wasn't she a different person than she'd been before the babies died, before his parents had gone to Central America, before he started seriously drinking?

She carried the stainless steel carafe to the kitchen faucet and turned on the cold water, letting it run for a minute. Noah had surprised her the other day when he'd spoken to Mallory so sternly in front of Snowden and the female officer. Rachel had been equally surprised by her own reaction, or lack thereof. She thought she would have been upset with him for reprimanding Mallory. She *wasn't* his child; she was Rachel's, just Rachel's. But she hadn't felt that way when he'd done it. She'd actually had been relieved to have him step in, if only for a minute.

She thought about him asking her about Snowden. She knew every time he looked at Mallory, he must be wondering who her father was. But she'd decided even before her daughter was born that she wouldn't tell Noah. That she would never tell him. He'd given up that right the night he had left the house drunk and shattered so many lives.

The carafe filled with water, Rachel carried it to the coffeemaker, poured the water in the reservoir, set the carafe in its place, and hit the black button. The red light popped on.

Barefoot, she walked to the door, unlocked it, and pushed open the screen door, stepping out onto the porch. The narrow floorboards, painted gray, were cool beneath her feet. She breathed deeply, pressing her hands to her lower back, contemplating what task on her list of a hundred she'd tackle first today. Trouble was, there was so much that needed doing that she never felt like she was getting ahead.

Preschool was out for the summer, though, and that would help. She wouldn't have to spend so much time driving back and forth to town. And Mattie would certainly be happy to have Mallory home all summer. He really missed her when she was in school.

Rachel walked to the end of the porch and let her hands fall to her sides as she surveyed the yard and surrounding outbuildings in the muted morning light. She loved this yard. It seemed like it had been her life for so long that she couldn't imagine leaving it. Not even with the job applications sitting on her desk in the office.

Her gaze shifted from one outbuilding to the next in the semicircle of the backyard. When she reached the garage, she took a step forward, down the front step. The garage bay door was open, and her car was half out of the garage.

Baffled, she walked down the steps, down the sidewalk, and cut across the grass. She'd parked the car yesterday afternoon after returning from Josh's house where she'd bought eggs, a weekly ritual. Rachel didn't really notice a difference in taste, but Mrs. Santori insisted on cooking with fresh eggs.

Rachel distinctly recalled that she had pulled her car into the garage, *all the way* into the garage, and hadn't moved it again. She walked around the back of her station wagon, dragging her fingers across the hatchback window. It was dirty and needed a wash. She walked around to the driver's side and peered inside. Sure enough, her keys were there. She always left them in the ignition. It wasn't like they lived in a high-crime area.

She walked away from the car, striding toward the house. What did Noah think he was doing? He wasn't allowed to drive a car. He wasn't allowed to go anywhere in the middle of the night. No one went anywhere in the middle of the night unless they were up to no good.

She walked into the kitchen and made a beeline for the spare bedroom. "Noah," she demanded, pushing open his door without knocking. "Just what the hell do you think you're doing?"

Rachel's voice startled Noah, and his eyes flew open.

"Well," she demanded, taking a step closer to his bed.

Chester, who'd obviously been asleep near the door, rose slowly and yawned, stretching.

Noah ran his hand over his face as he sat up, sliding his legs over the side of the bed. He felt funny sitting there in nothing but a pair of boxers, even though she'd obviously seen him in less. "What . . . what's the matter, Rache?"

"What's the matter with you is what I want to know!" She wasn't usually a shouter, but she was definitely shouting now.

"Wait . . ." He held up one hand, still a little groggy. He'd been having such a hard time sleeping at night that he'd taken some allergy medicine around midnight, hoping it might help him get some rest. Surely he couldn't have suffered a blackout and gone somewhere, done something while asleep and drugged on antihistamines. "I don't know what we're talking about here."

She crossed her arms over her chest. "My car. You moved my car."

He grimaced. "I did not move your car."

"You went somewhere in it last night and then you didn't even get it all the way back into the garage. What? You thought I wouldn't notice that you'd left the ass end hanging out of the garage?"

"Rache, I don't know what's going on with your car, but I didn't move it and I certainly didn't go anywhere."

She waited, that accusing look still on her face.

"Last night I played that matching card game with Mallory and Mattie after dinner, I watched the end of the Orioles game on TV, and then I went to bed. Remember? I was just shutting out the lights when you came downstairs to lock the door and get a glass of water?"

She glanced away, then back at him, one hand perched on her hip. She looked like she'd just gotten up; her hair hadn't been brushed yet, and she had the innocence about her face that seemed apparent only in the first minutes after a person woke.

"Don't lie to me," she said. "I don't understand why you would lie to me."

He looked up at her, hoping he wasn't lying. "Rache, I'm telling you, I didn't move your car. There's got to be another explanation. Maybe it rolled."

"The garage door is up. I closed it after I parked it yesterday afternoon."

"Anyone could have opened it. Maybe Mallory opened it to get her bike or her wagon out, or maybe Mattie did it."

She looked back at him, her jaw still set determinedly. "It was closed when we went into the house for supper. Mallory never went outside again, and I walked Mattie to the barn when he was ready for bed."

"I don't know what to tell you." He got up and walked past her, out the door toward the bathroom, trying not to be annoyed with her for accusing him. If the car had been moved, it was logical she would think he had done it. Shoot, he wondered if he *had* done it, but he wasn't going to tell her that. "There's got to be a logical explanation." He went into the bathroom and closed the door on her. When he came out two minutes later, she was still there.

She followed him back to his room. "Please tell me you're not drinking again, Noah. Please tell me you're not going to get liquor at night. That you're not drinking and driving."

He grabbed his jeans off the ironing board set up in the spare room and stepped into them. Then he chose a clean red T-shirt from a pile he stored on a cardboard box for lack of any better place to keep them. "I'm not drinking, Rache. I haven't had a drink in over five years. Not since the vodka that night."

To his surprise . . . to his shame, her green eyes filled with tears. "Noah, I can't go through this again. You can't." She clasped both sides of her face with her hands. "We won't survive it. Not a second time."

He grabbed her hands and lowered them to her sides, forcing her to look at him. His own eyes teared up. "Not a drink since that night. You have to believe me, Rache. I'll take a blood test, a lie detector test, anything to make you believe." He pressed his lips together when they began to tremble. "Because I need you to believe me."

Her eyes held his gaze, seeming to search for the truth. Slowly, she relaxed in his grasp, exhaling. "You really haven't been drinking, have you?"

He shook his head, releasing her, trying to give himself a moment to collect himself. "I haven't. I swear I haven't, Rachel."

"Then who moved my car last night?"

"I don't know." He sat down on the edge of the unmade bed to put on his socks. "Mallory, maybe? She's always asking if she can drive the tractor."

"That's ridiculous. She was with us last night."

"I don't know, then. Mattie?"

"He doesn't know how to drive a car, Noah. He can barely cut his own meat. Mallory would be more likely to move the car than he would," she scoffed.

Chester, standing in the doorway between the spare room and the hall, whined.

"Consuelo or Mateo?" Noah offered.

"Equally ridiculous." She looked down at the old dog. "Want to go out? OK, boy."

She walked out of the room, Chester rushing in front of her. Noah followed in his stocking feet, his sneakers in his hand. "Well, what other explanation could there be?"

Rachel let Chester out and stood by the door. "You think someone tried to steal my car last night and something spooked them? The keys were in it. I guess someone could have tried to steal it."

"It makes more sense than Mallory moving it."

"Think I should call the police?" She walked to the cupboard to the right of the sink and opened the old-fashioned glass-front door, removing two extra-large mugs.

"Might not be a bad idea."

"What am I supposed to say?" She went to the coffeemaker and poured them both cups of steaming coffee. "Someone trespassed on my property and moved my car?"

"And maybe your lawn mower," he pointed out, accepting the mug she offered.

She looked at him.

"I meant it when I said I hadn't left it out that night. I don't know how it got out in the yard after I put it away."

"I lock the doors in the house at night. I know we're safe and all, but that's a little creepy." She leaned against the counter and took a sip of coffee. Then she looked up at him. "Especially when the police don't know who killed Johnny Leager or Pam Rehak."

He took a seat at the kitchen table, turning the chair so he could face her. "I'm sure this has nothing to do with that."

"It's almost as if someone is doing it to scare me," she murmured.

"That doesn't make sense."

She lifted her gaze. "No less sense than someone beating Johnny to death with a brick, leaving a note accusing him of adultery, or hitting Pam in the head and then setting her on fire."

"And leaving a note accusing her of the same sin," Noah said, his thoughts now moving in the same direction as hers.

"My God, you're kidding." She walked over to the table, pulling out the chair at the end, sitting down to face him. "Is that what Snowden was here about yesterday?"

"He didn't actually come out and say there was a note, but they've definitely made a connection between the two murders, even though they were killed in different ways. Talking to them yesterday, I just had this feeling it was about the accusation of adultery. They were very interested in information I might know that others weren't privy to."

"So they suspect Johnny and Pam were having an affair and that you knew about it," she said softly.

"I never told you who he had been with, Rache."

"Guess I kind of know now," she answered, still holding his gaze.

He didn't know what to say so he took another drink, as did she.

Then she looked up at him again. "This is going to sound crazy, Noah, but . . . do you believe in evil?"

"What do you mean?"

"I . . . I don't exactly know." She fiddled with the handle of her cup, thinking about her nightmares, about the weird feelings she kept getting when she was in town, and then sometimes she felt it here, too, though only late at night. "I guess I'm talking inherent evil. The kind that makes people do things they don't really want to do. Lures people."

She had a strange look on her face that concerned him. "You mean like Satan?"

She stared into her cup of coffee. "Yeah, I guess so. My grandmother always used to say that he was present everywhere. Lurking. That we had to listen carefully to be certain it was God's voice and not Satan's, that Satan's voice could be very alluring."

"I used to believe Satan existed," he said evenly.

"But now you don't?"

He didn't want to get into this discussion with her right now. A man who professed not to believe in God certainly didn't believe in Satan, did he, but he knew how much it would upset her to hear him say so. Instead, he skirted the issue. "Rache, after the last few years, I don't know what I believe anymore." He hesitated, getting the feeling there was something more here than he was seeing. "Why do you ask?"

"I don't know." She shrugged, rising from the chair. "So you think I should call the police?"

"I doubt they need to launch a full investigation, but I don't think it would hurt to put in a report."

"I could stop by the station after I drop Mallory off for her playdate. I want to run a gift basket by for Sister Julie, anyway."

"For that fund-raiser they're having at Maria's Place?"

She nodded and turned around to put away the coffee canister.

"You're not going to go? Sister Julie was telling me about it; it sounded like fun. Mallory and Mattie would probably enjoy the picnic."

"I don't know. We don't usually participate in public things like that."

"Because of me? Because people look at you and point and say you're the one who used to be married to the priest who killed people."

Her face colored.

He smiled grimly. "It's OK, Rache. How about if we all go?"

"You'd go?"

Noah had no idea why he'd made such a suggestion, but the look on her face made him give up any chance of backpeddling now. "I guess. Sure. Why not? By now, the newness of being the town's latest released prisoner has probably died down."

"Mallory would love to go to the picnic." Rachel was grinning now.

"Just write a check to Sister Julie from the vineyard account for the tickets. I'm sure it's considered a tax-deductible donation." He got up, walking to the back door, his coffee cup in hand. He suddenly felt hemmed in, as if he couldn't breathe right. He needed to get outside and get a fresh breath of air.

"OK. I'll do that. Great."

Noah walked out of the kitchen and onto the porch, and his gaze immediately fastened on the Volvo, half in and half out of the garage. Carrying his mug of coffee, he walked off the porch and to the garage. He went around the driver's side, almost afraid to look inside for fear he'd see an empty vodka bottle or something else incriminating.

To his relief, there was nothing there, at least nothing obvious through the window. He opened the door and reached in, removing Rachel's car keys, leaving the car right where it was.

As he walked back to the house, he contemplated how the heck Rachel's Volvo had gotten there and hoped he'd had nothing to do with it.

Rachel waited until the police officer who had escorted her to Snowden's office retreated back down the hall and then she moved to take a seat in one of the chairs in front of his desk.

"Officer Lopez took your information?" Snowden asked from the other side of his desk. He had a stack of manila folders a mile high in front of him and a yellow legal pad he'd apparently been taking notes on when she came in. She could tell by the fine lines around his eyes that he was stressed and not getting enough sleep at night.

"Yes. It was fine. Quick. Easy." She nodded her head. "Listen, Noah doesn't—I really don't think there's any need for an investigation or anything. I just thought you ought to be aware in case anyone else calls with the same complaint. I know you guys are pretty tied up right now." She hesitated, gathering her courage to say what she'd come to say. "Snowden, why did you need to talk to Noah yesterday?"

"I told you, a few questions concerning the case."

"What could Noah possibly have to do with Pam Rehak's death? He didn't even know her."

"I didn't say he had anything to do with Pam Rehak's

death. We've questioned a lot of people in the last couple of weeks about both murders, and Noah was just one of them."

She looked at him for a moment and then rose to close the door before she spoke again. "Come on, Snowden." She turned around. "I know you better than that. You wouldn't question someone unless you had a damn good reason. And this is the second time you've asked him about Johnny. About his relationship with him."

"Rachel," he said calmly. "You know I can't discuss this with you. You can't become involved in any way."

"I feel as if I'm already involved. You know very well I know about the note that was left with Johnny's body. I wasn't supposed to know but I do, and nothing will change that." She grasped the back of one of the chairs. "So is the note the reason you're questioning Noah? Was there one left at Pam's, too?"

"You're being awfully protective of your ex-husband," Snowden pointed out.

She scowled, noting he hadn't answered her question. "Someone has to. He's in a very precarious position right now. He's barely been out of prison a month, and alcohol is readily available. You or I can only imagine how hard that must be for him. And then you start coming around, asking him about parishioners he counseled when he was a priest, knowing he can't give you any information. Pushing him anyway." She was quiet for a moment. "I just think it's wrong."

"It's my job to find out who killed these people, Rachel."

"That's fine, but it's not your job to make life any harder for Noah right now than it has to be."

"It wasn't my intention to—"

"Snowden!" She slapped her hand on the back of the chair. "This isn't just about the investigation and you know it. He knows you and I dated."

"Over the years, you've dated several people from this town, if I recall correctly."

"Yes, but you were the only one I—" She cut herself off

before she finished her thought. "Look, the truth is, I told Noah about the note left at the scene of Johnny Leager's death, and we're guessing one was left at Pam's place too." She went on faster, not giving him time to respond. "I just think you need to back off from Noah. Whether those two had an affair, you and I will never know for sure, but we both know someone thought they did. You need to figure out who that someone was on your own and leave Noah out of it."

Again, he was quiet for a moment. It was one of the things about Snowden that had made her crazy when they were going out. "You shouldn't have told Noah about what you overheard here."

"You're right, I shouldn't have, but he knew Johnny well and . . ." She let her gaze drift to his commendations on the wall. "And it just kind of came out. Obviously he won't say anything to anyone else." She paused. "I better go. It will be time to pick up Mallory in a few minutes." She started for the door and turned back. "You going to Sister Julie's benefit next Saturday?"

He frowned, picking up his pen. "My mother bought us tickets."

"Then I guess I'll see you there." When Rachel walked out, closing the door behind her, Snowden didn't go right back to what he was doing before she arrived. Instead, he pushed back in his chair, tucking his hands behind his head.

He couldn't believe he'd allowed a civilian to hear about a piece of evidence like that. It was just that he was so pleasantly surprised to see her that day and it all happened so quickly . . .

Regardless, Rachel had learned of the evidence and now she'd told someone else. A mistake like this one could really screw up a case, screw up his whole career.

CHAPTER 14

Rachel slid the pan of brownies out of the oven, switched off the timer, and noted the time on the digital clock on the back of the stove. The picnic didn't start for another hour, but she was pushing it, as usual.

"Can we put frosting and *sprinkewls* on the brownies?" Mallory asked from where she sat at the kitchen table, coloring. Mattie sat beside her, head bowed in concentration as he scribbled furiously.

"They have to cool a little first, but I think we have time for a little frosting and sprinkles." Rachel tossed the hot mitts into a drawer and pushed it shut before stooping down to look for a cooling rack she knew she had around the kitchen somewhere.

"Then we can eat them?"

Rachel could hear her daughter beaming. "No, we can't eat them. Remember? We're going to a picnic and they're auctioning off the desserts. We'll get a dessert, maybe even bring an extra one home for tomorrow, but we can't eat these brownies. Someone else will buy them."

"But I want brownies with *sprinkewls!*"

Rachel rooted around in the dark cabinet, pushing aside

cake and muffins pans. "Would you please get Noah to help you with your Ls, Mallory? You're driving me nuts."

"I'm driving her nuts, I'm driving her nuts," Mallory mimicked, grabbing another crayon from the box on the table.

"That's right, you are driving me nuts." Rachel stood, the rack she'd been searching for in her hand. "We work together for six months on your pronunciation, and Noah's here less than a week and suddenly you've found a whole basket of Rs."

Mallory giggled.

Rachel heard the sound of tearing paper, and she and Mallory both looked at Mattie.

"No, no." Mallory put her hand on Mattie's large one. "We don't tear the books. Books are our friends. That's what my teacher says," she told her mother.

"Your teacher's right." Rachel set the cooling rack on the counter, slid the brownie pan on top, and walked over to the kitchen table. It was so unlike Mattie to destroy anything.

When she moved around to stand beside him, she saw that he had taken a black crayon and scribbled all over a coloring book page of a monkey with a large M on it. On top of the black cloud of scribbling, he had drawn a big red blob and colored it in. Apparently, he hadn't torn the page on purpose, he'd just been coloring so hard that it had ripped from the pressure.

"What you doin', hon?" Rachel asked Mattie. He was usually pretty good at coloring. He didn't always stay in the lines, but she had never seen him scribble all over a page like that before. As she moved behind him to get a better look, she realized it actually looked like the red blob was exploding out of the blackness, giving the whole page an eerie appearance.

"It's OK," Rachel told Mattie, reaching over him to turn the page in the coloring book and fold it back, revealing the N page. "See, it's not torn out completely."

"*I'w* get the tape."

"No, Mal—" Before Rachel could get the words out, Mallory was leaping out of her booster seat and bounding across the floor, headed for the office.

Rachel looked down at Mattie again, who seemed visibly upset. "It's OK, Mattie," she assured him. "It was an accident." She looked up at Mallory rushing back into the kitchen, the Scotch tape dispenser in her hand. "Mallory, Mattie's upset. You need to tell him that tearing the coloring book isn't a big deal."

"But he keeps *scribbwling* in my books, and I don't want him to *scribbwle,* and I don't want him to tear out pages." She dropped the tape on the table. "Here, Mattie, you fix it. You know how."

Her hands still on the table leaning over the book, Rachel looked up at Mallory climbing back into her booster seat on the chair. "I've never seen Mattie scribble on a page before. He always colors nice."

"He does so *scribbwle.* He *scribbwled aw* over my Nemo book." Mallory gave the coloring book, one of several on the table, a push, and it glided across the table toward Rachel.

Rachel opened it, and sure enough, the pages had been scribbled all over. She turned the pages, one after another. Every single page filled in from the spine of the book to the edge of the page, cover to cover in red and black crayon. She looked up at Mattie with sudden concern. She was no psychologist, but the pages looked to her like demonstrations of anger. Rage. And they were just plain creepy.

Almost like her dreams . . .

She picked up the coloring book, taking it with her to the counter. Setting it down, she moved to the kitchen sink to look out the window. "Mallory, maybe you should go change. I left your clothes on your bed." Even though it was after eleven in the morning, Rachel had allowed Mallory to stay in her pj's, mainly to prevent having to make her change a third time when she spilled something on her clothes before they got out the door. "Noah will be back from the Pinot field any time now, and it'll be time to start getting ready to go. You and Mattie clean up the crayons and coloring books and put them away."

"Noah's going to the picnic, right?"

Rachel heard them picking up the crayons and dropping them into the box. "That's right."

"That's good. I *wike* Noah."

Rachel heard Mallory's bare feet hit the floor again.

"Do you *wike* Noah, too, Mama?"

Rachel continued to stare out the window, watching a fat yellow tabby cat stalk something in the grass in the yard. "Yes, I like Noah."

"Noah *wikes* you."

Rachel didn't answer, but that didn't stop Mallory from continuing the line of questioning.

"But he's not your boyfriend *wike* my friend Maria's new daddy?"

Mallory's words almost made her laugh. Or maybe want to cry. "No, he is not my boyfriend."

"But he *wivs* with us *wike Shawntewl wivs* with Maria and her mommy."

"Mal, please." Rachel turned around. She knew four-year-olds were inquisitive, and the brighter the child, the more curious they could be. She had just read an article on the subject last week in a parenting magazine. But sometimes Mallory's questions were almost more than she could deal with. The child was so perceptive. Even *she* had noticed a subtle change in Noah and Rachel's relationship since his arrival a month ago.

Mallory stood looking at her mother, her arms full of coloring books and crayons.

"Mal," Rachel said with more patience. "Could you please put your things away and go get dressed?"

The little girl stood there in lime green shorty pajamas, her hair already brushed and in pigtails, and looked at her mother as if contemplating whether or not to press the subject any further. Finally she offered a big smile and trotted off. "Time to get ready to go, Mattie. Go brush your teeth and your hair."

Mallory disappeared down the hall, and Rachel watched as Mattie slowly rose from his chair and pushed it back under the table. It seemed today as if he moved in slow motion, even slower than usual, if that was possible.

Something was going on with him. Rachel didn't know what, but something was definitely wrong. She glanced out the window again in frustration at her lack of ability to communicate with a man she had known her whole life. She looked back at Mattie. "You OK, buddy?" She leaned against the sink, watching him slowly shuffle toward the door. His face seemed heavier than before, and somehow sadder, although how she could come to that conclusion, she didn't know. When did Mattie ever express any emotion at all?

"If there is something wrong, I want to help," she said, watching him go. "I know Noah wants to help, too. But you have to let us know what's wrong. It's the only way we can help you, Mattie. Do you understand?"

He halted at the screen door that opened onto the porch, his hands hanging limply at his sides. He was dressed the same way he dressed every day in the summer—khaki-colored Dickie pants, a white T-shirt, and a ball cap. Today he was wearing one of Noah's old hats, one Noah must have dug out of the boxes he was apparently slowly making his way through.

Seeing Mattie standing there, head hung, made Rachel so sad. He was obviously upset, angry, something. And yet, she didn't know how to help him. On impulse, she walked up behind him and slowly reached out her hand to rest it on his shoulder.

He flinched when she touched him, but he didn't push her away the way he did sometimes. "OK," she said after a minute. "You go get ready, and could you make sure Chester's bowl of water on the porch is full?"

Mattie's ability to follow directions and complete tasks was limited, but she knew he liked helping out around the house. She imagined it made him feel like he was a part of the family—as odd a family as it was, especially with Noah the ex-prisoner home now.

Mattie shuffled forward, pushing the screen door open.

Rachel went to the pantry to get a tub of icing, glancing at the clock on the wall as she passed it. It was eleven-fifteen, and Noah had said he'd be in by ten-thirty so he could shower before they went. It wasn't like him to be late.

She grabbed the icing and a container of sprinkles, left them on the counter, and went up to her room to dress. On impulse, she pulled a lavender sundress over her head and found a pair of strappy brown sandals in her closet. She was usually a T-shirt and shorts kind of girl, capris or slacks to church. She didn't know what had possessed her to buy the dress the other day when she'd stopped at the Bass outlet to pick up a couple of T-shirts for Noah. She was tired of looking at him in the same three T-shirts he wore, day in and day out.

Standing in front of the mirror, she tucked a lock of hair behind her ear and made a face at herself in the reflection. "Not bad for forty," she said aloud with amusement. "Not bad at all."

On her way down the hall, she passed Mallory's bedroom door. "Need help?" she called.

"No," Mallory sang. "I'm coming, Mama. Almost dressed."

"OK." Rachel returned to the kitchen, looking at the clock again. Eleven-thirty. Noah was an hour late? Now she was beginning to worry.

Mallory appeared downstairs a couple of minutes later, dressed not in the cute yellow shorts and T-shirt Rachel had left out for her, but a pair of purple and pink polka-dotted knit shorts and a homemade red and green tie-dyed shirt they had bought at a spring festival. She had completed her ensemble with an orange Orioles ball cap Noah had given her and a pair of hot pink rubber rain boots with multicolored butterflies. Rachel blinked in exaggeration, holding up her hands as if the sight nearly blinded her. "Mallory, honey, those things don't match. Please put on the outfit that I left for you on your bed."

"But I *wike* this," Mallory ran her hands down the front of her outfit. "And I remembered a hat."

Rachel went to the cupboard where she stored paper plates and cups and plastic silverware. She grabbed a knife to frost the brownies. "You can't wear that. You have to change. You want to help me frost the brownies first?"

"Yeah!"

Rachel retrieved the stool her daughter used to reach the counter, and together they frosted the brownies that were still warm. Licking her fingers on her way to the sink when the task was complete, Rachel glanced at the clock again. He was more than an hour late. "Hey, honey, why don't you go ahead and do the sprinkles yourself? Not too many," she warned. "Then go up and get dressed. I'm going to go check on Noah."

"OK, Mama."

Out on the back step, Rachel shaded her eyes and glanced in the direction of the Pinot field. She didn't see Noah or the lawn tractor. She then walked down the driveway, her ankles a little unstable in the sandals on the loose oyster shells, to check to see if he was in one of the fields up front that ran along the road. Still no sign of him.

Wondering where he could have gotten to, she walked back up the driveway. Mallory spotted her through the kitchen window where she must have been washing her hands at the sink. She waved furiously.

Rachel waved back. "I'm going to take the truck and go back to the Pinot field to look for Noah. I'll be right back."

"*Si, Mama,*" Mallory called out the window. Mrs. Santori was teaching her Spanish.

Rachel walked over to the shed near the pressing barn and climbed into the old pickup. She fished for the key on the floor under the seat, started the truck, and backed out of the shed. First she drove to the Pinot field, then the Chancellor field, but there was no sign of him or the tractor at either place. Next, she cut through the backyard and drove down the driveway, thinking she just might not have been able to spot him in those fields. The grapevines on the trellises were thriving now, creating walls of bright green leaves and vines that might make it difficult to see him.

He wasn't there either, and she drove back up toward the house, contemplating what to do next. Could he have driven into town on the lawn tractor? She'd checked and it was gone.

But that just didn't make sense. He and Mallory had been talking about going to the picnic at Maria's Place while snapping green beans last night on the porch. She'd heard them through the window. He'd seemed as enthusiastic about going as the little girl had. He wouldn't disappoint her. Something was wrong.

Rachel parked the truck back in the shed and began to walk around the outbuildings. "Noah," she called. "Noah!"

She wondered if she should call the police.

She knew it was irrational, but Johnny and Pam's killer hadn't been caught yet. She knew Snowden thought their murders had something to do with the affair they had years ago, but what if he was wrong? What if Noah was in danger, or worse, hurt, lying in a field somewhere?

"Noah!" She walked around the storage shed where the oak barrels used for fermenting were stored. As she turned, she caught a glimmer of light out of the corner of her eye, a reflection off metal that seemed to twinkle in the bright sunlight. She turned toward the old hedgerow out beyond the last outbuilding. It was a tangled mess, left by the previous farmers, that needed to be cleaned out, although they had decided years ago to leave it standing to prevent erosion from the hill beyond it. "Noah?"

She hurried through the weeds, ignoring the scratches to her bare legs. She discovered a path the wheels of the tractor had made recently and ran in it, heading directly toward the hedgerow.

She spotted the lawn tractor, barely visible, behind the hedgerow, the wagon filled with brush. Noah had said he was going to the Pinot field to pick up a load of weeds and branches they'd pulled from the center rows between the trellises, but he must have decided to swing by the hedgerow and fill up the remainder of the wagon with brush cut the day before.

"Noah, Noah, where are you?" Rachel cried, hearing the panic in her own voice. She ran along the hedgerow. "Noah!" She almost tripped over the new machete she'd purchased the other day at the hardware store for him. She leaned over to pick it up, and when she drew it closer, she saw what could only be blood on the blade.

"Oh my God," she breathed, throwing the machete down and running along the hedgerow, trying to peer inside. It was a tangle of an old hedge with a fence buried in the middle, engulfed over the years by greenbriars, vined morning glories, and weeds. As she neared the end that abutted a small stand of silver maple trees, she saw a sneaker lying in the knee-high weeds.

"Noah!" She raced forward, tripping in her sandals. The sneaker was attached to a foot, to a leg. She threw herself down on the ground, grasping Noah's shoulders. He lay on his back, arms out. There was a tear on the right leg of his jeans, and blood stained the area in an almost perfect rusty-colored circle.

"Noah, are you—"

He blinked and opened his eyes, looking dazed.

She leaned over to smell his breath, the first thing going through her mind being that he'd drunk himself into a stupor and fallen on the machete. But his breath only smelled faintly of toothpaste.

"Noah, what happened?" She leaned over him, staring into his eyes.

He appeared groggy, almost as if waking from a deep sleep. "I . . . I don't know." He sat, running his hand through his hair, looking at her, looking around him. "I was cutting some brush and—"

"And what?" she asked, still kneeling over him.

"And . . ."

"You were drinking, weren't you?"

"No, no, I wasn't drinking, Rache."

"You promised me, Noah." She leaned forward, even closer this time to smell his breath again. "You swore to me you haven't had anything to drink since you—"

"It was a blackout, Rache."

It took a moment for what he said to register in her mind. "A blackout? I don't understand."

"Neither do I."

"You're still having blackouts after all these years?"

He looked away, wiping his mouth with the back of his hand. "I hadn't had one in years, not since I first went to prison. And then after I was released . . ." He looked at her again. Kneeling beside him, they were eye level. "It started again after I got home."

"And you haven't been drinking?"

He shook his head.

She covered her mouth with her hand, thinking for a moment, and then dropped her hand. "How many times, Noah?"

"I'm sure it's nothing. I just—"

"How many times has it happened, Noah?" she repeated angrily. But she wasn't so much angry as she was scared. She'd never heard of an alcoholic suffering from blackouts this long after he'd taken his last drink. Sure, she knew he'd suffered from them the last six months before he went to prison. It was why he remembered nothing of the night the Marcuses died. But blackouts didn't happen after a person stopped drinking. They just didn't.

"I don't know," he confessed quietly, hanging his head.

"Guess."

"I've been home a month. Eight, ten times? Maybe a dozen."

She grasped his hand that was scratched and bleeding. He wore a work glove on the other hand. "Noah, you have to see a doctor."

"Rache, I—" He didn't finish his sentence. "OK," he said, quietly.

"OK," she repeated, as if making a pact. She looked down at his leg. "You're bleeding."

He looked down as if seeing the wound for the first time, and when he put his hand to it, he flinched. "Ow. It hurts."

"I guess it does." She got to her feet, offering her hand to help him up. "It looks like you either sliced yourself with the machete or fell on it."

He took her hand and got to his feet, closing his eyes for a moment.

Rachel thought she saw him sway and put out her arms instinctively—like she was going to be able to catch him if he went down. "You OK?" she murmured.

He opened his eyes and looked down at her, surprising her with a silly smile. "Yeah, I'm good. I'm fine. Just dizzy there for a second."

She looked down at his leg, almost reluctant to release him. "It's starting to bleed again. I wonder if you need to go to the hospital. It looks like a pretty good-sized gash; you might need stitches."

"Don't be ridiculous. It'll be fine, and I had a tetanus shot last year." He started toward the tractor, forcing her to let him go. "What time is it?" He walked slowly, limping slightly.

"After twelve."

"I'm sorry. We're going to be late."

"I don't care about that, Noah. I care about you."

Rachel picked up the machete, and they walked back to the lawn tractor in silence, where she tossed it in the back of the trailer. When Noah climbed into the seat and slid over to make room for her, she hesitated and then got on beside him. "I'm not kidding," she warned him, shaking her finger the way she did to Mallory sometimes. "You're going to see a doctor."

"Yes, ma'am." He surprised her with a grin, then threw the tractor into gear and they lurched off.

CHAPTER 15

They arrived at the benefit picnic at the home for pregnant teens fashionably late. Maria's Place was located in a 1940s farmhouse set on an acre and a half lot, less than a mile from town but outside the city limits. The original farm's acreage had been sold off years ago, but the square, white two-story house with a large front porch was nestled in a beautiful grove of silver maple trees with sweeping front and backyards and plenty of places to picnic. The Benedictine sisters did their best to keep up the property, which included a detached garage and several outbuildings, all in various degrees of disrepair, but it was obvious more money was spent maintaining the house and its program rather than the buildings. Still, the entire place had a certain nostalgic charm.

Rachel parked along the road at the end of the long line of cars belonging to earlier arrivals and then began to unload the back of the Volvo. She handed Mattie an old-fashioned-style picnic basket she'd bought from one of those home basket parties years ago. To Mallory, she passed off the pan of brownies. "No snitching," she warned, reaching into the trunk again.

Mallory giggled, hopping up and down in nervous anticipation as she clutched the foil-covered pan. As they had approached the house in the car, she had spotted one of those large blow-up playhouses available at all the rental stores for parties. Even at this distance from the house, they could hear children laughing with glee as they bounced inside.

"How about me, can I snitch a brownie?" Noah took the canvas bag from Rachel's arms, leaving her nothing but the old quilt they would use to sit on when they had their lunch.

"No, you may not." Rachel locked the car and dropped the keys into the canvas bag. "Or you'll be in trouble, too," she warned playfully.

After they returned to the house earlier, after Noah's blackout episode, he had taken a quick shower, put a knee-sized Band-Aid on the gash on his thigh, and dressed in jeans and one of the new T-shirts she'd bought him. It was a golden yellow that looked good on him with the summer tan he was acquiring. On his head, he wore a light blue UCLA ball cap, which was fashionably frayed around the brim, bought when they traveled to California for a college reunion. With his hair shorter again, today he looked so much like he had ten years ago, as if no time had passed, that it was eerie. It was almost as if none of the terrible tragedies he had experienced had ever taken place. But Rachel had only to look at the tiny lines around his eyes and mouth to know that they had.

"Can I go in the bouncy thing, Mama?" Mallory asked, dancing along behind them as they walked back down the road, toward the driveway.

In the end, Rachel and the four-year-old had compromised on Mallory's picnic attire, at Noah's gentle suggestion. Mallory had shed the polka-dotted shorts for denim ones and sneakers replaced the rubber boots, but she was still wearing the tie-dyed T-shirt and ball cap that was too large for her head.

"I suppose you can ride the bouncy thing." Rachel tugged on one of her daughter's pigtails.

"And a pony ride?" Mallory looked up at her mother, her big eyes shining bright. "Noah said there was going to be pony rides and games for *chiwldren*."

"Well, thank you, Noah, for informing my daughter of all the ways she can spend my money today." Rachel cut her eyes at him, exaggerating her annoyance. Truthfully, she was so relieved he was okay that she couldn't really be annoyed with him about anything right now. She was very concerned about the blackouts, and she fully intended to make a doctor's appointment for him first thing Monday morning. She hadn't realized, until after it was all over, just how close she had been to panicking when she couldn't find him, how close she was to believing something horrible had happened to him as had happened to Johnny and Pam. Rachel knew it made no sense, but that terrifying, ominous feeling she kept experiencing in her dreams was now seeping into her real life, leaving her more than a little bit uneasy.

Rachel forced herself to rein her thoughts back in, looking down at Mallory, who waited patiently for an answer concerning what *Noah* had said about pony rides. She didn't know when Mallory had stopped calling him Mr. Noah, a tradition unique to the area, and started just calling him by his first name. But what else was she supposed to call him? Mr. Gibson? How silly would that be, especially since it was her surname as well. Uncle Noah? He wasn't her uncle.

Mallory giggled. "Do you think Mattie can bouncy-bounce too?"

"I don't know," Noah told her. "We'll have to check out the weight limits. Mattie's a pretty husky boy."

Mallory dropped back to pat Mattie, who was slowly bringing up the rear, carrying the picnic basket as carefully as if it were spun glass. "Don't worry, Mattie," she said with great seriousness. "If they won't *wet* you bouncy-bounce, I won't do it either."

Mallory's words brought a tightness to Rachel's throat. She was such a sweet little girl, her love so immense for a child so young. Rachel caught Noah's gaze and was surprised by the emotion she saw in his gentle brown eyes. The very same thought must have just crossed his mind.

Rachel focused on the blacktop driveway beneath her sandals, feeling foolish as she fought to hold back tears, thankful she was wearing sunglasses. Noah's growing attachment for Mallory had touched her in a way she hadn't anticipated. She just hadn't expected him to develop such an attachment to the little girl so quickly. It was almost as if . . .

She pushed the thought aside, thinking she must be PMS-ing to be so emotional today. First it was the scare with Noah, then this insignificant moment that almost seemed earth-shattering to her.

It was becoming more obvious to her with each passing day that she was going to have to rethink some decisions she had made before Noah was released. She was going to have to figure out what she *wanted* to do, and stop thinking about what she thought she *needed* to do. Life was too short not to embrace every possible glimmer of happiness; she of all people should know that.

As they walked up the driveway, they heard the sounds of a local bluegrass band playing from a makeshift platform built in the open area to the left of the house, where Sister Julie and volunteers usually parked. There had to be at least two hundred people milling around the property, all laughing and talking, adding to the old-fashioned hometown fair atmosphere.

As they walked up the driveway's incline, Mallory began to dance in and out of them, squealing with excitement. "Easy, there," Rachel warned, "or the brownies aren't going to make it to the auction table. You want me to take them?"

Mallory pushed the pan into her mother's hand and darted around her, weaving her way in and out of Noah and Mattie in a mad frenzy of anticipation.

"Rachel, there you are!" Mandy Thompson, one of the mothers who served on the preschool board at St. Paul's with

Rachel, rushed forward before they reached the front yard. "Gretchen has the best idea for the first day of pre-K in September. Come hear. She's manning the raffle ticket table right now."

"We just got here. I really need to—"

"No, you've got to hear this," Mandy gushed, gesturing with both hands, not paying a bit of attention to what Rachel was trying to say. "If we're going to do it, we've got to get right to work, but I just know you're going to love this."

Rachel looked to Noah, the brownie pan and blanket still in her hands, unsure what to do. She'd intended to grab a spot, lay out their blanket, and get Mallory and Mattie settled before she mingled.

"Give them to me," Noah said at once, taking the blanket and pushing it into the bag on his arm before reaching for the brownies.

Rachel looked to Mandy and back at Noah, still undecided as to whether to go now or just tell Mandy it would have to wait a minute. It had been so long since she hadn't had sole responsibility of Mattie and Mallory that she didn't know quite how to pass the baton, even for a few minutes. "I thought we should get a place in the shade before—"

"I'll take care of that," Noah insisted. "We'll find a perfect spot *with* shade, *without* ants."

"Without ants," Mallory sang, grabbing Noah's elbow and swinging around him as if she were square dancing.

"Well . . . all right." Rachel reluctantly followed Mandy, looking back over her shoulder. "Watch her," she warned. "She's as slippery as an eel at something like this. Before you know it, she'll be in the creek fishing for tadpoles or on the stage strumming a banjo."

"Go." Noah waved her off. "We'll be fine. We'll come find you later."

"OK, you," Noah said the minute Rachel was out of earshot.

"Me?" Mallory poked herself in the chest, turning to trot backwards in front of him.

He had to slow down to prevent running into her and knocking her over. "Yes, you. You stay with me and no taking off. I lose you and I'll be in big trouble with your mama."

"I *wost* my dino in the sandbox." She faced forward, falling into step beside him. "I wasn't in big *troubwle* with Mama."

Noah glanced over his shoulder to be sure Mattie was still following. He was, of course, as faithful as a pup.

"Not exactly the same thing, I'm afraid," Noah said, returning his attention to Mallory.

"Good to see you, friend."

Noah looked up to see Joshua Troyer approaching. He was a little surprised to see Josh here as he and his wife didn't usually attend town gatherings such as this one. His social life was based on his church life, and he and his wife rarely socialized outside of the church. He was dressed the same as every day in simple khaki work pants, a plain button-up short sleeve shirt, suspenders, and work boots, but he wore his wide-brimmed "Sunday" straw hat.

Noah accepted the hand Joshua offered and shook it. "Good to see you here," he said, genuinely pleased. "Your wife here, too?"

"Eeh-ya. Trudy's idea we come. Gone to get us lemonade." He stuffed his hands into his pockets, looking down at his boots. "Not much for parties."

"But it's a good cause, right?"

"Best there can be, protectin' God's little children."

"Can we ride the bouncy thing?" Mallory sang, circling Noah, arms at her sides like a toy soldier. "Can we? Can we?"

Noah looked down at the little bobbing blond head, then back at Joshua. "I better get this stuff put down and these brownies on the table before I have a mutiny on my hands."

He started to lead Mallory away. "But maybe I'll catch you later."

"Eeh-ya." Joshua nodded as he walked away, hands in his pockets.

Noah cut across the freshly mowed front lawn to the grassy plot that ran alongside the house, on the far side from the largest part of the crowd and the band, which was taking a break. Sometimes Mattie could get overstimulated at an event like this, with so many people and so much noise, so Noah wanted to be able to get him away from the bulk of the crowd if he needed to.

"How about here?" Noah halted at the base of a cluster of tangled lilac bushes that, untrimmed, had to be twelve foot tall. There were a few blankets spread out, scattered on the side lawn, but it seemed like a spot that would be less congested. It was past the time of year when lilacs bloomed, but he could have sworn he could still smell their faint scent in the air. Imagined or not, he loved the scent of lilacs, and this seemed like the perfect spot for his family to relax and share their picnic.

"Can we go bounce on the bouncy-bounce now? Can we, Noah?" Mallory tugged on his arm, jumping up and down as if she were already on a giant inflated pillow.

Noah set down the bag, took the basket from Mattie's hands, and pushed the brownie pan into them. "First help me with the blanket, then we'll find the dessert auction table—"

"Then *we'wll* jump on the bouncy-bounce?"

"Then we'll bounce," he assured her, unfolding the old patchwork quilt and giving it a shake before he allowed it to flutter to the ground. After placing the bag and the picnic basket on the blanket, he offered his hand to Mallory. "Ready?"

"Ready!" She grabbed his hand, bobbing up and down beside him.

As they came around the house, Noah spotted Snowden, dressed in his uniform, standing on the front porch. He was talking to Sergeant Swift, who was perched on the white porch rail, wearing cutoff shorts and a tank top, her back to Noah. As Noah crossed in front of the porch, Snowden nodded, watching him pass.

The way the police chief followed Noah with his gaze irked him. Like he was some kind of criminal or something. Well . . . he had been a criminal, but he wasn't one any longer, and he didn't appreciate that glare that Noah thought ought to be reserved for drug dealers, armed robbers, and Johnny and Pam's murderer, who very possibly lived in Stephen Kill and was possibly even at the picnic today.

Noah nodded coolly and kept walking. "Keeping up, Mattie?" he called over his shoulder.

Head down, almost cowering, Mattie followed, brownie pan clutched in his hands.

Noah looked back up at Snowden, then quickly glanced at Mattie again. He got the impression that Mattie didn't much like the police chief, either. Or that he was afraid of him. But why on earth would he be afraid of Snowden? Though they were all nearly the same age, the man probably hadn't spoken to him more than half a dozen times in the last ten years.

"I think I see the table where we're supposed to drop these off," Noah said, sounding more enthusiastic than he felt. "And the lemonade stand is right next to it. I think we better have some of the sisters' homemade lemonade before it's sold out for the day."

"*Wemonade!*" Mallory hung on to Noah's hand, skipping beside him. "I *wike wemonade!*"

Snowden watched Noah walk past the front porch, holding Mallory's hand, Mattie trudging behind him.

Delilah glanced over her shoulder, and when she saw who he was looking at, she picked up her paper cup of lemonade and raised it to her lips. "What?" she murmured.

"Him. Noah Gibson. Something about him." Snowden

shook his head. "I don't know. He's got an arrogance about him that a man who's done what he's done shouldn't have."

"He paid his debt to society, Chief. As long as he stays off the Jack Daniels, he's as harmless as the next man."

Snowden settled his hands on the gun belt on his hips. "He knows about Pam Rehak and Johnny Leager. He may very well have information that could lead us to the killer, but he won't talk. Why won't he talk?"

"You don't think it really is because of this whole privacy thing between a man and his priest?"

"They're dead. How much privacy do they need?" As Noah disappeared into the crowd, Snowden shifted his gaze back to Delilah.

She looked good in civilian clothes. Cute and younger than she did in her uniform. Young enough that standing here talking to her made him feel a little uncomfortable. Anyone walking by could see them talking, wonder what their relationship was beyond police business. Wonder if there had been any truth to the pornography that had been painted on the ball field dugouts when she'd first joined the force. It didn't matter that there was no personal relationship; people in small towns just liked to talk. Liked to conjecture.

Delilah swirled the ice cubes in her paper cup, watching them turn in the whirlpool of lemonade. He could tell by the look on her face that she didn't agree with him.

"What if it really is about principle?" She looked up at him with those big brown eyes of hers.

Snowden was beginning to realize that Delilah Frances Swift was a good deal more than the little blond package first suggested.

"Noah Gibson, a man of principle?" He met her gaze, unsmiling. "How many men of principle you know get into a car drunk and kill a mother and father of a two-year-old?"

"I know what you're saying, Chief. But it's not the same thing." The tone of her voice was almost dismissive.

Snowden couldn't decide if he was annoyed or amused by her. She wasn't intimidated in the least by him—the way his other officers were. The way most women in general were. "Not the same thing, how?"

"All I'm saying is that you and I know, anyone with half a lick of sense knows that alcoholism is a disease. Under the influence of whatever his poison of choice was, he made a bad decision. One that cost two people their lives. Maybe cost him his own life." She shrugged a suntanned shoulder. "That makes him a person who made a bad decision, not a cold-blooded murderer."

In the tank top and shorts, Snowden could tell Delilah had been out sunbathing. When she turned a certain way and the yellow shirt shifted on her shoulders, he caught a glimpse of white skin from a bathing suit strap. He wondered if she went to the beach. It would certainly make sense. They were less than ten miles from Cape Henlopen State Park. Or did she lie out in a chair around the pool in her townhouse complex? He wondered why he cared.

She caught him looking at her, and he glanced away.

"You're just pissed because he won't play your game," she said with amusement. "Maybe pissed because he's still a man of principle, somewhere beneath the skin of a struggling alcoholic." She sipped her drink. "Makes him a complicated man."

Snowden frowned. "You're missing the point."

"I don't think I am. You dated his wife, didn't you?"

"Ex-wife," Snowden corrected.

His radio went off with a hiss of static and then the voice of one of his officers on duty, but *almost* to his disappointment he didn't need to respond. He was monitoring the channel, as he often did on a day like today, when they had fewer officers on duty. Everyone had wanted off so they could come to the picnic, drink homemade lemonade, listen to the local talent on the makeshift stage, and talk with neighbors and friends. Snowden had been happy to pick up some of the slack and work a Saturday, because he hated these kinds of gatherings.

Delilah waited patiently for him to reply to her comment concerning Rachel Gibson. She swirled her lemonade.

"That was a while ago," he said.

She smiled smugly. "Good-lookin' woman, but anyone can see she's only got eyes for her husband. 'Scuse me, *ex-husband*."

He looked at her to find her grinning, and it was all he could do not to grin back. She had him that time.

They were quiet for a minute, except for the sound of swirling liquid and the click click of ice cubes hitting. "The good news," Delilah said after a moment, "is that even though it may take us a while to find who killed them—and we will find him—I don't think we have to worry about this nut job doing anyone else in. It was obviously personal. The killer had a beef with the two of them, with what they apparently did."

Snowden had been thinking the same thing. It didn't change the fact that he needed to solve these murders and do it fast if he wanted to retire from this police department someday, but at least he didn't have to worry about the safety of the townspeople he'd sworn to protect. "I best be getting back on the road, and I need to stop by the lemonade booth and say hello to my mother. I think she's taking a shift this afternoon."

"It's delicious," she told him. "You have to buy a cup."

"No doubt she'll force one on me whether I want it or not." He started for the porch steps that led down to the lawn. "Have a good day, Delilah," he said quietly enough so that no one else would hear him.

"You too, Snowden."

He didn't look back for fear someone would see them. See the attraction that he was trying hard to deny and not feeling very successful with at this moment.

* * *

Azrael did not expect the voice. Not here. Not now. It had never come in the daytime. In public. Before, it had always come at night. In private.

The sunlight seemed to brighten and then darken, but Azrael could tell by the faces of the townspeople that no one else could hear the voice, could see the light of the sun that was suddenly shadowed.

"Azrael."

Azrael wanted to turn away from the voice. To deny it. At least here, here in the warmth and brightness of the day. For some reason, it didn't seem as if it belonged here.

But there would be no denying the voice of God. Azrael knew that all too well. No matter what the voice said, what the voice told Azrael to do, God's will had to be done. It was not up to a mere mortal to understand the ways of God. God's punishment.

"It's time," the voice of God echoed in the Angel of Death's head.

"No." Azrael could feel the blackness swirling, but everything on the grassy lawn seemed the same. Neighbors laughed and talked in small groups beneath red, white, and blue streamers strung overhead between the outbuildings, fluttering in the warm breeze. The bluegrass band played a lively tune. Children ran through the grass, chasing each other, playing tag. All oblivious to the mighty presence of God.

Only Azrael. Only Azrael was blessed.

"That's right, you are blessed," the voice said.

In Azrael's ear? Or perhaps it was in Azrael's head. It made no difference, did it? It was still the voice of God.

"It's time," God repeated. "There is another who has sinned. Who must be punished."

"I must punish the sinner in your name," Azrael murmured silently. The fear was subsiding, and somewhere inside a confidence began to build. A confidence of such strength Azrael had never felt before. "If God is with me," Azrael mouthed silently. "Who can be against me?"

"Be prepared," God warned.

I'll be prepared to bring righteousness to the sinner, Azrael thought. *Prepared to do God's will, my duty. And through duty to God brings cleanliness of the soul. By doing the will of God, I will wash myself of my sins.*

The epiphany, brought by God's voice, no doubt, brought an overwhelming sense of joy, of relief, to Azrael.

The sunlight seemed to dim for a moment again, a chill rippling over Azrael, and then God was gone and the brightness returned. God's voice was gone, and there was nothing left but the sunshine, the warm embrace of friends, and the sweet, tart taste of homemade lemonade in Azrael's mouth.

CHAPTER 16

"Rachel, long time, no see!"

She turned around in line at the lemonade stand to see Ellen Hearn standing behind her. Stylish short hair bleached blond by the sun and sporting a dark tan and expensive designer polo and shorts, Rachel was taken aback by how put together Ellen looked. It had probably been at least six months since she'd seen her, maybe closer to a year. Two years ago she'd been appointed a Superior Court judge in the county, quite an accomplishment for a Stephen Kill girl.

Though two years older than her and Noah, Ellen had attended high school with them and then gone on to Georgetown University, where she'd graduated with a law degree. She'd returned to her hometown and entered into private practice in the Rehoboth Beach area, but had never forgotten her small-town roots. She still gave time as a volunteer for charities and good causes like Maria's Place, where she served as a board member.

"I've been around. Guess you need to start hanging out with us commoners at the preschool at St. Paul's or at the Five and Dime on Main Street," she teased.

Ellen smiled. "I haven't sold Mom and Dad's house on Main Street," she defended.

"I always loved that house." Rachel passed the big Victorian every time she drove into town. Ellen's parents had lovingly restored and preserved it, making it one of the best examples of late nineteenth-century architecture in the county.

"I'm still there a couple nights a week. I like being home when I can. Brings me back down to earth."

"Yeah, yeah, yeah." Rachel waved her off, teasing her. "Just admit it. Too good for us these days. You being a fancy judge now, name appearing in the *News Journal* all the time. Got yourself a condo in Rehoboth, right on the beach, I hear."

"Technically it's in Bethany, and it was an investment," she defended good naturedly. "Though I'll admit it is nice to relax on the balcony after a long day in court."

"Oceanfront, I would say so." They moved up in the line. The sisters were ladling chilled homemade lemonade as fast as they could, but there were so many people coming back for seconds and thirds that the line hadn't gotten any shorter in the two hours since Rachel had arrived.

"Seriously, it's good to see you." She lowered her voice. "I saw that Noah had been released last month. How's that going? I understand you're still staying at his parents' place."

"Guess it's Noah's now," she answered a little awkwardly. When Noah had been arrested, Ellen had been one of the first people to call her, telling her, obviously, she couldn't use her position to aid him in any way, but offering to explain anything to her she didn't understand regarding the legal process. From day one, she'd been nothing but understanding and supportive, unlike many in the town. "He's good." She nodded. "Attending AA meetings, working hard in the vineyard." She lifted her chin to meet Ellen's steady gaze. "I'm glad to have him home," she murmured.

"Then I'm glad for you." They moved a little closer to the lemonade table. "I know these last years have been hard for you, had to be."

"Not as hard as they had to have been for him." She looked away, blinking, again relieved she was wearing her sunglasses so no one could see the moisture in her eyes. "So how about you?" She gave Ellen a playful push. "Don't tell me you're still single."

"Yup. Don't know that marriage is in the stars for me."

"But I thought I heard you were dating someone. Some fancy attorney in D.C. or something."

Ellen shrugged. "For a while, but this job . . ."

"I know," Rachel said when the judge didn't finish her thought. "It's probably all-consuming."

"Can I help you?"

Rachel turned from Ellen to find she was next in line at the table. Monica Dryden, the only full-time paid employee at Maria's Place, smiled shyly. She'd come to town less than a year ago, apparently after a bad divorce, and was hired as general manager for the home for unwed mothers. The job entailed everything from paying the bills and washing dishes at the house to sitting up all night with scared teens in labor at the hospital.

In her late thirties and attractive in a wholesome, no makeup, simple clothing kind of way, Rachel had always wondered what the whole story was—where she came from, what had brought her to Stephen Kill, of all places. She'd gotten the impression Monica was running from something, maybe the ex-husband. But she never asked, of course. Interrogation of newcomers was strictly the Bread Ladies' responsibility.

"Yes, thanks," Rachel said, smiling across the table at her. "Three more lemonades. I swear, I think Noah's already drank a gallon of this stuff himself," she told Monica and Ellen, with a chuckle.

"Three lemonades, that will be six dollars, please."

"Two bucks a piece," Ellen declared. "We're being robbed by nuns!"

Rachel fished warm, folded bills from the cute little pocket on the hip of her sundress. "All for a good cause, though, isn't it?" She laughed with her.

"Sister Julie is in the kitchen making more lemonade with the girls as we speak." Monica accepted the money with plastic gloved hands, but even in the gloves, the burn scar Rachel had noticed before was still visible. Rachel had wondered if the burn was a result of an accident or abuse, but had never asked.

"You can pick up your lemonade to my left. Sister Margie, three more lemonades and a carrier," Monica called to the sixty-something nun wearing knee-length, frayed jean shorts and a purple T-shirt that said "Support Life."

"Three lemonades with a carrier, coming up," Sister Margie sang.

"Listen, it was good to see you." Rachel turned to lay her hand on Ellen's arm again. "I better get this lemonade to Noah. He's on bouncy-bounce duty and has been for the last two hours."

Ellen half waved, half saluted. "Say hello to him for me."

"Come over and say hello yourself." She reached out to steady the brown cardboard carrier Sister Margie was loading up with cups of lemonade. "I know he'd be tickled to see you."

Ellen checked her expensive wristwatch. "Unfortunately, I have to run."

"That's too bad." Rachel picked up the carrier of paper cups filled to the brim with ice and lemonade. "Have a great day."

"You too."

"Thanks, Sister," Rachel called over her shoulder as she dodged a little boy with a large bubble wand, trying to keep the full-to-the-brim cups from splashing over.

As Rachel wound her way through the crowd, she took in her surroundings: friends, neighbors, husbands and wives, children. Everyone seemed in such a festive mood that their excitement was contagious. Just watching Mr. and Mrs.

West, who had celebrated their fiftieth wedding anniversary this week, dance across the makeshift dance floor, made her smile. But as she halted in the side yard, tray of drinks in her hand, sunshine on her face, she got the strangest feeling. It was almost as if beneath the laughter and the glimmer of the summer sun, something lurked. Something dark. Something . . . evil.

Someone touched her shoulder and she whirled around, splashing lemonade over the sides of the cups.

"Whoa, there. Easy. Sorry, I didn't mean to startle you."

She looked up to find Jeremy Cary, the local dentist. Widowed more than a year ago, word at the diner, in line at the post office, and at the hardware store was that Dr. Cary was actively dating, and was more than a little interested in going out with Rachel.

"No, it's all right. You didn't startle me, I just . . ." She laughed, not bothering to finish her sentence, not knowing what the heck she was saying.

Jeremy, dressed in a pair of khaki shorts and a lavender polo, was a nice-looking guy in his early forties. He and his wife and two children had moved to Stephen Kill a few years back to take advantage of the inexpensive real estate inland and the business he could bring in from the high economic beach population only a few miles away. His wife had died in a drowning accident while the family was vacationing in the Carolinas, but he seemed to be picking up the pieces.

"So, nice day," Jeremy said.

"Yeah, great." She glanced around them. "This kind of thing is always fun, though. You know, the whole community getting together for a good cause."

"Right. Right. And great lemonade." He pointed to the cups she was balancing.

She looked down at the tray, then up at him and chuckled. "Definitely great lemonade."

"Well, I can see you're headed somewhere, so I'll let you go." He looked down at her through tortoiseshell sunglasses.

"But maybe . . . I was thinking you might . . . I don't know, like to grab a bite or catch a movie sometime."

Even knowing he was interested, Rachel hadn't been expecting an outright invitation. Well, it wasn't a specific invitation, but still . . . She wasn't sure what to say. Not sure how she felt. She'd been dating on and off occasionally the last few years, but nothing had ever gotten close to serious, except with Snowden. "I . . . Sure." She gave a nod. He was a nice guy. Smart, fun. Why wouldn't she go out to dinner or to a movie with him? It had been ages since she'd seen a movie in the movie theater with anything higher than a G rating. "I'd like that," she said, smiling up at him.

"So, I'll call you?"

"Sure. That'd be great. I'm in the phone book."

"Have a good day," Jeremy said, walking away.

"You too." Rachel paused for a second to catch her breath and then made a beeline for the backyard. She found Noah still on duty at the bouncy-bounce with no visible sign of Mallory, though she could tell by the gleeful shrieks coming from inside the lurching attraction that her daughter wasn't far. Mattie was seated under a tree up close to the house, and Father Hailey, the priest who had replaced Noah at St. Paul's, was leaning over speaking to him. She looked back at Noah. "Is she still in there? How many tickets did you buy?" She offered him the tray.

"You don't want to know." He took one of the cups and walked back to Mattie who sat under a large pin oak, his knees now drawn up to his chest and secured with his arms. Father Hailey had just walked away, his own cup of lemonade in hand.

Rachel watched as Noah attempted to give Mattie the cup, and when he didn't accept it, Noah placed it on the ground beside him and walked back to Rachel.

"What's going on with Mattie?" she asked.

"I don't know." Noah shrugged as they both studied him for a moment. "He seemed fine a few minutes ago. Almost as if he was having fun. He downed the last cup of lemonade before I had mine to my lips."

With a sigh, Rachel turned back to face the colorful inflated amusement. "I can take over here if you want to wander around, say hi to some people."

"Nah. I'd rather just stay here. I don't mind hanging out with Mallory and Mattie. Besides, it gives me something to do other than watch people watch me." He shook his head. "I swear, they look at me like they think I'm going to whip out an axe from my back pocket and start smiting them hip and thigh at any moment." He took the tray from her hands, removed a cup, and offered it to her before taking the last one.

"Oh, they do not. Joshua walked right up and started talking to you."

"That's because he wants me to come to church. I think he's thinking he can still possibly save my soul." He tossed the cardboard tray into the grass. "I'll take that back by the stand in a minute. They can use it again."

Rachel sipped the icy lemonade that seemed to be all the colder and more delicious in the heat of the afternoon. It had to be close to eighty degrees outside today. "Hey, guess who I saw a minute ago. Ellen Hearn." She had no intention of telling him she'd talked to Jeremy, too. Or that she'd sort of agreed to go out with him.

"You're kidding. I'd love to have said hello."

"I know. She said to tell you hi. She was on her way out. Had somewhere she had to be." She sipped her lemonade. "Did I tell you she was appointed a judge two years ago? Superior Court."

"You're kidding. Good for her."

"I know. It was what she always wanted."

"She doesn't live here anymore, does she?"

"Actually, she still does. Part of the time, at least. She's got a condo at the beach, too, though. Says she stays there some nights. Here others."

Noah nodded. "I'm glad to hear she's doing so well. She's a good woman. A good woman for the job, too."

A kitchen timer went off, and Harry Newton, who worked at the hardware store in town, got up from his lawn chair in the shade, walked over to the bouncer, and stuck his head inside. "Time's up," he announced.

A cacophony of childish oh no's and groans came from inside as the red, white, and blue blow-up bouncer came to a standstill and, one by one, kids began to hop out, with the assistance of the grandfatherly Harry.

Rachel had always liked Harry and his wife, Flora. They were good-hearted, hard-working people who always gave freely of themselves. Rachel had once attended a Bible study with them at St. Paul's and had formed a bond with them that never quite faded, though she had rarely seen them in the last five years. Sadly, their youngest son, now in his mid-thirties, had never molded to the Newton family values or morals as his parents and older siblings had. A late-in-life baby, as Flora had liked to call him, Skeeter drank, was involved in drugs, and never seemed able to hold a job for more than a few months at a time. He lived in an apartment over his parents' garage, and she knew both Harry and Flora worried about him, wondered where they had gone wrong in raising him. It was sad to see such kind people suffer so greatly at the hands of someone they loved.

"Got plenty more tickets, kiddies," Harry jovially told the children. "Ask your parents for more money. Tell 'em it's for a good cause. I'll be sitting right here waiting for you."

"Oh please, Harry." Rachel rolled her eyes. "No wonder this is one of the best moneymakers for the whole day," she told Noah, meaning for Harry to overhear. "Harry's practically blackmailing us."

The older man winked at her and offered a hand to the youngest Truman boy.

"I know." Noah passed her his cup, moving toward the open doorway in anticipation of Mallory's exit. "It's a miracle I didn't promise Harry next year's profits from the vineyard." He flashed a grin at Harry, who was still taking in their conversation with good cheer.

"You gettin' a lotta work done with that machete I sold you?" Harry asked Rachel.

"Putting me to work with it is more like it." Noah clapped his hands together. "Mallory," he called in a singsong voice. "Come out, come out, wherever you are."

"No *Mallworys* in here," Mallory sang in the same tone from inside.

"Get your butt out here," Noah ordered in a fatherly tone.

Mallory's head popped out at once, and with a leap, she landed on the ground in her stocking feet. "That was fun! Can I do it again? Can I? Can I?"

Noah squatted down in front of her, getting at eye level. He reached out with one hand to brush aside a damp, sweaty lock of blond hair that had escaped one of her pigtails. "How about a little lemonade and a quick rest?"

"I don't need a rest!"

"Well, I do." Noah gave her a push in Mattie's direction. "Mattie has your sneakers and some lemonade. You have some and then see if you can get him to drink a little. It's hot out."

"Hot out! Hot out!" Mallory bounced past Rachel, headed for the shade of the tree and the cup of lemonade.

At four, after the announcement of several raffle ticket winners and a warning that the silent auction would soon be closed to bids, everyone broke into groups to share their picnic dinner with friends or relatives. Rachel passed out paper plates to her odd little family—her daughter, Noah the ex-con, and the idiot savant who couldn't speak or read music but could play a pipe organ without ever having taken a lesson in his life.

They shared Mrs. Santori's fried chicken, spiced with

chili powder and cumin, pasta salad Rachel had made, and an assortment of cut-up vegetables and fruit. One drumstick and a few pieces of cantaloupe and Mallory had had enough of sitting on the blanket listening while Rachel and Noah discussed the necessary steps to be ready to start making wine in late August.

"Can Mattie and me go to the bouncy-bounce?" Mallory asked as her mother wiped her mouth with a napkin.

"Mattie and I." Noah reached for his lemonade. "And no, it's closed right now. Mr. Harry is having his dinner, fortifying himself for another round with you munchkins."

"Can Mattie and—*I* go ride the pony?"

"Pony is having his dinner, too." Noah, lying on his side, stretched out on the old quilt that had once belonged to Rachel's grandmother, reached for another piece of chicken. "You and Mattie need to hang around here for a little while and then, I promise, you'll get another pony ride and another bounce before we go home."

Mallory looked to her mother, hoping, no doubt, she would give in, but Rachel just smiled apologetically. "Why don't you and Mattie see if you can find any bugs while we finish up here?"

"Come on, Mattie." Mallory trudged off, head down, doing her best to look pitiful. *"Wet's* find some bugs."

Mattie just sat on the quilt, his knees drawn up. He'd barely touched his dinner.

"Come on, Mattie," Mallory repeated impatiently. "You don't have to be afraid of it. *I 'wll* protect you." She held out her hand.

Mattie rose slowly, accepted her hand, and the two ambled off.

"Not too far," Rachel called after them. "If you can't see me, you're too far away."

Rachel watched them go twenty feet and then plop down under a small red maple tree where Mallory had discovered dandelion flowers. "He barely ate," she remarked to Noah.

"And what in heaven's name is Mallory talking about? What's Mattie afraid of?"

"I don't know. I asked her again yesterday." Noah tossed a thigh bone on his plate and reached for his napkin.

In celebration of the day, Rachel had packed real cloth napkins from the mismatched assortment she kept in a drawer in the kitchen china closet. There was always something special about a meal when you used real napkins, even if it was a picnic meal on the lawn of a house that cared for teenaged girls who had gotten knocked up by their boyfriends.

"She just says he's afraid of the voice. Or of voices." He shrugged. "It doesn't make much sense, but she's four."

Rachel thought of the nightmare she'd had the previous night. For the first time, whatever the dark thing was that was plaguing her had possessed a voice. She'd woken in a cold sweat, disoriented and unable to remember what the dream had been about or what the thing had said. She could remember nothing, but there was no doubt in her mind that it had been accompanied by a voice this time.

She thought about the picture Mattie had colored this morning—the red, angry blob in the middle of all the black. As crazy as it sounded, something told her it was the voice of that blob that she had heard. Was Mattie hearing it in his dreams at night, too?

"Hey," Noah said gently. His hand brushed her arm. "You OK?"

She refocused her gaze, first on him, then Mallory. "Yeah. Fine." She offered a quick smile.

Mallory was seated in the grass, legs spread wide, with Mattie seated beside her. She was trying to tie the stems of two dandelions together.

"You sure you're feeling OK?" Noah persisted.

"It's not *my* health you should be worried about right now." She sat up on her knees and began to pack away what was left of their dinner. "I'm calling Monday to get you an appointment with Dr. Carson."

"Fine."

"I'm not kidding, Noah. You're going." She snapped the blue plastic lid on the disposable container that Mrs. Santori insisted they use again and again, and dropped it into the picnic basket. "This isn't something you screw around with. This could be serious. No one has blackouts five years after—"

"Rachel," Noah interrupted.

His tone made her glance down at him.

"I said I would go," he said gently. "If you want me to go, I'll go. I'll do it for you."

Her gaze was locked with his for a moment. She couldn't look away. He would do it *for her*. To alleviate *her* concern. The sound of his voice, the words, made her heart give a little trip. It had been a long time since anyone had done something solely for her benefit. To ease *her* mind.

"You should do it for yourself, not me," she said, getting to her feet, grabbing the stack of dirty paper plates. "I'm going to toss these."

"I'll do it."

She turned away from him. "I should check on Mallory anyway."

Rachel walked over to a rolling green trash Dumpster near the porch and lifted the lid to toss the plates in.

"Aren't you concerned?" a woman asked.

Rachel lowered the lid to see Cora on the porch, seated between Clara and Alice, all in old-fashioned lawn chairs. She looked like the queen to Rachel, perched there on the porch on her aluminum throne with her attendants, looking down on the townsfolk, her loyal subjects.

"Pardon?" Rachel half smiled, not even positive Cora was speaking to her. She had been an excellent secretary, serving Noah well for years, but Rachel had never taken a liking to her, and she couldn't even specifically say why. Sure, she was a gossip and Rachel didn't care for gossips, but her talk was usually harmless. There was something else that had always bothered her about Cora, something she could never quite put her finger on.

"That man, alone with your daughter." Cora rose, coming to the porch rail, pointing over Rachel's head.

Rachel turned to look in Mallory's direction. She assumed Cora was speaking of Noah, but it was Mattie who was still with Mallory. Mallory had tied several yellow dandelion flowers together into a crown and was placing it on Mattie's head.

"You mean Mattie?" Rachel turned back to Cora, puzzled.

"Yes, I mean Mattie." Cora leaned over the railing to whisper in a conspiratorial tone. "A full-grown man playing with a little girl. It's just not natural," she said in a stage whisper.

"Mattie?" Rachel looked at Cora as if she were crazy. She wasn't in the mood for this, not today. "Miss Cora, Mattie has been living with me since Rachel was born. He was there when I came home from the hospital. He would never harm Mallory. He'd never harm anyone. I can't even get him to swat flies in the kitchen."

Rachel heard Alice whisper to Clara, but she couldn't quite catch what she was saying. Rachel looked at Cora again. "I don't know what you're inferring by saying it isn't *natural*, but Mattie loves Mallory. He's loved her since she was a baby."

"But she's not a baby anymore." Cora cut her eyes in Mattie and Mallory's direction. "She's starting to look like a little girl. So pretty with that blond hair and big green eyes." She looked back at Rachel. "You just don't know what a man like that could be thinking about a pretty little girl like your Mallory."

"That's the most ridiculous thing I've ever heard," Rachel declared, not caring if she was short with her. "And it's totally inappropriate for you to say. For you to even think."

"I'm sorry, dear. I certainly didn't mean to offend." Cora

drew back, crossing her arms over her bright pink and green flowered blouse, not appearing to be the least bit apologetic. "It's just that a young mother like yourself, a young *single* mother, has so much to worry about."

"Well, if there's one thing I don't have to worry about, it's Mattie being with Mallory." She smiled stiffly. "Have a good evening, Miss Cora. Ladies." She nodded to Alice and Clara and stalked back to Noah, still lying on the quilt. "Are you ready to go home, because I'm ready to go."

He was on his feet in a second. "You all right?" He put his arm around her shoulder, glancing in the Bread Ladies' direction.

She removed her sunglasses, pressing her forefinger and thumb to her temples, closing her eyes. "I'm fine, I just—my head hurts. I'm not sleeping at night and I—" She didn't know what to say. How to explain to Noah everything that was going on in her head. It wasn't just what Cora had said, or how worried she was about Mattie, or about Noah's blackouts. It was everything . . . and something more. Something she couldn't quite put her finger on. Something oppressive here today.

"Just let me get this packed up and we'll go." Noah gave her a quick hug and released her.

Rachel wished the hug had lasted just a little longer. "No. I'm being silly." She opened her eyes, putting her sunglasses back on. "We promised Mallory another pony ride and one more trip to the bouncy thing."

"If you don't feel well, we'll go home anyway. Mallory will be fine."

"No, it's all right, really. Besides, we can't leave until we know what we won in the silent auction."

"With our luck, it'll be the wine basket we brought," he teased as he began to fold up the dirty napkins scattered on the quilt. "Or the surfing lesson gift certificate."

Rachel dropped to her knees beside him to give him a

hand. "I just bid on them to raise the prices," she defended. "I bid on a bunch of things."

He chuckled. "I'm telling you, we're going to end up with that basket." He tucked the napkins into the picnic basket. "And the surf lessons."

"Surf lessons would be OK." She smiled at him across the expanse of the quilt, already feeling better. She didn't know what was wrong with her, getting so worked up over something Cora had said. Anything Cora said. "You always said you'd like to learn to surf."

"Oh no." He pointed a finger. "We win the lessons, I pay, you surf. I'd pay good money to see that, for sure."

She threw a dirty napkin at him, hitting him in the face, and they both laughed. And the laughter between them felt so good. It felt so right that even the terrifying nameless voice in Rachel's dream couldn't, at this moment, make her feel anything but hopeful for what the next day would bring.

CHAPTER 17

Noah carried Mallory, asleep in his arms, into the kitchen, and Rachel followed behind them with a wine basket, a gift certificate for surfing lessons, and a new picnic basket identical to the one still sitting in the back of the Volvo, filled with dirty containers and napkins.

"Mattie go to his room?" Noah asked quietly, heading down the hall toward the staircase.

"Umm-hmm. I told him I'd check on him before I went to bed, but I wanted Mallory tucked in first."

Noah took the steps slowly, not wanting to jostle Mallory and wake her. Besides, he wanted to make this moment last as long as he could. She felt so good in his arms, smelling of baby shampoo, lemonade, and chocolate. Asleep, she appeared so angelic, with her halo of blond hair and pursed rosebud lips, surrounded by brownie crumbs. The truth was that holding Mallory in his arms made him feel like a man again. Rachel's allowing him to carry the little girl to bed made him feel as if he was capable of caring for someone other than himself.

"You get Mallory tucked in," Noah told Rachel softly, "and I'll check on Mattie and bring in the picnic basket. This isn't the time of year you want chicken bones sitting in the back of your car all night."

Rachel reached around him, flipping on the hall light as they reached the top of the stairs. "You sure?"

"Yup."

Rachel pushed Mallory's bedroom door open for him and let him pass her. Noah had seen Mallory's room from the hall before but had never come inside. It wasn't his place to come into her room. At least he had never felt it was before.

The bedroom, dimly lit by a whimsical lamp with a cone shade and pink tulle billowing off the top, was a magical place any little princess would have loved to rest her weary head. Everywhere Noah saw not only Rachel's artistic ability but her love for her child. The room was painted lavender and pink, and on one wall was a medieval fairy tale scene, complete with prancing horses and pink fairies. Mallory's unmade bed was covered in pink and white gingham sheets and a puffy, lavender satin quilt.

Noah laid her down gently, her head on the pillow. "There we go, sweetheart," he murmured. And without thinking, he leaned over to kiss her forehead.

Realizing what he had done, fearing he had crossed some invisible line Rachel had drawn in the sand, he stood up, looking over his shoulder at her. But Rachel was just standing there in the shadows, arms crossed over her chest. She wasn't smiling, but she wasn't frowning either. He passed her on his way to the hall. "I'll be in, in a minute. Anything else you need me to do besides check on Mattie and unload the car?"

When Rachel didn't reply, he looked back at her. "Rache?"

"No, that's it," she said, her voice choked with emotion.

Noah hesitated in the doorway, wanting to say something but as usual, not knowing what. He was unsure of what was going on here between them. "Be right back," he said at last, and hurried down the hall.

Outside, he walked toward the barn, the clear dark sky overhead, his path illuminated by the white driveway reflecting the soft yellow light of the security lamps secured on high poles in the barnyard. Chester trotted behind him, as faithful as he had ever been, seemingly unaware of the years that passed while his master was locked away in prison.

Noah breathed deeply and exhaled, realizing that for the first time he could remember, he had gone an entire day without thinking about having a drink. Without wanting one. Craving one. He couldn't resist a smile. Today was the best day he'd had yet since his release. Being there at the picnic with Rachel and Mallory and Mattie had made him feel good, feel proud. Today, what others thought of him, what they whispered behind his back, hadn't mattered. Only what Rachel, Mallory, and Mattie thought had been important to him, and today he felt as if he hadn't disappointed them. Maybe he hadn't made them happy, or given them exactly what they needed, or wanted, but he hadn't disappointed them, and that gave him a great deal of satisfaction.

Spotting the glowing eyes of the cellar windows, illuminated by the lamp in Mattie's room, Noah entered the barn. The red and white painted door swung shut behind him, and he hesitated for a moment. As the door closed, blocking the light from the security lamp outside, he was surrounded by darkness. Noah could feel the presence of the stuff piled around him: the winepress barrels, the cases of bottles, and the old milking staunches that had never been removed from the days when the farm had raised milk cows.

Everything seemed right, at first. He could hear nothing but the rhythmic pant of Chester's breathing and the muffled movements of Mattie down below, but as Noah took the first step toward the cellar door, a sound caught his attention. He halted, trying to filter out the sound from those made by Chester and Mattie and his own breathing.

The barn was silent.

He took another step, and this time it was not so much a sound as a feeling that halted him. He turned to peer into the darkness of the main room of the barn, where the cows had once been milked twice a day. As his eyes adjusted to the darkness, he began to make out the outline of the metal staunches, the stacked crates and barrels, other recognizable forms.

There was nothing there. His mind, his logic, his sight, even his hearing now told Noah there was nothing there, and yet, he felt a presence. A presence that carved a thin curl of fear from the pit of his stomach.

Suddenly, he was aware of the change in Chester's breathing. The dog was staring into the darkness, too, no longer panting. His breath came evenly, almost soundlessly, and then he emitted a small, anxious whine.

"What is it, boy?" Noah whispered, though why he was whispering he couldn't fathom. "Something there?"

Chester didn't respond verbally of course, but he continued to stare into the darkness, his side pressed against Noah's leg, his ears pricked.

Noah narrowed his gaze, staring into the darkness. Nothing moved. No sound. And yet . . . a presence. "Somebody there?" he snapped, sounding more menacing than he could ever be.

No response.

"It's OK, boy." He reached down to scratch between Chester's perked ears. "There's nothing—"

Out of the corner of his eye, Noah caught movement, and something fell, striking one of the metal staunches, the sound of wood hitting metal filling the darkness. Noah and the dog both jumped at the same time, as something came skittering toward them on the poured concrete floor, out of the darkness.

It streaked past Noah's leg, and Chester gave an excited bark, falling back on his one good rear haunch.

Noah burst into relieved laughter, pressing his hand to his thumping chest as the half-grown kitten slipped through the doorway leading down to the cellar and disappeared.

"OK, boy." Noah patted Chester's head and started for the cellar door. "No more late-night movies for either of us, I don't care how badly we're suffering from insomnia."

"Hey, Mattie, coming down," Noah called as he started

down the steps, the dog still at his heels. "Just wanted to say good night."

He descended out of the dark stairwell into the room, lit only by the lamp on the nightstand beside Mattie's twin bed. Mattie had already changed into an old shirt he slept in and climbed beneath the sheet.

The orange tabby kitten sat on the end of his bed, licking its paw.

Noah looked down at Mattie who lay stiff in his bed, his fingers curled around the pale blue sheet he had drawn to his chin. Because the cellar was below ground, the room was cool at night, cool enough that Mattie might need the blanket Rachel always left at the end of his bed. That was one of the nice things about the cellar bedroom Rachel had built for him. It was cool in the summer without the necessity of an air conditioner, and in the winter, he apparently rarely needed the electric space heater she'd had hardwired into the electrical system.

Mattie stared straight up at the ceiling, making no indication he even knew Noah was there.

Noah's gaze shifted to the Bible fort Mattie was building. It appeared larger than the last time Noah had been down here. The walls a little taller. His gaze shifted to the three Bibles piled on the nightstand beside the lamp. "Doing a little reading?" he asked. He didn't say it to taunt Mattie, but only as a matter of making conversation. One of the Bibles was open, face down, and Noah picked it up, glancing at the page. "Psalms," he said. "You like the Psalms, don't you, Mattie? You would. There've been so many beautiful songs to come out of Psalms." Noah found himself reading a passage. It was the first time he had read a word of the Bible since his arrest. "Psalm four," he said, his own voice sounding strange in his head. "David's." He pressed his finger to the page and read aloud. "I will lie down and sleep in peace, for you alone, O Lord, make me dwell in safety."

He smiled, looking down at Mattie. "That's nice, isn't it? Reassuring."

The words were barely out of his mouth when he frowned, looking down at Mattie staring at the ceiling, then at the page again. The verse was meant to provide reassurance to one going to sleep. Except that Mattie couldn't read, so he wouldn't know that.

A coincidence that the Bible was left open to this page? Left open to this page by a man who could neither read nor speak?

Looking down at Mattie, he returned the book to its place, still open to the page. "Anything you need, buddy?" He waited. "No? All right, well, Chester and I are going to head to bed, but we'll see you in the morning." He reached for the lamp. "You want me to shut—"

Mattie snapped his head around, staring at Noah, his dark eyes wide.

Noah pulled his hand back at once. "All right. That's fine, Mattie. We can leave the light on. That's not a problem. Leave it on all night, if you want."

He took one last look at Mattie and then went up the stairs, closing the door behind him and then securing the latch on the outside door as well. With Chester still following a few steps behind him, he went to the open garage, removed the picnic basket and quilt, and closed the hatch. Then he closed the garage door, specifically noting, in his mind, that he did it.

In the kitchen, he set down the picnic basket, draped the quilt over the back of a chair, and locked the back door, checking once he had turned the dead bolt to be sure it was secure.

He had no idea why he did it. He never had before.

Noah was just emptying the picnic basket, rinsing out the disposable containers, when Rachel appeared, barefoot, wearing a T-shirt and a pair of old gray gym shorts. He couldn't help but notice she was braless, her nipples small buttons pressing against the thin cotton fabric of the T-shirt. He turned away, feeling guilty for having noticed.

"She stayed asleep?"

"Down for the count."

"Hey, did you open one of Mattie's Bibles recently? Read a passage to him, maybe?"

She shook her head. "You mean in his room? No. Why?"

He shrugged. "I was just wondering." It was silly to tell her about the Bible verse. It was just a coincidence, he was sure. He was probably just feeling weird about it because it was the first time he'd touched a Bible in years. Rachel checked the lock on the back door, picked up the dog bowl, and walked to the sink.

As Noah leaned over to place the container in the top drawer of the dishwasher, Rachel stepped in front of the sink, flipping on the cold water. When he stood upright again, her hip brushed his thigh. He felt an electrical charge, something akin to what a person felt in the air on the cusp of a thunderstorm. He looked down to find her looking up at him, her green eyes wider than before.

The water trickled down the drain.

Noah lowered his head, and just as he was about to brush his lips against hers, she turned so that he missed her mouth.

"Noah," she whispered, pushing the heavy aluminum dish under the faucet.

Her voice was enough to snap him out of whatever peculiar spell he had fallen into, and he took a step back from the sink. "I . . . I'm sorry, Rache. I didn't mean—"

"Noah, it's OK." She held her hand up to him, her gaze fixed on the dog bowl filling with water. "It's been a long day. Neither of us has had enough sleep."

He took another step back, still watching her. The emotion in her voice made his chest ache. He wanted to pull her into his arms and stroke her hair, her back. He wanted to tell her that no matter what, no matter what happened between them, everything was going to be all right. He wanted to tell

her he loved her. That he loved Mallory and that he would always love them, no matter how far she went or how many
states she put between them in her effort to get away from
him.

But a lump rose in his throat and he found himself unable
to say a word. He turned away, leaving her at the sink, the
water still running. Chester followed him down the hall toward his lonely bedroom, and he wondered how he would
possibly sleep.

Skeeter stared blurry eyed at the empty vodka bottle in
front of him on the table, thinking they didn't make a pint
the size they used to.

His chin resting on the table, hands palms down on either
side of his head, his gaze shifted to the ceramic pipe and
empty Ziploc baggy. Fucking weed was gone. They didn't
make a dime bag the way they used to, either.

Skeeter needed more vodka. Or more weed. Or more of
both. He even had a couple of bucks in his pocket that his
old man had given him for mowing the lawn. Cheap bastard.
Twenty-five bucks for mowing and raking that whole fucking lawn when he had a wad in his wallet?

Skeeter figured his father was lucky he hadn't hit him
over the head with the rake and taken the wallet.

Skeeter turned his head so that his cheek rested on the old
gold-speckled Formica-top table. He couldn't remember sitting down at the kitchen table to smoke a bowl or finish off
the bottle, but he must have. That was his pipe, the blue glass
one he'd bought at the head shop at the beach last summer
when he worked that sweet construction job and had money
to blow on shit like that. If it hadn't been for the boss's son
who'd narked on him for pinching a couple of tools he'd later
hocked, he'd still have that job.

Skeeter closed one eye, then simultaneously opened it and
closed the other and watched the empty vodka bottle move.

He did it again and chuckled as the bottle hopped back and forth. When he laughed, drool came out of his mouth. He tried to pick up his head, but it felt like cement and he let it fall again, his cheek making a farting sound as he hit. That made him laugh harder.

He was more shit-faced than he realized.

Maybe he didn't need any more vodka or weed tonight. Maybe he'd just kick back on the couch and watch something stupid on TV. He was hungry and he vaguely remembered bringing home a pizza. It was on the cardboard box he used for a coffee table, but that was halfway across the room. The single-room apartment above his parents' garage wasn't that big, but it could seem big if you were drunk enough or stoned enough or, if you were lucky, both at the same time.

Skeeter closed both eyes. He was tired. Tired enough to sleep, but he hated to waste a good buzz like this on sleeping. He needed to get up. Get up and take a piss. Find that pizza box that he thought he could smell somewhere in the room. It was either the pizza he'd brought home or the garbage that needed taking out that he smelled. He stared at the vodka bottle, both eyes open, wondering just which one it was.

He heard a sound behind him. Footsteps?

Was Catty here? That slut. He couldn't remember if she'd just dropped him off or come upstairs for a quick fuck. Christ, he hated having to get a ride from his friends, or even worse, his seventy-year-old parents. But he'd lost his license again, this time for two years. Barely gotten out of having to go to jail. At least the lawyer his father had hired had been decent.

Skeeter heard footsteps on the stairs. Then he remembered he'd already heard them. Catty. Had to be Catty. She probably forgot something. Her keys. Her panties.

He grinned lopsidedly, raising his head so that his chin rested on the table again.

The door behind him opened. He waited for Catty to say something. One of her smart-assed remarks about what a fucking bastard he was, or something.

Catty didn't say anything. She just walked up behind him.

Skeeter thought about picking up his cement head, leaning back in the chair, and saying something to her. Telling her to take her cunt somewhere else. That she wasn't flopping at his place tonight. But it seemed like too much effort to Skeeter. She wasn't worth the concentration, the energy it would take to lift his head, push back with his hands, and sit up in the chair.

From behind him, Skeeter felt a slight breeze, almost like someone had run by him, but it was only across his face. Just his right cheek. He saw something out of the corner of his eye, something black. Like a bat or something.

Holy shit. Had Catty let a bat in the house?

The black bat appeared in front of him, swooping down across the table toward him. It occurred to Skeeter as he watched it that he should be more careful about taking pills when he didn't know what they were. Catty had given him something in the car before he got out, but he couldn't remember what she had said they were. Couldn't remember if she'd said anything at all.

The bat with its long black wings struck the table, going through his hand . . .

Skeeter watched as blood spurted from his arm, severed between his hand and his wrist. Had the bat bit him? A lot of blood for a bat bite. The fingers twitched, which creeped him out a little. They were his fingers. His hand. He knew it was his hand, not because he'd felt the bat bite him, but because he could see the tattoo one of his friends had put between his thumb and forefinger. D.B.N. They were his initials. Delbert Benjamin Newton. But he always told people it stood for "Die Bitch Now," which always got a laugh.

Suddenly, the bat, which had disappeared, swooped down again, and as it dove for his left hand, it occurred to Skeeter that he ought to move it. Maybe even hit the bat with something. Maybe the empty vodka bottle. But he stared in fascination as it swooped again and cleanly bit off his other hand.

More blood spurted. It ran across the sloping table, over the side, down onto the floor . . .

Skeeter felt light-headed, and it occurred to him as he sat there, chin on the table, staring, that a bite like that ought to hurt. But it didn't hurt. Just felt weird. Almost like he was dreaming. Maybe he *was* dreaming.

Then the bat spoke as it grew a hand and the hand placed a piece of paper on the table, setting the vodka bottle on top of it.

It was a deep, gravelly voice. "Thou shall not steal. And if your right hand causes you to sin, cut it off and cast it from you; for it is more profitable for you that one of your members perish, than for your whole body to be cast into hell."

What the fuck?

Skeeter meant to say it out loud, but he didn't hear his own voice. The words just bounced around in his head. Everything was beginning to get blurry, and the vodka bottle was beginning to fade. The hands were still now. His cement head had gotten even heavier until it rested, cheek down, in the pool of blood. All he heard was the sound of footsteps as the bat walked out of the apartment and quietly closed the door behind it.

CHAPTER 18

When he rolled onto his side to look at the digital clock beside his bed, Noah was startled to find that it was already 8:45. He never slept this late. As he dressed, he heard the sounds of a rushed Sunday morning breakfast out in the kitchen. Rachel was trying to be patient, but Mallory was obviously testing that patience. Apparently, like the day before, the two were not in agreement as to what was appropriate clothing for the day—for church, in this case.

After a quick stop in the bathroom, Noah entered the kitchen barefoot, sneakers and a clean pair of socks in hand. "Morning."

Rachel, dressed for church, leaned against the kitchen sink, coffee mug in hand. Her hair was still wet and pulled back, caught up in a plastic clip behind her head. "Morning." She walked to the coffeepot to pour him a cup. "You slept in."

"Yeah, I know." He tucked the socks into one of the sneakers and left them on the floor near the refrigerator. "I don't feel like I slept well last night. Weird dreams." He ran his hand through his hair, damp from where he'd pulled a wet comb through it, trying to remember, unsuccessfully, what he had dreamed about.

She pushed a mug into his hand. "Me too."

He took a sip of coffee, looking up at her over the rim of the white mug, stamped with the John Deere symbol and the words "Burton's Hardware." "Really. Like what?"

She lifted a slender shoulder, gazing into her cup. "Scary stuff," she said softly.

"Me too," he murmured, watching her, thinking. "Weird we'd both be having strange dreams, huh?"

"Yeah."

"Talk later, maybe?"

She gave a slight nod. "Maybe." Her attention shifted to Mallory, seated in her booster, eating the last spoonfuls of cereal from her bowl. "Finish up, because you're going back upstairs to change, Missy."

Mattie sat beside her, methodically spooning cereal into his mouth, staring at the box in front of him as if he could read it.

"So what are we wearing today?" Noah stood between the sink and the table, trying to keep things light.

"Snow pants," Rachel said dryly.

Noah almost choked on his coffee. "Snow pants?" He leaned over, tilting his head to see under the table. Sure enough, Mallory was wearing hot pink snow pants and flip-flops. Her shirt was an ordinary lavender T-shirt with an orange butterfly appliquéd at the neckline.

"I *wike* them," Mallory declared defiantly.

"Mal, hon, I told you, they're too hot."

"I'm not hot." Mallory picked up her bowl and drank the milk left in the bottom.

"And snow pants are not appropriate for Sunday School."

"I wore them to Sunday School when we had the big snow."

"Yes, you did." Rachel exhaled. "You wore them to church in February when we had the big snow. Because it was cold. Because it had snowed. And you were wearing pants under-

neath so you could take them off once we got to church, remember?"

Mallory pushed back from the table, the chair legs scrap-
ing on the wood floor. She climbed out of her booster seat
and reached up to retrieve her bowl and spoon and carry
them to the sink, snow pants making a swooshing, crunching
sound as she walked. "It's too hot for pants under. Just panties."
She walked past Noah and her mother and dropped the plastic bowl into the sink. The spoon clattered as it hit the stainless steel.

Rachel surprised Noah by turning to him and gesturing
with one hand as if to say, "Do something with her, because
I can't."

Noah hesitated, debating whether or not further discussion was necessary. He understood the purpose of talking
with kids, even if he'd never been a father longer than a few
months. He also understood that kids needed structure and
that, ultimately, someone needed to be in charge, that someone being the parent rather than the child.

"Mallory," he said firmly, but not unkindly, "your mother
asked you to change out of the snow pants into something
more appropriate for church. When you get home, you may
certainly put the snow pants back on, but I would suggest
you get up those stairs and change, and do it quickly or there
will be consequences."

She came to stand in front of Noah, and it was all he could
do not to smile. The little, blond ponytailed girl in a T-shirt,
flip-flops, and snow pants was almost more than he could
stand.

"What's *con-see-quences?*"

"Consequences for disobeying your mother are probably
something along the lines of no DVD movies or Wiggles on
TV for a few days."

"No *Wiggwles!*"

She looked so shocked that Noah really had to fight to
keep from laughing out loud. "Hurry," he whispered to her.

She turned and ran, hot pink marshmallow legs pumping.

Rachel turned to him the minute her daughter was out of sight and smiled. "Thanks."

He smiled back. "No problem. See you after church." He walked out onto the front porch, still barefoot, and took a deep breath, thinking that despite his restless, nightmare-filled night, the day had a promising start. Very promising.

Snowden was standing on a stepladder at his mother's house, changing a light bulb at the top of the stairs, when his cell phone went off. She was just telling him how ridiculous it was that he thought he needed to change her light bulbs. She'd been changing them for fifty years on her own just fine. She thought that the fact that last year she had fallen off the ladder, halfway down the stairs and dislocated her shoulder, resulting in three months of physical therapy, was irrelevant.

He almost welcomed the call, though from the display screen on the phone, he could see it was the station. "Chief Calloway," he said into the phone, handing his mother the dead light bulb as he stepped off the ladder.

She immediately lifted the bulb to her ear to shake it as if not believing him when he said the reason the light wouldn't come on was because the bulb was out. "I bought the three-year kind," she said indignantly.

"Chief, Johnson here," the voice on the other end of the line said. "Sorry to call you on a Sunday, but it looks like we got us another one."

Snowden turned his back to his mother, cradling the phone on his shoulder as he began to fold up the ladder. He fought the eerie chill that snaked up his spine. "Another what, Johnson?"

"Murder, Chief. Another ugly one."

For a moment Snowden didn't respond, he was so shocked. He released the ladder, leaving it to stand at the top of the stairs as he walked away, circling in the hallway. He had so completely convinced himself that whoever had killed Leager and Rehak had done it for personal reasons that it really hadn't occurred to him that the rest of the town's residents might not be safe.

"Chief?"

Snowden found his voice, resting his hand on the top of the stepladder. "Who?"

"Skeeter Newton."

Snowden knew the victim. He was a real bum, into drugs and alcohol, and he got into fistfights in bars. He dabbled in criminal activity, mostly in other towns, but nothing big. Nothing they could ever pin on him. Snowden had seen his name go by his desk recently when his driver's license had been revoked for a DUI.

"Bled to death at the kitchen table in his apartment," Johnson continued. "Hand cut right off at the wrist. Mother found him when she and her husband came home from church."

"Something wrong?" Snowden's mother asked, still holding the light bulb.

"You sure he didn't kill himself?" Snowden felt a glimmer of hope. Maybe Skeeter had gotten drunk or high and tried to commit suicide. Or maybe he'd been high or drunk and tried to do something stupid like open a can of beans with a pocketknife. He'd seen stranger accidents.

"Both hands, Chief," Johnson said dully. "Cut right off, laying there on the table in front of him. Mrs. Newton was hysterical when she called 911. They had a hell of a time figuring out what she was saying."

"OK, OK." Snowden cradled the phone on his shoulder again and grabbed the ladder, folding it as he went down the stairs.

Tillie hustled after him. "Someone else has been murdered, haven't they?"

"I'll be there in five minutes," Snowden said into the phone. "At the parents' residence, right?" They lived only two streets over, in an older house very similar to his mother's, though larger and nicer.

"Yeah. He was livin' over his parents' garage, the parasite."

"I want the parents out of there." Snowden entered his mother's laundry room. "And no one else at the scene except those who have to be there."

"Right. EMTs are on their way, of course. Gotta send them and an ambulance no matter how dead the poor sucker is. I've got two cars in route, the third on its way as soon as Billings finishes writing a speeding ticket, but I knew you'd want me to call you."

Snowden slid the stepladder into its proper place between the wall and his mother's ancient washing machine. "You did the right thing, Johnson. I'm on my way."

Snowden hung up the phone as he went out his mother's back door. He was wearing a pair of gym shorts, a gray Rutgers University T-shirt, and sneakers, but he didn't want to take the time to run home and change into his uniform. "I've got a problem, Mom. I've got to go."

"You said less than five minutes." She followed him out the door. "It's one of my neighbors, isn't it? Who's been murdered?"

"Mom, you know I can't say." He hurried to his police car. "I'll call you later."

Snowden started up the black and white Crown Victoria and shifted it into reverse, ignoring his mother, who remained in the driveway, the bad light bulb still in her hand. Only once he was out on the street, seat belt fastened, car in drive, did he reach for his cell and call Delilah.

"Jeez Louise, that's a lot of blood," Delilah breathed.

"A man this size has around five liters," EMT Jason Cline told her, looking on with interest.

She took care not to step in the large pool of congealed blood on the floor around the cheap kitchen table as she studied Skeeter. Remarkably, he was still sitting in the chair, slumped forward, bloody wrist stumps on each side of his head. He was wearing cutoff jean shorts and a Harley David-son T-shirt with the sleeves torn off. His thinning brown hair was pulled back in a ponytail, but wisps of hair partially cov-ered his face. The waxen hands, sprinkled with dark hair on the backs, fingers slightly flexed, lay on the table, appearing to Delilah to be exactly where they had come to lie when they'd been cut off. His skin was the color of white wax, so inhuman looking that she almost had to remind herself this was a real body and not a mannequin posed for some cheap horror film kids were making in their parents' garage.

"Five liters, huh?" Delilah asked. "It looks like we've got close to that on the table and on the floor."

"Nah, probably only half that. It takes a few minutes to bleed out from the wrists. Blood coagulates," remarked Jason, dressed in the paramedic's uniform of a navy blue jumpsuit and stethoscope. "Most people don't realize that. You want to kill yourself, there are a lot smarter places to cut like the jugular or femoral artery." He demonstrated with the blade of his index finger across his neck, then his inner thigh.

She stood on the other side of the table, looking down on the victim. "Something tells me Skeeter here didn't do this himself."

Delilah had had the pleasure, or the displeasure in this case, of knowing Delbert "Skeeter" Newton. She'd met him the first week on the job here in Stephen Kill when she'd been called to a domestic disturbance. Turned out Skeeter had gotten pissed at his mother over her not allowing him to take her car keys and borrow her car, and he'd given her "a couple of little pushes" according to the drunken Skeeter. It was Mr. Newton who'd called the police when he'd gotten scared. In the end, Mrs. Newton had refused to agree to press charges, and Delilah and Lopez had ended up escort-ing him upstairs to the apartment over the garage where she stood now. She couldn't say she was too sorry to see the punk dead, but her heart went out to the parents downstairs, sitting on their front stoop, arms around each other, sobbing uncontrollably.

Jason walked around the table to stand beside Delilah. "So," he said quietly, "what do you think? You wanna maybe go out or something sometime, *Sergeant* Swift?"

She studied the angles of Skeeter's wrists and detached hands, only half listening to Jason. He was nice enough, cute enough, but she just wasn't interested. It was almost as if he *paled in comparison* to someone else she found herself thinking about way too often. She almost laughed aloud at the morbid phrasing that had gone through her head. "I . . . I don't think so, Jason. Thanks, I appreciate the offer, but I'm kind of seeing someone right now."

Someone cleared his throat, and Delilah looked up to see Snowden standing there. He'd been downstairs talking with the Newtons when she arrived and sent her up to start collecting evidence.

"Well." Jason clapped his hands together, moving back around the table toward the door of the filthy apartment. "Guess I'll be waiting downstairs. Give a holler if you need me, Chief."

Snowden muttered something under his breath, and Delilah had to fight to resist a smile. Snowden intimidated Jason. Shoot, he intimidated everyone in this town.

"So what's your initial take on this, Swift?" Snowden asked, all business and attitude.

If she hadn't known better, she'd have thought he was annoyed by Jason's flirtation. But Delilah didn't have time to think about such nonsense right now. She had a dead man sitting in front of her at his kitchen table with his hands cut off, lying right there in front of him.

"Obviously a homicide, Chief."

He grunted an affirmation.

"No weapon on the scene. I've got men beating the bushes around the property, but they're not going to find anything."

"What makes you say that?"

"The club, bat, whatever it was that was used to kill Rehak wasn't left at the scene."

"And you're assuming that this murder is connected with Rehak's?"

She pulled a pair of disposable gloves from the back pocket of her jean shorts. She'd been shopping at the Wal-Mart on Route 1 when Snowden had called. She'd left her cart right where it stood, half-full of cleaning supplies, chips, and an assortment of frozen breakfast items. It had still taken her, in Sunday traffic through Rehoboth, almost half an hour to make it to the Newton residence.

Gloves on, she gingerly reached across the table and picked up the piece of ordinary white typing paper from under the empty bottle of cheap vodka. The sheet had two Bible verses—cut from an actual Bible by the look of the almost transparent paper they were on—taped to it. "Thou shall not steal," she read aloud. "And if your right hand causes you to sin, cut it off and cast it from you; for it is more profitable for you that one of your members perish, than for your whole body to be cast into hell."

She looked up at Snowden. "The verses accuse him of a sin, just like the verses left behind at Rehak's and Leager's accused them of a sin. Killer goes a step further here by offering the form of punishment."

"Thou shall not steal is one of the Ten Commandments, right out of the Old Testament," Snowden thought aloud, studying the page she held in her hand. "But the other verse comes from the New Testament, one of the Gospels, I'm pretty sure. It doesn't refer to a thief, though. It's been taken out of context."

She looked up at him again. "Snowden, the killer is obviously a nut job. Bright, sane Christians take verses out of context all the time. Why would we expect an insane murderer not to?"

He scowled. He knew she was right, whether he'd admit it to her face or not.

"The note is different than the others." It was a statement more than an argument against her theory that the other murders had been isolated incidences.

"So he's on a learning curve." She shrugged, carefully setting the note down outside the pool of blood on the table so that she could bag it in a minute. "First time, note is handwritten. Maybe an impulse thing," she theorized aloud. "Second time, the plan is better laid out. Killer tears the page from a Bible before going to commit the murder. This time, the killer likes two verses but they're not together in the Bible. Inconvenient. So, he does what's logical—cuts them out and tapes them on a piece of paper."

"Plain old printer paper," Snowden said. "Plain old Scotch tape."

"Could have come from any household or office in the United States," she murmured. Her gaze shifted upward to meet his again. "Could have come from my house or yours."

"Ah, hell," Snowden murmured, running his hand over the top of his head, over his closely shorn, dark hair.

It was the first time Delilah had ever heard him swear. "Yeah, ah hell," she agreed. "At the risk of sounding paranoid or overly dramatic, Chief, I think we've got us a serial killer right here in little ole Stephen Kill, Delaware." She took a breath, her gaze shifting to the dead man sitting in the kitchen chair, dismembered. "May God save his sorry soul," she said solemnly. "Save us all."

To her surprise, Snowden reached out and caught her hand, giving it a squeeze before he let it go. "All right," he called, walking away. "Get the evidence bagged, the photos taken, and let's get Skeeter out of here."

Sunday afternoon, Noah entered the small den that had become an office years ago, when his parents had decided to turn the old farm into a vineyard. It was still much the way it had appeared in his childhood—walls painted white, an accordion shade on the single window, but no curtains, only a valance. Sometime in the late eighties, his mother had added a wallpaper border along the top of the walls—yellow with white daisies and dancing yellow and black bumblebees. The paper was faded and peeling in a couple of places and completely missing in one corner where Rachel had mentioned she'd had a leak through the ceiling four years ago. There in the corner, the ceiling had been patched and painted, though the entire ceiling had not been repainted so it stood out, stark white against yellow.

The furniture consisted of a giant oak desk and old wooden chair behind it, a round oak table that had once stood in one of his grandmother's kitchens, a wall of bookcases filled with books, stacks of yellowed paper, and various bits of junk that probably needed to be tossed. As he passed them, headed toward the new metal file cabinets on either side of the windows, a can roped in colorful yarn caught his eye. He had made the pencil can for his mother in elementary school, though what grade he could no longer remember. The pencil can made him a little sad, sad to think of the potential he once had and what he had done with it. But it also made him happy inside as he recalled the life he had led growing up here, the only child of Joanne and Mark Gibson. He had been loved, cherished. A lump rose in his throat as an image of his parents riding in that Jeep in Nicaragua crossed his mind. He couldn't help but wonder if they had been afraid in the last moments of their lives, if his mother had cried.

Usually, these thoughts took him down a road of despair and to a burning desire for a drink, but today they didn't. Today, he felt a strange, overwhelming sense of peace.

Caught a little off-balance by his feelings, Noah walked to the file cabinets and pulled open the top drawer of the first one he came to. He was looking for information on the warranty of the stainless steel tanks his parents had used to regulate the temperature of the wine in the primary fermentation stage. His father had been meticulous about keeping files, but in the years since he'd passed away and Rachel had found herself responsible for the entire operation, she had admitted to Noah, over tuna sandwiches at lunch, that she had allowed the order of the office to disintegrate. However, she swore to him that if his father had kept the warranty information, it was somewhere in one of these file cabinets. After the leak, she'd replaced his father's stacked cardboard file boxes with real filing cabinets.

Noah began to flip through the papers in the top drawer, some in hanging files, some in file folders, others just tucked inside. As he dug deeper, he couldn't resist a smile. His ex-wife was not quite the neat, controlled woman she liked everyone to believe she was. Inside the drawer he found envelopes with old bills in them, napkins with notes, user's manuals for appliances, and a myriad of other junk. He found the same in the second drawer, although mixed with manuals for a breast pump, a DVD player, and the directions on putting a purple tricycle together, he discovered notes and receipts in his father's handwriting. The same in the third drawer. He moved to the next filing cabinet. Apparently, when Rachel had moved the papers from the damp boxes, she'd made no attempt to file in any sort of order that would allow her to find anything later.

He was still chuckling as he reached the second drawer of the third file cabinet, where he'd been fortunate enough to find some information on acidity tests his father had done on the must from the Chancellor grapes he had planted the first year. It wasn't the warranty he was looking for, but the information would certainly come in handy when he began making the must that would eventually become wine.

The phone rang but he didn't bother to try to uncover the old black dial-style phone he knew was buried somewhere on the desk. Elsewhere in the house, he heard Mallory answer it, "Gibson residence," then the clip-clop of her feet in her cowboy boots as she ran to find Rachel, hollering "Mama! Phone!"

With a smile, Noah turned his attention to the next drawer. Behind directions on how to set an answering machine and a pile of long-expired diaper coupons, he came across a folder with the name of a fertility clinic in Baltimore on it. The cover was a pale blue with pink clouds and smiling babies, and inside were several pamphlets explaining all the services they offered a new patient—in vitro fertilization, sperm bank access, and a number of other procedures. Tucked in the top, in slits cut just for the purpose, was an appointment card with Rachel's name printed on it in someone's handwriting other than her own. It was dated a week before the accident that had taken the Marcuses' lives.

Noah took a step back, feeling as if he'd just been sucker punched. For a moment, he stared at the folder, not even wanting to touch it again. A fertility clinic? In the months leading up to the accident, he vaguely remembered discussing the possibility of he and Rachel using someone else's eggs or sperm to get pregnant to prevent the deadly combination of their genes, which might produce another baby that would not survive. But Noah had been against the idea, hanging on to the ridiculous notion that everything happened for a reason, that it was all part of God's plan.

The part about God's plan had shattered the morning he woke up in jail, charged with a DWI and two vehicular homicides.

Noah took a shuddering breath and grabbed the appointment card, leaving the drawer open as he left the office in search of Rachel.

CHAPTER 19

Rachel was surprised to hear Jeremy Cary on the end of the line, and for a moment she sputtered. "H . . . hi."

"Not catching you at a bad time, am I?"

"N . . . no, not at all." She glanced at Mallory, seated at the kitchen table, busy with colored playdough and plastic cookie cutters. Mattie was in the living room, playing the organ. She slipped out the back door, and onto the porch so she could hear Jeremy better.

"It was good to see you yesterday," Jeremy continued. "And I was thinking maybe we could go out this week. Catch a movie, grab a bite to eat?"

It took a moment for it to register that he was asking her out on a date. She'd had a hard time focusing all day. She'd had another disturbing night's sleep last night, riddled with nightmares she couldn't remember. She'd awakened at three in the morning seated out in the hallway wearing an old flannel robe over her T-shirt and panties, having no recollection of how she'd gotten there. Even more disturbing had been the fact that she'd found sand in her bed this morning, sand from her bare feet. Apparently she'd been outside during her little sleepwalking adventure.

"A movie?" she repeated, like an idiot.

"If there's something playing you'd like to see. Otherwise, just dinner, a walk on the boardwalk, whatever you'd like to do, really."

She lowered herself to sit on the top step of the porch, running one hand through her hair. She had a pounding headache. It had been a long day. Upon their arrival at church, Mattie had refused to get out of the car. He'd dressed for church and gotten into the car quite willingly, but once they'd reached the parking lot, which had been filled with parishioners entering the building, he'd curled up on the backseat and wouldn't budge. Finally, she'd ended up sending Mallory into Sunday School, and she'd sat there for an hour with Mattie. As far as she could remember, it was the first time he hadn't played the organ in church on a Sunday morning since they had attempted to send him away to live in a group home after Noah went to jail.

Rachel tried to switch gears. Jeremy sounded so nice on the phone, so sincere, and she did like him. God knew she could use a night out. So why was she hesitating?

"So what do you think?" Jeremy asked tentatively.

Apparently she was taking too long to answer. "Um . . . a movie or something would be fun. Yes, thanks. That would be great," she said with more enthusiasm than she felt. "When?"

"When's good for you? Wednesday night? A Friday or Saturday better?"

"Um . . . Friday, I guess. I . . . I'll have to get a babysitter for Mallory and Mattie."

"Right. Sure. Mattie and Mallory."

She could hear a question in his voice and she knew what it was without him having to say it. Her ex-husband was living in her house, or she was living in his house, or whatever. Why couldn't he watch them? And it was a good question.

But Rachel just didn't feel right asking Noah if he could baby-sit Mallory so she could go on a date. It was just too weird.

"So, Friday sounds great," Jeremy said, picking up the lag in the conversation again. "How about if I check the paper, see what's playing in Rehoboth and call you, what, tomorrow night?"

"Sure. Sounds good."

"Sounds great to me," he countered. "Hey, did you hear the news in church this morning? Pretty scary stuff."

Rachel felt a prickle of fear at the back of her neck. "No, I didn't hear anything. Mattie was having a bad morning. Mallory went to Sunday School and walked out with a friend. I never got out of the car."

"You're kidding. You didn't hear? There's been another murder in town."

Rachel felt her chest constrict as a flash of the previous night's dream appeared on the viewing screen of her mind. Blood. A swirl of blackness. The voice. "Y . . . You're kidding." She pressed her free hand to the solid wood of the step as if to steady herself. But it wasn't her body that had been caught off balance. "A murder related to the others?"

"Gotta be. Poor guy had his hands cut off. My neighbor responded to the call. He's an EMT. Said it was a bloody mess, just like at Johnny Leager's place."

"He was stoned to death?" she breathed.

"His hands were cut off at the wrists and he bled to death, apparently."

She wanted to ask if a note had been left, but she didn't. Jeremy wouldn't know anything about the Biblical references the killer had left behind with Johnny and Pam. "Who?" she managed.

"The Newtons' youngest son. The one with the bad tattoos. Lived with them, apparently."

"Oh God," she breathed, thinking of Harry and Flora. "I saw Harry yesterday. He was volunteering at the picnic."

"Don't really know them. Not patients of mine."

Rachel clutched the phone, thinking she needed to go see Harry and Flora. She didn't know what comfort she could offer, she just felt as if she needed to see them, to let them know that she cared. Everyone knew their son was no good, they of all people knew, but that didn't mean he deserved to be murdered, and it certainly didn't mean they deserved to suffer the loss of a child. Rachel knew all too well how devastating that tragedy could be.

"Anyway, I'll give you a ring tomorrow?"

"Yeah, sure," she said, "talk to you then." As she hung up, she heard the porch door swing open behind her.

"Rachel?"

"Noah . . ." She turned to him, the phone still clutched in her hand. She felt slightly light-headed. Scared.

He halted halfway between the door and the step. His brow creased and he stared at her for a moment. "What's wrong?" He slid something into his back pocket.

Rachel turned on the step to stare straight ahead. Noah had hooked a water sprinkler to the hose and was watering a flower bed next to the house, where fat, orange tiger lilies were blooming. Tiger lilies always made her think of her grandmother because she had always loved them. She remembered her grandmother stopping the old truck along the side of the road so Rachel could jump out and pick lilies from the edge of ditches to place in a vase on the kitchen table.

"Rache?" Noah repeated.

She watched the water, like raindrops, beat on the petals of one of the lilies. What was wrong with her? It was certainly a terrible tragedy that Skeeter Newton was dead, murdered in such a heinous way, but why should that frighten her? Why should that make her afraid? Afraid for her own life, for the lives of those on this farm whom she loved.

Noah sat down beside her and took her hand, gazing into her eyes. "Are you sick?" he asked. "Do you need to lie down? You're white as a ghost."

She met his gaze. "Skeeter Newton was murdered. Someone cut his hands off and he bled to death."

Noah glanced away, then back at her. "That's awful, Rache. Poor Harry and Flora."

She nodded. "It's the same killer," she whispered. "And there's no way Skeeter was sleeping with Pam Rehak or Johnny Leager."

He smoothed her hand with his. "You don't know that it's the same person."

"I *know*," she whispered.

"How?"

She shook her head. "I don't know how. I just know it is, either the same person or the same thing. . . ." She looked away, knowing how ridiculous she sounded, unable to help herself. She turned back to him. "Noah, I know this is going to sound crazy but there's something evil out there. Something evil in this town. I . . . I can feel it."

She half expected him to laugh. Noah didn't believe in God any longer and he certainly didn't believe in Satan or any inherent evil spoken of in the Bible. But he didn't laugh. He just sat there.

"You feel it, too, don't you?" Her voice was barely a whisper.

He lifted her hand to his lips and kissed it. She didn't pull away.

"I don't know what I feel."

"Today, Mattie wouldn't go into church. Did I tell you?" She covered his hand with hers. "He was afraid to go inside, Noah. Afraid of something or someone." She was silent for a moment. "I'm afraid now. I don't know what I'm afraid of, but I'm afraid. Afraid for Mallory. For all of us."

"It's only natural," he said, putting his arm around her and drawing her to his shoulder. "Parents lose a child, no matter how old he is, and it's natural that you should worry about losing your own child." He kissed the top of her head. "Especially after what you've been through."

"*We've* been through," she corrected.

He sighed, and though he didn't agree with her verbally, she could feel it in his body posture. She knew he still felt the loss of their little boys, even after all this time. She pressed her lips together, refocusing her thoughts, trying to think logically.

Pam Rehak and Johnny Leager had been killed for the sin of adultery. If the same killer had murdered Skeeter Newton, for what sin? She knew he was a derelict, a drunk, into drugs, but the Bible wasn't clear on punishing those types of behaviors.

She looked up at Noah. "Did . . . did you counsel Skeeter?"

He shook his head, but there was something about the look on his face that worried her. He was watching the water sprinkler, his face a mask, yet there was something in his dark eyes that told her there was more to his answer.

"No, he never came in for counseling," he said, as if it was a ridiculous notion. "I don't think Skeeter's been in church since he got kicked out of Sunday School for smoking pot in the boy's bathroom when he was in the seventh grade." It was one of the many Skeeter stories most of the town knew and would probably be repeating for days to come.

The screen door opened behind them and Rachel felt, as much as she heard, Mallory behind her. When she turned, her daughter was standing there, hands blue with playdough, studying her mother and Noah.

"Mallory." Rachel moved out from under Noah's arm and rose off the step quickly, dropping the phone from her lap. She chased it as it skittered across the porch. "Done with the playdough?" she asked, feigning great interest.

"Can we have cookies? Mattie's hungry."

"No cookies. Dinner in an hour and a half. Noah's cooking shish kebabs on the grill."

"But Mattie's hungry for cookies, not *kish-ka-bobs*," the little girl argued.

Noah rose from where he'd been seated and stepped off the porch. "I'll be back in a little while, OK?"

Having captured the runaway phone, Rachel turned to him as she took Mallory by the wrist, trying to avoid the blue playdough. "Where are you going?"

"I won't be gone long. If you guys get hungry before I get back, though, just throw the marinated chicken and cut-up veggies on the skewers and grill them on medium heat, about four minutes a side."

"Noah—"

"We'll talk about it later," he said, striding down the sidewalk.

Rachel was tempted to go after him, to demand to know where he was going, why he was going somewhere on a Sunday afternoon. But the determination of his stride made her turn away instead.

"OK, Cookie," she said, trying to sound cheerful. "How about if we get this playdough cleaned up off you and the floor and get those green beans snapped?"

"Mattie wants cookies, not green beans," Mallory argued stubbornly as she allowed her mother to lead her into the house.

"Well, Mattie is just going to have to wait until after his supper for cookies."

It took Noah twenty-five minutes to make the jaunt to town on the lawn tractor. All the way there, he kept trying to figure out what he was going to say, how he was going to word it without incriminating himself in any way. A part of him had been tempted to just turn back, to return to the farmhouse, have dinner with his family, and wait for the police to come. It was certainly what he would have done a month ago. But a month ago Rachel hadn't looked into his eyes the way she looked into them now. A month ago, he had not loved Mallory so fiercely that it hurt. A month ago he had been without hope, but no longer. Hope was what spurred him on now. And maybe a little anger. Anger that such a thing as this could happen now, now when there was hope.

It was hard for Noah to cross the threshold of St. Paul's, but he made himself push through the heavy doors into the narthex, which was always unlocked. Seeing the sanctuary beyond the glass doors to be dark, he took the familiar staircase to the basement, trying not to allow his emotions to get in the way of his mission. His whole life he had walked this long corridor, and now in his dreams, he still walked it. Only, in his dreams, it was no longer the safe sanctuary it had once been and the doors no longer led to colorful classrooms and a cozy nursery. In his dreams, each brightly painted door opened into a hell unto itself: raging flames, the dark voice, death, destruction, all his past failings.

He moved soundlessly down the corridor, his gaze fixed on the dark blue short-pile carpet beneath his sneakers. The office door was open and he walked in, passing the desk where Cora Watkins had reigned for the last forty years.

"You're early," Father Hailey called from behind the half-closed inner door that led to the office that had once been Noah's.

Noah halted, swallowing hard. He had known it would be difficult to walk in here, but he hadn't realized just how hard. He was flooded with memories, good and bad, overwhelmed by the passion he had once felt for this place and by his own sense of failure.

"But that's fine, come in anyway." The door swung open and Father Hailey appeared. He was at once taken aback by the sight of Noah. "I'm sorry," he said, glancing behind Noah. "I thought you were someone else."

"It's all right. This will only take a minute." Noah met Father Hailey's gaze. It was obvious the man was at least momentarily unsettled by Noah's presence.

Noah didn't blame him. "Could we . . ." He indicated the open door. If the priest was expecting another parishioner, Noah didn't want anyone walking in on this conversation.

"C . . . certainly." Father extended his hand in invitation.

Noah entered the small, darkly paneled office that hadn't seemed to have changed much in the last five years. The items on the walls and the desk were different, the books on the bookshelves were somewhat different, perhaps, but it was the same place.

Father Hailey closed the door and walked to his desk, sliding into his chair. His trembling hands found the cover of an open Bible and he closed it, resting one unsteady hand on the black leather cover. "Please, have a seat."

Noah walked to one of the two chairs in front of the desk and rested both hands on the wooden back. "You have an appointment. I understand. I'll only take a moment of your time."

Father Hailey smiled apologetically. "If you like, Noah, we could schedule some time to talk, this week, perhaps."

Noah shook his head. "That won't be necessary." He looked down at the stained cushion of the seat cover and then back up at the priest. "I understand there's been another murder. Skeeter Newton."

"Terrible tragedy. Terrible. I intend to visit with the Newtons this evening.

"I just wanted to remind you that you are not at liberty to discuss any information that might have been left behind when I . . ." Noah searched for the right words, and when he couldn't find them, he grimaced. "Hell, you know what I mean."

Father Hailey blinked at Noah's utterance, perhaps because the office had rarely heard such words, or maybe because the good father had not heard them often spoken from a fellow priest's lips.

Ex-priest.

"I'm not certain what information was left behind, what kind of records Miss Cora kept, but you have no right to turn them over to the police."

As what Noah was saying began to sink in, Father Hailey started to rub the cover of the Bible. "Do sit down." He raised one hand from the worn Bible cover long enough to gesture to one of the chairs.

"I don't want to sit down!" Noah grasped the chair by its arms, lifted it, and slammed it down.

Father Hailey sat back in his chair, eyes widening.

Noah took a deep breath, not knowing where his anger came from or why he had channeled it toward Father Hailey. "I'm sorry," he said. "I just want to be clear on the fact that what passed between Father Noah Gibson and those parishioners—now your parishioners—stays behind these doors."

"I . . . I gave the police no information r . . . regarding the previous murders," he stammered, acting as if he was afraid Noah would come across the desk at him. "No one has even said if his death is related to the others. I . . . I would imagine the police don't know yet."

"Right. Fine." Noah straightened. "You're absolutely right," he said, knowing in his heart of hearts that he was wrong. "I'm just telling you, I made a commitment when I offered this room as a refuge to those in this town who were troubled, and as a priest of the Episcopal Church, as a man of God, you are obligated to support that commitment."

Somewhere in the church, a door opened and closed.

Noah moved toward the door. There was no reason to stay—he'd said what he'd come to say. Besides, he preferred not to be seen here by anyone else if he could help it. Not like this, not feeling as vulnerable and shaken as he was now.

"Good day, Father. Thank you for seeing me, and again, I apologize." He glanced at his sneakers. "I think these murders have us all on edge."

Before Father Hailey, rising to his feet, could respond,

Noah was out the door. Father Hailey heard him walk through the office and out the door, going in the direction of the choir room, rather than the stairs leading to the narthex and sanctuary, the route usually taken by parishioners. He heard the man take the short flight of steps two at a time to the door meant only as an emergency exit. The clang of the steel door echoed as it swung shut and was followed by footsteps coming from the opposite direction.

Father Hailey's appointment.

Taking a handkerchief from his pocket, he wiped the sweat from his brow and returned it to his pocket as he picked up the Bible to return it to the shelf. As he took the three short steps to the wall, the Bible, of its own accord, yawned open to reveal a page from which a verse had been neatly cut. The leather suddenly hot to his touch, he shoved the Bible onto the shelf, quickly pulling his hand away.

"Father Hailey," a voice greeted from behind him. "Thank you for seeing me on such short notice."

He turned, forcing a smile. "It's my pleasure. It's what I'm here for. Please, have a seat." He took his own chair, leaning forward, tenting his hands where they rested on the desk. The door clicked shut as the parishioner moved forward hesitantly to take the chair. "Tell me, now," Father Hailey said, "about what's been upsetting you."

CHAPTER 20

"Chief."

"Sergeant Swift." Snowden nodded but didn't make eye contact.

He was making himself a cup of coffee in the lounge, which really wasn't much of a lounge at all. Although the small station had outgrown itself years ago, city employees were forced to make do because there wasn't the estimated million dollars in the city budget for a new building. Subsequently, the only furniture in the lounge was a couple of office chairs pushed under a table and a microwave cart that held the microwave and the coffeepot. Other than the dormitory-size refrigerator, the rest of the ten by ten room was taken up by two copiers, two floor-to-ceiling bookshelves filled with manuals, a couple of four-drawer file cabinets, and boxes stacked upon boxes, some containing old files, others rolls of paper towels, toilet tissue, and Kleenex.

McGee, one of the good old boys on the force who didn't care for his chief or Delilah, grunted a morning greeting and walked out, carrying a box of chocolate and marshmallow Pop-Tarts and a cup of coffee.

"Do you have a minute?" Delilah asked Snowden, thinking he looked like he needed more than just a cup of coffee to get his morning going. Although he played a good game and she doubted few others suspected, she could tell by the circles under his dark eyes that he wasn't getting enough sleep, or enough to eat, and that this case was starting to get to him. It was as if it had completely blindsided him. He had truly believed that the Leager and Rehak murders had been isolated cases and that the town and the people he had sworn to protect were safe. Now, he had to deal with the distinct possibility that he had a serial killer on his hands.

He checked his stainless steel watch with a flick of his wrist and went back to stirring his coffee with a red plastic stirrer. "I've got a budget meeting over at city hall in half an hour."

"I need five minutes. The ME's report was just faxed in."

"That was quick."

"It's just an initial report. I think the folks up there realize we haven't got time to waste."

He met her gaze and lifted his chin in the direction of his office. Delilah didn't take a cup of coffee; she'd had three before she left her place this morning and she was already wired. She followed him out of the lounge and down the hall, trying to assess him from behind.

In the four days since Skeeter Newton's murder, she'd spent hours with Snowden working on the case, but there had been no contact in any personal way. She still didn't know what to think about his gesture that day in Skeeter's apartment when he'd taken her hand. Was it just an older, wiser male officer offering support to a younger, less-experienced female officer at a gruesome crime scene, or was it something more? And if it was something more, how did she feel about it? She knew she was attracted to Snowden, had been since the first time they shook hands at her initial interview for a position on Stephen Kill's police force, but a romance was out of the question. He was the chief of police and her boss. And she didn't even want to approach the threshold of her being young and white and him being older and black. The fact that this was the United States in the year 2006 wouldn't mean a thing to her relatives back in East Jesus, Georgia, and despite the attempts to appear otherwise, Stephen Kill wasn't exactly the most broad-minded of towns. Inside Snowden's office, out of habit, Delilah closed the door. He walked around his desk, setting his large coffee cup with a U.S. Army emblem on it down on his desk. He remained standing, flipping open a file marked *Budget* in his neat, block print. She couldn't tell if he was trying to avoid eye contact with her or if he really was just overworked and overstressed.

She decided to jump right in. "The ME in Wilmington says the tox screen on Skeeter Newton came back positive on a whole host of goodies—cocaine, some prescription painkillers, and get this"—she read the report that was a little blurry because the station's fax machine needed toner or something—"*methadone*." She looked up. "And, of course, our friend the wacky weed."

He knitted his dark brows, gazing up at her. "Wacky weed, Sergeant?"

She couldn't tell if he was amused or annoyed with her. She decided she better play it straight. "Marijuana, Chief."

He grimaced, shaking his head as he glanced down again at the file on his desk. "Wacky weed? Sounds like something my mother would say."

She thought she detected a trace of a smile on his sensuous lips, and she silently heaved a little sigh of relief.

"Tell me about the methadone." He used his police chief voice again. "That's odd to find in a small town, in a small town punk."

"It is," she agreed. "But I did a little research into his sometimes girlfriend and found out she's in an outpatient drug rehab program in Baltimore. She had a heroin habit, and methadone is used in treating her withdrawal."

"So she was sharing, how kind."

On some men, sarcasm was unbecoming, but with Snowden, it worked. She liked a clever, slightly cynical man.

"I talked to the ME briefly," she continued. "Guess what she says is one of the possible side effects of methadone abuse, especially if taken with a cocktail of alcohol and other assorted drugs." She checked the report. "He had a .13 blood alcohol level, by the way."

Snowden closed the file, giving her his complete attention. "Hallucinations," he said.

She half frowned, half grinned. "How did you know?"

"For a brief time in college, I had this noble notion I'd like to be a drug rehab counselor, or something like that." He shrugged his broad shoulders. "I took some courses."

She studied him for a moment, trying to imagine him seated in a circle in the basement of a church talking with crack addicts. She just couldn't see him in the chair.

"What makes you think he was hallucinating?" Snowden asked.

"No sign of struggle. Who knows, but why else would a guy let someone cut off his hands and then sit there and bleed to death without calling out for help or at least getting up out of the darned chair? The EMT at the scene said that blood loss of that volume kills you pretty quickly, but it's not instantaneous. He was in some altered state, had to be, and not just drunk or high. Frankly, I've been both in my lifetime, I'm not proud to say, but no matter how drunk on whiskey I got, there was no way in heck anyone could cut off my hands and I'd just sit there and let it happen."

"There was evidence from his posture that his head had rested on the table prior to death. Maybe he was asleep."

"Snowden, I think that if he was asleep, that first hack would have woken him, don't you?" Sarcasm wasn't only for the tall males of the species.

"I'm just trying to get you to think out loud. Trying to get you to draw good conclusions. " He crossed his arms over his chest. "What did the ME have to say about the wounds?"

"The killer was strong. One cut, each hand. Very clean. Weapon would have had a relatively thin blade, but it had to have some size to it to snap the bones like that. And very sharp."

"What kind of weapon does she say the wounds suggest?"

"You're going to laugh, but a sword," Delilah said.

"So we've got a ninja killer in our town?" He didn't smile.

"There're some other possibilities. I thought I'd go down to the hardware store and see what I can see. A sample of the flesh at the wrists was sent to a lab to see if there was any type of residue or foreign bodies that might give us a better idea what the weapon was, but it could take weeks to have results, and the ME didn't seem too hopeful we'd get anything concrete."

"OK. What about the note?"

She shrugged. "It is what it is. It's our guy all right, his signature. Doesn't take a Biblical scholar to see that Skeeter was being accused of being a thief. Of course, we already know from his record that he was never charged with any type of robbery. I can't even find his name in the computer bank showing he was questioned on any."

Snowden exhaled, pushing back his chair and sitting down, hands on his knees. "So, like Rehak and Leager, the killer believes him to be guilty of a crime no one seems to know about or at least be willing to admit actually took place."

"A sin," she said softly. "It's about sin, Snowden."

He glanced away. "Gives me the chills."

"Me too."

They were silent for a moment, both lost in their own thoughts, their own dreads. Snowden spoke first, turning back to her. "If we don't know about a robbery he committed, who would?"

"Well, he doesn't strike me as the type to confess to his priest, if that's what you mean." She thought for a moment. "I don't know. Friends, I guess. Maybe his girlfriend. Of course we have no idea how long ago this could have taken place. With Rehak and Leager, it could have been as long as seven or eight years ago. Skeeter had a record going back as far as twenty years."

Snowden checked his wristwatch again. "I need to go." He rose, taking the file with him, leaving the cup of coffee, untouched. "What's your plan for today?"

"Go to the hardware store and check out the sharp, heavy, thin-bladed weapons I can find. Start interviewing Skeeter's friends and acquaintances. I might go back to the apartment and look around. Be sure I didn't miss anything in all the hullabaloo Sunday."

He nodded, coming around the desk. "You need help? Someone to ride along?"

She almost piped up with a "sure," thinking she'd like to have Snowden along today, but then she realized he meant another officer. He was headed to his meeting in city hall.

"Nah, I'll be fine." She waved him away with the faxed report.

He opened his office door. "Check in with me later."

"You bet." She watched him go, admiring his broad back, thinking to herself how hot that back would be, minus the uniform.

"Good morning," Dr. Carson greeted his patient, who sat nervously on the end of the paper-covered exam table, dressed in a cloth hospital gown. His linen service bill was ridiculously high. Again and again, his CPA suggested he could cut overhead in his practice by going to the cheaper paper gowns, but it wasn't a concession Edgar was willing to make. His father, a GP here in Stephen Kill for fifty years, had used cloth gowns until his dying day—on the 18th hole at the country club—and he would too.

"I hope you didn't have to wait too long." Edgar moved to the sink on the far wall and pumped the soap dispenser.

"It's quite all right," the patient said, hands folded, gaze fixed awkwardly straight ahead. "I didn't wait long."

"Been busy all week." Edgar washed his hands thoroughly under warm running water. "You'd think summer would be a slow time, no flu, no colds, but this time of year we've got your allergies, your bug bites, your sunburn." He grabbed a paper towel and turned to face his patient, smiling. "Honestly, I think we're busier."

He tossed the damp paper towel into the trash can and reached for the medical record his nurse Irma Jean had left on the counter beside the sink. Irma Jean was closer to retirement than sixty-three-year-old Edgar, but she still ran a tight ship, and there were certain procedures she'd instilled in him years ago. Medical records went on the counter beside the sink in each examining room. Not in a nice plastic holder on the door, not on the wall inside the room, not even on the perfectly nice foldout desks he'd had added to the rooms a few years ago. He picked up the new, black ballpoint pen Irma Jean always left for him with each record in each room. Irma Jean expected him to make accurate notations in the charts, and it was always in black ballpoint pen, never in blue, and God forbid, never with one of those fancy roller-ball pens he admired in the drugstore.

Edgar grabbed his rolling stool from under the desk, sat on it, pulling his white lab coat over his expanding middle, and rolled toward the end of the exam table. He liked to sit down during an exam, when he could, seating himself below the patients sitting nervously on the end of the table. It seemed to help put them at ease. He glanced at the sentence under "Complaint" that Irma Jean had noted when the patient called to make the appointment. It was a little vague.

"So, can you tell me a little bit about this trouble sleeping?" he asked with a warm smile. Edgar loved what he did. He loved the people of Stephen Kill, and he despised the thought that any one of them could be sick or hurting physically or mentally.

"I . . . I just can't sleep." Fingers intertwined on the patient's lap. "Bad dreams."

"I see." Edgar nodded. "Insomnia is a relatively common phenomenon these days. We're all under more stress than we once were. Are you under any stress?"

"Not really. Not any more than usual."

Edgar rested the medical record on his lap, giving the patient his complete attention. "Any other changes you've noticed? Appetite? Bowels? Any feelings of sadness?"

"No, well . . . it's as if time doesn't seem to be what it once was."

Edgar touched the frame of his glasses, pushing them back up on the bridge of his nose, thinking that was an odd statement. "What do you mean by that?"

More nervous finger movement. "I . . . almost feel as if I'm losing blocks of time. I know I am."

"Now, is this at night?"

"Yes." The voice was quiet. Almost ethereal.

Edgar felt the hair prickle on the back of his neck. Suddenly, he felt . . . uncomfortable. "You mean, you're falling asleep. Losing hours that way."

A shake of the head.

"I'm sorry." Edgar picked up the black ballpoint pen. "Could you explain a little further?"

"Some nights, I try not to sleep. The nightmares." The patient did not meet Edgar's gaze. "But the hours disappear anyway. In the morning, I realize I've been out of bed, only I don't remember getting out of bed."

"Sleepwalking. How interesting." Edgar made a notation. "Have you sleepwalked in the past?"

Head shake.

"Maybe even as a child?"

"Not that I know of. But . . . but this is more than sleepwalking. I . . . I think I'm doing things."

Edgar paused, trying to decide what question to ask next. How to best assess the patient's concern. "What about during the day? Have you noticed anything different during the day?"

"I lose time then too." The patient looked up apprehensively. "Only not as often."

Edgar studied the patient's troubled face for a moment and then pushed his stool over to the desk, walked his way back to the examining table, and reached into his lab coat pocket for his stethoscope. "Well, I'm sure we can get to the bottom of this in no time. Let's check you over and then we'll talk about our options, how does that sound?"

"I just want it to go away."

Standing, Edgar warmed the end of his stethoscope in the palm of his hand. "Want what to go away?"

"The voice."

CHAPTER 21

Noah sat on the front porch in his father's rocking chair, a glass of iced tea left untouched on the table beside him. He watched Mattie as the man slowly pulled a red wagon around the raised beds of the garden. Mallory sat inside the wagon, dressed in a bathing suit, a tutu, and a red felt cowboy hat, "steering" her horse and buggy with a jump rope she had looped through Mattie's belt.

Noah had worked only half a day today, but he was exhausted. Too much to think about. Not enough sleep. He was still carrying the fertility clinic's card in his back pocket. Five days and he hadn't found the right time to ask Rachel about it.

It hadn't occurred to him before he found the folder that Mallory might have been conceived any other way than the way most babies were conceived. The idea that she had come from a sperm donor appealed to him. If Mallory was the result of artificial insemination, he could still hold on to the unrealistic notion that Rachel had not been with another man these last five years. But the possibility also angered him. Why didn't she just tell him how Mallory was conceived if it had been a fertility clinic? Why let him walk around town looking into the face of every eligible man, wondering if he resembled Mallory? Wondering if he was Mallory's father.

Noah heard the phone ring inside the house, followed by Rachel's melodious voice. She had been upstairs showering, but she must have come down. She had a date tonight with the dentist, Jeremy Cary, but that was about all he could get out of Rachel. Not that it was any of his business.

The porch door opened and Noah heard Rachel's voice clearly. "No, I understand, Amanda. Your mom's right. If you have a fever, you should stay home." She paused. "Not a problem. Thanks for calling, and please wear your sunscreen next time you go to the beach, OK?"

Noah heard Rachel's footsteps, and she appeared around the corner of the porch. "Mal—" she started to call. "Oh, there she is." She halted, phone in her hand.

"There she is," Noah repeated, taking a quick look at the short khaki skirt, lavender T-shirt, and heeled sandals Rachel was wearing. She looked ten years younger in the outfit and about as good as he had ever seen her. With some women, age and childbirth wore them down, but it seemed as though his Rachel only got prettier as the years went by.

Noah turned back to watch Mattie and Mallory. "I think it's a horse and buggy."

"Tutu goes nicely."

"As do the fuzzy purple bedroom slippers," Noah piped in.

Rachel smiled and then looked down at the phone.

"What's up?" he asked. "Babysitter sick?"

"Went to the beach with some friends and apparently attempted to get sun poisoning."

He grimaced. "Ouch."

"Yeah. So, I guess I spent all this time getting dolled up for nothing. I'll have to cancel with Jeremy."

He glanced at her, then back at Mallory. "Why don't you just let me keep an eye on them?" As soon as the words were out of his mouth, he wished he could take them back. Was he crazy, making it easier for Rachel to go out on a date? He didn't want her dating Dr. Jeremy Cary. He didn't want her dating anyone.

"I don't know," she hemmed, still cradling the phone.

"Come on. I don't know why you got a babysitter to begin with," he continued with his good-guy shtick. "I'll be here anyway. It's not like I can go anywhere."

She twisted her mouth. She was wearing a sheer pink lipstick. "It's kind of weird, isn't it? You babysitting Mallory while I go out on a date?"

"What's not weird about us these days, Rache?"

She chuckled, seeming to catch his drift. She, too, had been noticing the subtle changes in their relationship. "You have a point there."

"Go on, go out with the dentist. Just don't have too good a time."

"OK." She smiled. "Thanks."

He looked away, not fully trusting himself not to betray his true feelings. He watched as Mattie pulled the wagon around the apple tree. "No problem."

"Say, what did Dr. Carson have to say when he called earlier?"

He shrugged, still not looking at her. "Not much. I need to go over to Beebe and get a CAT scan and some other equally ridiculously priced tests."

"So he didn't seem too concerned?" She moved to lean on the porch rail, standing directly in front of him, blocking his view of Mattie and Mallory.

"No, not really. But you know how he is—if you walked in with your head tucked under your arm, he'd be calm. Said it was nothing to worry about." He hesitated. "What did you tell him? Your appointment was before mine yesterday."

She shrugged. "I didn't tell him anything about you. Don't be so paranoid. He had a cancellation and I thought I'd save myself a trip if he could see both of us in the same day. I needed new allergy medicine."

He wasn't sure he believed her, but he had no evidence to support the suspicion. It was just that Dr. Carson had looked at him oddly a couple of times during the exam. He wondered what Rachel had seen the doctor about if it wasn't to discuss him, but didn't know how to justify asking her.

Out of the corner of his eye, Noah caught a glimpse of Mallory's blond ponytail, bobbing higher on the horizon than it should have been. He got to his feet to get a better look. "Mal! No standing in the—"

Just as Noah spoke, Mattie lunged forward, pulling the wagon, and Mallory, standing up and reaching for a tiny green apple, was hurled backward off the end, her red cowboy hat flying off her head.

Noah pressed his hands to the porch railing and vaulted over it, landing in the grass on the far side of an old rhododendron bush.

Mallory squealed in pain as she hit the ground.

"It's OK," Noah assured her, sprinting across lawn grass, reaching her a moment later. He went down on his knee, wrapping his arms around her. It was only a minor tumble, nothing serious, but he was terrified of losing her. Maybe it was the death of his sons, or the murders in town, or how far he had fallen in life, he didn't know. All he knew was that this little girl, this family, was his world now.

Mattie just stood there, wagon handle still in his hand, staring with wide, dark eyes.

"It's OK, sweetie," Noah soothed, lifting Mallory out of the grass. "What hurts?"

"My head," she cried, laying her hand on the back of her head.

Noah found an egg rising quickly.

"What are you doing out here?" Rachel asked, squatting beside them, phone still in her hand. Her voice was calm, but she'd come running. "There's no diving into the grass, Mal, only into pools."

Noah brushed a stray lock of blond hair out of her eyes. "I give you an 8.5 for that backward somersault, though, Missy."

Mallory laughed, then grimaced, bringing her hand to her head again. "Owww! It hurts."

The sound of tires in the driveway resonated in the still twilight air.

"Shoot. He's early." Rachel stood.

"It's OK. Go. She'll be fine." Noah stood, Mallory still in his arms. A bag of frozen peas on your head, a Popsicle in your tummy, and you'll be all better, won't you?"

"Grape. I want grape."

Rachel looked at the black BMW pulling up behind the garage and then back at Mallory.

"Go," Noah insisted. "It's just a bump."

Jeremy the dentist got out of his car. Waved. He was dressed in khaki pants and a peach-colored polo shirt, making Noah feel self-conscious in his dirty jeans and T-shirt.

"Go," Noah insisted. "We'll be fine." He shifted Mallory onto his hip so she could sit up. She'd already stopped crying. "Won't we, Princess Buttercup?"

"*We'wwll* be fine," Mallory mimicked, holding on to Noah's shoulder.

"I won't be late." Rachel leaned to kiss Mallory, and Noah caught a faint hint of her perfume. It was light, airy, fruity rather than floral. It suited her.

"Stay out as late as you want." He took the phone from her hand and watched her hurry across the grass.

"Rachel." The dentist's face lit up and he flashed teeth that were entirely too white not to be man-made.

Noah turned away. "Let's get those peas on this head." He started for the porch. "You coming, Mattie? Grape Popsicles," he called over his shoulder.

It wasn't until Noah had gotten Mallory settled into the easy chair in the living room, TV on, bag of peas on the back of her head, and Popsicle in her hand that he realized Mattie hadn't come inside. He set the remote control on the arm of the chair and readjusted the kitchen towel he'd tucked into the neckline of her Little Mermaid bathing suit. "I'm just going to run out and check on Mattie, OK?"

She craned her neck so she could see the TV screen, not in the least bit interested in where he was going.

He covered her hand with his, raising the bag of peas from where she had let it fall to her neck to the blue-green knot appearing on the back of her head below her ponytail. "Be right back."

Outside, the light was beginning to fade quickly. Fat, iridescent green june bugs buzzed, hovering over the grass. Gazing in the yard for any sign of Mattie, Noah walked over to the yellow water sprinkler, moved it ten feet down along the flower bed next to the house, and then walked around to turn on the faucet.

Water sprayed in a semicircle arc, falling on the new zinnia seedlings he and Mallory had planted two weeks ago. "Mattie?" he called, walking around the front of the house, to the garden side.

The wagon sat where they'd left it. He walked over to pick up out of the grass the jump rope that Mallory had been using for reins and dropped it into the wagon. He added the red cowboy hat, forgotten in the commotion. "Mattie? You here?" He grabbed the handle of the wagon and pulled it around to the garage. The weather channel was calling for possible thunderstorms this evening.

He opened the side door and pulled the wagon into the semidarkness of the garage. Just as he was turning to go, he halted, gazing back over his shoulder. The garage was quiet and smelled faintly of gasoline and mouse droppings. He felt like someone was there, though. "Mattie?" he called again.

He saw a flash of motion out of the corner of his eye and turned to the Volvo parked in the single bay. The doors were closed, no interior lights shone inside, and no one appeared to be in the car, but that was the direction of the movement he knew he had seen.

Noah walked around to the passenger side of the front seat and opened the door. Mattie laid face down on the seat, obviously trying to hide, the keys to the car in his hand. Noah could have sworn he'd seen them earlier in the day on the kitchen counter.

"Mattie, what's going on, buddy?" He drew back to give him a little space.

Noah waited for a minute and then hooked his thumb over his shoulder. "Come on, out of the car."

Mattie looked up at Noah and then, with obvious reluctance, crawled across the seat and out of the car. Noah waited until Mattie closed the door and then he put out his hand.

"Let's return those keys to the kitchen before both of us get into trouble, OK?"

Mattie stared at his feet. He knew what he'd done was wrong.

"Come on," Noah said. "I need to go inside. You come too. We'll talk."

Head hung, Mattie followed Noah obediently into the house. In the kitchen, Noah dropped the keys on the counter where Rachel had left them and pointed to the kitchen table. "Sit. I'll make popcorn."

Noah turned his back to Mattie and squatted to fish the heavy aluminum pot out from under the counter. He knew Rachel bought microwave popcorn, but he still liked making it the old-fashioned way, the way he'd done it as a kid with his parents. "You've got to tell me what's going on, buddy. You know you're not allowed to drive the car. Just like me." He stood, pot and companion lid in hand. "Either of us gets caught driving Rachel's car and we are in serious trouble."

He put the pot on the stove and walked to the pantry, coming out with a bag of popcorn and a plastic bottle of vegetable oil. "So why were you trying to take off? Not because Mallory took that little tumble, right?"

Mattie had pulled the chair up to the table and sat, meaty hands palms down. He didn't meet Noah's gaze.

Noah groaned inwardly in frustration. He wondered if he needed to take Mattie to see a psychologist, a psychiatrist, someone. Obviously something was going on here. Mattie's behavior was becoming more and more erratic . . . unpredictable. If Noah couldn't reach him, maybe someone with more experience dealing with adults like Mattie could help.

"Because that wasn't your fault, you know. It was just an accident. If anyone's at fault, it's Mallory, because she knows better than to stand up in the wagon."

"Wasn't my fault," Mallory said, entering the kitchen. She deposited her wooden Popsicle stick in the trash can and walked to the refrigerator, opening the freezer side. "It was an accident. Accidents happen."

"Yes, it was an accident, but you need to be more careful." Noah poured a little oil into the pan and lit the burner beneath it.

Outside, Chester began to bark. It was a strange bark, though, as if someone was there. Except Noah had not heard a car in the driveway. "What's up with him?"

"What's up with him?" Mallory repeated, depositing the bag of peas in the freezer and walking to the kitchen table. She placed her elbows on the table, her chin to her hand, and looked up at Mattie. "What's up?"

Chester continued to bark.

"Stay away from the stove," Noah warned with a finger, cutting the flame off beneath the pot. "Both of you." He stepped outside on the porch, and the screen door slapped behind him. It was almost dark, and though he could still hear Chester, he couldn't see him. "Chester, here boy," he called, walking down the porch steps.

Oyster shells crunched under his sneakers as he walked down the driveway. The security lamp in the barnyard was just beginning to come on, emitting a soft, luminescent green glow but not yet providing light. It sounded like Chester was near the largest of the outbuildings, the barn where Mattie made his home.

"Chester, come on boy!" He spotted the dog. The dog spotted him, but instead of loping in Noah's direction, he ducked into the barn. Mattie must have left the door open, which in itself was odd. Mattie was a creature of habit. He wore the same clothing each and every day. He ate his meat before he ever ate anything else on his plate. He closed doors he opened.

"Chester," Noah called, annoyed now. "What are you doing, dog? Have you lost your mind?" He opened the door and stepped into the dark barn. "You come when I call, you hear me?"

Chester stood three feet away, between two old milk staunches. He was staring into the darkness, deeper in the barn. Suddenly uncomfortable, Noah halted. "What's up, boy?" he said softly.

The dog surprised him with a rumble deep in his throat, the closest thing Noah had heard to a growl in the old retriever since his return home.

"Something there, boy?" Noah hesitated, then took a step back, reaching for the light switch. His hand hit a cobweb, and he resisted the urge to pull back. He felt along the wall, his fingers finding the cold plate of the industrial switch box. He flipped the switch, and two light bulbs suspended from wires from the ceiling came on. There were at least three more toward the back of the barn, but they were apparently all burned out.

Noah studied the shadowed interior of the barn for a moment. He couldn't see anything or anyone that didn't belong there, just the piles of stuff that really needed to be sorted. "See, nobody's here. Come on, Chester." He slapped his thigh. "You chasing cats again? I told you that was bad for your health, a dog as old as you are and already missing one leg."

The dog finally turned to Noah.

"That's right, come on boy." Still feeling a little unnerved, even with the lights on, Noah stepped out the door, flipping off the switch as he went. Chester followed in his awkward gait.

"Good boy. That's right." It wasn't until Noah nearly reached the porch that he glanced back at the barn. There's nothing there. So why did he feel like there was?

Shaking off the foolishness, he crossed the porch and entered the kitchen, Chester following in his wake. "OK. Let's make some popcorn." Noah clapped his hands together.

Mallory was still standing beside Mattie, who stared straight ahead at the basket of napkins and vase of wild flowers in the center of the table.

"Mattie knows it wasn't his *fauwlt* I *fawled*," Mallory announced.

Noah turned the flame on under the pot again. "He knows it's not his *fault* you *fell*?" he repeated, unobtrusively correcting her grammar. "That right? How do you know?"

"He *towld* me," she said matter-of-factly.

"Told," Noah repeated, putting the emphasis on the *l*. "Say it."

"*Tooold*," she repeated.

"Excellent." He swirled the oil around in the pot, glancing back at her. "And he told you this out loud, like with words."

She crossed her arms over her chest stubbornly. "He *tolllled* me."

Smiling to himself, Noah reached for the bag of popcorn kernels and poured some into the pot. "Did he tell you why he had the keys to your mother's car?"

"He says he was afraid. He was going to drive away."

Noah still didn't know if he believed Mattie told Mallory anything, but the possibility that he might be communicating with her, communicating this kind of information, was alarming. "Mattie knows he's not allowed to take the car. It would be dangerous. What's he afraid of?"

She groaned with exasperation as only a four-year-old could. "I *told* you before. He doesn't know." She spoke each word slowly as if Noah might better understand her that way.

"But something is scaring him."

She nodded. "Bad dreams at night. Bad dreams in the day sometimes. I don't have bad dreams," she continued, now in a singsong voice. "Because I have my pwastic sword under my bed, and if any bad dreams come, it cuts them up."

"That's nice, sugar bear." He slid the pan back and forth across the burner, securing the lid with his other hand, and was rewarded with the first pop. "Can you tell me anything else about what Mattie's afraid of?"

"Um-hmmm." She was walking leisurely around the table now, dragging her hand. When she reached Mattie, she drew her hand across his T-shirt, reconnecting with the table when she reached the other side.

"And?" Noah prodded.

"And what?" Mallory started around the table again. She'd removed her tutu but was still wearing the green Little Mermaid bathing suit and the purple fuzzy slippers.

"And what else is Mattie afraid of?" Noah took care to show no impatience in his voice. For Mallory, this was all matter-of-fact, and he knew he needed to keep it that way too. Kids had a way of knowing when adults were getting anxious, and that was the time they often chose to clam up.

She stopped beside Mattie and put her small arm around his broad back. "He's afraid of the voice too."

"Whose voice?"

"He doesn't know." She leaned over to look at him. "You don't know, do you, Mattie?" she crooned as if he were a small child or one of her baby dolls.

The popcorn had begun to pop in earnest now, and Noah had to raise his voice to be heard over the din. "How about you? Do you hear the voice?" he asked, not even sure why he would ask such a thing.

"No, but Mattie says he *wiwll* protect me from it if it comes, won't you, Mattie?" She peered into his face. "Mattie says he wiwll kiwll anybody with a sword that tries to hurt me."

CHAPTER 22

Snowden turned the block, still jogging at a decent pace, though he'd been running almost an hour. It felt good to be outside, even if it was ten o'clock at night and the sun had long set. The temperature had cooled to seventy degrees, and though it was muggy, there was a slight breeze that invigorated his sweaty body. It felt good to push himself physically, giving his mind release.

He'd decided to take an unplanned run after arriving home following a quick stop at his mother's house. Her arthritis was bothering her again and he was worried about her. She seemed frailer than usual. But after the typical conversation he usually shared with her, he arrived home antsy and unable to concentrate on the fat file he needed to look over. This "sin killer" case, as he'd begun calling it in his mind, was beginning to get to him. He kept going over the details again and again; he'd even spoken with an FBI agent in D.C. today who was also a forensic psychologist, hoping for some insight. He just felt as if he was missing something when he read the facts.

Snowden needed to get into the killer's head, but he didn't

know how. All he saw when he looked at the file were the gory photos, the facts. He didn't see the man, and his gut feeling told him he needed to see the man to find the man.

Snowden turned the corner, intending to jog up this next block and then loop back home, but as he passed under a streetlamp, he realized he'd turned onto a different street than usual. In fact, he'd overshot his usual path by three blocks. This was a newer section of town, where an apartment building and a cul-de-sac of townhouses had been built in the last two years. Delilah lived on this street.

He hadn't consciously come this way on purpose. Had he subconsciously?

He found himself thinking entirely too often of Sergeant Delilah Swift these days, time he needed to be spending on trying to figure out who the hell was murdering Stephen Kill citizens. But he couldn't get her out of his head sometimes; the blond hair, the clear brown eyes, the sweet southern drawl that could turn authoritative at the drop of a pin. He liked the way she worked, and he liked to watch her work. She knew procedures and she followed them, but she had a way of picking up nuances, details not obvious to most cops. She knew people, understood what made them tick, and she used her knowledge to make herself a better cop.

Snowden considered turning around in the middle of the street and heading for home. He needed to get a shower, grab something to eat, and do a little reading before bed. He'd wasted half his day at city hall today and intended to be in the office early tomorrow, even though it was Saturday.

But he didn't turn around. Instead, he jogged into the cul-de-sac. The townhouses were nice, moderately priced, attractive, and seemed to be built well. On the small, well-kept front lawns he saw a plastic Big Wheel trike, an abandoned basketball, a couple of lawn chairs. Lights glowed behind pulled draperies and mini-blinds. Someone passed him going the opposite way, walking a cocker spaniel. "Evening," the middle-aged man greeted.

Snowden recognized him as one of the men on the volunteer fire squadron. "Evening, Mr. Kemp."

"Long way from home, Chief," he said as he passed Snowden.

"Nothing like a change of scenery," Snowden panted.

Mr. Kemp walked on and Snowden slowed his pace, suddenly feeling winded. He gazed at the townhouses he passed. He didn't know which one Delilah lived in. He followed the sidewalk, making the turn at the end of the cul-de-sac, headed out again.

That was when he saw her. She was just a silhouette on a dark front porch that was really no more than a stoop with a railing. She was dressed in shorts and a T-shirt, leaning over the black wrought iron rail, a cigarette glowing in the dark.

He couldn't just jog by.

"Eve-ning, Chief," she said in that accent of hers that could be smooth as silk.

"Delilah." He halted and walked in a circle on the sidewalk in front of her house.

She drew slowly on the cigarette. "You don't usually run in this direction."

He shrugged, still walking in tight circles, letting his heart rate lower slowly. "Something different."

"Late to be jogging, but you can't sleep anyway, can you?"

He halted in front of her, leaning forward, hands pressed just above his knees. "I didn't know you smoked."

"I don't, so don't tell my mama." She leaned over and ground the cigarette butt on the brick step. "I bummed it off my neighbor. Figured it was better than the fifth of Jack Daniels I was contemplating earlier."

He laughed.

"You want to come in, have a glass of water?"

"I should probably get home." Snowden gazed down the street. Mr. Kemp had disappeared. He doubted anyone would see him go inside.

"Come on, Snowden. You're already here. You've already

seen me in my underwear, you might as well come in." As she reached for the door handle she tugged on the hem of her shorts. "Well, maybe not my underwear, but my brother's. Boxer shorts. Good for sleeping."

Snowden followed her inside. The front door opened into a small foyer where an antique side table stood, an old wavy-glassed mirror hanging over it. To the left was a staircase leading up. She led him down the short hall, lined with family photographs. To the left lay a dimly lit living room, sparsely furnished. To the right, a brightly lit eat-in kitchen, dominated by another antique table, this one a dining table big enough to easily seat eight. On it lay stacks of folders, legal pads, and newspaper clippings as well as several assorted tools such as machetes and saws.

"Plan on clearing the farm or opening a tool store?" he asked, looking down at the table.

She went to a cupboard and opened it to reveal six glasses, all neatly lined up. She took one and carried it to the refrigerator, filling it with ice and then water from the automatic dispenser on the door.

He picked up one of the tools, the oldest of the collection. It had a stained wooden handle and a thin, curved blade.

"Scythe," she said. "My granddaddy called it a sling-blade. He used it to keep the woods from encroaching on his fields."

"Where'd you get it?"

"I ran into old man Pickering at the hardware store. He overheard my conversation with Leroy, who works the counter. He insisted on running out to his farm, bringing it back in. He said if he was to kill a man, a scythe would do it."

"Wrong shape to cut off a man's hands," Snowden said, running a finger over the curved, rusty blade. He set it back on the table.

She pushed the glass of water into his hand. "I know. But he wanted to help out, and I thought it wouldn't hurt to have a look. Compare different types of blades." She rested one hand on her hip, surveying her collection.

In the light, he could see that she was, indeed, wearing a pair of men's boxer shorts. Striped, white and green. Her T-shirt was a men's V-neck undershirt, white and transparent. Through the fabric he couldn't help but see her small, firm breasts, the dark areoles showing through.

His mouth felt dry and he concentrated on swallowing a mouthful of cold water. "You've been busy. I don't even recognize all these things. What are they?"

One by one she picked them up. Some were brand new, still with price tags, others had obviously been used a long time. "What we've got here, Snowden, are implements meant to trim, prune, chop, split, blaze trails, brush out lines, and clear campsites," she said with great authority. "We've got your axe, your hatchet, your pruning saw and shears, a pruning knife"—she tapped a long-bladed, short-handled knife he'd never seen before—"your bow saw and your lopper. But here"—she picked up the last tool on the table—"here we've got your common machete."

He watched her slice the air with it. This one, with two-inch-wide, thin blade and molded, blond wood handle still had a price tag on it, as well as a cardboard sheath on the blade to prevent injury. "If I were a woman looking to lop off a man's hands, I think I'd use this nice machete." It made a swishing sound as she sliced the air again.

"You'd be a pretty sick woman."

She smiled. "Exactly." She set it down, crossing her arms over her breasts, not seeming in the least bit uncomfortable to be standing with him in her kitchen, only half dressed. "Guess what I found out at Burton's today? They have a brand spankin' new computer system they're using to track inventory, what comes in, what goes out."

Snowden finished the glass of water and walked it to the sink. "Do they know who buys what?"

"Darned straight they do." She grinned. "Been eleven sales of this kind of implement in the last two months, which is when they started keeping track. I crossed off any saws because the wound was obviously sliced rather than sawed, which left me with only five."

"The killer could have had one of these things lying around. We don't know that he bought the weapon, or if he did, that he bought it around here."

She frowned. "I know that, Snowden, but we have to start somewhere. Do you have any idea how many times a crime is solved by tracking down who bought a pistol, or rope, or the rat poison? Don't you ever watch true crime TV?"

"I try not to," he said with a teasing, superior manner. "So who bought something they could use to chop off a man's hands?"

She grabbed a legal pad off the top of a pile of files on her desk. "I'm hungry. You want some ice cream?" She walked out of the dining area, back into the kitchen area, bare feet padding on the clean tile floor.

"No, I don't want any ice cream, Delilah. I want to know who's on that list."

She opened the freezer, tucking the notepad under her arm. "I've got Ben & Jerry's Cherry Garcia," she sang.

If Snowden had to choose his favorite ice cream, it would have been Cherry Garcia. "And I took you for a Phish Food kind of girl," he quipped.

She removed the cardboard pint and set it on the counter, pulling the legal pad out from under her arm. "Once I crossed off the serrated-edged saws and any type of shears, I was left with only four names. One bought an axe, two bought hatchets, and one a machete."

"I thought the ME said the wound was caused by something with a narrow blade. Wouldn't an axe show chop marks in the table?"

She set the legal pad on the counter and retrieved two bowls from the cupboard over her head. "Blasted table was old-school Formica. Probably came from the parents' house. Had to be at least forty years old. There were nicks on it, but nothing definitive." From a drawer, she fished out an ice cream scoop.

Snowden walked into the kitchen area but resisted leaning over the counter to read her chicken scratch. "OK, you've got my rapt attention."

She didn't need the piece of paper to recite the names. As she scooped ice cream out of the cardboard container into the delicate glass bowls, she spoke softly. "Joshua Troyer bought an axe."

"The man uses wood to heat his home."

"Dr. Cary picked up a hatchet two weeks ago. Actually bought it from Mr. Newton, who works there part-time." She dropped a scoop of ice cream into a bowl.

"Cary bought an old house on the end of Sycamore. Backyard is overgrown. It's going to take more than a hatchet to clear."

"Cora Watkins bought a hatchet too."

"What would she be doing with a hatchet?" Snowden wondered aloud.

"I thought the same thing." She put the ice cream container back in the refrigerator and pointed. "Spoons in that drawer. Come on in the living room and sit down." She picked up her notepad and the bowls of ice cream.

He grabbed two spoons from the immaculate drawer, neatly stacked with eating utensils. "I can't imagine Cora lifting anything heavier than a loaf of pumpkin bread." He followed her into the living room.

She sat down on the end of a small, paisley print couch, and setting everything on an old piano bench that served as an end table, she turned on a lamp.

Snowden stood in the entryway to the living room, spoon in each hand.

"Come on, sit down." She reached for the ice cream bowls.

"Delilah, I don't want to sit on your nice couch. I'm all

sweaty." And the couch was small. She'd be sitting beside him, close enough to touch. "I probably stink."

She laughed. "Snowden, I grew up with six brothers, remember? There's no way in heck you smell half as bad as six Swift brothers come back from fishin' on the lake on a hot August day."

He glanced at the couch that looked very expensive. She had incredible taste for a woman as young as she was. The old polished furniture, with nothing quite matching, was striking against the blond hardwood floor, the faded Oriental carpet, and the rich, dark design of the couch.

"Sit," she ordered.

Snowden sat, passing her a spoon.

"You'll never guess who bought the machete," she said, drawing her shapely legs up under and diving into the bowl of cherry vanilla ice cream.

He slipped a spoonful into his mouth, and it was cold and sweet. "I'm listening."

She licked her spoon, smiling provocatively. "Name on the account is Gibson."

"Noah Gibson." He halted his spoon midair, lowering it to the bowl. "You've got to be kidding."

She bit down on her lower lip. "Not Noah, but Rachel."

"Jesus H. Christ," he whispered, looking away. *Rachel a killer?* Impossible. An accessory to murder? Even that idea seemed far-fetched. When he realized he'd cursed aloud, he turned to Delilah. "I apologize. Excuse my language."

She laughed, pushing another spoonful of ice cream into her mouth. "I know it's supposed to be Jesus Holy Christ, but in my family, the H. stands for Henry. Old Henry was my daddy's daddy and a real son of a bitch, so the stories go."

He couldn't resist returning her smile. She was so beautiful—sitting on this couch in her brother's underwear, not wearing a stitch of makeup, legs tucked under her, eating ice cream—that Snowden, for the first time in as long as he could remember, actually wished he had a woman to jog home to tonight. Sitting here with his sergeant, who he had no business fraternizing with, made him realize how damned lonely he was.

He glanced away, his gaze settling on a large upholstered chair nestled in the shadows of the far side of the room. It was a big, cozy, comfy chair with a matching hassock, the kind men had once slept in on Sunday afternoons in the days before La-Z-Boys. He imagined Delilah curled in the chair in her boxers and T-shirt, eating ice cream, pouring over the files she had constructed on the case.

"So what do you think?" he asked quietly, setting his bowl on the hardwood floor beside the couch.

"This is about sin, Snowden, I know it is." She moved closer to him on the couch, drawing him in as if telling a story. Her voice was soft but compelling. "It's about punishment for sin, real or imagined. It's about religion. Miss Watkins and the Gibsons all have close ties to the church. To St. Paul's."

"Which takes us back to Noah Gibson knowing about sins his parishioners committed," Snowden said. It still pissed him off that Noah, in the name of so-called principle, refused to give information that could help solve the crimes. That certainly made him a suspect in Snowden's book. Snowden told himself that the fact that he had dated Noah's ex-wife and been disappointed that she still had a thing for Noah in no way came into play. At least he hoped it didn't.

"The priest who listened to confessions, the fallen priest who went to prison for his sins, is too easy," she whispered, reaching out to rest her hand on his. "We're barking in the wrong *holler*. Who else in that church would know about the sins people in this town have committed?"

"No one. Confessions are private," he answered softly, making no attempt to remove her hand from his. It seemed so small, so pale, resting on his large, black hand. Seeing it there made him want to cover it with his other hand, bring it to his lips.

"But they're not, Snowden." She patted his hand. "Think

about it. You go to the church to talk with your minister or priest. People in the town see you pull into the parking lot in your car. People at choir practice see you slipping out of the priest's office. The church secretary enters your appointments in the priest's book. Shoot, the janitor lingers outside a closed door a moment too long, overhearing a conversation."

Snowden sat back on the couch, his hand sliding out from under hers. "That takes you back to the idea that anyone in this town could have killed those people."

"Yes and no."

"How so?"

"We do have some possible suspects. Some leads. All I'm saying is that we keep our minds open. Right now, the priest looks so obvious that it can't be him."

"Or it is because he's right under our noses. It fits perfectly. He went to jail for a sin he committed, Delilah. Johnny and Pam weren't punished for their sins. Apparently neither was Skeeter. Maybe he's seeing that they're punished for what they did, as he was punished."

"Maybe. But we can't decide it's him just because you want it to be him."

"I don't want it to be him," Snowden defended.

"Sure you do. You think he should have spent the rest of his life in prison for what he did. He doesn't deserve to return home, go back to his pretty wife."

"I keep my personal feelings to myself when I'm conducting an investigation."

"I know you do." She sat back, pointing a finger at him. "Which is exactly why first thing next week, I want to talk to everyone who bought one of these tools from Burton's, including Rachel Gibson. Just a friendly visit. I also need to find out why the killer thought Skeeter was a thief. When I tried to address the subject with his parents, something strange was going on there. It seemed like Mrs. Newton wanted to say something, but not in front of her husband." She shook her head. "I could be wrong. Grief does funny things to people, but I think if I can catch her alone, she might have some more information for us." She looked up at him. "So what do you think?"

"Good a direction as any to head." He rose from the couch. "Maybe I'll ride with you Monday."

"That would be great." She popped off the couch. "I mean, sure." She pressed her hands to the small of her back, seeming a little flustered. "That might be a good idea, you know, just in case Noah Gibson comes after me with a machete or Miss Cora tries to beat me over the head with a loaf of zucchini bread."

"So I'll see you at the station Monday morning." He leaned over to pick up his bowl. "And not before, Sergeant. You're already working too many hours."

"I don't need to be paid the overtime."

"What you need is rest and time away from this. Monday morning will come soon enough."

"All right, fine." She took the bowl from his hand.

He headed for the door. "Thanks for the ice cream."

"Any time."

He opened the door, stepped out into the humid night, but his hand still rested on the doorknob.

"I'm glad you came by, Snowden, even if you didn't do it on purpose." She held the dirty bowl in her hands. "I mean, I know you didn't but—"

"It's OK," Snowden said, half smiling. "I know what you mean. I don't know why I came this way, but I'm glad I did."

"See you Monday, then." She rested her hand on the doorknob he'd just vacated. "And we're off our even/odd days. You have to buy the coffee."

He glanced back at her over his shoulder as he walked away and was glad the porch light was out. Glad she couldn't see the dumb look on his face and know how ridiculously smitten he was with her.

*   *   *

Noah saw the headlights through the window over the kitchen sink. He'd been sitting at the table in a pair of plaid cotton sleep pants, using the excuse that he was waiting for the wash to be done rather than waiting up for Rachel. They were divorced. She had a right to go see the latest Brad Pitt movie with whomever she wanted to see it with.

He debated whether or not he and Chester should hightail it to bed before Rachel walked in the house. But the dryer was still running and he hated to leave the load of clothes for her to fold herself when he'd started the load in the first place.

The BMW stopped in the driveway, and he heard a car door open and then close. He doubted there had even been time for even a quick good night kiss. He smiled to himself, reaching for his glass of iced tea.

Rachel came up the steps, across the porch, and in the front door. The BMW turned around and headed back down the driveway.

"Hey," she said when she saw him sitting at the kitchen table. She didn't seem particularly surprised he was there. "You didn't have to wait up for me."

"I know. I wasn't really. Dryer is still going." He hooked his thumb in the direction of the laundry room. "I thought I'd hang the shirts before I went to bed. Mallory's swimsuit is in there too. Grape Popsicle. I know she'll want it tomorrow."

"That's nice. Thanks." She smiled, walking to the refrigerator. As she went, she stood on one foot and then the other, removing her sandals. "Ah. That's better." She dropped them on the floor and opened the refrigerator, grabbing a bottle of water.

"So, you have a nice evening?" Noah kept his tone light.

"Yeah, it was fine." Leaning against the refrigerator, she pushed silky hair from her eyes and tipped back the water bottle.

"How was the movie?"

"We ended up skipping it." She lifted one shoulder and let it fall. "Had dinner. Went for a walk on the boardwalk."

He nodded.

"How's Mal's head?"

"Fine. Just a bump. Not even a headache when she went to bed." He swirled what was left of his iced tea in the bottom of his glass. "I, uh . . . had a little thing with Mattie tonight."

She drew the bottle away from her mouth. "A little thing?"

"I'm sure it's nothing." He thought for a moment. "I hope it's not anything." He turned in his chair to face her. "After you left, I came inside with Mallory. Got her settled. Mattie never came in so I went back out to find him, and he was hiding in the front seat of your car in the garage."

She wrinkled the end of her freckled nose and took another sip of water. "Odd place to hide."

"Rache, he had your keys."

This time she lowered the water bottle to her side. "You're kidding me. Had he started the car?"

"I don't think so."

"Why would he take my keys? He doesn't know how to drive . . . does he?" She walked to the table, taking the chair across from him. She pressed her hand to her mouth. "Oh, Noah, that morning the car had been moved. I accused you of—"

"It's OK. Logical conclusion. As for Mattie actually driving the car, I doubt he can. I certainly never taught him."

"I certainly didn't either."

Noah's brow furrowed. "But I don't recollect ever teaching him how to drive the lawn tractor, do you?"

Rachel thought for a minute. "God, no." She met his gaze, her concern shining in her eyes. "I don't, but he drives it around the yard all the time."

Noah pressed his palm to the table. "Anyway, I tried not to make a big deal about it. I just told him it would be dangerous for him to even move the car."

"Mallory know anything about him driving my car?"

"Well, not really, but that got interesting too. According to Mallory, Mattie's still afraid of *the voice.*" He hesitated. "She also said that he had promised to protect her from the voice. That he would kill anyone who tried to hurt her."

Rachel's eyes grew rounder. "She said he said *kill?*"

He nodded. "With a sword."

She looked away for a minute. "I don't know . . ." She turned back to him. "What do you think we should do?"

"Probably nothing other than watch him. Honestly, you know what an imagination Mallory has. This wouldn't be the first tall tale she's told." He said it gently, not wanting her to think he was criticizing Mallory or Rachel's parenting. "And neither of us has ever heard Mattie say a word."

"You're right." She nodded in agreement. "We'll just keep an eye on him." She covered his hand with hers. "I'm sorry. I knew I shouldn't have gone out tonight. You shouldn't have had to deal with this alone."

He gave a wave with his hand, careful not to move his other hand out from under hers. "It's fine, Rachel. Everything is fine."

"And how about you?" she asked softly, gazing into his eyes. "You feeling OK? No more blackouts?"

He shook his head. Of course, he wouldn't have told her for the world that he'd experienced another bad one Saturday night after the picnic. That he'd woken up outside in the Pinot field, lying between two rows of trellises. He'd had one last night, too, though he'd never made it out of his bed, as far as he knew.

"I'm fine," he insisted, wondering what she would do if he leaned forward and kissed her. Their faces were barely a foot apart. It would be so easy—

The dryer buzzed loudly, startling them both. She straightened in the chair, pulling her hand away from his. He sat up, feeling like an idiot.

"I'll get it," he said.

"No, I will." She was already on her feet.

Noah watched her disappear into the back, heard her open the dryer and the buzzing alarm ceased. He carried his glass to the sink. Rachel had wanted him to kiss her. He had seen it in her eyes. Seen the way she pursed her lips.

He turned on the faucet and watched his glass fill with water. He didn't know what to do. Did he need to just follow his instincts and kiss her the next time the opportunity presented itself? Or did they need to talk this through like—

"Noah." Rachel startled him, coming right up behind him. He hadn't even heard her come back into the kitchen. "Where the hell did you get this?" she demanded.

He turned to find her shaking a business card at him. "Where did I get—" Then he realized what she had in her hand. He'd left it in his pocket. How could he have been so stupid as to have left it in his pocket and then washed his jeans?

"Well?" She planted one hand on her hip, still shaking the fertility clinic appointment card. She was as angry as he believed he had ever seen her. "I'm waiting . . ."

CHAPTER 23

Noah turned around to cut off the water, then back to face Rachel . . . not wanting to face her. He was angry and confused, and angry and sad. Sad that his genes mixed with hers were never able to produce a child who could live more than a few months. Confused as to why she would have been inseminated with another man's sperm without consulting him. But mostly he was just angry that she didn't tell him at the time. She didn't tell him then and she hadn't told him now, even after he returned home.

"You had no right to snoop in my personal papers," she accused.

"I wasn't snooping. I was looking for those warranties the other day where you told me to look. The file cabinets are a mess, Rachel. It was just there." He motioned lamely.

"You mean you've had this since Sunday and not said anything?" Her mouth tightened into a thin line.

He looked down at the hardwood floor, scuffed by time and his beloved family who had treaded here. "I meant to say something to you that day, as soon as I found it, but you were upset about Skeeter Newton and . . ." He let his sentence trail off into silence.

She was quiet for a second.

He looked up. "I'm sorry, Rachel. I'm sorry I found it. I'm sorry I didn't say anything that day." He hesitated. "But now I have to ask. Did you go through with it? Did you get a sperm donation so that we could have a child of our own?" He went on faster than before, unable to conceal the emotion in his voice. "Rache, that appointment was only a week before I went to jail."

She folded her arms over her breasts, the card still in her hand. "It's none of your business." She sounded on the verge of tears.

"I know it's not."

"You abandoned me, Noah. You gave me up for a bottle of vodka," she charged, her voice choking with anger. Pain.

"I know. You're right, I did and I'm so sorry. I don't know how many times I can say I'm sorry, but I mean it every time, Rache, I swear that I do." He reached out to her, but she pulled away.

"Do you have any idea how angry I've been with you?" she demanded. "How you broke my heart? For sweet God's sake, Noah, I've loved you since I was in the eighth grade!"

He just stood there and listened, not responding, because what was there to say?

"You left me, you left me with this house, the vineyard, your parents' estate to settle. Then there was the baby."

"I didn't know you were pregnant. If I had known—"

"If you had known, *what?*" She met his gaze with fiery green eyes. "You'd have stopped drinking? You'd have realized how ridiculous your assumption that God had forsaken you because your parents were murdered was? Because our sons died? Are you telling me you would have gone to AA like I'd been asking you to, for a year? What would you have done differently?" she demanded. "If you had known I was pregnant, you wouldn't have taken the truck that night, after I begged you not to?" She sniffed, wiping her nose with the back of her shaking hand, still looking at him. Beseeching him.

"I don't know," he whispered.

Again, she was silent for a moment. "Well, at least you're honest. I'll give you that." She threw up her hand, still clutching the appointment card, and then sniffed.

Noah grabbed a paper towel sheet off the roll on the counter and offered it to her.

She snatched it out of his hand. "Thank you."

"You're welcome."

She blew her nose.

Noah just stood there, hands at his sides. "You want to sit down?" he asked quietly. "Talk about this?"

She took a deep breath, sounding calmer when she spoke again. "No, Noah, I don't want to sit down. I don't want to talk about it." She wadded the paper towel up in her hand. "I didn't even know I was pregnant the night of the accident. Then, everything happened so fast and I was so angry with you. So hurt . . ."

Noah could feel his gut twisting inside. How could he have done this to Rachel, to the one person he loved more than anyone on earth? "No, it's all right. I understand." His voice was stronger than he expected. "If I'd been in your shoes, I don't think I would have told me either. I didn't deserve to know." He exhaled, realizing he shouldn't push her any further, but realizing that he had to, just the same. "So that's how Mallory was conceived? You never slept with another man, Rache?"

Her eyes were filled with moisture, but she was no longer crying. "I never slept with another man. There's never been anyone but you."

Noah was still overwhelmed by his sadness, but somewhere inside, he felt a warm glow. There had never been anyone else but Rachel for him. Never would be. "I'm sorry I asked that. I just had to know. I don't know why, but I did."

She nodded, wiped her nose again with the paper towel, and walked to the trash can to throw it away. "I'm going to bed."

He considered suggesting again that they talk, but he sensed this wasn't the time. They were both too emotionally wrought. There would be time to talk later. A great deal of time, he hoped. "OK. I'll finish up the laundry and turn out the lights."

She stood at the garbage can and studied the card in her hand for a moment, then tossed it in.

"See you in the morning." He watched her walk out of the kitchen, and then something made him turn around. Something on the porch. A movement?

No.

He peered through the window over the sink, trying to see beyond his own reflection in the glass. There was nothing there. No one there, just . . . shadows. Darkness. But there was a feeling. A feeling of something evil lurking.

A shiver trickled down Noah's spine.

Evil lurking? That was ridiculous. Where did those thoughts come from? It had been a long time since he had believed in any evil beyond the evil of men.

He checked the lock on the door, flipping off the kitchen lights. Despite his own reassurances, he walked out of the kitchen, resisting the urge to look over his shoulder.

Afraid of what he might see . . .

"Mrs. Newton." Delilah smiled.

"Sergeant Swift." The woman in her midsixties, still in her polyester church dress, pushed open the back door. "Come in."

"Just for a second. I stopped by on my way home from

church to see how you were. See if I could do anything for you."

Mrs. Newton led Delilah into a pretty, old-fashioned kitchen. "You just missed Harry. He went down to the store for bread and the newspaper."

"I'm sorry I missed him," Delilah smiled, wondering if there was extra punishment for telling lies on Sunday. In truth, she'd been sitting in her car down the street watching their house, debating whether to try to see Mr. and Mrs. Newton together, or wait to see if Mr. Newton left the house. She'd gotten lucky in less than an hour.

"So you're OK, I mean . . . I know you're not *OK*," Delilah said, her empathy genuine. "I just wondered if there was anything we, the police department, could do for you."

"The funeral's tomorrow." She took a pitcher of iced tea from the refrigerator. "Would you like to sit down, Sergeant? Have a glass of tea?"

"No, really, I can't. I have to get home and give my mama a ring. We always talk on Sundays."

"Delbert and I always talked on Sundays. I'd bring him the paper after Harry was done with it." Her eyes clouded with tears and she turned away, setting the iced tea pitcher on the counter. "You'll need to add sugar or sweetener. Delbert always said that my tea was . . ." She averted her gaze and sank into a chair, catching a fold of her flowered dress and rubbing it between her thumb and forefinger. The woman's arthritic hands were swollen and must have been painful, but she didn't seem to notice.

Delilah let an appropriate amount of time pass and then pushed forward. "Mrs. Newton, if you don't mind, I have a question. And . . . if you don't feel like you want to answer it, that's fine. It's just that the more information we have, the faster we'll find out who did this to your son."

She turned to Delilah. She had obviously been a very pretty woman once upon a time, though her hair was white and her skin wrinkled, she had incredible blue eyes. "Delbert always made poor choices with friends," she murmured.

"So you think a friend did this?" Delilah took a step closer.

"I don't know, Sergeant. If I did . . . if I had an idea . . ." She opened her arms in a plea.

"That's all right." Delilah walked around the small kitchen table, moving closer to Mrs. Newton. "When we talked, ma'am, and we briefly discussed why someone might accuse Delbert of being a thief, I . . . I got the impression you wanted to tell me something."

"He was never charged with anything," she said quickly.

"I understand that." Delilah moved closer, keeping eye contact. "But . . . could he possibly have been involved in some kind of robbery?"

Her lower lip trembled and she clasped her hands, one thumb massaging a swollen knuckle.

"Mrs. Newton, any information might help."

She was quiet for a moment, and then she glanced up. "I overheard him one night talking to friends in the driveway. It's been years, Sergeant."

"It's all right." Delilah reached out and took her hand.

Mrs. Newton looked away, then back at Delilah. "They were talking about holding up a store," she whispered. "A mini-mart or something. About how little money they had gotten. They . . . they were angry."

Delilah nodded.

"I asked Delbert about it later." Her jaw trembled. "He said I misheard."

"Did anyone else know about it?"

"I don't know. His friends, I suppose. The ones he did it with. I don't even know who they were." Her voice took on a somber tone. "One died a couple of years back, another . . . another went to prison, I think."

"So you never mentioned this to Mr. Newton, to a female friend, perhaps?"

She shook her head, seeming to refocus. "No, no one." She glanced up. "Well, I did talk with one person about it at the time. I didn't know what to do."

Delilah held her hand. "Who did you talk with?"

Mrs. Newton smiled, that far-off look in her clouded eyes again. "He was always so nice to me, so understanding of how difficult it was to have a child like Delbert."

"Who did you discuss the matter with, Mrs. Newton?" Delilah repeated.

Her blue eyes settled on Delilah. "Father Gibson."

"Thought about how you're going to phrase your question?" Snowden walked behind Delilah, allowing her to take the lead entering the dental office.

She appreciated his confidence in her, but at the same time, she appreciated his presence. In truth, she really didn't know what she was going to say to Dr. Cary. How did one tactfully ask if he'd purchased a hatchet to murder someone?

"I just thought I'd be honest with him. Tell him we're following every lead, no matter how far-fetched or how certain we are that it's taking us in the wrong direction. Tell him he's not a suspect, but it's only fair that each person who purchased certain implements in town be interviewed. She glanced over her shoulder at Snowden as she reached for the door. "That sound OK to you, Chief?"

"Sounds OK to me, Sergeant," he answered, in an equally tempered tone.

When they'd climbed into the patrol car that morning, Snowden supplying the coffee from the diner, neither had mentioned his visit Friday night. Delilah still didn't know what to make of it, though she'd stayed up half the night measuring possibilities, coming to no conclusions. But now it was time to set aside whatever was going on between them, if anything was going on between them, and concentrate on their jobs.

Delilah entered the waiting room to find half a dozen patients waiting in upholstered chairs. She recognized most of them by their faces, even if she didn't know their names. She approached the receptionist's window as Snowden stopped to speak to an older woman.

"Good morning," the receptionist said from behind the glass as she slid it aside. She was an attractive African American woman about the same age as Delilah.

"Good morning. Sergeant Swift and Chief Calloway here to see Dr. Cary. I called earlier."

"Yes, of course." Her gaze flitted to Snowden, and there was no doubt in Delilah's mind that she found him attractive. "Come on back. He's with a patient right now, but you can wait in his office. I'm sure he won't be long."

"Thank you." Delilah glanced at her nametag on her bright pink smock covered with dancing toothbrushes. "Chandelle." She forced a smile and headed around the corner, through the open door. Snowden followed.

"Right this way," Chandelle flashed bright white teeth at Snowden. "I'll let Dr. Cary know you're here." She opened a door with a name plaque that read JEREMY CARY D.D.S. and stepped back to let them pass. "Anything I can get for you, Chief Calloway? Coffee? A soda? Sergeant?"

Extending the invitation to Delilah was obviously an afterthought.

"No, thank you." Delilah looked at Snowden, raising her eyebrows, cutting her eyes in Chandelle's direction as she bounced back down the hall. "I think you have an admirer, Chief."

He scowled. "You contacted Miss Watkins and the others?"

"I called Miss Watkins and Mr. Troyer. Thought maybe our visit with Mrs. Gibson ought to be impromptu." She gazed at the diploma encased in a frame on the wall behind the large walnut desk and fancy black leather executive's chair.

"Sorry to keep you waiting." Dr. Jeremy Cary entered the office, closing the door behind him.

"Thanks for seeing us. We apologize for the inconvenience."

"Not a problem. I'm always happy to assist our town's finest." He slipped into his chair. "Have a seat."

"This will just take a minute." Delilah remained standing. She was so short that she never liked to sit when interviewing a man, for fear her size would put her at a disadvantage. "We're following up on leads on the recent murders, Dr. Cary, and one of our tasks is to account for every sharp instrument or tool purchased in the last month or so here in Stephen Kill." She removed her little notebook from her breast pocket under her brass nametag. "I understand you purchased a hatchet from Burton's Hardware in June of this year."

"I don't remember the day," he said, at once sounding defensive. "But yes, I bought a hatchet." He scrutinized her. "Why, again, did you say you were asking?"

She could almost see the man's hackles go up. "It's part of our ongoing investigation. A routine interview."

"This doesn't have anything to do with my wife's death, does it? Because it was my understanding that the inquiry was closed almost a year ago."

Delilah wanted to sneak a peek in Snowden's direction, but she didn't dare. She knew the dentist was single, but she hadn't known he was a widower and she certainly hadn't been aware his wife's death had been investigated by the police. Her screwup. She should have looked closer into these people's lives before she began her interviews.

She paused for a moment, wondering if Snowden thought the doctor's response was as odd as she did. "No, sir. I don't know anything about an inquiry into your wife's death. As I said—"

"Because it was ruled an accident," he interrupted. "The death certificate was issued." Though he remained seated, he pressed both large hands down on the ink blotter on the desk, his knuckles turning white. "I understood from the state of North Carolina that the matter was closed."

"Could you tell me why you purchased the hatchet at Burton's Hardware, Dr. Cary?"

He stared at her for a minute and then rose. "No, no, actually, I don't think I can. I believe I should speak with my lawyer first."

"Dr. Cary, I assure you this has nothing to do with your wife's death," Snowden said calmly, watching him.

"Just the same, I'll have my attorney contact you." He walked around the desk, moving toward the door. "Is there anything else I can help you with, Chief, Sergeant?"

"That'll be all," Delilah said. "Thank you for your time."

She waited until he was out the door before she followed. "OK, that was weird," she whispered under her breath, turning her head so that only Snowden would hear her. "I think I just might be looking into Mrs. Cary's *accidental* death, soon as this is over."

Mrs. Troyer, dressed in a plain, shapeless blue cotton dress, knee-high white socks, brown orthopedic shoes, and a small white cap pinned on her head, directed Delilah and Snowden to the hog pen at the rear of the property. She continued to hang a stained men's white T-shirt with wooden clothespins as they headed off across the lawn. At the corner of the barn, Delilah glanced back, catching Mrs. Troyer watching them from behind a threadbare bed sheet. When she spotted Delilah, she dropped the sheet, disappearing from view.

"Really, Snowden, you should have warned me this town was full of crazies before I signed a year lease on my townhouse," she murmured under her breath. "I'm beginning to think I walked into the Stepford Wives' hometown."

Either he hadn't heard her or chose to ignore her. He led

the way toward the hog pen. Back at the car, they had agreed it would be better for him to question Mr. Troyer because of Joshua's notorious fundamental disapproval of women in any occupation that didn't involve the home and hanging laundry on the line.

They found Joshua Troyer standing at a three-foot-high fence, tossing heads of cabbage and assorted produce from a basket at his feet into a muddy pen. The stench from the mud and manure in the heat rose up in great waves. Hogs grunted, snorted, fighting for the tidbits of the not-so-fresh vegetables, sounding almost human in their antagonism or delight.

"Mr. Troyer, thanks for letting us stop by." Snowden halted a couple of steps from the hog pen.

Delilah stayed back, not because of the smell but because she harbored an immense dislike for hogs that bordered on fear. Growing up, her parents had raised them for market, as had her grandparents and most families in the county. It had been her experience that they were savage animals that would eat anything thrown in their path—stale donuts, box and all, from the local bakery; fish heads; dead chickens; each other; and, word had it, the occasional human who wandered into their path. When she was young, her brothers had always threatened to feed her to the hogs if she tattled on them for smoking or stealing Papa's rye whiskey, and she'd half believed them. Everyone she knew could tell the tale of some good-for-nothing who had disappeared in the night and was said to have been murdered and thrown in a hog pen. Hogs didn't leave much behind, not even bones if you gave them some time.

"Eeh-ya," Mr. Troyer muttered, not looking up at Snowden.

It was an odd response, in Delilah's book, but everything about this town, about the people who lived here, was getting odder by the day.

"As I told your wife on the phone, we're working on an investigation and—"

"Tryin' to find who killed that boy, ain't ya?" Troyer interrupted.

"We just have a few questions, Mr. Troyer, and then we'll let you get back to work," Snowden said.

Troyer continued to toss vegetables over the crude board fence—half a head of lettuce, a soft tomato, some kind of greens. He had no intention of halting his work for police questioning.

"We're tracking down all the farm implements bought in the last two months," Snowden explained, "and we understand that you purchased an axe last—"

"Got your work cut out for you, you do," Troyer continued in his slow, methodic cadence. "If yer looking for a man of flesh, though, not sure you're going to find one."

Delilah listened carefully, fighting the urge to shrug off the weird feeling that kept nibbling at the base of her spine. It was a hot day, humid, and growing hotter by the minute. The barnyard was surrounded by fields planted in feed corn, and though the crop was only knee high, she felt hemmed in, as if she couldn't breathe. She remembered a horror movie she'd once seen with her brothers, something about cornfields and creatures that lived within.

"Wouldn't say this to many, but I known your mother's family a long time." Troyer spoke to Snowden, giving no indication he even knew Delilah was there. "Known they was good, God-fearing people. Bible talks about it, you know." He leaned over the fence to watch two black-and-white spotted hogs fight over half a head of cabbage. "Talks about the wrath of God. Of punishment."

Delilah rested her hands on her hips, her handcuffs clanking as she took a step closer. "You think whoever killed these people is punishing them, Mr. Troyer? What makes you say that?"

"Eeh-ya. Bible talks about it," he repeated. "Talks about how he'll send an agent, an angel. We pay for our sins. We all pay for them someday."

She knew the Bible pretty well, and she had no clue what he was referring to. Something in Revelation, no doubt. People were always misinterpreting, misquoting the book of Revelation. "Did you purchase an axe, Mr. Troyer?"

"Lester Burton says I did, reckon I did." He lifted up the half-bushel basket, scattering the last leaves and a carrot butt over the side of the fence. One of the hogs hit the fence in its keenness to snatch up the last tidbits, and the old boards bowed out, then popped in. Troyer turned away and started across the grass, carrying the basket.

"Can I ask you what you purchased the axe for, Mr. Troyer?" Snowden followed him.

"You can ask. No law says I have to tell you. Man's got a right to buy an axe if he needs one."

Delilah took up the rear, sidestepping a pile of chicken crap in the grass. Mrs. Troyer's laying hens were apparently left free during the day and only penned up at night. "We'd appreciate any help you can give us, sir. We're simply doing our jobs. It's only fair that we question everyone."

"No need to 'mister' or 'sir' me. We don't believe in putting on airs. Joshua will do." He stopped and looked back at Delilah. "Bought it to chop wood. Old axe, my daddy's, finally met its maker." He entered an open lean-to shed and deposited the basket upside down over a stack of identical baskets. A red and white chicken scratched in the dirt, making clucking sounds. "Take it if you want."

He pointed and Delilah spotted a shiny new axe hanging on two old nails banged into the decaying wood wall of the shed. "Eeh-ya. Take it if you want." He turned to face Snowden, removing his hat, then a white handkerchief from his back pocket. "Run your fancy tests." He took his time, mopping his brow. "I didn't kill that bad seed, any of the three, but if God had sent me, I'd done it." He looked to Snowden and pointed again, almost as if daring him. "Take it."

"That won't be necessary, Mr. Troyer. As I said, we're

only following every lead. Thank you for your time." Snowden glanced at her. "Anything else, Sergeant?"

She grimaced. Anything else? The man had practically offered to kill the next person caught slipping a candy bar into his pocket at the drugstore or not claiming tips on her tax return. "I think that's all we need, Chief," she answered, managing to sound the way a cop ought to sound.

Snowden tipped his hat the way Delilah saw men do in the old black-and-white movies. "Thank you for your time, Mr. Troyer. We'll see ourselves off."

Delilah walked a step behind Snowden, following him to the cruiser parked under an elm tree in front of the house. As they crossed the lawn, she gazed back in the direction of the clothesline. The laundry basket, still half full of wet clothes, was still in the grass. She didn't see Mrs. Troyer, but she could feel her watching them. "What if it's a community thing, Chief?" she said quietly.

"What?"

She took one last look at the clothesline flapping with wet clothes, and the rippling cornfields that surrounded them. She waited until she climbed into the passenger seat to speak again. "A community thing. You know, like in *Murder on the Orient Express*. What if they all did it?"

"All who?" He started the car, turned it around in the dirt driveway, and pointed it toward the blacktop county road.

"I don't know! A whole group of them. The dentist, the ex-priest, the Amish guy."

"He's not Amish. He's Mennonite. Big difference."

"Whatever!" She turned to him in the seat. "Snowden, I'm serious. What if they're in on it together?"

"Pretty unlikely group."

"Maybe, but not if they have similar motives."

"Such as?"

"Sin, of course. Mr. Troyer's religious, obviously the priest is—"

"And the dentist whose wife drowned in an accident in Myrtle Beach?"

"An accident? So why the investigation?"

He shrugged. She tried not to take notice of what fine shoulders he had to shrug.

"Mitigating circumstances. Big, ugly fight in a restaurant the night before. Threats were made—getting full custody of the children, ruining his reputation, taking him for everything he had in the divorce settlement. Then she drowns the next night, and his alibi is perfect, almost too perfect. In the end, there wasn't enough evidence for a prelim hearing so the case was closed; her death was ruled an accident, and he walked away with the kids, the money, and the reputation, for the most part intact, and he looks like the poor grieving widower. "

"Think he killed her?" Delilah asked.

"If you'd known her, there'd be no doubt in your mind." He took his eyes off the road long enough to glance her way, an uncharacteristic half grin on his face. "Half this town probably would have held her under for him."

She laughed, not completely sure he was kidding. This was a different side of the straight-laced, trying to be better than everyone else, Snowden Calloway she knew, and darned if she didn't like it.

"Next stop, Miss Cora Watkins' place." She pointed back in the direction of town. "Zucchini bread central."

"Yes, ma'am," he said, imitating her southern drawl.

CHAPTER 24

Miss Cora Watkins, age fifty-nine and never married, was waiting for Delilah and the chief of police. Probably been waiting all morning. The moment they pulled up to the curb in front of the modest, two-story home that Cora and her sister Clara's parents had left to them, someone was at the door.

The house, built in the forties, was square with a four-sided pyramid roof, faded green asbestos siding, and striped green and white canvas awnings over each window. The lady of the house stood on the front porch, sporting a flowered, full apron and a smug smile of self-importance.

"I don't know what it is about this woman," Delilah said as she logged onto the computer mounted on the dash, noting the time of the interview. "But she bugs me. Something about her bugs me. I've never liked a gossip."

"I've known her my whole life; she's harmless." Snowden rested his hand on his nightstick to keep it from catching on the car seat and unfolded his tall frame, stepping out the door.

Delilah climbed the painted white porch steps ahead of him, knowing they must have made quite a sight for the Stephen Kill born and bred, old-maid Watkins sisters—she a petite blond packing a .38 automatic and an attitude, him a six-four black man with blue eyes, on a mission, once again, to prove he was as good as his white counterparts.

"Clara," Cora sang through the porch screen door. "Our guests are here. Have Alice bring out the tea." She turned back to Delilah. "I thought we'd take refreshments on the front porch while we chat. It's going to be such a hot day." She patted one plump cheek, then the other with an open palm.

Cora sounded to Delilah as if she thought the little house were Tara and she the southern belle of the ball.

"That won't be necessary," Delilah said. "We won't take up more than a few minutes of your time, Miss Watkins."

"Nonsense." She hustled to the side of the porch, where four aluminum porch chairs, old but in good condition, looked to have been arranged specifically for their visit. "You must sit and have a tall glass of my tea. Tell her, Snowden." She took the closest chair, rearranging her apron over her lap as she sat. "This may not be the *deep* south from where you came, but we still have our manners." She lifted her chin almost haughtily. "It's how we do things here in Stephen Kill."

Delilah was about to refuse the offer again when Snowden walked past her, taking the far chair. The look he gave her as he passed told her to take the chair and drink the darned tea. Anything to get the information they needed and get out of there.

Reluctantly, Delilah sat down across from Cora. The screen door opened and the sister, Clara, also in a flowered apron, walked onto the porch. Like her sister, Clara was short, with the lumpy, bumpy figure of a middle-aged woman, round faced and wearing her gray hair in a tightly permed helmet. "Chief Calloway, how nice of you to call."

"I told you, Clara, the chief and his little deputy are here on official business." Cora tapped the chair beside her. "Have a seat, dear. Isn't Alice coming with the iced tea? Alice!"

"Actually, it's Sergeant Swift, Miss Watkins." Delilah tried to keep the annoyance out of her voice as she produced her notepad. "We don't have *deputies* on the force."

"We just have a few quick questions, ladies, and then we'll be on our way," Snowden said, sounding as if he was trying to smooth things over.

Delilah didn't need him smoothing anything. This was her investigation; she could run the interview the way she wanted and she didn't have to like this woman, didn't have to drink her damned sweet tea if she didn't want to. "As I'm sure you know, we're investigating the Newton homicide in which—"

"Terrible tragedy, just terrible." Cora turned to the door. "Alice! Alice, is the tea coming?" Her voice reached an impatient crescendo by the end of the sentence.

"Coming," called a voice from inside, followed by a clatter that sounded like a glass hitting a countertop.

"As part of the investigation," Delilah continued, this time with less patience, "we're taking an inventory of various tools purchased in Stephen Kill in the last few months."

The screen door opened and Alice Crupp appeared, a tray with a pitcher and four glasses filled with ice balanced in her hands. She apparently bought her clothes from the same store and had her hair permed in the same beauty salon as the Watkins sisters. They could have been triplets.

"Nice to see you, Chief Calloway, Sergeant Swift." She nodded shyly as she set the tray on a small table beside Cora's chair. "Would you care for iced tea?"

"Of course they'll have tea. That's why I had you bring tea out, Alice dear." She glanced up at Snowden. "Would you care for a little snack, Chief Calloway? Some zucchini bread? Chocolate chip cookies, maybe."

"No, thank you," Delilah said firmly. "Now, if we could just ask you a few questions, Miss Watkins—"

"Please, call me Cora, Miss Cora." She watched as Alice poured the tea. "Everyone does, don't they, Chief Calloway?"

"We're questioning everyone who purchased a certain

type of tool," Delilah forged on. "Now, just a little background information first. You work as the church secretary for Father Hailey, is that not correct?"

"Part time, now. Just part time. I told him you'd be stopping by this morning, so I just thought I'd go in this afternoon. There's so little for me to do these days, you know. What with that new fancy computer." She raised both hands. "I'm just at a loss with that thing. I told Father Hailey that he would just have to start doing the monthly newsletter himself."

"Your name came up as having made a purchase at Burton's Hardware. Let's see . . ." Delilah pretended to check her notes, although she already knew when the item had been purchased.

"Come, come, Alice, the officers don't have all day."

Alice, having poured tea into each of the four glasses, set the pitcher with the orange butterflies on the table, picked up the tray, and offered it to Cora. Delilah leaned one way, then the other, trying to see around the middle-aged woman's rump as she served Snowden next, then Clara.

"Do you recall making a purchase at Burton's, ma'am?"

Alice moved in front of Delilah, offering the last glass of iced tea, her gaze darting to Cora and then back to Delilah.

No longer seeing an expedient option, Delilah accepted the tea, mumbled a thank-you, and then set the glass on the floor beside her chair. "Ma'am, do you recall making this purchase?" she repeated.

"Thank you, Alice." Cora smiled, shifting her gaze back to Delilah. "I don't believe I do, Deputy. You know, Harry Newton's older than I am. I asked him what he thought he was doing, trying to pretend to be able to run that fancy computer that's supposed to be a cash register. I liked it better the old way, myself. When we were growing up, Clara and I, Daddy would send us to Burton's for a dime's worth of seeds or a twist of twine, and it would go on our account. Daddy would pay at the end of the month, or when he got to it."

Delilah watched Cora sip her tea, a little amazed. "You don't recall buying a hatchet at Burton's Hardware?"

"No."

Delilah looked to Snowden, not certain how, at this point, to proceed. She hadn't expected someone to deny a purchase recorded by the store. Certainly not an old lady. "Are you certain you don't remember buying a hatchet?"

"No, I don't. I don't remember any such thing. And I certainly would, wouldn't I? I may be of a certain age, but I'm not dotty yet, young lady."

"Thank you so much for cooperating." Snowden had politely drank a little of the tea before setting it down beside his chair where he left it when he rose.

"That's all the questions you have for me?" Cora got up from the chair, glass still in hand. "But I thought you'd have more questions . . . about Skeeter Newton. I've known him his whole life, you know. Knew he was a bad seed from the beginning—we all knew, didn't we, Clara?"

"We all knew," the look-alike repeated.

"I just feel so sorry for Harry and Flora. I was telling them only yesterday," Cora went on. "We stopped by just before supper, just to check in, to see if there was anything we could do. Clara and I stop or call every night. It's just so tragic."

"If we have any more questions, we'll call, ma'am." On her way to the steps, Delilah passed Alice, who stood, back to the screen door, with the tray in her hand. Their gazes met for just a split second, but there was something in her eyes that caught Delilah's attention. Alice seemed to want to speak, but something held her back.

Delilah waited until Snowden had pulled the car away from the curb before she said anything. "Did you see the way Alice looked at me?"

"Looked at you?"

"She knows something about Cora, something about the hatchet, something about something."

"That certainly narrows down the field, *Deputy*. I was discussing the other day with the city council our need to have at least one in-house detective on the force. If they can find the money, I had a mind to suggest you for the position. Deductions like *she knows something about something* will certainly sway the city council into hiring its first female police detective."

Delilah didn't know if she wanted to hug him or kick him. Police detective? When she was a little girl, she'd always wanted to be Sherlock Holmes, or maybe Maddie Hayes, the investigator on *Moonlighting*, that old show with Bruce Willis. But he was teasing, making fun of her, so she couldn't tell how serious he was. "You really think I'd make a good detective?"

"I think you would, *Deputy*."

"Stop calling me that. You're not funny." She glanced out the window, unable to resist grinning. "You want to grab a sandwich at the diner before we head out to the Gibson place?"

"Sounds good to me. I need to get the taste of that iced tea out of my mouth."

She glanced back at him, trying to hide her amusement. "Not good?"

"Worse than the zucchini bread."

Delilah watched Noah Gibson set down a wooden case of green wine bottles and wipe the sweat from his brow with the heel of his hand. He didn't appear nervous as they approached from the car Snowden had parked behind the Volvo in the garage, but he did look pissed. When they'd pulled into the driveway, he must have heard the sound of the tires on the loose, oyster shells. He stepped out of the barn, glanced in their direction, and then turned and went back inside.

He was cleaning out the large barn that stood closest to the house and appeared to be original to the property. An area around the door was stacked high with assorted junk;

some items she recognized, like the wine bottles and some kind of wooden kegs, and others she had no clue what they were, but guessed they were all used in the process of making wine.

Word at the diner was that Noah Gibson had decided to begin making wine again, as his parents had before their deaths. Some were taking bets as to how long it would be before he tied one on. Delilah didn't honestly see what one had to do with the other, but she hadn't spoken up the morning she had heard the gossip, while waiting on a fried scrapple sandwich and coffee. She was still considered an outsider by most people in the town so she kept her mouth shut. It was amazing the things a person heard when she was an insignificant fly on the wall.

"Noah," Snowden said as they approached him.

"Snowden. Sergeant." Noah nodded to one and then the other as he adjusted the brim of his faded ball cap.

"Mr. Gibson, we're here to—"

"I know why you're here." He scowled at Snowden. "I didn't know Skeeter Newton, and I never counseled him. He wasn't the churchgoing kind, but then I suppose your investigation has already shown that."

"What about anyone in his family?" Delilah questioned, figuring if he was willing to talk, she might as well ask. If she didn't, Snowden would. When she'd told him about her conversation with Mrs. Newton the day before, on the ride to the vineyard, he'd seemed a little smug.

"Who I counseled is none of your business, Sergeant."

"It is if it's related to our investigation," Delilah countered.

Noah turned to Snowden, which pissed her off. "We've been through this before. For ethical reasons, I'm not discussing any private discussions I might have had with my parishioners."

"You will if we get a court order."

He turned back to Delilah, amazingly calm. "So get one." She was beginning to think she might have misjudged

Noah Gibson. In her mind, she had seen him as the fallen priest, a broken man, but this was not a broken man who stood before them. This was a confident, strong-minded man, determined to stick to what he saw as his ethical or moral obligations. She also saw something defiant in his eyes; it was that defiance that worried her.

"I'd like to speak to Mrs. Gibson. Is she here?"

"What about?"

The porch door of the farmhouse slapped closed. "Noah?"

All three turned to see Rachel Gibson hurry across the cut grass, calling over her shoulder to her daughter who'd followed her onto the porch. Mallory Gibson was wearing a purple rain slicker, hood up, despite the heat of the day and the lack of precipitation. Her feet were bare. "Go back inside with Mrs. Santori, bubble butt. I'll be in, in a minute."

The little girl reminded Delilah of her nieces. She reminded her how much she missed them.

"What's going on?" Rachel Gibson asked, tension in her voice.

Delilah couldn't help but look at Snowden, look to see how he reacted to her. His face remained stony. If he still felt anything for the ex-priest's ex-wife, he wasn't showing it. "We have a few questions for you, Mrs. Gibson."

"You don't have to answer them," Noah said.

Rachel glanced at him, then back at Delilah. Delilah couldn't tell what she was thinking.

"Did you purchase a machete, Mrs. Gibson?"

"Who says she did?" Noah pulled his ball cap off. "Is that how Skeeter Newton was murdered? Someone cut off his hands with a machete? You think I bought a machete, went to his home, and cut his hands off, leaving him to bleed to death?"

Delilah ignored him. "Records at Burton's Hardware store indicate, Mrs. Gibson, that you purchased a machete two weeks ago." She let a silence fall between them. "You want to show us the machete?"

Rachel Gibson stood there for a moment, hands at her sides, and then shrugged and walked away, indicating they should follow.

"This is absurd, Snowden, and you know it is." Noah stalked off after Rachel, and Delilah and Snowden followed.

"What, you think Rachel killed Skeeter? Or are you thinking she went to the hardware store to buy the machete for me so I could do it? Is that it?" He shook his ball cap at Snowden. "You know, every moment that you waste harassing me is a moment lost finding out who did kill them."

Rachel led them across the yard to the garage they had parked in front of. Inside, it was cooler. It was a typical detached garage—car, a lawn tractor, a kid's tricycle, a wagon. On the right-hand wall, out of reach of small hands, were various tools and farm implements hanging on the wall— hammers, levels, an axe, pruning shears, a hatchet. Delilah began to quickly take a mental inventory.

"You know what," Rachel said, turning around suddenly. "No, no, you can't see the machete purchased at Burton's Hardware. You want to see it, you get a court order." She stepped toward them, partially blocking Delilah's view.

"Rachel, please," Snowden said calmly. "Do you realize how this looks?"

"I don't care how it looks. I resent you making assumptions about me or my family, Snowden," Rachel said, emotion in her voice. "You know, this comes close to police harassment."

"No one's being harassed here, Mrs. Gibson," Delilah defended. "We've been making calls on folks all day, simply tracking down certain tools purchased in the town in a certain time frame."

"You have to have a court order to make me show you the machete I bought, don't you? Doesn't she?" Rachel asked, turning to Snowden.

She was pretty. Slender, a sleek dirty-blond ponytail, and

expressive green eyes. Eyes that right now showed a fury lurking just beneath the barely polite surface.

"Rachel, we're just doing our jobs," Snowden responded patiently. "Conducting a thorough investigation. The Newtons deserve our best, as do the Leager and the Rehak families."

"You're right, I'm sorry." Rachel slid the hand on her hip into her back pocket. "It's just that . . ." She glanced back at Noah, then at Snowden again. "It's just hard, Snowden. People seem to see Noah as someone he isn't, and now I suppose it's beginning to rub off on me. You know, he's paid his dues. Noah's stopped drinking, he attends AA, and . . . and we're trying to put our lives back together."

"Could we just see the machete, Rachel?" Snowden hooked his thumbs in his gun belt. "It would make things easier."

Delilah watched as Noah caught Rachel's hand and squeezed it. She didn't look at him. "No, Snowden. I'm sorry, but it's a matter of principle. You'll have to get a warrant."

Delilah looked to Snowden, then back at Noah. "Guess we're done here, then, at least for now," she said coolly. "Have a nice day."

Noah and Rachel stood hand in hand in silence until they watched the back of the police cruiser disappear down the driveway. Only then did he turn to her. "You all right?"

She squeezed his hand. "Yes. No. Noah, I fully intended to hand over the damned machete, but it's not here."

"Not here? What do you mean?"

"I mean it's not here." She led him by the hand back into the garage, pointing above his head at the wall.

Noah stared at the empty place where it should have been. "I left it there, after we came back from the hedgerow, before we went to the picnic that Saturday," he said. "I haven't had a chance to get back to clearing that brush. I haven't used it since."

She studied the wall as if she could somehow conjure up the machete if she stared hard enough. "You're sure you didn't use it again, and maybe you just don't remember?"

"I'm sure I don't remember using it."

She looked at him for a moment and then, on impulse, threw her arms around him. "Noah, listen to me." She smoothed his cheek with the palm of her hand, gazing into his dark, troubled eyes. "Don't worry about this. It's around here somewhere, and I bought the stupid machete, not you."

"But maybe they'll try to implicate you."

"That's ridiculous." She looked at him for a moment and then caught his cheeks with the palms of her hands. "Listen to me. I know what you're thinking. The blackouts. Time you can't account for. But you didn't kill Skeeter and you didn't kill the others either. Do you hear me? I *know* you didn't do it."

His smile was sad as he reached out to stroke her hair. "Thank you," he whispered. "I need that right now. I need you to believe in me, to help me believe in myself."

Rachel felt her chest tighten. She let her eyes drift shut and she met his mouth halfway. His kiss was gentle, a kiss of apology, of deep regret, but also a kiss of yearning. All too soon, he pulled away.

She rubbed her lips together, savoring his taste. "What do you think we should do about the machete?" she whispered. A million thoughts were tumbling in her head. What was she doing? Why had she kissed him? Where did she think this could go? Where did she want it to go? But there wasn't time to think about that now. What mattered was the safety of her family, of those she loved, and she knew, as God was her witness, that she still loved Noah. Or maybe she was just falling in love with him again.

"I think we need to stay calm."

He stroked her hair again and she felt her eyelids flutter. Forty years old and a man was making her weak kneed.

"And then," Noah said, holding her gaze with his. "I think I need to have a look in Mattie's room."

CHAPTER 25

Delilah was waiting in the dark on her tiny porch when Snowden jogged up her street. It was almost eleven. The night air was heavy and humid, and it smelled like rain. "I was beginning to think you weren't coming," she said.

He walked in a tight circle on the sidewalk in front of the steps. "I shouldn't have," he panted.

She smiled. "Come on in before someone sees you." She took a quick look up and down the street; it was a good thing her neighbors were early to bed, early to rise.

He followed her into the kitchen. She got him a glass of water and pushed it into his hand. There was still a thin sheen of sweat across his forehead, but his breathing was coming back to normal.

She watched him walk in a circle around the kitchen, sipping the water. Tonight, he wore navy running shorts and a plain gray tank that showed off his beautiful dark skin and the corded muscles of his shoulders and biceps.

She decided she could use a glass of cold water herself. She went back to the dish cabinet. "I called Alice Crupp this afternoon after we got back to the station."

He turned to her, halting. "And?"

Delilah leaned against the refrigerator, filling her glass from the dispenser. She'd taken more care with her evening attire than usual. She was wearing a pair of her brother's plaid boxers, but tonight she'd chosen a T-shirt that was clean and without any tears or stains. She'd brushed her hair and her teeth too. "Alice is the one who bought the hatchet, not Cora . . . at Cora's request. That's why she looked at me so funny this morning. The hatchet was put on the Watkins' sisters' account, but it was actually Alice who went into the store and made the purchase."

"You're kidding." He knitted his dark brows. "Why didn't Cora just say so this morning?"

She rested her hip against the refrigerator, sipping her water. "Gets better. I called Miss Cora and asked her that very question. Know what she said?" She waited a moment, not really expecting a question from Snowden. "She hemmed and hawed, and then she said she'd had Alice buy it for the priest."

"Noah?"

She shook her head. "Father Hailey."

"I'll be damned." He looked away, studying the pattern on her kitchen floor.

"I'll be double-damned," Delilah echoed. "I asked Miss Cora why she hadn't just come out and told us she'd sent Alice to buy the hatchet when we asked about it." She shrugged. "All she said was that it had slipped her mind."

"Slipped her mind?"

"That's what she said." Delilah tilted her head, beckoning him. "Come on in, sit down for a few minutes."

He hesitated. "I shouldn't."

"Neither should I." She walked past him, headed for the living room. "But I think that train's left the station, don't you?" She smiled at him over her shoulder. "Oh, come on, just a couple of minutes, Snowden. I think I can control myself for that long, keep myself from ripping your clothes off."

She felt her cheeks grow warm the minute the words came out of her mouth. What had possessed her to say such a thing? She was almost afraid to look back for fear she'd see him bolting for the door.

He wasn't. He followed her into the low-lit living room. "Cora have any idea what Father Hailey needed a hatchet for?"

She sat down on the couch, tucking a bare, size-six foot beneath her, leaving plenty of room for him beside her. "Nope. Said not, but have no fear. I intend to ask him."

Noah lay awake in his bed for what seemed an eternity. He listened to the sound of Chester's snoring and of the house settling. The sound of the toilet flushing upstairs. Light footsteps. Doors opening and closing. When he shut his eyes, he could see Rachel walking down the hall in one of her skimpy T-shirts and a pair of old gym shorts, looking in on Mallory, kissing her good night on her forehead. He wished he was up there with them, wished he could kiss Mallory good night. Kiss them both good night.

He opened his eyes again, surprised that such domestic thoughts could find their way into his head tonight.

After the police had left, he'd looked everywhere for the new machete—in Mattie's room, in the barn, in the garage again. He'd asked Mateo, who vaguely recalled seeing it hanging in the garage, but that was right after Rachel had bought it. Noah had even attempted to question Mattie at dinner, but of course he had gotten no response. What he had gotten was a strange comment from Mallory just before she'd trotted off to bed. She'd come to give him a hug good night. He'd had to hug her stuffed meerkat, too. Just as she was pulling out of his arms, she had whispered in his ear, "Mattie doesn't want to talk about the *ma-chet-tee.* He's afraid of it."

Noah hadn't questioned her; what was he going to say? There was no proof Mattie had said a word to Mallory about the machete. But her puzzling words worried him now. Tonight, after Mrs. Santori had gone home and they'd been left to themselves, he and Rachel had a cup of herbal tea on the front porch while Mattie and Mallory ran in the grass, in the fading light, attempting to catch fat, shiny green june bugs in their hands.

Rachel had told him she wanted to talk to him about Mattie, but she'd obviously been reticent to say what was on her mind. Noah had wanted to talk to her about Mattie too, and it had only taken a moment for them to realize they had both come to the conclusion that, for the present, Mattie wasn't to be left alone with Mallory.

They had absolutely no reason to believe he would ever harm the precious little girl, but it wasn't a risk either Rachel or Noah was willing to take, no matter how badly they felt about such a decision. There were just too many unanswered questions concerning Mattie right now. There was the matter of him moving both the lawn tractor and the car, his odd behavior, the strange drawings and colorings Rachel had been saving, and now the missing machete. What if he really had somehow spoken or communicated to Mallory? What if he really had said he would kill someone with a sword to protect her? To a man like Mattie, a machete could look like a sword, couldn't it?

Rachel and Noah had also agreed this evening, over mugs of Lemon Zinger tea, that they would take Mattie to a doctor, a psychologist or psychiatrist with experience dealing with idiot savants. Perhaps a professional could help them navigate through the halls of Mattie's mind to discover what he was afraid of. Noah was also interested in knowing if it was possible that Mattie could talk and that he simply chose not to.

After such a serious discussion, the conversation had drifted pleasantly. Noah and Rachel hadn't talked about anything in particular, just good times they remembered. They had laughed about the time Noah had tried to catch a lizard in their student apartment in California and broken three lamps in the process. Then he'd reminded her of the time they'd taken the youth of St. Paul's to the beach at Rehoboth to surf and she'd lost her bikini top and had to stand in shoulder-deep water while he went back up on the beach to find her a T-shirt. It had been their early days, when they'd first returned to Stephen Kill, and the incident had made both the new priest and his wife a hit with the teens. It was the first time in a long time that Noah had been reminded of one of the good times when he'd been a priest.

Noah smiled at the thought of Rachel standing in the water trying to shield her bare breasts, exhaled, and let his eyes drift shut. Today had exhausted him. He was so tired that he didn't seem to be able to quiet himself long enough to fall asleep. He felt as if every muscle in his body was jumping under his skin.

He'd made a serious dent in cleaning the barn, finding some stainless steel equipment they would need for the wine-fermenting process come fall. Then there had been the visit from the friendly Stephen Kill police force, the discovery that the machete was missing, and Rachel's kiss. He was as occupied with thoughts of that single kiss as he was with the machete. She'd kissed him, he hadn't kissed . . . not initially . . . he was sure of it. What did it mean? She hadn't said a word about it, but she'd definitely acted differently with him tonight. She'd made the tea, pulled her chair up close to his so they could talk without Miss Nosy Mallory overhearing them. And as they had talked, she had touched him several times— tapped his knee, brushed her hand over his arm, toyed with his fingers while his hand rested on the table between them.

Noah wanted Rachel back. He'd been afraid to admit it to himself. Afraid even to think it, but now, it was all he could think about. *She* was all he could think of. The taste of her lips . . . the warmth of her hand as she caressed his cheek.

Her touch took him back to their first years together when they had been happy. When life had been good. . . .

The dream started out innocently enough. Rachel and Noah were walking on the beach; he recognized the place as a lonely spot in Cape Henlopen Park. It was just growing dark, and they were walking hand in hand, bare feet in the surf. One moment the ocean was calm, the next it turned white and stormy, the waves rising up in a manner that seemed physically impossible.

Rachel turned to him, her green eyes wide with sudden terror. They both turned, still hand in hand, toward the ocean. What was it, he wondered. A tidal wave? The results of a nuclear blast that would alter the surface of the earth forever? Had the end of the world as outlined in Revelation finally come?

But as he turned, as the waves rose over his head, higher and higher, it began to take form. It was a creature that possessed a voice, a booming, terrifying voice. Out of the rising wave he began to see human limbs—arms, legs. People were screaming, trapped inside the rising water creature, crying out to Noah and Rachel. As the water rose higher, as high as a two-story building, it began to turn red. One moment it was an angry ocean wave, the next a sea of blood. The arms and legs became people—his parents, his babies, Pam Rehak, Mr. and Mrs. Marcus, Johnny Leager, and Skeeter.

Noah and Rachel looked up to see the wave of blood begin to tumble downward, pressing down over their heads, death imminent, and as it closed in, he saw a face clearly in the tumble of bodies. It was Clancy, his roommate from jail. His lips were moving; he was trying to tell Noah something, but Noah couldn't hear him above the crash of the wave and the voice of the creature.

As the blood washed down over Noah with bone-crushing force, he lost contact with Rachel's hand, and that was when he screamed.

* * *

"Noah. Noah, wake up." Rachel sat down on the edge of the twin bed and rested her hand on his shoulder. He was still asleep, but it was obvious by the way he was thrashing around that he was in the middle of a nightmare, that or perhaps it was one of his blackouts.

She herself had been having a nightmare. She'd woken shaking, in a cold sweat, and come downstairs to get a drink of water. Just as she was walking into the kitchen, she'd heard Noah call her name. The sound of his frightened voice, the way he had cried out to her, had scared the bejesus out of her. All she could think of was that someone was in the house, someone with the missing machete, and that Noah was in danger. As she sprinted down the hall toward the spare bedroom, she'd grabbed the broom from behind the refrigerator. It was ridiculous, of course. How was she going to defend Noah or herself with a wooden broom handle? But there was no logic in her response. It came from her gut. Her heart. She'd lost Noah once; she wasn't going to let it happen again.

Relief had flooded her when she burst through the door to find Noah alone, flailing in his bed. Chester had bounced up on his feet and whined, pushing his wet nose up against her as if to say, "Thank goodness you're here."

Rachel had patted the dog's head as she flipped on the overhead light, just to be sure no one was lurking in the dark behind a storage box or the ironing board. Neither the sounds she made nor the light woke Noah. Satisfied they were alone, she'd come to his bed.

"Noah, wake up." She shook him again.

His eyes flew open; he was shaking all over. "Rachel," he rasped, reaching out to grasp her arms.

"It's all right," she murmured, a tenderness coming over her that she didn't realize she still possessed for him. "You were having a bad dream."

He blinked, glanced around the room, and then looked up at her again. "Just a dream?"

She nodded.

The room air conditioner hummed in the window. Because of cross-ventilation, the old house was relatively cool. Most of the time they could keep the windows and doors open and rarely had to use the large window unit in the living room that cooled the kitchen and living room. But last week when the temperature had risen dramatically, Noah had retrieved the small room air conditioners from the attic and installed one in each bedroom.

"I . . . I was in the kitchen getting a drink," she said. "You called me."

"I did?" He closed his eyes. Exhaled. "What time is it?"

She glanced at the digital clock beside the bed. "Twelve thirty-five."

He opened his eyes again. "What were you doing up so late?"

It was her turn to look away. She debated whether or not to tell him. He had enough things to worry about right now; he didn't need to be concerned with her mental state. But the dream had scared her, scared her enough to want to tell him. She met his gaze. "Another nightmare. I've been having them for weeks."

"You have?" He seemed more awake now. More himself. "Come here." He slid over in the bed, putting out his arm for her. He wasn't wearing anything but a pair of boxers. In his struggle in his sleep, he'd thrown the pale blue flowered sheet aside.

She hesitated, then threw caution to the wind and slid in beside him. The moment her head hit the pillow beside his, she let her eyes drift shut. She'd been so alone for so long that just the feel of his warm body pressed against her made her light-headed. His arm around her shoulders felt so good.

Noah kissed the top of her head, and she shifted so that

she could rest her head on his shoulder. He was still thin, but work in the vineyard had been good for him. He had developed arm and chest muscles a priest would never have.

"Tell me about your dream."

"I don't want to." She snuggled against him.

"Tell me anyway."

"It's more of the same thing, Noah. It . . . it's beginning to scare me. You've got to listen to me, got to believe me when I tell you there's something evil in this town." She couldn't keep the sound of terror out of her voice this time.

"Shhhh," Noah soothed, smoothing her hair, kissing the top of her head. "It's all right. Tell me about the dream."

She exhaled, feeling as if she needed a moment to prepare herself. Any more, just thinking about the nightmares frightened her. That was why she kept herself so busy all day, so she wouldn't have time to remember. "They never start out like nightmares," she whispered. "This time, you and I were on the beach." She couldn't help but smile. "You know, there on that stretch near the watchtowers in the state park."

"Where we used to walk at night."

She nodded. "We were just walking, talking, holding hands."

He kissed her bare shoulder. It was the first time she remembered she wasn't wearing anything but a tank top and a pair of bikini panties.

"The water was beautiful," she continued cautiously, almost fearing that to repeat the story would bring back the horror of it. "A calm surf, that refreshing breeze off the water. Then suddenly a wave rose out of nowhere."

"A wave?" He looked down at her, seeming surprised. No, more than surprised. Shocked. Disturbed.

"A huge wave," she continued, unable to tear her gaze from his. "Like, I don't know, one of those tidal waves in the movies that wipes out Manhattan or something."

"Go on," he breathed.

"What's wrong, Noah?" She turned toward him in the narrow bed, one of her knees slipping in-between his.

"Just go on."

"It was that thing again. That . . . monster . . . creature. It was like the thing Mattie keeps drawing, only worse. Scarier. The water, Noah, it turned to—"

"Blood," he finished for her.

Her brow furrowed. "How did you know?"

"This is unbelievable," he whispered. "What was in the wave?"

"Bodies. Some I knew—"

"Some you didn't," he finished for her.

She felt her chin tremble. "You were dreaming about it too, weren't you?"

"Yes. No." He closed his eyes, smoothing her hair with his hand. "It's impossible."

"Apparently, it's not," she said after a moment.

He opened his eyes again, looking down at her. "Power of suggestion can be a strange thing, Rache. We were talking about the beach last night. We've both been having nightmares. Somehow—"

"Noah, listen to me." She rolled onto her side, resting her hand on his bare chest. Her mouth was only inches from his. "I can't explain this. I don't understand it, but I'm telling you, it's some kind of warning. There's something evil out there. It has to do with the killings in town and it somehow has something to do with us."

He was quiet for a moment before he responded. "There is something evil out there, a man who is murdering in some sort of righteous fugue."

She shook her head. "I think it goes deeper than that. What . . . what if it's something satanic?"

He glanced away.

"No, I'm serious, Noah."

"I don't believe in Satan."

"You used to," she challenged. Now that she had reached this point, she felt like she needed to tell him what had been running through her mind for days. Even if he thought she was crazy, at least she would have said it. "You believed in Satan when you believed in God."

He rolled his head on the pillow to stare straight up at the ceiling. "Rache, I don't want to talk about this."

"I know you don't, but at least think about it. All these weird feelings you and I have both been getting lately. And you can deny them all you want, you know what I mean. Now Mattie's strange behavior. That eerie music he keeps playing on the organ. The pictures he's drawing of a thing that looks like the thing in my dreams. Now in yours."

He closed his eyes. "There can be no Satan if there's no God," he said, seeming to be thinking out loud.

"So what? Because you're ignoring God's presence in your life, you're willing to take the chance of ignoring Satan?"

"Rache—"

"No, I'm serious. What if this is somehow about you? Think about it. The police actually see you as a suspect in the murders. You've even suspected yourself. What if . . . if someone or some*thing* wants it to look like you?"

"Rache, it's crazy."

"You're right, it is. A good reason to ignore the facts, right?" She leaned over him. "Look at me."

He shifted his gaze.

"Please tell me you'll at least consider the possibility. Please?"

"But why? Why would—"

"Because of who you are. What you were. You were almost lost, Noah," she cried passionately. "But now you've come back. You're a threat to all that is wrong and bad in this world."

"That's ridiculous."

"Maybe," she agreed after a moment. "But you need to

consider the possibility. For me." She paused. "Please, Noah. For me?"

"OK. For you." He lifted his head from the pillow and pressed his lips to hers. "Only for you," he whispered against her mouth.

Rachel hesitated for only a second and then she lowered her mouth over his, parting his lips. This had been coming for days. She'd felt the sexual tension between them every time they touched innocently, passing Mallory from one to the other, handing him a glass.

As Noah deepened the kiss, rolling her onto her back, bringing his hand under her aching breast, she wondered if she was making a mistake. If she would regret this later. But Noah slid his hand under her tank top, and any thoughts she might have been trying to process flew out the window. As he pressed her into the mattress, she moaned with pleasure, tears filling her eyes. For the first time in longer than she could remember, the tears were of joy.

"Don't cry," Noah murmured, lifting his head over hers, gazing into her eyes as he stroked her damp cheek with his fingers. "Please don't cry. If only I could go back . . . I never meant to hurt you, Rache. I swear, I—"

"Shhh," she hushed, looking up at him through her lashes heavy with tears. She took his hand from her cheek and began to kiss each fingertip. "No more apologies, Noah. I'm tired of living in the past. I want to live here, now." She drew his hand across her cheek again. "Make love to me," she whispered.

Noah had to blink to keep his own eyes from tearing up. He was so filled with thankfulness, with love for her right now. And no matter what they were facing beyond the walls of the old farmhouse, he felt as if together, they could beat it.

"Make love to me," she said again.

He was mesmerized by her lips and the pleasure she sent coursing through him as she spoke the words. "Make love to you," he said. "I can't tell you how many times I've thought about making love to you." He drew his hand along her ribcage and over the swell of her breast.

He heard her breath catch in her throat and watched as her eyelids lowered. "I can't tell you how many times I've thought of touching you like this." He swept his hand over her breast, his thumb catching the nub of her nipple. "How many times I've thought of kissing you like this."

He covered her mouth with a hunger he thought he had left behind long ago. He wanted to tell her he loved her, but instead, when they were both breathless, he drew his mouth over her chin, down the length of her slender neck and over the thin fabric of her tank top. He slid his hand beneath her shirt and heard her moan softly as his fingertips found her nipple. He pushed the shirt up further and lowered his mouth to her breast.

She stroked the back of his head, ran her fingers through his short cropped hair. "Noah," she whispered. "Noah, I've missed you so much. Missed this so much . . ."

"Missed you so much," he repeated.

Once again, they were gazing into each other's eyes. He couldn't get enough of her eyes . . . her eyes *on him,* filled with tears and what had to be some form of the love they had once shared.

Rachel moved beneath him, lifting her hips with urgency, molding them to his. Any fear he might have harbored that he would not physically be able to make love to her drifted from his thoughts. That was the past. The alcohol. The depression he only now was beginning to realize he had been suffering from.

He grasped the hem of her top and pulled it over her head, letting it drift over the side of the bed. Next, she raised her hips, allowing him to slip down her panties. His boxers joined her clothes on the floor.

Noah entwined his fingers with hers and she raised her

hands over her head until he was pushing them into the pillow. He covered her face, her throat, her breasts with kisses.

"I've waited so long, Noah," she breathed, closing her eyes. "Missed you so much . . ."

Fingers intertwined, she raised her hips to meet his and he slipped inside her. She gasped and he studied her beautiful face for a moment, wishing he could still time. But her urgency was contagious. He couldn't hold back. They fell and rose again and again, meeting each other in that ageless dance that had always been so perfect. So right between them.

Noah had never made love to another woman and he knew as he lowered his body over Rachel's, taking her fully, that he would never bring another woman to his bed. No matter what happened after today, she was his one true love.

He tried to make the moment last, but the sounds of her moans drove him deeper. Faster. She pulled her hands from his and dug her fingernails into his bare shoulders.

He breathed deeply, trying to think of anything except her beautiful body beneath his. The scent of her clean hair. The sound of her voice. But the pleasure that coursed through him was too strong. Their need too great.

Rachel cried out, her body tensing, her hips arching against his and he pushed into her again and again, seeking the release only she could give him. "Rachel," he moaned.

"Noah . . ."

Later, after they made love and Rachel was cuddled in Noah's arm, her back pressed against his chest, she listened to the sound of his steady breathing as he drifted off to sleep, and she prayed fervently to God that He would help them make their family whole again. That whatever evil lurked beyond the house, human or otherwise, they would have the courage to fight it together.

CHAPTER 26

When Noah woke in the morning to the sound of clinking dishes and Mrs. Santori fussing with the dog in Spanish, he put out his arm for Rachel. The moment he did it, he remembered she was gone. Just before dawn, she'd slipped out of bed, pulling on her panties and T-shirt, and kissed him one last time before returning to her own bedroom. All she had said was something about being confused enough herself and not wanting to confuse Mallory.

Noah quickly showered, dressed, and arrived in the kitchen in time for Mrs. Santori's homemade waffles. Rachel had already showered, had dressed in a T-shirt and shorts, and was leaning over Mallory, cutting up a waffle for her. "Want coffee, hon?" she asked him.

It took a moment for it to register in his mind that she was talking to him. "Um, I'll get it." He spotted her cup on the table. "Need a refill?" He gave Mattie's shoulder a squeeze as he passed him, sitting at the table, eating. "Hey, buddy."

"Please." Rachel looked up, knife and fork in hand, and smiled. "I definitely need the kick this morning. I don't feel like I got a bit of sleep last night."

Noah turned away to avoid making eye contact with her. When he'd heard Rachel's voice in the kitchen, he'd almost been afraid to come out of the bathroom. He'd feared that she would call him outside to tell him the previous night had been a mistake or, worse, that she would pretend it hadn't happened at all. He was thrilled that she was obviously acknowledging their lovemaking, even teasing him about it, but the idea also scared him. If he truly wanted Rachel back, it would mean taking a great deal of responsibility, not just for the past but for their future. It would mean being certain he would never drink again, being certain he could be the man she deserved . . . the man only a short few weeks ago he had feared was gone forever.

"*Día hermosa*," Mrs. Santori remarked, watching the exchange between Noah and Rachel as she poured a scoop of batter into the electric waffle iron. "Lovely day."

Noah didn't know exactly when Consuelo had changed her attitude concerning him, but sometime in the last few weeks she had gone from scowling disapprovingly at him to making him his favorite dishes. Rachel had said last night that he had changed since his return home. The housekeeper must have seen it too.

"It is a beautiful day." He flashed her a grin as he filled two cups with hot coffee. "So what have you two ladies planned for today?" He carried the mugs to the table and sat down at his place, looking to Rachel and Mallory.

Rachel handed the knife and fork to her daughter and took her chair, accepting the mug he slid across the table to her. "The rows need to be mowed between the Pinot trellises. I thought I'd do that before it got too hot and free up Mateo to continue tying those stray vines in the Delaware field. It's amazing how a little rain can make the vines grow so fast." She sipped her coffee.

He stabbed two waffles from the serving plate in the middle of the table and dropped them on his plate. "How about you, Miss Mallory? What do you plan to do today?"

She shrugged. "I don't know. *Pway.*"

"*Play,*" he repeated, emphasizing the diphthong. "That sounds like fun. Wish I could play."

"You can *play* with me and Mattie, if you want." She licked strawberry jam from the corner of her mouth. "Mama said we could run in the sprinkler if I don't wear my cowboy boots again."

He looked to Rachel, fighting a grin. "She did, did she?" He turned to Mattie. "And how about you? You going to play in the sprinkler today?"

Mattie kept his gaze focused on his plate.

Noah met Rachel's gaze. "Maybe while I'm at the hospital getting those tests tomorrow I'll see if they have any referral programs. See what we can do about making one of the appointments we talked about."

Rachel used her fork to take a waffle from the serving plate, still looking into Noah's eyes. *Thank you.* She moved her lips without speaking aloud.

You're welcome he mouthed, and then he turned back to Mattie and Mallory. "My appointment's early tomorrow. Josh is taking me. When I get home, how about if we do something fun like go to the beach?"

"Go to the beach," Mallory squealed. "Me and Mattie love the beach, only Mama never has time to take us."

Noah passed Rachel the syrup. "I think we'll just have to make her take the time, then, won't we?"

She stuck her tongue out at him, but as she took the syrup from his hand, she caressed one of his fingers with one of hers.

He smiled.

"More waffles?" Mrs. Santori carried another plate to the table.

"I think we have enough, Consuelo, thanks." Rachel poured syrup over her waffle.

Noah hadn't gotten two forkfuls in his mouth when he heard a vehicle coming up the driveway. Recognizing the pickup, Chester gave a half-hearted bark from the front porch. "Gotta go." He pushed another piece of waffle into his mouth as he rose out of the chair. "I already put gas in the mower last night, but there's an extra can in the garage if you need it," he told Rachel, washing the waffle down with a gulp of coffee.

"Thanks for breakfast, Consuelo." He walked around the table, headed for the door. "See you all later." On impulse, he leaned over Rachel and kissed her on the mouth.

Mallory gave a squeal, dropped her fork on her plate, and covered her face with sticky hands. Mattie lowered his head so far that his forehead was almost in his plate.

"Bye," Noah whispered.

"Bye," Rachel answered.

Noah walked out of the kitchen whistling.

"No, I don't have an appointment," Delilah told Cora Watkins, who sat behind a desk in St. Paul's office. "I was hoping Father Hailey would have a moment for me anyway."

Cora glanced nervously at the closed door to the priest's office. "Father Hailey likes people to make appointments. He's not like Father Gibson. Father Hailey likes order in his life."

"I'm sure he does." Delilah studied a series of photographs of St. Paul's building and grounds displayed on the wall. The first, by the look of the cars in the background, was a very old one. Late twenties, early thirties. Successive photos showed, as years passed, the changes in the structure of the church and the additions made. "Could you see if he has a minute, Miss Cora?" Delilah pressed. "I promise I won't be long."

Cora rose from behind her desk and hurried to the door, tapped and let herself in, closing it behind her. Delilah heard voices behind the door, Cora's and Father Hailey's. He didn't sound pleased. Cora came out a second later.

"He has an appointment in fifteen minutes."

"Not a problem." Delilah glanced back at the photographs, pointing at one in particular. "Is that Joshua Troyer?"

Cora moved closer, lifting her glasses on a jeweled chain to her eyes. "Is indeed. That was the year we had the new air conditioning put in. He moved some walls for us, made room in the basement for the new unit, and helped put in the new air ducts." She pointed over her desk to an intake vent.

Delilah nodded, the wheels of her mind turning. She wondered if voices could be heard through the air ducts. "And this man?" She pointed to an earlier photograph showing an extension being added to the stone wall that encircled the church and the surrounding graveyard. The large, burly man wearing overalls and standing beside the wall, holding up a mason's trowel, looked vaguely familiar, but she couldn't place the face with a name in the town.

"Oh, that's Jack McConnell."

The name, too, sounded familiar, but Delilah still couldn't place it.

"Mattie McConnell's father," Cora told her, seeming excited to be able to inform someone of something they didn't know. "He fell off a ladder while trying to replace some shingles on the roof after a storm, broke his neck."

"And when was that?"

"Hmmm, let's see. Can't remember what year, but Father Gibson was already here."

"What an awful tragedy," Delilah murmured.

"Terrible tragedy. Left that retarded boy of his all alone. We had no choice, the congregation, but to take up the care for him. Father Gibson did a lot, of course, but we all supported him financially. Cora and I always saw he had a nice sweater at Christmas." She frowned. "Of course, he would never wear it, not even on Sundays to play the organ."

"So Mattie grew up here?"

"Lived here his entire wretched life. Jack was from Stephen

Kill. Everybody thought he'd make something of himself. Went off to college on a football scholarship back in the days when boys didn't do that. Must have got some poor girl pregnant, though, because a short time later he was back, beggin' the church for a job as a handyman, carrying that retarded boy of his under his arm." She shook her head. "Loved that boy something fierce, he did."

"And you never knew who Mattie's mother was?"

"Jack kept to himself after he came back. Never was the same man he'd been before he left. We dated, you know, Jack and I. He was a good-looking boy, in those days. Some thought he'd ask me to marry him." Her mouth twitched. " 'Course, then he started runnin' with Alice."

Delilah couldn't help but notice the change in the pitch of Cora's voice. Was that bitterness she heard? "So you grew up here in Stephen Kill?" She wondered how Cora and Alice had become such good friends if Cora was still holding the grudge she sounded like she was holding against Alice.

"My whole life." She stood taller, bringing her hands together. "Clara and I were raised in that house on Oak Street. Our papa was the postman. He built the house himself, he and his brothers."

"You seem to be close friends with Alice Crupp," she said, still curious about Cora's relationship with Alice. "Did she grow up on Oak Street too?"

"Certainly not." She took on a superior tone in her voice. "Her father rented a farm on the edge of town, close to Gibson's. He was a no-good drunk. After Alice's mother left them, Alice began to miss a lot of school. We . . . lost touch. Later we heard she'd run off and got married, but when she came back to town years later, all she said was that she'd worked in Washington as a secretary. She never married." Cora seemed to be thinking out loud now, barely aware of Delilah's presence. "It always seemed a shame to me—"

"Miss Watkins," Father Hailey interrupted from his office doorway.

"I'm sure Sergeant Swift doesn't have time for a complete history of each of our parishioners."

Delilah shifted her attention from the church secretary to the priest. "Thank you so much for seeing me, Father Hailey. I apologize for not calling ahead of time."

"No apology necessary." He linked his hands. "Won't you come in?"

Delilah entered the office and waited for the priest to close the door behind her. Her gaze settled on the intake vent above the large desk, and she wondered where the floor vents were.

"Please, have a seat." He indicated a chair as he walked around her, slipping in behind his desk.

"No, thank you. Really. This will only take a minute." She wandered to the bookshelves she'd noticed weeks ago when she'd come to his office with Snowden. "This is just a routine visit. It's silly for me to even be here, but if I'm not thorough"—she flashed him a cute, southern girl grin—"my boss will have my hide."

"Yes, Chief Calloway can be a stickler for procedures and rules, can't he?" Father Hailey offered a thin smile.

Delilah rested a finger on one of the books on the shelf. It was a narrative on the Gospel of Luke. "May I?"

"Certainly." He cleared his throat.

"I've always been a fan of Luke."

"Most women are."

She opened the book, glancing over the cover at him. "I'm following up on purchases made at Burton's Hardware in the last few weeks. Did you buy a hatchet?"

"No, no, I don't believe I did." He reached for a book on his desk, slid it over a few inches, and straightened it.

"Oh, that's right. You didn't buy it. You asked Miss Watkins to get it for you." She met his gaze over the book.

"Oh, that hatchet. Yes, yes, I suppose I did."

She slid the book back into its place and moved along the

shelf, closer toward him. "Could I ask why you, or rather, your secretary, purchased it?"

"Yes, certainly." He hesitated, his eyes crinkling at the corners. "Exactly *why* are you asking, Sergeant Swift?"

She lifted a shoulder, running her finger along the spine of several books. "Just routine police work."

"Was the Newtons' son murdered with a hatchet?"

"We don't know yet what was used in the homicide." She drew her hand along the spines of several different versions of the Bible—New Revised Version, New American Standard, New International. Her favorite was the good old King James version. She'd been milk-fed on it since she was an infant.

She slid the King James Bible from its place.

"It was all those pesky branches." Father Hailey rose suddenly from his chair.

There was something in his tone of voice that made her glance over at him. He looked pale.

"Pesky branches?"

"On the elm tree in the parking lot. Tree limbs and branches hanging right over my parking space." He gestured stiffly. "If I've asked our maintenance man, Mr. James, once I've asked him a dozen times to please cut those branches back. They scratch my car and . . . and they leave sap on the hood." He pressed both palms to his desk. "Sap isn't good for the paint on a car, Sergeant."

His answer and the way it was delivered were so bizarre that she couldn't help but believe him. She wasn't sure what she stepped into, but obviously the man had issues with his car and this Mr. James. She opened the timeworn leather cover of the Bible in her hand and began to flip through the pages.

"You're welcome to . . . to see it. To take it, if need be," Father Hailey went on. "I'll cooperate in any way I can, of course. Anything to catch this monster."

"We're not confiscating the—" Delilah halted midsentence, glancing down at the page of the Bible in her hand. For a moment, she thought for sure she was mistaken. The Bible was obviously old . . . pages tear in old books.

But this page of the Old Testament was not torn. Someone had neatly cut a verse from it. . . .

"So how were the tests?" Rachel asked, seated beside Noah on a towel, dressed in a skimpy red bikini.

After Noah had returned home at one, Rachel had given Consuelo the rest of the day off and they had packed up and come to the state park to enjoy the sunshine and the surf for a few hours. When everyone got too hot and too sandy, they thought they'd take Mattie and Mallory up on the boardwalk for a while. Maybe they'd let Mallory ride a few rides in Funland, and they would have pizza for dinner at Grotto's.

"Tests were fine." Noah shrugged. He had a serious farmer's tan going that Rachel had been teasing him about since he pulled off his T-shirt—tanned face and neck and arms below the elbows with lily white chest and legs. "You know, boring like medical tests are."

She dug into the sand with her bare toes. "And I don't suppose anyone said anything . . . about how they went?"

He frowned. "Of course not. Dr. Carson will call in a few days." He glanced at her. "Don't worry about it. I'm sure it's fine. I'm fine."

"Passing out, blacking out, whatever it is you're doing isn't being fine, Noah."

"Why don't we wait and see what the tests show, OK?" He covered her hand with his. "Once we have a diagnosis, then we'll worry."

She closed her eyes and nodded, exhaling.

Noah watched as Mallory approached them carrying a bucket half full of broken shells she and Mattie had been collecting along the stretch of beach. The little girl was wearing a pink bathing suit with an old leather belt cinched around her waist and the ball cap Noah had given her the first week he'd returned home.

"Hey there," Noah greeted as she halted in front of his bare feet stretched out in the sand.

"Hey there," she echoed. Then she cocked her head, studying him seriously, the bucket swinging in her hand. "Are you mommy's boyfriend, Noah?"

He glanced at Rachel, who seemed as surprised by the question as he was. "Well . . ."

"That's really not an appropriate question for a little girl to ask," Rachel said, getting up off the beach towel.

Mallory's face fell. "He isn't your boyfriend?"

Noah got up. "Why are you so full of nosy questions today, Missy?" He took her hand, leading her down toward the water.

"I was wondering," she said, looking over her shoulder at her mother, who was following behind them. "Because if you *was* Mommy's boyfriend, maybe you could be my daddy. Maria's mommy has a boyfriend and he's her daddy now." She halted at the edge of the water. "I never had a daddy."

He looked up to see Rachel pressing her lips tightly together, trying to control her emotions. "I know, sweetie," he said softly, squatting to pick up a shell to add to her bucket.

"Well, I think you should be Mommy's boyfriend," Mallory declared.

"You'd like me for a daddy?" He squatted in the wet sand.

She set down her bucket. "And Mattie, too, because he don't have a daddy either. The voice killed his daddy."

Noah felt a tingle of fear. "The voice killed his daddy? What are you talking about, Mal?"

Rachel knelt in front of Mallory. "No one killed Mattie's daddy, hon. He fell off a ladder. It was an accident."

Mallory picked up her bucket and started up the beach toward Mattie. "That's not what Mattie says," she sang. Then she waved. "Hey, Mattie! You want Noah to be your daddy? He's going to be my daddy."

Noah stood, reaching out to catch Rachel's hand.

"What's she talking about?" she murmured. "Jack fell off the ladder, right? You were there that day."

"I was there," he said, taking a step closer, meeting her gaze. "I didn't see it, but there was no reason to think it was anything but an accident." He searched her eyes carefully. "The police never suspected it was anything other than an accident as far as I know."

Rachel glanced at Mallory, who had plopped down in the sand beside Mattie. "I'm beginning to worry about her. You think I need to take her to a doctor? A psychologist?"

He slipped his arm around her bare waist, remembering the touch of her warm skin, naked beneath the sheet. "Let's hold off. I got the name of a psychologist up in Wilmington who has some experience with idiot savants. Let's make an appointment, talk with her, and then see if we can decipher where the problem here is."

"I mean, she seems like a perfectly normal child, doesn't she?" Rachel asked, concern in her voice. "She's been healthy since the day she was born."

"I'm sure she's fine. Worse-case scenario, she's got an even better imagination than we thought."

"And she's making up all this stuff about what Mattie tells her."

"It's certainly possible."

Rachel halted, pulling off her dark sunglasses. "What kind of little girl makes up things like people's fathers having been murdered and voices no one else hears?"

"It's going to be OK," Noah insisted, leaning down to brush his lips against hers. "Don't worry. We're going to be OK."

"See, Mattie!" Mallory cried at the sight of her mother and Noah kissing. "I told you Noah was going to be our daddy!"

* * *

"This is a bad idea." Snowden stepped through Delilah's front door.

"So why'd you come again?" she teased lightly. She walked through the dark hall to the kitchen, knowing he'd follow her. She got him a glass of water before she turned to him.

"I keep thinking about you." He accepted the glass of water. "I need to be concentrating on the case and instead I'm thinking about a woman." He raised one hand in frustration, making a fist and drawing it down to his side.

Delilah hated to see him in such anguish over something so simple as coming to her place, sitting on the couch, talking. There'd been nothing between them anyone could possibly say was inappropriate . . . not that she hadn't had some inappropriate thoughts. But she understood what he meant. As the chief of police, her superior, and the only black man on the force, he was held to a higher standard.

"I think about you, too, Snowden," she said softly. "And I think about the fact that my daddy and my brothers would skin us both alive if they saw us together like this." She held his gaze for a moment, trying to read what he was thinking in those dark blue depths. She smiled. "Fortunately, between thinking about you stripped down to your undershorts and my daddy lynching us, I've been going over this case in my head. Now I know you like the ex-priest. I know what's logical, maybe even the direction the evidence points, what little we have, but I want you to hear me out."

"I just don't want to see you waste your time. Every minute that passes that we don't find this guy, we're moving closer to another killing. We both know he's going to kill again."

"I understand that. But I'm telling you, Snowden, this is getting weirder by the day. I talked to Father Hailey."

"And?"

Snowden didn't appear convinced they needed to look

beyond Noah Gibson, but at least he was willing to listen to her. It occurred to her that maybe he was willing to listen to her as long as she was willing to stand in her kitchen in her brother's boxers, but she had a feeling what was going on between her and Snowden was something more than simple lust.

"Father Hailey sent Cora to get the hatchet to cut away some tree limbs hanging over his car in the church parking lot." She rolled her eyes. "Not sure why Cora sent Alice and lied about it. I discovered a couple of interesting things while I was paying my visit to St. Paul's, though." She leaned against the counter, arms crossed.

Snowden sipped his water. "Care to fill me in?"

"Had quite a scare, for one thing. Seems Father Hailey cuts passages out of Bibles."

Snowden arched a dark brow.

"I'm standing there in his office, flipping through the pages of a Bible and I come to a page that's been cut up." She shook her head. "Yeah, I was hoping for an instant that we'd gotten lucky. No such luck. Not the verses we're looking for, and he was able to show me a scrapbook he keeps of them."

Snowden frowned. "Why would a priest be cutting verses from a Bible and keeping them in a scrapbook?"

"Apparently, it's for his little book of temptations. Something tempts him, a bad thought, bad desire"—she gestured—"he cuts the passage out and adds it to a scrapbook."

Snowden drained his glass and crossed the kitchen to place it in the sink. "That's a little weird."

"I thought so too." She shifted her posture slightly so that she was turned toward him. "But that doesn't make him a killer."

"What else did you find out?" He leaned against the counter beside her.

"That Joshua Troyer helped do some work on St. Paul's a few years back when Gibson was the priest there and was counseling people in his office."

"So?"

"Apparently he moved some walls to make room for a new central air conditioning system, but get this." She raised her hand to hold her finger practically under his nose. "He helped install heat and air ducts. The project must have taken months." She shrugged. "A person wonders what could be heard through those ducts."

"Joshua Troyer is a peaceful man. I've never heard him say a cross word about anyone in my life. Never heard him so much as even utter a curse word."

"OK, but you still have to admit, he's a little weird, and so's the wife with the doily on her head." She thought for a moment. "They ever have any children?"

He shook his head. "She's not able to conceive. It's been a difficult issue in their lives. Children are very important to the Mennonite community."

"And they didn't hit the in vitro clinic like other infertile couples? Adopt?"

"God's will, Joshua says."

Delilah let that idea settle in her head before she went on. Snowden didn't seem to mind the silence. "You never told me that someone died working at the church when Noah Gibson was there."

"Jack McConnell, Mattie's father. He fell off a ladder. That has nothing to do with this case."

"I know," she thought out loud. "Just interesting, I guess. That's all."

"Interesting, yes, all of it is. Maybe even a little questionable, but . . ." He reached out to touch her hand with one finger. "None of this information takes us in any direction."

"Maybe not." His finger brushed hers, and she found herself holding her breath. "But it tells us that we need to be careful not to be so confident it's the ex-priest that we don't see someone else right under our noses. I mean, honestly, what have we got on Gibson?"

He took her hand in his, but he was still leaning back

against the sink. He didn't look at her. "What we've still got is the fact that he, to our knowledge, is the only person who knew about the 'sins' the victims committed."

"OK." Delilah exhaled, her mind divided between the feel of Snowden's touch and the subject at hand. "So he knew about the sins, but—"

"And motive." He turned toward her. "I'm telling you, the guy has motive."

"Maybe." She swayed her head one way and then the other. "It's just that, besides you, he seems like the most ordinary, sanest guy in this town."

Snowden half smiled. "I should go."

"Why?" She tugged on his hand, wishing he would kiss her or she'd get up enough nerve to kiss him.

He searched her gaze for a moment and she found herself lost in the gentleness of his eyes. "You know why," he whispered.

Then he let go of her hand, walked out of the kitchen, and out the front door.

Azrael moaned, gripping the bed sheet, forehead beaded in sweat. The dream had begun so pleasantly. Sunshine. Warmth. The comforting touch of a hand. It felt so good to be loved, to be wanted, that a joy filled Azrael's heart.

Then, suddenly, the sun grew brighter until it was a spotlight overhead, so intense the angel could not see. The bright white room filled with voices. Strangers. The joy gave way to terror and an overwhelming sense of being alone in the world.

Azrael had disappointed God.

The angel cried out, twisting in the sweat-soaked sheets, the pain now excruciating. "No! No . . ."

Waves of blood. Waves of pain. Sin washing down on God's chosen one.

From the blood tumbled a baby. Not a baby at all, but a two-headed monster.

Azrael screamed and awoke to a dark room and the pleasant hum of the air conditioner.

CHAPTER 27

"Dr. Carson." Irma Jean walked into his private office, with its rich, dark wainscoting and diplomas and medical degrees framed grandly on the walls. "You're certainly in early." She glanced at her watch, a gift from Edgar many years ago, before they'd both become widowed, before they'd become lovers. "Your first appointment isn't for another half an hour."

He glanced up from the open file on his desk. He looked tired, the lines around his mouth more pronounced than usual. "I know. I couldn't sleep, so I came in to get some paperwork done." He tapped on the file with his pen. "I'm concerned about this patient."

She glanced down at the record, noted the patient's name, and walked to the windows to open the mini-blinds so that the sun poured through the cracks but wasn't blinding. "Test results?"

"They showed nothing organic." He sat back in his chair, tucking his hands behind his head. "I just keep going over the conversation we had during the initial exam, and something troubles me, but I can't put my finger on it."

"You don't often miss a diagnosis." She straightened several large medical textbooks that had begun to slide on a shelf under the windows.

"I'm not thinking medical so much as psychological. This isn't the first patient I've had this summer to complain about nightmares, but there's something odd here. I feel like I'm missing a red flag or something."

"You think there could be an undiagnosed psychological disorder?"

He thought for a moment. "Very possibly."

"You've always been honest with your patients, and they've always trusted in that honesty." She moved to the door. "Maybe you need to express your concerns to the patient and suggest an appointment with a physician who deals with this type of thing."

He removed his bifocals and rubbed his eyes. "I suppose that wouldn't hurt. I just don't want to offend anyone. I mean, we all say odd things, act a little crazy sometimes, rationalize inaccurately. The deaths in the town this summer have everyone on edge. I know I'm not myself." He gestured toward her. "Even you said you've been doing things you never did before—checking the locks on the windows and doors five or six times a night."

She rested her hand on the doorknob. "It could very well be nothing, but you've always been good about your gut instinct. If your instinct tells you something is wrong, Edgar, you need to address the matter with the patient."

He thought for a moment. "You're right." He nodded. "You're absolutely right, Irma Jean."

She smiled. "Coffee?"

"Please." He put his glasses back on, and as she closed the door behind her, he made a note next to his list of phone calls for the day.

* * *

"Hey, where is everyone?" Rachel walked out onto the front porch, barefoot but dressed, cup of coffee in her hand. It was overcast and a light rain was falling. Though it had cooled off slightly, the air was still heavy with the July humidity of southern Delaware.

Noah glanced over his shoulder, smiling at the sight of her, a smile that she had to admit made her warm from the tips of her toes to the top of her head. As crazy as it sounded, she was in love and there was no denying it. In the week and a half since the first time she and Noah had made love in more than five years, they had been tentatively working through their new relationship. Testing the waters, as it were.

Rachel wasn't foolish enough to think they could ever go back to the early days when they were first married and so happy together, before all the bad stuff began, before Noah's drinking, but she was hopeful that maybe, just maybe, they could make this new relationship work.

He was not, of course, the man she had first fallen in love with in high school. How could he be? Everything he once was, in his mind, was gone. He had lost the church. He had lost his children. His parents. He had taken lives and given up five years of his life as payment. The new Noah was not as trusting of himself or others, certainly not as sweetly naïve. He was quieter, more introverted, at times. But he also spoke up sooner when it came to expressing his thoughts and feelings. He was more focused. More intense in many ways.

There were things about Noah that hadn't changed too. She reveled in those attributes—his tenderness; his work ethic; his interest in anything new, different, or challenging; and his solid belief in family. Watching Noah with Mallory sometimes brought tears to her eyes. Noah was becoming the father Rachel had always dreamed her daughter would have, and it was becoming obvious she adored him. Finding a father for Mallory certainly wasn't a good-enough reason to make a commitment to Noah a second time, but it would be impossible for Rachel not to take that into consideration.

She and Noah, and later, she as a single parent, had always believed in the importance of two parents in a child's life, and right now she couldn't imagine a better father, a father who loved Mallory more than Noah.

Noah scooted over from where he sat on the top step of the porch and made room for her. She sat down beside him.

He gave her a quick good morning kiss on her cheek, which was more endearing than a kiss on the mouth first thing in the morning, because it wasn't a kiss of desire, it was a kiss of commitment, of friendship and trust. A kiss of love.

"Let's see, it's Friday, so it's Mrs. Santori's day off. And Mattie and Mallory are lying on the living room floor, putting wooden puzzles together. And I'm here." He raised both hands and then reached down to pick up his coffee cup with his left hand. "Just watching the rain fall, thinking how lucky a man I am."

He turned to face her, and she couldn't resist brushing her lips against his. Last night, she'd sneaked down to his room in the middle of the night, after another one of her nightmares, and she'd woken him and they'd made love. When she closed her eyes, she could still feel his hands on her breasts, and the tremors of pleasure they yielded.

Rachel rubbed his knee through his blue jeans and sipped her coffee. "It was nice of you to let me sleep. I guess Mallory and Mattie already had breakfast."

"Well, you didn't go back to bed until almost six." He grinned. "I thought you could use a little sleep. And yes, they have eaten. Cap'n Crunch with Crunch Berries."

She wrinkled her nose. "Yuck. Glad I missed that."

He gazed out at the rain again, quiet for a moment. "Mattie was sitting on the porch this morning when I let Chester out at six-thirty. I don't know how long he'd been out here."

"That's the third time this week."

"I know. It's as if, all of a sudden, that room that has been his sanctuary scares him." Noah was quiet again. "I was wondering if we should consider bringing him into the house."

She exhaled, drawing her hand over her head, pushing her hair back. "I know, I was wondering the same thing. I only wish we didn't have to wait so long for that psychologist's appointment. September seems like a long way off right now."

"Another month and a half is all." He rubbed her arm. "That's really not unheard of. And I understand Dr. Powers has an excellent reputation for helping people like Mattie."

"You're right. I'm just concerned with whether or not it's safe to have him in the house." She lifted one hand and let it fall to his knee. "I hope Dr. Powers can give us some better insight into what he's capable of doing." She paused, thinking. "And even if we wanted to bring him into the house, where would we put him? Your parents' room is too big; you know how he prefers small spaces. Not to mention it's full of their things."

"I thought about that." Noah swirled the coffee in his cup. "And I have an idea."

She could guess what his idea was going to be by his tone of voice, and she couldn't resist a smile because she'd been thinking the same thing. She just hadn't been ready to voice it. "Yes, I'm listening . . ."

"I could move upstairs with you," he whispered into her ear, nipping at her earlobe. "And Mattie could have my room."

"I suppose that could work." She looked into his eyes, amazed that he could still make her feel this giddy inside. "We'd hear him if he came up the stairs, wouldn't we?" She pressed her lips together, trying to consider what was best for Mattie, and not think about having Noah all to herself in her bed each night.

"We could hear him. And honestly, Rachel, we have no proof there's any reason to be worried about having him in the house in the first place. He hasn't done a thing wrong."

"Except move the car and tractor. Possibly go somewhere in them. I swear the car was moved again two nights ago."

"Well, if Mattie is taking the car, we'd be able to keep track of him better if he was in the house. There's no way Chester would let him leave the house at night without barking and waking us both up. You heard how he carried on with me the other night when I went out to the car to get the checkbook after you'd gone to bed."

She chuckled. "And I thought watchdogs were supposed to keep people out of the house, not in the house."

Noah smiled slyly. She was thinking about sleeping together, too. "This plan could work."

"I don't know," she hedged. "There's no way Mallory is not going to notice your sleeping in my room. I'd have to talk to her, and honestly, I don't know what I would say." She made herself meet his gaze. "I'm not sure what I'm ready to say because I'm not sure I'm ready to . . ."

"Not sure you're ready to give me another chance?"

She held the warm coffee cup between both her hands, watching the rain fall on the bright green grass. "It just hasn't been that long, Noah. I mean, I know you've been good about going to AA. I know you haven't been drinking, but—"

"Rache, I stopped drinking the night I was arrested. Remember, I've had five years to dry out."

"I know." She felt tears burn the backs of her eyelids. "I just . . . I just can't live through anything like that again, Noah. I can't subject Mallory to it, and with everything else that's going on right now . . ." Against her will, her voice raised in pitch. "What with Mattie and . . . and this crazy killer and these nightmares that won't go away. This awful feeling of impending doom . . ."

"It's all right." He set down his cup and put his arm around her, drawing her closer. "Rache, it's all right. I didn't mean to push you. We don't have to rush things. Mattie can just move into the bedroom with me."

"There's too much junk in there," she moaned. "I can't

believe I was so mean as to have put you in there to begin with. I should have cleaned your parents' room out."

"It's been fine. I think I would have been overwhelmed in Mom and Dad's room, too. Remember, I slept in a jail cell for five years," he teased.

She managed half a smile.

"Come on, Rache." He rubbed her upper arm. "We'll clean out the spare room today. Look, it's a perfect day for it." He gestured to the falling rain. "Weather channel says it's going to do this all day. We can make it a family project."

She took a deep breath, pressing her cheek to his shoulder. "I don't mean to sound so indecisive. I don't mean to lead you on and then turn you away." She made herself look into his dark eyes. "I do love you. Guess I never stopped, as much as I might have wanted to."

"That's all I need." He continued to look into her eyes. "It's all I want, Rache. Your love. Mallory's. I'll take you any way you're still willing to have me."

His words were so sweet that she felt tears well in her eyes again. "Let's think about it. In the meantime, we could clean up that mess, move some of the stuff, like that sewing machine I'm never going to use, up to the nursery." She thought for a minute. "You could go through all those boxes still up there. You haven't touched them in weeks."

He scowled, but it only seemed half-hearted. "How did I know that sooner or later you were going to make me do that?"

"Well, you need to do it. If you want to put what happened behind you, you need to go through that stuff. There's nothing there to be afraid of, Noah," she told him. "You've seen pictures of the boys around the house here. I know it hurts, but they're a part of us."

"It's not the boys' pictures." He drew his arm from her shoulder and picked up his coffee cup again, staring into it.

"What is it then?"

"If I unpack the boxes . . ." He halted and started again. "If I unpack those boxes, it's like I'm going to stay."

"I don't understand. You told me the first day you got home that you weren't moving."

"I mean here," he said softly, gently tapping his chest, over his heart. "It means I'm going to live. I'm going to move on. I'm going to make it."

It had never occurred to Rachel that Noah had ever feared he might relapse. Certainly the first days he had been home from prison he had seemed withdrawn, lacked much confidence in himself, but that had faded so quickly. He had been working so hard, trying so hard.

"Oh, Noah," she breathed, holding his gaze. "Of course you're going to make it. I think . . . I think *we're* going to make it."

He took a deep breath. Exhaled. "OK," he told her, rising from the step and offering his hand to her to help her up. "So today we clean out my room, we go through those boxes of mine upstairs, and we think about what our next move is going to be. I don't know. Maybe we shouldn't sleep together right now; maybe we should wait until we're both ready to recommit to marriage again."

She walked across the porch, looking back over her shoulder. It was the second time this week he had mentioned them remarrying. "You're just talking about sleeping, right?" she teased. "We just shouldn't *sleep* together?"

Noah tipped back his head and laughed.

"Hey, what's so funny?" Mallory thrust open the screen door to let them in.

"None of your business, Miss Nosy." Rachel touched her daughter's upturned nose with the tip of her finger. "Now go find Mattie and bring him here. We've got work to do."

Rachel had been putting off, dreading, cleaning the spare room downstairs for years and yet, somehow, Noah made it fun. He assigned tasks to each person, allowing Mattie to carry boxes and Mallory to fill bags with trash or items to go to the church thrift store. Rachel found new homes for the items they decided to keep while keeping up a steady conversation with Noah. They didn't talk about anything important—the weather, how the grape crops were faring, what kind of wine they would make this fall. It was the kind of stuff a husband and wife—partners—talked about, and it felt good.

When the time came, after lunch, when Mallory and Mattie had crashed on the living room floor to watch a Disney movie, Rachel climbed the stairs in front of Noah. She led him to the tiny room at the top of the stairs that had once been their nursery, but after the death of their sons had become a storage closet.

They had to turn on the overhead light and borrow a lamp from Rachel's bedroom because it was so dark in the small room on the overcast day. They sat on the floor side by side and began to pull through the boxes. Once they started, Noah seemed to relax a little.

Several boxes held clothes; some he decided to keep, but much of it was outdated enough that she convinced him to donate it to the thrift shop. They went through books, mostly religious, most he decided to get rid of. The box of keepsakes was the hardest for Noah . . . and for Rachel. She had packed away the two framed photos of their little boys that he'd kept in his office at the church and the wedding photo of them and his parents, as well as a photo taken on the beach before they were married. There were more ball caps, a tin lunchbox from his childhood, several yearbooks.

They were laughing about a photo taken their senior year in high school when the phone rang. Rachel picked up the cordless phone and scooted back on the floor so that she was leaning against the wall. After a day of pulling, sliding, and carrying stuff all over the house, her back was beginning to ache.

"Hello."

"Good afternoon, this is Dr. Carson's office calling," said the nurse in a very cool, efficient voice. "May I speak with Mr. Gibson?"

"Sure, just a minute, please." Rachel covered the mouth-piece with her hand. "Dr. Carson's office calling." She handed the phone to him.

"Hello, this is Noah Gibson." He got up off the floor and walked a few steps across the small room. "Yes, thank you, I'll hold." He waited. "Dr. Carson . . ."

Rachel rose on her knees, eager to hear what the doctor had to say. According to Noah, his blackouts were becoming less frequent. She hadn't witnessed another, and he said he'd only had two, that he knew of, in the last ten days. Still, she was worried because even one or two wasn't normal. She couldn't bear to think what she would do if he had a brain tumor or something horrible like that, but she couldn't to-tally dismiss the possibility either, until they knew for cer-tain.

"Um-hmm. Um-hmm."

"What's he say?" Rachel whispered.

"I see." Noah walked out the door into the hall.

Rachel stared at the empty doorway for a second, unsure if she should follow him. She was a little hurt that he felt the need to walk out of the room, away from her, but she knew that was silly. A lot of people paced when they talked on the phone. She paced.

"Um-hmm. OK, what does that mean?" she heard him say. He was getting farther away; he had to be nearly to her bedroom door.

She had to fight the urge to get up and follow him, or at least crawl to the doorway to see if she could hear any better. She could still hear Noah say the occasional word, but she couldn't make out what he was saying. Mostly he was just listening.

She heard him turn at the end of the hallway and start back toward her.

"No, I don't think that will be necessary."

She wrapped her arms around herself, suddenly feeling chilled. The dampness from the rain seemed to be seeping through the exterior wall. Through the small, rain-splattered window.

Noah was quiet for a moment. "Entirely," he said, surprisingly forceful. "Listen, I appreciate you calling, Dr. Carson. I won't take up any more of your time."

Another pause.

"Certainly. I'll let you know."

Rachel heard the phone click. He didn't even say goodbye. She realized that her heart was beating faster. She forced herself to stay right where she was until he came around the corner.

"What did Dr. Carson have to say about the test results?"

"He said everything looked fine. CAT scan. MRI." He set the phone on a cardboard box and leaned over to pick up one they'd marked with a black magic marker. *Books. Give away.*

"There's nothing? It was completely normal?"

"Yup. Healthy forty-year-old brain." He carried the box out of the room.

Rachel followed. "So what did he say about the blackouts? Why are you having them?"

"He doesn't know." Noah started down the steps.

"He doesn't know? That's it?" She fought the panic in her chest. "I don't understand. Aren't there more tests?"

"I suppose there are, Rachel, but I'm not taking them. It's already better." At the bottom of the stairs, he turned into the kitchen. "Could you get the back door? I'm going to put this stuff in the back of the car. We can take it to the church on Monday."

She held open the door for him. "So that's it?"

"That's it. If they get worse, I'll call him again. He'll send me to someone else."

"Like a neurologist? And you don't think you should see one now?"

"No, Rache, I don't." He turned back toward her, box in his arms, rain falling, wetting his shirt, his hair. "I'm telling you, it's going to be all right." He stared hard at her. "Just let it go."

She started to say something, then pressed her lips together, cool rain hitting her face. Maybe he was right. Maybe she did need to let it go. She turned to go back into the house, mumbling something about getting another box. As she climbed the porch steps, she wondered what the real reason was that she didn't press him any further.

Was it because she thought he was right, he was fine, or because she didn't want to consider any other possibilities?

CHAPTER 28

The phone rang and Delilah danced her way from the stove toward the opposite counter, a wooden spoon in her hand. It was Motown night and she was listening to Aretha Franklin, her idol. If Delilah could have been granted one wish, it would have been to have had a voice like Aretha's.

"R-E-S-P-E-C-T, find out what it means to me," she sang into the spoon, picking up the handset. " 'llo."

"Delilah."

She smiled, licking the tomato sauce from the spoon as she parked her fanny against the counter. "Hey, I wasn't expecting to hear from you until later," she said, referring to Snowden's almost nightly late-night visits. He never stayed long, they talked almost exclusively about the murder cases, but there was no doubt in either of their minds that things were heating up between them. They just hadn't decided yet what to do about it.

"Delilah, we found it," Snowden said, his voice thick with emotion.

"Found it?" She walked back to the stove to stir her home-made spaghetti sauce. "Found what?"

"The murder weapon. The machete Rachel Gibson bought."

Delilah dropped the spoon into the pot of sauce and it splashed up, burning her finger. "Holy crap," she muttered, licking the hot sauce from her finger. "You're sure it's the machete she bought? Sure it was used to cut off Skeeter's hands?"

"Well, it's the same model Burton's sells in their store. The only model, and it looks like blood on the blade."

"Where is it?" She cut the flame off under the pot and headed out of the kitchen.

"It's sitting on my desk in an evidence bag."

"Where was it found? Who found it? The rain today—"

"We got lucky," he interrupted. "Some kids found it under the Horsey Mill Pond Bridge. Killer must have driven over the bridge and thrown it over the side, thinking it would go into the water, but the pond's water level's been down for weeks."

"So it stayed dry, preserving any evidence," she whispered, as if it were a miracle.

"I hope so."

"I'm coming." She flipped the light on in her bedroom and reached for a pair of shorts from her dirty clothes basket. "Don't go anywhere. I'll be there in ten minutes." She hung up, tossed the phone on her bed, and grabbed a bra out of the top drawer of her dresser.

It was difficult for her to believe that Noah Gibson could be such a gruesome, cold-hearted killer but Delilah knew he was a more realistic suspect than Rachel. And Delilah was usually such a good judge of character. But wasn't that what people always said about serial killers? Wasn't that what all the neighbors had said about Wichita's BTK Strangler when they discovered how many people the devoted husband, father, and church leader had tortured and killed? These men weren't ordinary criminals; they were bright, often articulate, friendly. They had a way of convincing people they were who they wanted other people to believe they were.

Delilah threw a T-shirt over her head, slid her feet into a pair of flip-flops, and grabbed her personal firearm off the top of the dresser. She dropped it into her purse as she went out the front door, into the dark. A girl just couldn't be too safe these days. If a man like Noah Gibson could be a murderer, anyone could.

"So how do you want to proceed, Sergeant?" Snowden sat back in his chair behind his desk, looking to her. His office door was open, but the building was quiet. Almost eerie quiet. The cops on duty, just three on a Sunday, were out on patrol. The only others in the building were the dispatcher behind the safety glass in the room out front and the woman who worked as the evening janitor.

Delilah met Snowden's gaze. He wore a pair of blue jeans and an eggplant-colored polo shirt. It was one of the few times Delilah had ever seen him in anything but his uniform or running clothes, and it gave her a different perspective on him. In the civilian clothes, he didn't quite appear to be the cool hard-ass he liked people to think he was.

"Sergeant?"

She shifted her attention to the machete in a large plastic evidence bag on his desk in front of her, shifting gears. There was no denying those rusty stains were blood. "It goes to the lab, of course. We have the blood tested to see if it matches Newton's. We check fingerprints." She looked up, unable to smile, despite the fact that they might have the killer. "Won't be a problem matching Noah Gibson's fingerprints, if they're on it. We know he's on file."

"You want to bring him in?"

"Tonight?"

"Certainly within our rights. He refused to turn over the machete when we asked to see it."

Delilah hesitated. "Actually, it was Rachel Gibson who

refused to show it to us without a warrant. She was the one being uncooperative."

He frowned until a crease formed on his forehead. "You think she killed these people? You think she's strong enough to have held Skeeter down while she chopped off his hands?"

"There was no evidence of a struggle at the scene."

His frown moved downward to tug at his sensual, full lips. "You're serious? Delilah, I know this woman. She couldn't do something like this. Women aren't serial killers."

"Tell Aileen Wuornos's victims' families that." She got up out of her chair to pace. "Two percent."

"Two percent?"

He was obviously annoyed with her. She didn't care. Her job was to look at the evidence objectively. She wasn't sure how objective he could be when it came to Rachel Gibson. Even if she was unobtainable and he knew it, he still had a soft spot for her. The funny thing was, Delilah wasn't even jealous. She was kind of glad to know he *could* have a soft spot for someone.

"I've been doing some research on the Internet, and two percent of all serial killers are female. So it's not unheard of." She laced her fingers together and pushed her arms out to stretch them. "That's all I'm saying."

"You still don't think it's him."

"I don't think it's him." She began to pace behind the chair in front of his desk. "But I'll keep an open mind. I'll look at what the lab says the machete tells us. I'll interview him again."

Snowden pushed back in his chair and stared at the white ceiling tiles.

"What?" she asked after a long moment of silence stretched between them.

"I didn't say anything."

She dropped both hands to her hips, halting beside the desk. He could be such a . . . such a *man*. "No, you didn't have to say anything. I can see the look on your face. What are you thinking?"

"I'm thinking that Noah Gibson still looks like our best suspect because I don't know who else we've got. Most serial killers have been interviewed by police as possible suspects, often multiple times, but are released for lack of evidence. The Wichita strangler was interviewed. So was Ted Bundy."

"I disagree that we don't have any other suspects. What about Joshua Troyer? He worked in the church for months and could have overheard a lot of things. He knows everyone in town, but he's kind of invisible, isn't he?" She narrowed her eyes. "Quiet. Good natured. Always the neighborly type, willing to lend a hand. He's also religious. And you heard what he said about being willing to kill people for their sins." She shuddered. "He certainly gave me the creeps."

Snowden folded his hands behind his head.

"And what about Cora Watkins?" she continued.

"What about her?"

Delilah perched herself on the edge of the chair in front of the desk and leaned forward, pressing both hands on the smooth, polished wood. "She's certainly overheard things over the years. Saw people come and go in that private church office. She's the town gossip, for heaven's sake. If she doesn't know people's secrets, no one does!" She threw her hands up in the air in emphasis.

"She's sixty years old, Delilah. Overweight."

"She's pretty darned spry when she's trying to cut in line in front of you at the grocery store."

He surprised her with a smile. "You're good at this. Observing people, reading them."

She sat back in the chair, watching him. He was such a handsome man, such a good man. But somehow, he always seemed sad to her. "Apparently I'm not good enough, otherwise I'd have this guy . . . or gal, by now."

He smiled again. "You should go home. I'll lock this up in the evidence locker and have one of the guys personally carry it over to the crime lab in Baltimore in the morning."

"So you don't think we should bring Noah Gibson in tonight?"

He shook his head. "We have his machete, but he'll only say that's meaningless. That someone stole it from their place."

She got up. "Maybe someone did."

He rose out of his chair and walked around his desk. "Go home, Delilah."

She looked up into his eyes. "What are you going to do?"

"Process this evidence, go home, take a shower, have something to eat, and go to bed."

"You promise?"

He nodded.

She hesitated and then lifted her lashes. "You want me to come with you?" she whispered, holding his blue-eyed gaze.

He caught her hand in his and lifted it to his lips, kissing it gently. "I can't tell you how much I'd like that right now."

She closed her eyes for a moment. "But we can't."

"We can't," he murmured as he let her hand go.

Her heart still in her throat, she grabbed her purse off the edge of his desk and walked out of the office. "See you tomorrow, Chief."

"See you tomorrow, Sergeant."

Ellen set her empty soup bowl in the sink, filled it with water, and then grabbed the dog leash on the counter. "Jetson," she called.

The red and white corgi bounced into the kitchen.

"That's a good boy. Such a good boy. I know it's late, but how about that walk?" She leaned over to drop the bright blue cinch collar over his head. Ellen had returned home to Stephen Kill that night, even though she usually spent Sundays at her place at the beach. Jill had often stayed over until Monday morning before returning to her office in D.C. "Summer hours," she called it.

But Saturday, Ellen and Jill had had a huge blowup. The kind from which relationships didn't recover. Jill had accused Ellen of not paying enough attention to her, of taking her for granted. Ellen maintained that Jill didn't have enough respect for the importance of her job. What it all boiled down to was that Jill thought Ellen ought to come out. Ellen didn't think Sussex County or her coworkers were quite ready for that. The argument had gotten ugly and ended with Jill packing her bag and walking out.

"They're just not ready for a lesbo judge, are they, boy?" Ellen asked her dog, giving him a pat on the head. She rose. "OK, let's go, but just a short potty walk."

As she walked out the back door, she grabbed her keys with the pepper spray canister on the keychain. Like everyone else in town, she was a little uneasy with a killer on the loose. But that didn't mean she was going to alter her life in any way; that would just be giving in to the criminal. That was definitely something she'd learned in the last two years on the bench. A person had to fight, *society* had to fight, against these individuals trying to ruin the lives of those who were good and kind and faithful.

Ellen led Jetson out the back door, through the garden and out the front gate, onto Main Street. Well lit, with sidewalks, it was the central street that ran through Stephen Kill. Turn-of-the-century Victorian houses painted in bright pastel colors dotted both sides of the street. She headed east, out of town, past the well-tended lawns and minivans and SUVs parked in the driveways.

It was warm out, and the humidity was so high that the air was oppressive, but Ellen walked at an energetic pace. Jill, a health nut, was always telling her she needed to exercise more, eat better. In the last six months, thanks to Jill's nagging, Ellen had actually lost a few pounds and toned up. She supposed she'd pack it all on again now that Jill was gone. And Ellen knew she wasn't coming back.

A lump rose in her throat and she forced it down. She didn't know if she'd been in love with Jill or not, but she had certainly cared deeply for her.

She took a deep breath. She didn't have time for foolish sentiment. This really was for the best. Jill was right—Ellen was married to her job; she didn't have time for a good relationship.

Jetson halted on the sidewalk and looked over his shoulder.

Ellen glanced in the same direction. There was very little breeze, but the ground-sweeping branches of the weeping willow tree in the Belkens' front yard swayed. A cicada chirped. There was nothing there. Shadows.

"Come on, boy." Ellen tugged on the dog's leash. "If you have to go, you better go. I'm not taking you out in the middle of the night. I'm warning you, now. I'm not in the mood."

They walked the last half a block to where the sidewalk ended, and Ellen turned around and headed back home. Their progress was slowed as she allowed Jetson to stop to investigate several times—a squashed, dry toad; a little pile of squirrel excrement.

Walking up the street, Ellen glanced at the hand-carved welcome sign on a small patch of grass between the two lanes of the street. As one entered the town and was greeted by the sign, the street narrowed considerably, dating back to the original establishment of the town in the seventeenth century.

The sign was usually well lit by a spotlight. The light was set by a timer, and Ellen was sure it had already been glowing when she arrived in town. Maybe the bulb had burned out, or maybe the timer in the box at the base of the sign needed to be jiggled. Earlier in the summer she and Jetson had stopped to do just that on one of their evening walks.

Ellen tugged on the dog leash and crossed the pavement
to the grassy island.

Azrael cut across the Belkens' backyard, knife in hand,
hidden beneath the sleeve of the yellow rain slicker. Someone's dog barked. Not the Belkens' German shepherd, a
smaller dog. The summer air was warm and thick, suffocat-
ing, but it did not slow the Angel of Death. There was a task
to be done. The offender had to pay for the sin. God had given
His order. God had spoken.

At least, Azrael thought, God has spoken . . .

The Angel could not remember the sound of God's voice
or when the order had been given. Last night? This morning?

Everything was getting so confusing. It was the nightmares. The two-headed baby kept coming back again and
again, and Azrael knew something would have to be done
about it soon. End it soon.

And it wasn't just the baby, it was the pressure of being
God's servant but no one knowing. No one understanding.
The whole town was in an uproar. The whole state. There were
articles in the newspaper every day. Earlier in the week,
CNN had come to town to tape a short piece on the serial
killer stalking the small, all-American East Coast town.

Why did no one see the truth? This was not the work of a
serial killer. It was the work of a vengeful God. Mankind had
been warned. The Bible was clear. Punishment would be
handed down to those who disobeyed God's laws.

Azrael reached the sidewalk but did not look up or down
the street. Was not afraid to be seen. God protected His ser-
vants.

The Angel spotted the judge crossing the street. She had
left through the back door of her house, her dog with her. It
was a cute little red and white dog with a long body and
short legs. The kind the Queen of England had.

As the judge reached the town sign, she loosened the

dog's leash and went down on one knee to examine the spotlight that usually illuminated the sign.

The little dog turned and barked in greeting as Azrael crossed the street. The judge turned, recognized the Angel, and smiled. "Spotlight's out." She turned back, gesturing. "I'm wondering if it's the bulb." She started to turn back toward Azrael, seeming surprised now. "Expecting rain?"

Azrael reached out and around, and before the judge realized what was happening, the kitchen knife tore across the soft flesh of her neck. Ellen's eyes widened in surprise, but she did not scream. The leash fell from her hand, and her dog darted across the street with a little yip of fear.

The judge rocked back on her heels, and Azrael caught her under the armspits. Blood pumped from the open wound into the soft grass and the neatly trimmed azalea bushes. There were gurgling sounds.

Azrael dragged her around the spotlight, trying not to dig up any more of the mulch than necessary. City workers had to rake the mulch by hand; it wouldn't be very nice to make more work for them.

The judge was surprisingly light. Surprisingly limp already.

The Angel moved the judge's body into position and sank the knife through her neck again, this time to secure her so she wouldn't fall forward. Tucking the verse into the pocket of the dead woman's shirt, Azrael rolled off the disposable gloves and pushed them in a pocket in the rain slicker for disposal later.

The Angel then recrossed the street, not bothering to look in either direction. The dog was sitting there under the streetlamp, looking frightened.

Azrael glanced back at the judge and at the little dog. God wouldn't want to see the animal harmed. What if it ran out into the street in front of a car or something?

Speaking soothingly, the Angel moved slowly toward the

dog. It barked, scooted over a couple of feet on the sidewalk, and then plopped down again and whined.

"That's right. Good boy," Azrael crooned. "Don't be afraid. I won't hurt you."

The Angel caught the end of the leash and tugged. "Come on, good dog. Let's get you back safe in your house."

A police officer moved an orange barrier set up across the street, and Snowden made a U-turn in his cruiser. As he wheeled back, his headlights fully illuminated the WELCOME TO STEPHEN KILL sign. "Sweet Jesus," he beseeched, hitting the brake and shifting into park.

The call had come through from the dispatcher just after midnight. Snowden had talked to his shift commander as he dressed. He knew what to expect, and yet words couldn't justify the horror. Police cars and other emergency vehicles had pulled up in a semicircle around the neatly trimmed and manicured center island of grass. Flashing red and blue lights on the top of an ambulance cast a sickening pulse of light and shadow on the crime scene.

Snowden's first impulse as he climbed out of the car was to look away. It seemed disrespectful to stare, and yet he couldn't help himself.

Judge Ellen Hearn stood propped up against the welcome sign, her arms outspread, her hands draped behind it. She was covered in blood, her head lulling forward, what appeared to be a large kitchen knife protruding from her neck, holding her fastened to the wooden sign.

From Snowden's point of view, twenty feet in front of the sign, the judge appeared to have been crucified.

CHAPTER 29

"Prints came back on the kitchen knife and the machete," Delilah said, walking into Snowden's office without knocking.

He looked up from his desk; it seemed to be sinking in paperwork. In the two days since Judge Hearn's murder, Delilah had been working practically around the clock. She'd reread every file on each of the murder cases and reinterviewed half the people she or one of the other officers on the force had already interviewed, as well as the victims' families, friends, and neighbors.

She had also somehow convinced or coerced Father Hailey into checking old appointment books stored in the basement, and sure enough, he discovered that Ellen Hearn had gone to Noah Gibson for several private counseling sessions two years before Noah went to prison. There was no way to know what they had discussed from the appointment books, but it was enough evidence to link the fourth victim to the ex-priest.

Delilah had also done some prying into Ellen Hearn's personal life that most officers would have been hesitant to do, considering the judge's position in the state judicial system and the fact that she was already dead. The revelation that Judge Ellen Hearn was a lesbian, as accused, according to the Bible text left in her bloody shirt pocket, had taken Snowden completely by surprise. Like most of the folks in town, he'd known her, admired her his entire life, and never known. Apparently, the judge had been extremely discreet when it came to her private life, and it was only by looking through her personal belongings in her condo in Bethany that Delilah had been able to locate Miss Jillian Parquay of Washington, D.C., and learn the story of their affair that had lasted more than a year.

"And what does the crime lab tell us?" Snowden asked, tenting his fingers.

"No prints on the kitchen knife, except the judge's. Killer probably watched from her garden until she left the house to walk the dog and then he slipped inside, wearing disposable gloves you can buy at any Wal-Mart, and took the victim's knife from a rack on the counter."

"Neighbors said she routinely walked the dog, though usually a little earlier in the evening, and rarely on Sunday nights," Snowden recalled.

"She probably hadn't planned on spending the night in Stephen Kill Sunday night. Girlfriend thought she must have decided to stay here after a big fight they had the night before. And if you ask anyone in town, they'd probably be able to tell you that the judge leaves by her back door to walk the dog any night she's in town."

Snowden frowned. "I still can't believe the killer took the time to return the dog to the house."

"Apparently he was concerned for the dog's safety," she said.

"What kind of person kills someone and then walks their dog back to the house, risking getting caught?"

"I'm wondering if he wants to get caught. If the blood is getting the best of him. Maybe he wants us to end it. Maybe finding the machete wasn't a mistake. Maybe he wanted us to find it. Find him."

Snowden met her gaze. "Can we?"

"We're getting closer." She slid one sheet of paper in her hand behind another. "We've got better evidence off the machete. It's definitely Newton's blood, and we've got Noah Gibson's prints, along with at least three other sets of prints, maybe four. None of them other than Noah's are in the AFIS computer bank, though."

"That's a lot of unidentified people handling one weapon," he thought aloud. "Gibson's prints actually in any of the blood?"

Delilah shook her head. "Too easy. But one good print *was*. I'm thinking maybe someone helped him out, at least disposed of the weapon for him. We've definitely got enough to bring the Gibsons in." She almost sounded deflated.

With yet another connection of Noah Gibson to a victim, Snowden knew Delilah was struggling with the conclusion that she was wrong and that Noah might very well be the killer. "Both of them?"

"Who better to ask to dispose of a weapon used in a crime than your ex-spouse? I thought we'd ask Rachel to voluntarily allow us to take her fingerprints and compare."

He shrugged, still not mentally, or at least emotionally, ready to consider Rachel might be involved. He reached for his coffee cup. "She bought the machete, her prints should be on it."

"But they shouldn't be in the blood," Delilah countered.

Snowden was silent for a minute. He sipped his coffee; it was cold. He'd had a none-too-pleasant call from the governor's office this morning. A state police task force was being formed to *aid* the Stephen Kill force in the apprehension of the killer preying on the town. It was a barely veiled method of saying the governor no longer had confidence that Snowden could head up the investigation or catch the killer. The task force would probably mean Snowden's job. If the governor's office didn't believe in him, neither would the city council come time to renew his contract.

"OK, send Lopez out to the vineyard. Tell him to bring in Noah, but let Rachel drive herself in. Give her time to get a babysitter if the housekeeper isn't there. Just don't let them talk to each other."

"Right." Delilah halted in the doorway and turned back, lowering her voice. "I know you don't think Rachel had anything to do with this, and I hope you're right. But you might not be. When we were going over the list of people who might have known what the priest knew, we didn't consider Rachel. What if he talked about his work to his wife? It would seem only natural to me, no matter what code of ethics binds you. I mean, even the law recognizes the special relationship between spouses."

She has a good point.

Snowden picked up a folder full of documents his secretary had brought in for him to sign. He didn't look up at Delilah. "Have someone come for me when they arrive, Sergeant."

Noah forked straw from the back of the wagon into the aisle between the two rows of Delaware grape trellises. "See, Mattie, just like this. We put the straw between the rows and it keeps the weeds from growing." He stepped back, leaning on the handle of the pitchfork. "You try."

Mattie stood beside him, holding the wooden handle of his pitchfork in a death grip, and stared at his sneakers.

Mallory stood to the side, an orange plastic shovel in her hand. "Come on, Mattie," she encouraged brightly. "You can do it. Just like this." She scooped straw into her shovel and threw it down. "You try it."

But Mattie just stood there.

Noah exhaled, leaning the pitchfork handle against his leg and removing his ball cap to wipe the sweat off his brow.

Mallory, wearing her pink tutu, a hand-crocheted green vest over shorts, and a Wiggles tee, imitated Noah by propping up her plastic shovel and removing the ball cap that was too big for her head. She even copied his unconscious sigh of exasperation. "He's afraid," she said, wiping her forehead.

"Of what, hon?" Noah could barely hide his frustration.

They'd moved Mattie into the house two nights ago, and so far it hadn't gone well. The first night he'd seemed okay when they'd carried his bed into the house, but when they had tried to move some of his Bibles, he'd ripped them out of Noah's and Rachel's hands and thrown them on the floor. Then they'd had to wait while he picked them all up and stacked them methodically in their places on the floor.

Later, when they'd tried to settle Mattie in bed in the spare room where Noah had previously slept, he'd insisted on taking his pillow into the hallway and sleeping at the bottom of the stairs. All night, Noah and Rachel had taken turns leading him back to his room, which wasn't exactly the way Noah had envisioned his first night with her again. Ultimately, after too little sleep and too much frustration, they had given up and let him sleep on the floor, reminding him he couldn't go upstairs. Noah had barely slept.

This morning, Noah and Rachel had actually discussed locking Mattie in his bedroom at night, but the fear of fire made them both hesitant to do so. Noah didn't know what was going on in Mattie's head, but something was building inside him. His behavior showed it; his music certainly showed it. When he played the organ in the living room, he played heavy handed, choosing the strangest pieces—some he'd memorized, others he seemed to be composing. They all sounded so angry . . . so ominous, even to Noah's untrained ear.

It had been Rachel's idea this morning that Mattie come with Noah to work on spreading the mulch. She had thought maybe some physical exercise might be good for him. It had been Mallory's idea that she tag along. She had told Noah that Mattie didn't like her to be too far away. That it made him scared.

"Mallory, you have to tell me." He looked to Mattie. "One of you has to tell me. This is getting out of control and it's beginning to scare your mommy. Who is Mattie afraid of and why?"

Mallory pulled her ball cap back on her head. "He doesn't know who it is. He just knows she's bad."

"Who's—"

Mattie suddenly stabbed at the straw in the back of the trailer and threw it down, making a strange, guttural sound. The deep timbre of his voice startled Noah into silence. He hadn't heard Mattie make any sounds like that since he was a kid.

"That's right!" Mallory squealed with delight. "That's how you do it!" She dug her little shovel into the straw and threw some onto the ground.

Mattie did it again, his movements jerky but accurate.

"See, I knew you could do it," Mallory encouraged. "What a smart boy!"

"Noah!"

The sound of Rachel's voice caught Noah's attention, and he looked up in the direction of the house, shading his eyes with one hand.

Rachel was hurrying up the dirt road that led to the Delaware field and the Pinot field beyond it.

Something is wrong.

"What a good job," Noah said, trying to keep his concern out of his voice. "You just keep doing that, Mattie. Mallory, you help him. I'll go see what Mommy wants." He leaned the pitchfork against the wheel of the tractor, well out of Mallory's reach, and hurried up the trellis row. He met Rachel at the edge of the field.

"What's wrong?" He reached out, taking both her hands in his.

She was out of breath. "Officer Lopez is here for you. He

says you need to come with him to the station." Taking his hands in hers, she squeezed them. "Noah, he says I need to come down, too. To let them take my fingerprints."

He glanced in Mallory and Mattie's direction and then back at Rachel, his mind turning. "Did he say why?"

She shook her head. "He wanted to come get you himself. I told him I'd point him in the right direction, I just needed to run into the house and turn the iron off. I went out the back door."

"You left him waiting for you on the front porch?" Noah asked incredulously. "Rachel, why did you do that? That makes it look like we have something to hide."

"I . . . I don't know." Her voice rose and then fell in pitch as she struggled to hold herself together. She looked down at the ground and then up at him again. "I . . . I guess I wanted to warn you. I wanted to see you."

Down the row of flourishing grapevine trellises, Noah could hear Mallory laughing. Her voice was so light and airy that it sounded like a bell tinkling in the wind.

"Rachel, it's going to be all right." He fixed his gaze on her. "Snowden just wants it to be me."

"That isn't true. He isn't like that."

Noah remained calm. "No matter what Snowden thinks, he doesn't have the evidence to back it up and he knows it. Otherwise, he'd have arrested me before now."

"I don't understand." She shook her head. "Surely you . . . you and I aren't the only people who knew these things about the victims. Surely the police realize that." She looked up at him. "I don't remember you ever saying that Ellen came in to talk to you. She was a judge, for God's sake. What sin could the killer possibly have accused her of?"

"Probably homosexuality," he murmured.

She bit down on her trembling lower lip. "Oh no, Noah. I had no—"

"No, you didn't have any idea." He glanced over her shoulder in the direction of the house, then looked into her eyes again. "Now, I'm going to go in and see what they have to say. But you stay here. You don't have to give them your finger-prints, not without a court order."

"But I want to. This is ridiculous. They can't keep—"

"You stay here with Mattie and Mallory for a few min-utes; let me go up to the house and go with the officer. Mallory and Mattie don't need to see me being taken off in a police car."

"I'll come just as soon as I can get Mrs. Santori over here. I know she's home, she just—"

"No, Rachel." He gripped her shoulders. "Do you hear me? I want you to stay home." A strange coldness came over him, and he glanced at the house again. Nothing seemed out of place. The sun was shining and it was hot; there was no way he could be cold. And yet he couldn't shake it, couldn't reason his way out of it.

He gave her a quick kiss and released her hands, walking away. "I'll get someone to bring me home as soon as they're done with me."

"Noah—"

"I love you, Rache," he interrupted. "Just wait for me, OK?"

She started to speak and then didn't. Tears filled her eyes as he started down the road. "I love you," she called after him.

He raised one hand and then turned to jog down the dirt road toward the uniformed officer striding in his direction.

"Snowden, Sergeant Swift and I have already been over this," Noah said, still trying to remain patient. He'd been at the station two hours and had somehow still managed to hold his temper. But the questions, the insinuations, were beginning to wear on him. "My prints were on the machete because I used it to cut down part of the hedge on the back of my property. I used it the day of the Maria's Place benefit picnic." He gestured with one hand. "Then, when you guys asked for it, it was gone."

"And you didn't tell us it was missing the day we inquired because . . ."

Noah groaned, shifting in the hard chair behind the desk where he'd been instructed to sit. "Help him out, will you, Sergeant?" he asked.

The pretty blond cop was leaning against a wall. "According to Mr. Gibson, they didn't know until we asked for it that it was missing. He's guessing that Mrs. Gibson panicked when she didn't see it where it was supposed to be."

"She wasn't trying to cover anything up," Noah told Snowden. "She just didn't know where it was, and frankly, she was a little pissed off that you'd come asking for it."

"And the machete was never located?"

"No. It was not."

"And you or Rachel didn't come to us and give us this information because—"

"You know very well why." Noah pressed his palms to the smooth table and leaned forward, making eye contact with the imposing black man. "Because you've already got it in your head that I have something to do with these murders because I counseled each of the victims or a family member."

"So you do acknowledge that you knew secrets about the victims."

"I acknowledge no such thing. I shouldn't even be acknowledging that I counseled them. It's none of your damned business."

There was a knock on the door, and Sergeant Swift answered it. Someone spoke softly to her and she responded. They spoke for over a minute and then she glanced over her shoulder. "Mrs. Gibson is here."

"Oh, Rache," Noah whispered under his breath, slumping back in the chair. He should have known she wouldn't stay at home.

Swift glanced at Noah and then at her boss. "You want me to talk to her or do you want to do it?"

He hesitated long enough to make Noah nervous. Rachel told him she had dated Snowden, that she had liked him very much, but that she had known she could never love him. That was why she said she had broken up with him. She'd also said that Snowden had been very hurt when she stopped seeing him.

"You go," Snowden said at last. "Noah and I will sit here and chat."

He waited until the door shut behind her and then he walked to the table and took the only other chair, opposite Noah. When he spoke again, his adversarial tone was absent. "I wish you could help us out here."

"I wish I could, too."

"Governor's office is sending a task force down. I may be pumping gas to make my house payment shortly."

"I'm sorry to hear that." Noah folded his arms over his chest. Snowden was so different than him that Noah couldn't fathom why Rachel would have been attracted to him. Maybe the fact that Snowden *was* so different had been his most endearing quality.

Snowden studied Noah. Noah didn't look away.

"You have to admit, the evidence is incriminating."

"Not really. All you've got is that I know something about the victims that the murderer also knew."

"Things no one else in this town knew," Snowden emphasized.

"We don't know that for sure. I mean really, think about it." Noah leaned forward. "There are no real secrets, are there? Not in a town like this. We just like to pretend no one knows. I know that's how I was. I thought no one knew I was an alcoholic." He pointed at Snowden. "You knew."

"I knew," Snowden conceded.

"So did most of my congregation."

"OK, I get your point. But you have no alibi for any of the

nights these murders took place. You say you were asleep in your bed, but because you sleep alone, because you and Rachel are divorced, you don't even have proof of that."

Noah didn't know if he had meant it unkindly, but it hurt just the same. "You're not married. No girlfriend. You live alone. Where were you the night Ellen's throat was cut and she was nailed to that sign, accused of being a homosexual?"

Snowden glared. "How the hell did you know how he left her? No mention has been made of the note."

"As far as how he did it, again there are no secrets in a small town. Firemen, EMTs, neighbors. People talk. It doesn't matter who told me. And the note?" Noah said. "A guess. I know he left notes behind before. Bible verse, wasn't it? I could even guess which one and probably be very close if not correct. Still doesn't make me a murderer," Noah challenged.

Snowden sat back in his chair, letting his gaze drift. "OK, for the sake of argument, let's say you didn't do this. Who could? Who would?"

"I imagine a lot of people could do something like this," Noah thought aloud. "We don't like to consider the idea that we're capable of committing such awful transgressions and yet . . ."

His mind went back to the night he got into the truck, went down the lane, turned onto the county road. . . . A moment before, if someone had asked him if he could kill someone, he would have said no. And yet he learned he was, indeed, capable of murder.

Noah refocused his attention on Snowden. "Obviously the murders are tied into the sins these people committed. Adultery, theft, homosexuality. As for who knew about them, obviously more people than the victims or we realize."

"If you were the only person the victims ever confessed to, who could have overheard?"

Noah shrugged. "Anyone in the church who wanted to, I suppose. I mean, we make the assumption no one would listen under the crack of a priest's door, but do we know that for sure?" He let his mind drift back to the days when he had been St. Paul's priest, when he had served as a marriage counselor, a family counselor, a spiritual advisor. "I imagine there isn't a secret in this town that Miss Cora doesn't know."

Snowden frowned. "The church secretary? Come on. She's sixty years old and overweight. She doesn't have the physical capabilities to have committed these murders."

"Joshua Troyer did work at the church, but he wouldn't hurt a fly."

"That right?" Snowden glanced up, arching an eyebrow. "I interviewed him after Skeeter Newton was killed. Joshua told Sergeant Swift and me that some people deserved to die for their sins, that if God told him to punish someone for their sins, he would do it."

"Just talk."

Snowden was quiet for a moment. "I know Jack McConnell and Mattie lived in the church basement after they had a fire at their place. Mattie would have been around most of the time." He looked up. "Could he have overheard conversations you had with your parishioners?"

"Mattie?" Noah scowled. "I guess he could have overheard, but I don't know how much he would have understood."

"I remember the way Jack was always preaching at him. Reading to him from the Bible, warning him against sin. Jack got a little crazy there in the end. A little obsessed."

"Snowden, you know Mattie. He . . . he can't communicate."

"He plays the pipe organ as well as anyone I've ever heard, and I understand he's never had any lessons."

"He's an idiot savant. You know that. It's ancient history. But a very low-functioning savant." Noah shrugged. "He has a gift, that's all."

"Could Mattie have taken your machete?"

It wasn't until the words came out of Snowden's mouth

that it occurred to Noah that Mattie's strange behavior possibly could have something to do with the murders in Stephen Kill. "No, he would never . . ." Noah let his sentence trail off into silence.

Mattie's fear. His anger. Mallory's talk of a voice he heard.

Noah's heart began to race. It wasn't possible. . . .

The car, the lawn tractor. The strange feeling that Noah and Rachel both kept getting at the house. Their nightmares.

It wasn't possible, and yet . . .

"What?" Snowden asked.

Noah shook his head. He wasn't ready to say anything yet. If he did, Mattie would be in Sussex County Correctional Facility before morning. That was no place for Mattie. No place for any human being.

"Couldn't be Mattie," Noah said firmly. "I've lived with him my whole life. So have you. So has Rachel. He can't speak, he can't read, he can't write. He can barely pour his own Cheerios." He looked at Snowden beseechingly, as if saying the words could make them so. "Mattie couldn't have done this."

A knock sounded at the door, and a nicely dressed young woman Noah didn't recognize poked her head through the door. "Got the governor's office on the line. I asked if you could return the call, but they weren't going for it."

Snowden scowled. "All right. I'm coming." He rose from the chair, unfolding his long limbs. "Can I get you something? A soda, cup of coffee?"

Noah shook his head. "What you can do is either arrest me or let me go. You and I both know this conversation isn't going anywhere and you haven't got enough to hold me legally."

The police chief pushed his chair under the table. "Be back after I take this call." He closed the door behind him, and Noah heard the door lock.

He shuddered at the sound of it and rose from his chair to

pace, trying hard not to think about the years he had spent in prison, the years he had lost locked behind a door. The thought that he could actually end up being charged for these murders was so ludicrous, it was laughable. And yet, the possibility was beginning to scare him. There was no direct evidence pointing to him, and yet, he had to agree with Snowden, that from the outside looking in, he could see how someone would think he looked suspicious.

But Noah knew he couldn't face the situation this way. Not with fear, fear that would eventually paralyze him. He couldn't just be defensive. He had to be offensive as well. And that meant trying to look beyond the evidence the police had.

So if he wasn't the killer, then who was? Not Mattie. Not Joshua. And Snowden was right, no matter how much Cora knew, she was too old, too out of shape to have committed these crimes.

As Noah paced, he kept glancing at the door. The tiny, white-walled room was beginning to make him claustrophobic. He could hear voices beyond the door, but he couldn't make out what anyone was saying.

He kept thinking about Rachel being out there somewhere, allowing someone to take her fingerprints. He really wished she hadn't agreed to do that. At this point, anything they gave the police might be used to direct guilt. What was Rachel thinking? Her fingerprints were going to show up on that machete, too.

Time seemed to drag until Noah began to wonder what had happened to Snowden. He didn't know exactly how much time had passed because he'd given up wearing a watch in prison and hadn't reestablished the habit since his release, but it had to be going on an hour. Was this some kind of strategy of Snowden's, to leave Noah locked up in this little cell-like room until he went so stir-crazy that he was willing to confess, confess to anything, just to get out?

At last Noah heard someone unlock the door, and he turned expectantly. It wasn't Snowden, but the officer who had come for the woman cop earlier. "The chief would like to see you in his office."

"His office?" Noah questioned. But he hurried toward the door. "I understand my wife is here. Do you think you could—"

"She's already in with the chief," the Hispanic officer said. "Come with me."

Snowden now wanted to see him in his office instead of the interrogation room? He had Rachel in his office? What the hell was going on here?

The officer led him down a corridor and pointed to a door left slightly ajar. Noah pushed it open hesitantly, but when he saw Rachel sitting in front of Snowden at his desk, her face ashen, he rushed to her.

"Rache—"

"Noah." She came out of the chair, reaching out to him. "They've arrested Mattie."

"What?" Noah wrapped one arm around her. "I don't understand." He looked to Snowden, trying hard to keep his temper. "You and I discussed this. I told you there's no way Mattie is capable—"

"They found something in his room in the barn," Rachel interrupted, clutching his arm. She suddenly sounded close to tears. "It's bad, Noah."

He took one look at Snowden's solemn face and walked her back to the chair, forcing her to sit.

Snowden pushed a book sealed in a plastic bag across his desk toward Noah. "This yours?"

Noah picked it up. "No. It's not mine. I don't own any Bibles anymore."

"The officer found it in Mattie's room in the cellar."

"What officer? Why was anyone in Mattie's room? I didn't give anyone permission to search my property." He took a step toward Snowden behind the desk, panic fluttering in his chest. "You have to have a warrant to search my place without my permission."

"Housekeeper told my officer he was free to have a look around."

"What officer? When? You mean to tell me that someone went back to our place after I was brought in, after Rachel agreed to come and let you fingerprint her?"

"The officer was just told to have a look around the outbuildings. Your employee gave him permission to go into the barn."

"An employee, *exactly*. She had no right to give anyone permission to trespass on my property."

"It's not Consuelo's fault, Noah." Rachel slid to the end of the chair but remained seated. She was trying to calm him, warn him he needed to remain reasonable. "She was trying to help."

Noah continued to hold the Bible in the evidence bag in his hand, amazed by its weight, but not so much its physical weight as the weight it levied on his heart. "Mattie has hundreds of Bibles," he argued. "He builds things with them. You know that, Snowden."

Rachel laid her hand over Noah's. "There's been pages torn out of it. Verses cut from it," she said softly.

It took a moment for her meaning to sink in. "No," he whispered. "That's not possible. What verses?"

"The ones our killer quoted," Snowden answered. "A whole page on adultery is missing, and cut from Exodus is 'Thou shall not steal.' Then there's a verse missing from a page that says something about if your right hand causes you to sin, it should be cut off, snipped out of the book of Matthew."

"That's not possible." Shocked, Noah set the Bible down on Snowden's desk. "Mattie can't read. He couldn't possibly have known what verses to cut out. He doesn't even understand what *adultery* is. He couldn't . . ."

Noah suddenly felt off balance. It was as if one more belief he had held to be truth was crumbling in front of him. *Mattie couldn't have done those terrible things . . .* he thought wildly. *Could he?*

"My officer brought the Bible in, but he didn't search the remainder of the barn. I'd like your permission to search the rest of your property, Noah." Snowden hesitated and then went on before Noah had time to respond. "I understand how hard this has to be for you, for you both." He shifted his gaze to Rachel and his eyes seemed to soften. "But if Mattie has committed these murders, I know very well you don't want him anywhere near that beautiful little girl—"

"Where is she?" Noah asked Rachel suddenly.

She drew her hand down his arm to comfort him. "She's fine. I just called and checked on her. She's worried about Mattie, of course, but she's OK. She and Consuelo are making fajitas for dinner."

Noah couldn't resist a bittersweet smile at the thought of Mallory standing on a chair beside the housekeeper at the kitchen counter, chopping vegetables for dinner. She was so precious to him. It frightened him to think that Mattie could have done these terrible things, and he had allowed him to be alone with Mallory.

But he *couldn't* have killed those people. Noah's mind kept going back to that impossibility.

"We just want to have a look around, Noah." The police chief spoke to him as if he were Noah's friend. Of course, they both knew they would never be friends. "The weapon used in the Rehak case was never recovered. Forensics say we're probably looking for something like a baseball bat. Does Mattie own a bat?"

"I think I'd probably have noticed a bloody baseball bat lying around the place," Noah snapped, pacing behind the chair.

He wasn't sure what to do. Even if Mattie did do this, as

beyond belief as that was, it was his responsibility to see that the man was treated fairly.

"Noah," Rachel chastised softly.

Noah looked to Snowden. "I need some time. Maybe I should talk to a lawyer for Mattie. Did you already have him brought in?"

Snowden nodded, almost seeming apologetic. "I had to. It's the most incriminating evidence found so far."

"You mean more incriminating than my fingerprints on the machete?"

"I'm just doing my job. It's not personal."

Not personal, right, Noah thought. He spoke his next thought aloud. "It wasn't personal when you dated my wife either, was it?"

"Noah, please," Rachel murmured.

Noah's gaze shifted to the man behind the desk. In all fairness, Snowden had neither done nor said anything out of line, not before Noah was released from prison and not since. "Is he going to have to go into a jail cell? He shouldn't be with other prisoners." The thought of Mattie in prison made Noah shudder.

"I already thought about that. I've got a call in to the state to see if we can put him in some kind of psychiatric unit, rather than sending him over to Sussex Correctional."

"Thank you. I appreciate that. Can I see him, just to make sure he's OK?"

"It might be easier for him if you don't. Not yet."

Rachel rose from the chair, reaching out to him. "Snowden says we can go home. I think we need to get back to Mallory."

"Of course. Right." Noah drew her under his arm protectively. "Can you hold off on the warrant to search the place until tomorrow?" He glanced at the institutional clock on the wall. "It's probably too late today for me to speak with a lawyer, but I'll put some calls in first thing in the morning."

Snowden hesitated.

"Look, you've got Mattie. If he really is the killer, time is no longer of the essence, is it?"

The chief of police thought for a moment. "I suppose we can wait until tomorrow, but you understand, any evidence you tamper with could make you an accessory."

Noah set his jaw. "That mean I'm no longer a suspect, Chief Calloway?"

He rose from his chair, and Noah had to admit he was intimidating. "No, it doesn't. You're free to go, but you shouldn't be making any trips out of state right now."

"Come on, let's go." Noah ushered Rachel out of the office. "You know where to find me. I'll give you a call in the morning after I talk to a lawyer."

Delilah passed the Gibsons on her way into Snowden's office. He looked pissed, she just scared. Everyone nodded, but no one spoke. She felt bad for them, but she was glad that the evidence pointed toward Mattie, someone they had not considered before, and not Noah.

Delilah tapped on Snowden's open door and walked in.

"Nice work," he said. "Close the door."

She didn't like the tone of his voice. "Thank you."

"You sent Lopez back to the house after Noah was brought in?"

"I just wanted him to have a look around. The housekeeper gave him permission to go into the barn."

"Someone might argue that Officer Lopez entered that barn illegally, which would mean the evidence obtained is inadmissible in court."

"No way," she argued, resting both hands on her hips. "I didn't screw up this case, Snowden. I might have broken it."

"OK." He sat down behind his desk. "So the Bible was in the room Mattie slept in."

"Well, yeah, he slept there up until a few nights ago.

Housekeeper told Lopez the Gibsons brought him into the house to sleep in a downstairs bedroom. I don't know the whole story yet."

"Are you aware of Mr. McConnell's IQ?"

"No, but I understand he's . . . handicapped," she said, not sure where the conversation was going. "But I've heard people talk about him being some kind of musical genius or something. They say he can play anything on an organ, he just has to hear it once."

"Mattie's what's called an idiot savant. I grew up with him. We all did. Delilah, he is musically gifted, but he can't read or write. He can't care for himself."

"The mentally handicapped have killed before."

Snowden folded his hands. "Have they also miraculously developed the ability to read? How could Mattie have cut those exact scriptures out of that Bible when he can't recognize his own written name?"

Delilah pressed her lips together. "I don't know," she said. "And I know where you're going with this, but I'm telling you, Noah Gibson is not our man. Mattie McConnell might not be either, but I'll warrant you, we're closer to this killer than we were this morning."

Snowden exhaled, sitting back in his chair. "I hope you're right." He reached for his pen. "Because if you're not, in the very near future, the two of us might be seeking employment elsewhere."

CHAPTER 30

In silence, Noah and Rachel got into her Volvo parked behind the police station. It wasn't until they passed the welcome sign as they left town, which no longer seemed so welcoming, that Noah finally spoke up.

"I just can't believe this is happening. It's like a bad movie."

She glanced at him sitting beside her. Every muscle in his body seemed to be tense. This was a side of him she hadn't really seen before. "We'll get through it."

"Mattie did not kill those people. He couldn't have." He balled his hand into a fist and brought it down hard on the leather seat.

"I know." Keeping her eye on the road, she laid her hand on his fist. "But you have to stay calm. We need to think this through rather than letting our emotions get the best of us. I think you're right. We need to get Mattie a lawyer."

"I just feel so . . . so inadequate." He seemed to be talking as much to himself as her. "Mattie must be scared to death, and they wouldn't even let us see him."

"Snowden will make sure he's taken care of. No one's

going to hurt him. And if he does have to be locked up some-where, a hospital psychiatric ward would be much better than a prison cell."

"I know." He groaned aloud. "But it shouldn't be like this. Something isn't right here. I know Mattie didn't do this. You don't think he did it, do you?"

Rachel dared a quick glance at him. "No, I don't. But if he didn't tear out that page, cut those verses from the Bible, who did? Snowden said he would have to send the Bible off to a crime lab, but he saw the notes left by the killer. He's sure they were cut out of that same Bible. He recognized the print."

"An NIV published by Oxford," Noah scoffed. "Do you know how many of those are printed in the United States every year?"

"I understand that." She nodded, looking at him, then back at the road. "But it's too much of a coincidence that the very same quotes left at the crime scenes are the ones miss-ing from Mattie's Bible."

"So someone's been cutting verses from one of Mattie's Bibles." He threw up one hand. "Hell, Rache, three quarters of the people in this town know Mattie collects Bibles. A quarter have given him one. If you were a killer and you wanted to cover your tracks, wouldn't you cut your verses from someone else's Bible instead of your own?" He looked at her and then away. "I know I would!"

"Noah, you're right." She continued to speak softly, re-maining composed. "I know that, but we have to stay calm. Being angry, lashing out at Snowden, at the police, isn't going to make this any easier, not for us and not for Mattie."

"I'm not lashing out!"

She glanced at him again, hesitating, unsure if she wanted to say what she was thinking. At the stop sign, she signaled to turn right instead of left to go home.

"Where are we going?"

"Noah, you're angry and you have a right to be, but you have to figure out how to deal with it."

"I'm not angry." He almost shouted the words and then, to her surprise, her relief, he actually chuckled. "OK, so maybe I am a little angry. And it feels so weird." He looked at her. "I was never an angry person before I went to jail. Not growing up, not through my teenage years, not even when the boys and Mom and Dad died."

"I know," she murmured. "Maybe that's why you drank."

"Why I drank?" He stared at her for a moment, then looked away, concentrating on the dark pavement rolling under the car. "What do you mean by that? You reading up on psycho-analyzation now?"

Rachel signaled and pulled over into the tall grass on the side of the road, refusing to be hurt by his biting comment. There wasn't any way she could hurt as badly as she knew he was hurting inside right now.

The shoulder where she pulled over wasn't wide, but there was usually little traffic that ran up and down this road, one of the reasons why she liked living on it. She slid the car into park, hit her flashers, and cut the engine so she could give him her complete attention.

"I wonder, Noah," she said, trying to choose her words carefully, "if that was why you started drinking so much. Because I never thought it was because of me."

"No, of course not." Quick to answer, he released his seat belt buckle and slid over closer on the bench seat. "Rachel, it was never because of you."

Tears stung the back of her eyelids, but she made herself look at him. If they were going to try marriage again, if they were going to have any chance at all, she knew she had to say it. Had to try to make him understand. "I think you were angry at God, maybe even at me, at the boys, at your mom and dad."

"Rache—"

She pressed her fingertips against his lips. "Hear me out," she said. "I think you were angry at all of us, but mostly with yourself, and because you had never been an angry person, you didn't know what to do with those feelings." She fought the emotion in her voice, the sadness in her heart. "Looking back, I think you drank to drown the anger because you didn't know what else to do with it. You were always such a good person, so happy, that when those bad things started to happen, you didn't know what to do with them."

He didn't look at her, but his hand slid out and he took her hand. He stared straight ahead, through the windshield. "I haven't been this way since I came home."

She looked up at the curve in the road ahead of them, choking back her emotion. "I know. But maybe it's time to let this go, too. Accept your anger as a valid emotion, and forgive yourself for what happened here."

To this day, Noah couldn't actually remember what happened that night, but in his mind's eye he had played it over and over again, until he saw it more vividly than a memory, as vividly as if it were a scene rerun again and again on a TV screen.

He was headed east, but had already passed the road into town. He had no idea where he'd been going. The beach, maybe. Most likely a liquor store outside of town. He never bought liquor in Stephen Kill. He was headed east in the truck; the Marcuses were headed west, for home. They'd been at her mother's house in Fenwick Island. Their two-year-old was asleep in her car seat in the backseat.

Noah lost control of the truck on the curve. He was going too fast. He couldn't stay in his own lane. Joel Marcus came around the curve in the opposite direction in his Dodge Caravan. They hit head-on.

Although he remembered nothing from the accident, in his mind Noah could hear the sound of squealing breaks, the impact, the breaking glass. Pattie had not been wearing her seat belt. In court, speculation was made that maybe she had unfastened it to reach back for the baby. Pattie was ejected from the car and died before the first emergency vehicle arrived on the scene. Joel suffered internal injuries from the impact, despite the presence of an air bag. He died on the operating table of a ruptured spleen. Only the baby, strapped safely in her car seat survived without injury.

Well . . . and Noah. He woke the next day in jail with nothing more than an egg on his head. There was a theory that drunk drivers were rarely injured in collisions because they had such loose muscle tone that they just bounced around on impact. Noah had his own theory, and that was that death was too good for drunk drivers. They lived to be punished for the rest of their days with the knowledge that they killed another human being. One of God's sick little jokes.

God.

Noah's eyes filled with tears. No matter how he tried to get rid of *Him*, He was still there.

"Oh, baby, it's OK," Rachel whispered, scooting over closer to him. She put her arms around him.

"I'm so sorry," he murmured into her hair.

"I know you are."

"I didn't mean to hurt you." He choked on his words. "I didn't mean to hurt anyone."

"I know," she soothed.

She held him tightly, and they were quiet for a minute. Quiet long enough for him to get himself together again. Then he leaned back, looking into her eyes. "Let's go home to Mallory."

She smiled, her own eyes filled with tears. "OK, let's go home."

They kissed and he brushed her cheek tenderly with his fingertips before releasing her. "We'll go home and we'll have fajitas with Mallory, and we'll put her to bed and then we'll sit down and try and look at this logically," he told Rachel as she started the car engine. "If the police can't figure out who's killing these people, maybe we can."

* * *

Snowden walked slowly up his mother's driveway, dreading going in. It was dark except for the glow of her porch light, and the air hung heavy with the promise of rain. In the distance, to the west, thunder rumbled.

His mother would want to talk about the case, about Judge Hearn. About what the police knew and what they didn't know. She'd want to know why he wasn't eating enough and why he didn't ask out that pretty blonde on the force. It was always the same with her, and his answers were never good enough.

She met him at the back door. "You said you'd be here by seven."

"I'm sorry. I was waiting for transport for a prisoner."

"Mattie McConnell." She held the door open. "Hard to believe. You know, he used to come to the library with his father. He liked animal books. I always—"

"Mom, how did you know we arrested Mattie?" He kicked off his shoes and left them in the mudroom.

"Scanner."

Snowden walked into the kitchen. There was a pot of chili on the stove. He hated her chili. No spices. Cheap ground turkey. It tasted like beans and burger and ketchup to him. "You don't have a police scanner."

"Calvin and Trudy next door have one. They came over to tell me that Officer Lopez brought him in."

"Of course they did." He sighed, reaching up in the cabinet for a Corelle bowl.

"There's corn bread on the table."

He scooped out a little chili and carried his bowl to the place she'd left set for him at the dinette table.

"That's not enough to feed a fly."

He sat down, folded his hands, thanked God for the food, prayed for patience, and picked up the soup spoon set neatly on a folded paper towel.

Tillie opened the refrigerator and brought him a stick of margarine in an old-fashioned butter dish. Snowden always made it a point to buy real butter, whipped in a tub for easy spreading. He loved real butter on corn bread.

"I hope you're not sending that poor boy to jail."

"He's not a boy. He's my age, Ma. And you know I can't tell you where they're taking him."

She slid the butter dish across the table and folded her arms over her flowered apron. Her mouth puckered sternly. "You know very well Mattie McConnell didn't murder those people."

"I know no such thing." He took a large square of corn bread from under the cloth napkin and began to butter it. "And neither do you."

"Mattie would never hurt anyone. Of course there were rumors, how his daddy fell off that ladder and broke his neck."

Snowden took a big bite of the corn bread. His mother did make good corn bread, the dry kind that was cakey, not the wet, southern kind. "What rumors? The police report said it was an accident. No one ever thought Mattie had anything to do with his father's death," he defended.

"Police don't know everything."

"Ma—"

"Some say he didn't fall off that ladder. Jack was like a monkey on ladders. And he wasn't that old either. They say he was pushed."

Snowden groaned. He should have just stayed at the station and waited to be sure Mattie was in that state police transport van to take him up to the hospital in Wilmington. He should have just called his mother and told her he couldn't make it. But the van had gotten a flat tire on Route 1 and had been delayed. His shift supervisor assured him he had everything under control. He didn't think he'd have any problem transferring him. Mattie hadn't been the least bit resistant since his arrest. In fact, all he'd done since he'd been put in the cell was pretend to play a keyboard.

The truth was that Snowden had left because he'd felt so guilty about sending Mattie off to the nuthouse. But there he could be evaluated. Maybe even questioned about the murders. Snowden certainly didn't have the capability to communicate with him. He doubted Mattie had the capability to communicate at all.

That was what was worrying him about the arrest. As much as he hated to admit it, Noah had made some good arguments. It was too easy. Mattie had possession of the Bible from which the notes the killer left behind had been cut. Mattie couldn't defend himself. Did the killer want to see the mentally handicapped man go to a mental hospital for the rest of his life for something he didn't do? Would that then be the end of the murders? Would they ever really know if Mattie did it?

Snowden took a mouthful of chili and another bite of corn bread.

"You shouldn't eat so fast. It's bad for your digestion." Tillie crossed the small kitchen. "You want something to drink?"

"Yes, thank you." Snowden took another bite of chili.

Delilah had left the station without saying good night. He wondered if she would be expecting him tonight. He wondered if he should go. He couldn't continue his visits to her house. He knew it. She had to. Maybe tonight was the night to put an end to it. But he felt like he needed to see her. Tonight, of all nights, he needed her.

"Bathroom door's squeaking again." Tillie set a glass of water in front of him.

"I'll have a look at it just as soon as I'm done, Ma."

It was ten by the time Snowden left his mother's house. After supper, he'd used WD-40 on the squeaky hinge. Then she'd found another. Then she'd needed him to change the filter on her dehumidifier.

He'd called the station once while he was there to check

to see if Mattie McConnell had been picked up. He hadn't yet, but Johnson said he'd been assured someone would be there anytime. Snowden debated whether or not to call again, but he didn't want his shift commander to think he didn't think he was capable of handling a prisoner with the IQ of a preschooler. It was just that guilt was beginning to get the better of him. Maybe he shouldn't have had Mattie arrested yet, not until he had someone look at the Bible to be sure it was a match to the evidence they already had in custody.

On the way home, Snowden had to turn on the windshield wipers. Lightning zigzagged the dark sky. Thunder rumbled. Inside his house, he moved around mostly in the dark, only turning on a few lights. The more time that passed, the worse he felt. Noah had insisted Mattie wasn't capable of cutting those verses from the Bible. If he had been trying to cover for himself, he wouldn't have argued in Mattie's behalf, would he? Or was he so clever that he knew how to make himself seem innocent, even to a chief of police?

He kept reminding himself of what all the literature said about serial killers. They were always bright. Clever. Convincing.

Snowden changed into sweatpants and a T-shirt. Barefoot, he made himself a cup of mint tea and went into his living room where he had his computer set up. He signed onto the Internet, deleted e-mails offering him quick weight-loss pills and increased penis size, and then Googled *idiot savant*.

The storm continued to hang over Stephen Kill, rain hitting the windowpanes of the house, thunder rumbling. There were occasional flashes of light in the living room, which was illuminated only by the computer screen. Once, the screen clicked off, but then it clicked right back on, the battery backup beeping twice before electricity was restored.

It occurred to Snowden that he ought to shut down his computer. The storm seemed to be getting worse. But time got away from him as he read about what doctors knew about idiot savants and what they didn't know. He was watching a film clip of the movie *Rain Man* when his phone ran, startling him.

When he picked up, he half expected to hear Delilah's sweet southern drawl, asking him where the hell he was. It was Johnson.

"Sorry to call you, Chief, but we've got us a situation here."

"Situation?"

"I think you need to come down to the station."

Noah heard the thunder rumble, felt it deep in his bones. He rolled over in the old bed he and Rachel had shared as newlyweds. They had just set it up the other night after moving Mattie into the spare room downstairs.

He moved away from Rachel, curling up in a ball, half awake, half asleep, fighting the acrid scent that always came to him just before a blackout. "No," he mumbled.

Darkness seemed suddenly to close in on him. Someone was calling his name. Lightning flashed and someone, some-*thing,* was in the room. A large, dark shape in the corner of the room.

Noah tried to roll over. To warn Rachel. But his limbs wouldn't obey. He could feel himself being sucked into the darkness. He tried to resist, to cry out, but there was no fighting it.

"What the hell do you mean he got away?" Snowden climbed out of his police car, which he had pulled around to the back door where prisoners entered and exited. He'd taken the extra five minutes to put on a fresh uniform; he had a feeling it might be a long night.

Lieutenant Johnson held a large golf umbrella over them both as they walked to the building's overhang to get out of the rain. Johnson, fifty, built like a fireplug with a crewcut, was an Air Force retiree and a good cop. Solid. Went by the book. He wasn't a creative man, and he didn't seem to have a head for investigating, but he understood the role of the police in keeping the peace in a small town and he did it well.

"It was my fault, Chief." Johnson drew himself up to his full five-foot-eight height. "I . . . I underestimated the prisoner. When we went to transfer him, there was a problem. Apparently, the spare tire the bozos put on the van was soft, so they ran down to the gas station to put some air in it. Instead of putting McConnell back in a cell, I had him put in the interrogation room. He just seemed so scared, like a kid."

"And someone didn't lock the door."

"No, sir." Johnson shook his bulldog head. "I did not. Same time, an alarm was going off at the post office. I was shorthanded and I was scrambling to get someone over there. Apparently, Mattie just walked right out. By the time I found out the post office was secure and got back to the room, he was gone."

Snowden stood beneath the overhang, watching the rain pour over in rivulets. The night air had cooled off with the storm, but it was still humid out, the air so close that when you inhaled, you didn't feel like you could quite get a full breath.

"What time was this?"

Johnson checked his watch. He had a ruddy face that reddened when he became irritated or anxious. It was bright red. " 'Bout an hour ago now. We've looked everywhere. I mean, how far could he have gotten? He didn't act like he knew enough to find his way out of a wet paper bag."

"Biggest mistake you can make, underestimating a prisoner."

"I know that, Chief. Like I said, I screwed up."

Snowden stared out into the darkness, watching the rain illuminated by one of the security lights in the back parking lot. He saw Delilah pull into the parking lot in her little red pickup. He'd called her as he left the house, woken her. This was her case; she had a right to be here.

"You're sure he's not still inside somewhere, cowering in a corner?" Snowden studied the shadows of the parking lot, hoping against hope that he might see Mattie's hulking form huddled in the rain.

"He's a big guy, Chief. Outweighs you by fifty pounds. He's not inside."

"Did you call the Gibsons? See if he turned up there? They should be warned that he might."

"No answer, but I can't tell if it's ringing through or not. We've got some phones out in the area. Lot of cable TV out. Had two calls from people wanting to know what we were going to do about the cable being out. Apparently there's some kind of John Wayne movie marathon on tonight." Johnson shook his head, chuckling, but he really wasn't that amused.

"Well, let's send a patrol car out to the Gibsons. Have a look around. Maybe he just went back to their place and he's sitting on the porch soaking wet, scared to death."

Delilah ran across the parking lot. She was dressed in jeans, a T-shirt, and a yellow rain slicker, wearing her badge on her hip the way detectives did. Snowden was quite sure she was wearing her gun belt. She looked good, even in the dark, in the rain, her hair messy from sleep and only a quick comb-through.

"Chief, Lieutenant." She nodded to them both as she darted under the overhang.

"Johnson will fill you in. I'll be in my office." Snowden nodded toward her, turning away. Then he turned back, suddenly thinking of something. "All our vehicles accounted for, Johnson?"

"Sir?"

Snowden pointed into the parking lot at the black-and-white cruisers parked in two rows, side by side. As officers came in and out, cars were checked out off the end of a row, returned at the end of a row. The third space on the second row was open. It shouldn't have been open.

Johnson stared at the cars for a moment and then swore under his breath. "He's retarded, Chief. To steal a car, a person would have to get a key. He'd have to—"

"Check the log." Snowden glared.

Johnson grabbed the back door, left propped open with half a cement block, and stepped inside.

"I think I'll take a car, ride out to the Gibsons' myself," Delilah said, taking care not to meet Snowden's gaze directly.

"I was thinking the same thing." He glanced down at her. "Let's take mine."

CHAPTER 31

Unlike so many nights, nothing startled Rachel awake. She woke slowly to the sound of the rumbling thunder, now farther in the distance than it had been before. She could hear the rain pattering on the old farmhouse window. The storm was letting up.

Then she realized the air conditioner was silent; it had been on when they went to bed. Now it was hot and sticky in the room.

Still half asleep, relieved not to have woken in the terror of one of her nightmares, she pushed the hot sheet off her naked body and reached out to Noah in the bed beside her.

He wasn't there.

She sat up, looking around in the dark room, drawing the sheet up to cover her bare breasts. It was almost pitch black. Not even the light from the security lamp in the yard shone through the windows. "Noah?"

Despite the warmth of the room, she shivered. Something wasn't right. Something didn't *feel* right in the room. The sense of dread she had been experiencing began to slowly seep through her. "Is someone there?"

She reached out and turned the switch on the bedside lamp. It clicked, but the light didn't come on.

Electricity must have gone out in the storm. That explained why the window air conditioner was off. The digital clock beside her bed wasn't illuminated either.

Had Noah gone downstairs to check the breaker box? Years ago, his parents had hired an electrician to rewire the house, and the old glass fuse box had been replaced with a proper regulation switch box. They rarely lost power these days. Unless, of course, power lines went down in a storm like this, she reminded herself, fighting the feeling that something was wrong, very wrong.

Rachel slid her feet onto the rag rug on the floor beside the bed and felt for her clothes. She didn't feel as if she'd been asleep long. After they had tucked Mallory into bed, they had sat side by side at the kitchen table and talked about who might possibly be killing parishioners Noah had counseled. Who might be trying to frame Mattie. They hadn't come up with any clear-cut answers, but they had a lot of questions, which were all jotted down on a legal pad downstairs on the table. They'd gone to bed, too tired, too scared to make love, but Noah had held her in his arms until she drifted off to sleep. That was the last thing she remembered.

Rachel finally located the clothes she'd tossed on the floor when she'd gone to bed. She stepped into a pair of denim shorts and pulled her discarded T-shirt over her head. Then she fumbled for the drawer pull on the bedside table, slid it open, and felt for the flashlight she always kept inside. She found a pack of tissues, ChapStick, something small and square she couldn't make out, a book light, and a magazine. Finally, in the back of the drawer, she felt the hard plastic tube of the flashlight.

"Aha," she said aloud, trying to shake that spooked feeling a person had when they were alone in the dark. She flipped the switch and the flashlight clicked on, but the light was feeble. The batteries were running low. Figured. She didn't know the last time she'd used it. At least a year ago. It was just here for emergencies like this one.

Not that this was an emergency.

"Shoot," she muttered, thinking that if she spoke aloud, the heaviness in her chest that was the fear of something she couldn't quite pinpoint wouldn't seem quite so real. She shook the flashlight, and the dumb thing went out. She must have dislodged the batteries. "Well, that's much better," she chastised herself. She shook it again, and the dim light shone once more from the barrel.

Holding it gingerly in her hand, she took a quick swipe of the room, though why, she had no idea. There was nothing there out of the ordinary, of course. Clothes thrown over the doors of the open antique armoire. Shoes on the floor. Some of Noah's clothes in a laundry basket, for lack of a better place to put them presently. Nothing had been disturbed.

Noah must have closed the bedroom door behind him when he went downstairs to check the box, Rachel told herself.

She entered the hall, moving the flashlight beam as she walked slowly toward Mallory's bedroom. She and Noah had moved into the house with his parents six years before their deaths. When the old church rectory they'd been living in had been determined to be infested with termites, the council had voted to demolish it and use the space for the additional parking needed. Noah was offered a stipend for housing, and he and Rachel had moved into the farmhouse. Some women might not have liked the idea of moving in with their in-laws, but not Rachel. She'd loved this house, this family, since she was child. She knew it as well as she knew her own body.

Yet for some reason, now in the dim yellow beam of light, nothing looked quite familiar. Everything seemed slightly strange—the striped wallpaper, the carpet runner, even the family photographs on the wall. That heavy feeling in her chest seemed to be growing weightier by the minute.

Rachel opened Mallory's bedroom door and flashed the beam quickly over her bed, just to be sure she was there. The diffused round beam caught the form of her little body curled up in her bed under a tangle of sheets. Rachel continued to move the beam across the room. Everything was as she had left it when she and Noah had kissed Mallory good night, assuring her that Mattie would be all right. Nothing was different, except that the night-light and the room air conditioner were both off.

Satisfied, she passed the beam over the room one last time. As she moved it, she must have wiggled the batteries because it went off again. "Come on," she groaned softly, shaking it.

The flashlight came back on, directing the light directly on Mallory's bed. That was when Rachel realized something wasn't right. Not trusting her own judgment, she started to walk slowly toward the bed, beam fixed on the rumpled covers that looked just like Mallory's sleeping form.

Only not quite. . . .

Reaching the bed, she put out one hand, expecting to feel the warmth of Mallory's little body. An arm, a leg, maybe her hip. But the blanket collapsed under Rachel's touch. Mallory wasn't there. It had just looked like she was because of the way the sheet and blanket were piled.

Rachel felt a flicker of apprehension, but she squelched it. There was no need to panic; her daughter was here somewhere. The little imp was probably on the floor on the other side of the bed. When she was younger, Mallory had fallen out of bed in the middle of the night on a regular basis. Or maybe she was curled up in her chair, asleep. In the large closet where the door was always propped open with a dollhouse?

But as Rachel checked each possibility, her heart raced a little faster.

Mallory wasn't in her room.

"She's probably downstairs with Noah," Rachel murmured aloud, in the hopes of convincing herself.

The storm probably woke her, Noah got up with her, letting Rachel sleep. Rachel had always known he would be that kind of father. Together, they must have gone downstairs to investigate the electricity situation.

More determined than afraid now, Rachel went back into the hall, letting the lousy flashlight lead the way. Normally, she walked around the house in the dark. She didn't need a flashlight. But tonight, she did.

"Hey, guys?" she called softly as she came down the stairs, flashlight in one hand, railing under the other. She could hear the battery backup for her computer beeping, but otherwise the house was silent. "Noah? Mal?" Her voice got louder as she reached the bottom of the staircase, that unnamed dread growing again.

No one answered.

"Noah?" she called loudly. She turned right, entering the hall, passing the spare room and the bathroom on her way to the utility room. She flashed the beam of light. The dryer was open, clothes visible. There was a laundry basket on the floor and another on top of the washing machine. No Noah or Mallory, and the door on the breaker box was closed.

"Noah, where are you?" She walked back out into the hall, checking the spare room and the bathroom on her way back to the kitchen. Now she was scared.

Where were they? She looked around the kitchen, flashing the light beam that seemed to be getting dimmer. Chester was asleep under the table. But where were Noah and Mallory?

Could they have gone outside?

But why would they have done that? It was still raining. There was no way to turn the electricity back on from outside.

Rachel moved slowly toward the kitchen door, studying every familiar object in the kitchen, looking for something out of place. She saw the chairs pushed in, legal pad of notes she and Noah had made still on the table. Two mugs on the counter beside the sink. Nothing was out of place or had been disturbed.

Without thinking, she picked the phone up from its cradle on the wall and held it to her ear. She was a little unnerved but certainly not surprised when she heard no dial tone. They lost phone service out here more often than they lost electricity.

She slowly hung up the phone, thinking she had her cell upstairs in her purse. But who was she going to call? The police? What was she going to say? She couldn't find her daughter and her ex in the dark? Considering the fact that Noah had already been hauled into the police station once in the last twenty-four hours, that wasn't a call she wanted to make if she didn't have to.

They had to be outside.

Rachel started for the door, and the flashlight beam waned again. Remembering there was another flashlight in the kitchen junk drawer, she backtracked, pulling open the drawer near the phone. The dim light showed a jumble of pens and pencils, baggie ties, a toothbrush, paper clips, and coupons, but no flashlight.

She shoved the drawer shut in annoyance. Where was the red flashlight? She could have sworn she'd seen it there earlier in the evening when she'd grabbed a pen out of the drawer.

Noah. He must have taken it. But where was he?

Rachel went to the door again. As she reached for the doorknob, she stepped into something cold and wet on the hardwood floor. She immediately flashed the light downward, and the beam waned dangerously low.

It was rainwater, tracked in from outside. And . . . she leaned over and, on closer inspection, spotted pieces of grass, or weeds, some dark soil. A large, muddy footprint. Footprints.

She stepped back for a better look, leaning over to lower

the pathetic flashlight over the little puddle. Definitely foot-prints . . . leading into the house.

Snowden wanted to drive, and Delilah didn't argue with him. It was his car, he was the chief of police, and he was the one who had left someone in charge who had screwed up the prisoner transfer.

As they climbed in, she glanced at him in the semidark-ness. He hadn't gone jogging tonight, at least hadn't come by her place. It was probably because of the rain. Or because he was annoyed that she had sent Lopez back to the Gibson place without getting his okay on it first. Truthfully, she hadn't expected him to find anything, or she would have thought it through a little better.

Snowden was upset with himself, though. She could tell he was by the way he held his mouth, so tight that his sen-sual lips were almost pursed.

"You mad at me?" she asked as he pulled out of the sta-tion.

"Put your seat belt on."

She grabbed the belt, clicked it securely.

"No, I'm not angry with you, Sergeant Swift. It's just that we have a chain of command and you should have come to me before sending Officer Lopez back to the Gibsons."

"That's not what I mean and you know it." She didn't know what made her do it, but she slid her hand across the seat to rest it on his thigh.

His muscles tightened beneath her fingertips at once.

"Delilah—" Her name seemed to catch in his throat.

"I'm sorry," she said, keeping her hand on his thigh. "You're right. I got ahead of myself. I guess I was so sure Noah didn't have anything to do with the murders that I was hoping I could prove it to you."

"You still sure?" He glanced at her quickly.

They were just passing the WELCOME TO STEPHEN KILL

sign. There were still a couple of spots of Ellen Hearn's blood on it, but no one but the police and the emergency workers knew that. If you stood back, it just looked like variations in the wood stain of the sign.

"Sure what?" She pulled her hand back.

"Noah's not involved."

"I don't know what I'm sure of anymore. I went home thinking I shouldn't have locked Mattie up. He looked so bewildered when they brought him in. So scared. He didn't look like a man who could have done to the judge what was done to her."

"They never do," Snowden said softly.

For a moment Delilah was quiet. She listened to the steady swish, swish of the windshield wipers. The storm was passing. She couldn't hear thunder any longer, and the sky was dark.

"I don't know what I think," she finally said. "About this case. About anything." She looked at him. "About you and me."

"There can't be a you and me, Delilah."

"I know that. I keep telling myself that." She stared straight ahead at the pavement illuminated by the cruiser's high beams. Toads hopped on the wet blacktop. "But I can't stop thinking about you," she murmured, almost mesmerized by the rhythm of the windshield wipers, the smell of his clean, starched uniform and the masculine scent that clung to him.

"If it's any consolation," he spoke so quietly that she had to listen hard to hear him, "I think about you too. About your hair, about your eyes, the sound of your voice—"

"Alpha 1-A, come in," interrupted the dispatcher's voice over the radio.

Delilah hit the speakerphone button. "This is Alpha 1-A, Sergeant Swift here."

"You with the chief, Swift?"

"Affirmative."

"Got a call from a motorist on County Road 307 who reported one of our cars in a ditch, quarter of a mile west of the Route 22 intersection. Hit a pole. Some power lines are apparently down. We've got a call into the electric Co-op."

Delilah looked at Snowden. "Sounds like our missing car. Any reported injuries?" she asked the dispatcher.

"Motorist said the car had been abandoned," came the crackly voice.

It always amazed Delilah that as far as technology had come in the last decade, police radios were still sometimes plagued with static. She glanced at Snowden. He nodded and mouthed "backup."

"We're headed for the Gibson property. We'll check out the car as we go by and then continue on. Send a car out to the site of the abandoned cruiser, tow truck, you know the drill, and send backup to the Gibson property."

"Ten-four."

"Out," Delilah murmured, and punched the speakerphone off. "So our mentally retarded boy can't read or write, but he can drive a car?" She glanced out into the darkness. "What the hell's going on here, Snowden?"

"I want my mommy!" the little girl whimpered out of the darkness.

"Shhhhh," Azrael shushed, heart pounding, hands shaking.

This wasn't the way this was supposed to happen. It was all wrong.

A lump rose in the angel's throat. It was all wrong, but there was no way to right it. No way to turn back. God had spoken. God had ordered that Mattie must die for his sins . . . or was it for his mother's sins?

Azrael couldn't remember.

It was all so confusing. God's voice had gotten lost in the

storm somehow. Lost in the driving rain. The pain that wouldn't cease.

"I want to go. I want my mommy," the little girl repeated.

Azrael stood in the dark, the beam of the red flashlight pointed down on the wall of Bibles that separated the Angel from duty to God.

The child began to cry softly, reminding Azrael of another child's cry. No, not a child. A monster! A creature with two heads.

"Mattie, come out here!" the angel demanded angrily.

There was movement behind the wall of Bibles.

"Leave him alone!" The little girl's voice was surprisingly strong.

Azrael did not want to injure the child. It was not the child God had ordered His Angel of Death to kill. Not tonight, at least. But Azrael could not disregard the order. Could not fight the need that burned inside.

The Angel of Death gripped the knife tighter and took a step forward.

"Our car, all right." Delilah stood beside Snowden, staring at the wrecked police car in the ditch, illuminated by the headlights of his cruiser. "Nobody here. I checked the car again. Can't see on the other side, but until we know power's been cut, no one belongs over there. No way to tell if any of the downed lines are hot."

He glanced away, his stomach balling into a knot. This just kept getting better and better. There wasn't a chance in hell he was going to keep his job. A serial killer he couldn't catch. A murdered judge. A shaky arrest of a mentally incompetent man. Then he escapes, steals a police car, and wrecks it. He might as well start sending out resumes now. The only bright spot in the whole lousy picture was the thought that if he was no longer a member of the force, there was no reason why he couldn't date Delilah.

She came to stand beside him and waited in silence, looking up to him. In the distance, he could hear the whine of a police siren approaching.

"I think we need to get to the Gibson place," she said. "That's got to be where he's headed."

Snowden walked to the car in silence, and she climbed in on the other side. "Call in and let them know we're leaving the scene."

As chatty as Delilah could be sometimes, she seemed to recognize his need for silence. He shifted the car into reverse, cut off the bubble lights so Mattie wouldn't see them coming, shifted into drive, and hit the gas, fishtailing on the wet pavement.

Car headlights appeared in the driveway, and Rachel halted, barefoot in the wet grass. Who could be coming in the middle of the night?

She clicked off the flashlight, suspicious. The car came around the slight bend in the road, the headlights illuminating the grape trellises that ran along both sides of the drive. The bright white light reflected off the broad, wet grape leaves and she caught a glimpse of the side of the car. It was a black-and-white police cruiser.

Against her will, her heart fluttered. The police had come at night to tell them that Joanne and Mark were dead and that they needed to contact the State Department. The police had come the night Noah had been arrested.

Rachel didn't know that she could stand any more loss. Any more pain.

A thousand thoughts flew through her head as she fought the urge to bolt, waiting for the car to pull up in front of the garage.

Had Noah taken Mallory somewhere to use a phone, perhaps, and been involved in an accident?

But that didn't make any sense. She rarely used her cell

phone, but he knew she had one. And there was no way he would leave the property with Mallory, take the risk of being caught driving with a suspended license. He would have woken her.

Maybe this had nothing to do with Noah and Mallory. Maybe it was Mattie. Had something terrible happened to him in police custody?

By the time Sergeant Swift and Snowden approached her, Rachel was fighting tears.

"What's going on?" She rushed toward them. "Have Noah and Mallory been hurt?"

Sergeant Swift took her outstretched hands. "Are they missing, Mrs. Gibson?"

"Yes. No." She shook her head. Confused. Scared out of her wits now. "I mean, I don't know. I woke up and the electric was out and—" She lifted her gaze suddenly, pulling her hands away. "You're sure this isn't about Noah and Mallory? Why are you here in the middle of the night?" She looked to the police chief. "Snowden?"

"Mattie escaped. We think he took a police car. We've got a wrecked cruiser out on 307. We were hoping maybe you had seen him."

"No. No, Mattie isn't here." Rachel fought to control her emotions. "You arrested him. He was in your custody. I trusted you, Snowden!"

"Mrs. Gibson . . ."

Sergeant Swift's voice, laced with a southern drawl, drew Rachel's attention again.

"Mrs. Gibson, you mentioned Mr. Gibson and your daughter. You don't know where they are?"

"No. The electricity went out." She pointed lamely toward the dark farmhouse. "When I woke up, Noah was gone from bed." Her gaze strayed to Snowden's face, illuminated by the headlights of the car. She couldn't tell what he was thinking, but she knew the fact that she and Noah were sleeping together again had registered in his mind.

Rachel focused on the small blond woman in the yellow rain slicker. "I thought he must have gotten up to check the breaker box but I can't find him."

"And your daughter?"

"I . . . I don't know where she is either." The words, the realization of their meaning, caused bile to rise in her throat, and for a moment Rachel thought she might vomit. She swallowed hard, suddenly feeling as if that sense of dread she couldn't identify had just increased tenfold. God, was she losing her mind?

"She must be with Noah. She must have woken in the storm and he . . . they . . ." Rachel couldn't think of an explanation, and her voice trailed into silence. But then she looked up suddenly. "But there were footprints in the kitchen. I . . . I don't know whose, but someone came into the house. Do you think it was Mattie? Could Mattie and Noah and Mallory be together?"

"I'm going to check the house," Snowden told Delilah, walking back to the car. He removed a flashlight from the front seat. "Keep her out here."

"They're not inside," Rachel called after him as he strode away. But now she wasn't sure. Not of anything. "I don't think they are. I already looked."

"Stay here with her," Snowden repeated, clicking the flashlight on. "Radio me if you see or hear anything. Backup's on the way."

CHAPTER 32

Noah woke slowly, disoriented, confused. He was surrounded by a darkness that was so devoid of light that it almost seemed velvety. As he became more aware of his own body, he realized he was lying on a floor, his face pressed against floorboards. He could feel the ridges under his cheek.

He rolled onto his back, trying to focus on something, on anything. He thought he was in the house, but he wasn't entirely certain.

He ran his hand over his chest and downward. He was wearing a T-shirt, shorts. Something on his feet. Last he remembered, he was naked in bed and had Rachel curled asleep in his arm. There had been a storm, and he had been listening to the rumble of the thunder over the hum of the window air conditioner. Every few minutes, a drum roll of thunder had been followed by a flash of light that illuminated the bedroom, as lightning zigzagged across the sky. He remembered he had been thinking. Even as worried about Mattie as he was, as scared as he was about being a suspect in multiple homicides, he knew he was very lucky. He remembered thinking that he was being given the gift of a second chance at life, something many people desired but few were given.

He remembered wondering who else, what else, could give such a gift but God.

Noah sat up and rubbed his mouth with the back of his hand. He could tell he was in an enclosed place. He could feel walls, objects, something fairly close. Wherever he was, it was hot and humid. The storm seemed to have passed; no thunder rumbled, no lightning flashed, no rain pattered. It was as if he were in the midst of nothingness, and it was one of the most disturbing feelings he'd ever experienced.

He rose to his feet, but forced himself to take his time. It always took his head a couple of minutes to catch up. He still felt a little dizzy, his stomach queasy, but that always happened after a blackout.

Dr. Carson had told him on the phone last week that the scans had shown no organic explanation for the blackouts. He had recommended Noah see a psychiatrist. He had suggested there was a possibility that the blackouts might not be real, that they might be a device his mind was using to cope with all the changes in his life.

Noah didn't care how good a physician Edgar was, there was no arguing this wasn't real.

Noah put out both hands, feeling the still air around him, then in front of him, before taking a cautious step forward. Still nothing. He couldn't feel anything with his fingertips, couldn't hear anything. He took another step.

A sound somewhere beyond him made him freeze. . . .

What was it? A steady, familiar sound, muffled by the walls or whatever was between them. . . .

Noah tried hard to concentrate, still feeling off balance but not sure if it was because of the utter darkness that surrounded him or because he was just coming out of a blackout.

It came to him almost like a light bulb popping on over a cartoon figure. *It is footsteps. . . .*

Noah's heart began to pound as he was overcome by an unidentifiable sense of terror. Terror of something unknown to him, yet so close he could almost taste its squalor.

No. Feelings can't always be trusted. You have to be logical. You have to think, he told himself. He made himself re-focus.

Where were the footsteps?

On hardwood. He *was* in the house. Had to be.

But they were footsteps too heavy to be Rachel's or Mallory's. Mattie wasn't in the house. He was locked up somewhere in a hospital ward. No one should be in the house in what had to be the middle of the night.

As the muffled footsteps moved closer, Noah's anxiety rose. It wasn't just fear and disorientation, it was . . . an overwhelming sense of the need to protect his family. Of threatening evil.

He slid a foot forward, turning his head slightly. As he did, he thought he caught a flash of light. Just a sliver. From under a door?

Had to be.

He must have blindly reached for the door at the same instant as the intruder. It came back so quickly that it struck the toe of Noah's shoe as he stumbled backward. Light blinded him, and he threw up his hands. The moment he recognized who it was, his fear went down a notch, but his anger rose. "What the hell are you doing in my house in the middle of the night?"

"There's something wrong," Rachel muttered, suddenly chilled. She turned and looked toward the house again, and then across the surrounding yard. It was so dark she couldn't see anything beyond the shape of the eaves and the trees around it. Something evil was here . . . someone. She could feel it. She could taste it, like ashes in her mouth. She wrapped her arms around her waist to warm herself, trying to will herself to be reasonable. To think logically. "This shouldn't be taking this long."

"He's searching the house thoroughly." Sergeant Swift's demeanor was relaxed, but she, too, kept looking back at the house. "It takes a couple of minutes if you do it right, and I can guarantee you the chief is doing it right."

"I'm beginning to get scared," Rachel admitted. "I can't imagine where Noah and Mallory could be. The car's here. Even the lawn tractor is here."

"So you think they're together?"

"They've got to be." Rachel heard the tremor in her voice and fought the sting of tears. "Mallory's just a little girl. She won't be five until December. She has to be with Noah. Where else could she be?"

"We have backup coming, ma'am. As soon as another car arrives and the chief comes out and let's us know the house is all clear, we'll find them. They can't be far."

Rachel turned to her, the bright headlights of the car making her squint. "You think Mattie is here, too?" She glanced in the direction of the barn, feeling drawn to it.

"I think there's a good possibility." Sergeant Swift looked over her shoulder, then back at Rachel. "You see something near the barn, ma'am?"

Rachel shook her head, returning her gaze to the police officer. She hadn't seen anything, but she couldn't help thinking there was something there. "He wouldn't hurt them, you know. I don't know why or how that Bible had verses cut from it, but Mattie didn't do it. He can't read."

"Did you know he could drive?"

Rachel bit down on her lower lip, thinking back to the mystery of the tractor and car being moved. "That's different. He's watched us do it a thousand times. It's relatively simple."

The sergeant frowned. "Well, I hope so, ma'am. For his sake."

She rested her hands on her hips and studied Rachel. "Your little girl, Mr. Gibson gets along with her?"

Rachel dared another quick look in the direction of the barn. If Mattie had run away, if he'd tried to come home, wasn't that where he would go? Not to the house, but to his room in the cellar? To the place where he felt safe? "Of course they get along. Noah loves Mallory."

"Not his daughter, is she?"

Rachel set her jaw, wondering where this questioning was going, afraid she knew. "Why do you ask, Sergeant?"

She shrugged. "Just wondering."

"Noah loves Mallory. He would never hurt her, if that's what you're thinking," she insisted, her tone changing from defensive to angry. "Never."

"Prison changes a man." The policewoman glanced casually at Rachel. "I'm just saying . . . a man comes home to find his wife, ex-wife or not, has a child by another man. Could make him angry. Could make him—"

"Sergeant!" Rachel almost shouted it. "I won't stand here and listen to this, do you understand me? You don't know Noah. You don't know what kind of person he is. How good a person he is. All you know is what people have told you."

"I know the facts. I know . . ."

Sergeant Swift's last words were lost to Rachel's ears as she caught a flash of light in the barn cellar window. "Mallory!" she cried, taking off at a run. "Mallory! Noah!"

"Mrs. Gibson, stop. Halt!" Sergeant Swift ordered.

But all Rachel heard was her own pounding footsteps as she ran barefoot through the wet grass toward the barn.

Ah, hells bells, Delilah thought as Mrs. Gibson took off.

Delilah didn't know what to do. Short of tackling her, there was no way she was going to stop this woman. She knew the look in her eyes too well.

So, now what? Go after her? What if McConnell was in there? There was no way to say, at this point, whether or not he was dangerous. Or should she stay with the car as Snowden had ordered? Either way, he was going to be pissed.

Delilah jerked the car door open and leaned over and grabbed her flashlight. As she stood, she heard a door slap shut and spun around. Two people with a single flashlight were approaching. At once, she recognized Snowden's tall, broad-shouldered form.

"Mrs. Gibson just took off," she called, jogging toward them. The rain had ceased but the ground was saturated, and her shoes slipped in the wet grass.

"Took off where?"

"Where's my wife? What's going on here?" the man with Snowden demanded.

It was Noah Gibson; Delilah recognized his voice.

"She saw something, Chief." Delilah eyed Gibson. Snowden didn't have him handcuffed, but he had him on a pretty short lead. "She just took off toward the barn. I guess she's looking for the little girl."

"Mallory? Mallory's missing? And you didn't tell me?" Noah exploded.

Snowden halted on the end of the sidewalk where Delilah met them. "Noah, I need you to have a seat in the patrol car."

The ex-priest looked up at Snowden. "You didn't tell me Mallory was missing. Why the hell didn't you tell me?" he demanded. "What's going on here? What else aren't you telling me?"

"I'm sure she's here somewhere, Mr. Gibson," Delilah said, trying to defuse his anger. She looked to Snowden. "We need to find Mrs. Gibson. I'm thinking McConnell could be in the barn."

"Where's the backup we called for?" Snowden strode toward the car parked in the driveway between the house and the barn. "If you'll just have a seat in the back, Noah, we'll check out the barn, send Rachel back—"

Delilah caught movement out of the corner of her eye and turned back to see Noah cut behind Snowden and sprint into the darkness.

"Halt, Noah," Snowden shouted. "You can't go in there. I'm ordering you to halt."

"So shoot me," Noah hollered as he disappeared behind the garage.

"Goddamn it!" Snowden barked, startling Delilah. "Where's our backup? We need more men out here."

Delilah ran for the car. "I'll call it in again, Chief.

Noah crept through the back door of the barn, praying no one heard the squeak of the ancient iron door hinges. He had to find Mallory and Rachel. He didn't know what was going on, but the sense of imminent danger pressing on his chest pushed him forward in the pitch darkness.

Snowden had said little in the house beyond the fact that the power was out and that Mattie was missing and suspected to be on the property. He said Mattie had stolen a car and that the police were looking for him. He'd suspiciously asked Noah why he was in the spare room in the dark with the door closed, but luckily Noah had been able to offer the lame explanation that he was looking for a flashlight.

When Snowden told him that Rachel was outside with Sergeant Swift, Noah began to get the uneasy feeling that even though he didn't know what was going on, something awful was about to happen. Nothing Snowden was telling him made sense, but he had feared that if he questioned Snowden too hard, he'd wind up in handcuffs, and then what good would he be to Mattie?

But Snowden had said nothing about Mallory. He hadn't told him that Mallory was missing.

Dear God, he prayed as he crept through the barn, hands thrust out to prevent running into anything. *Please don't let anything happen to her. Please protect her.*

All Noah could think of was that Mattie had come to the house, somehow gotten in, and taken Mallory with him. Why, he didn't know, except that Mallory had always been there to comfort him. Maybe he just wanted her. As scared as he was, he still couldn't believe Mattie would hurt Mallory.

But he wouldn't have believed Mattie could outsmart the police and steal a police car either.

Thankful he had cleaned out the main level of the barn recently, Noah made his way to the front in the dark, feeling his way. He needed to get downstairs to Mattie's room before Snowden and his sergeant busted in.

In the distance, he heard the soft but distinctive cry of a police siren.

Noah's toe hit something hard, and he had to bite down to keep from crying out. Elsewhere in the darkness, the air seemed to stir, and he froze. There was someone else there. Question was, who? He knew it wasn't Snowden or the female officer. He had no doubt they'd enter the barn with flashlights and guns blazing.

Once again, he was overwhelmed by a feeling of something oppressive. Frightening. Vile.

He took another step forward, his heart hammering in his throat.

Again the air stirred, and he halted. He thought he could hear breathing. There was definitely someone there. Suddenly, he caught a scent. It took a moment for his brain to identify it, and then he felt as if a weight fell from his shoulders. "Rache?" he called softly.

"Noah?" Her muffled cry came from directly in front of him.

He threw out his arms, walking forward, and found her soft form. He pulled her against him. "It's Mallory," she whispered, seeming on the verge of a breakdown. "I woke up and you were gone and Mallory was gone. I thought she was with you."

"I had a blackout and somehow I ended up in the nursery.

I haven't seen her. I woke up dressed, in the babies' room. I had photo albums out. Of the boys, of you and me. Of Mom and Dad. I don't remember even taking them out."

"It's OK," she whispered, her voice seeming to get stronger. "We'll figure it out."

Still holding on to her arms, he took a step back. He still couldn't really see her face. "You think Mallory's with Mattie?"

"I saw a flash of light through the cellar window. I wanted to get to Mattie first. I couldn't bear it if the police hurt him. He might not understand." Her voice trembled again.

"I know. It's going to be all right, though." His arm around her, he turned in the direction of the door that led down to the cellar. "We'll turn him over to the police. We'll make Snowden swear he'll be taken care of."

Noah stopped where he thought the door had to be and reached out with his free hand. At first, he found nothing but still air, but as he probed the darkness, he was rewarded with the rough surface of the door. He found the knob and opened it.

A faint light shown from somewhere downstairs, beyond the tunnel vision of the staircase, and again Noah's heart tripped in his chest. It had to be Mattie. He must have had a flashlight. "Mattie?" he called. "Mattie, it's Noah. You down there?"

Rachel caught the waistband of Noah's shorts and followed him down the steps. "Mattie?" she called softly, obviously trying not to frighten him. "Is Mallory down there with you?"

"Mama! No—"

Mallory's voice was cut off suddenly, as if someone had clamped a hand over her mouth.

"Mallory!" Noah ran down the steps, still unable to see anything. Just as he reached the bottom of the staircase, the flashlight went out, and they were again in the dark.

CHAPTER 33

As the light was extinguished, Rachel stepped off the last step, reaching out to grab Noah's arm. She made a tiny sound but managed to choke it back.

"Shhh," Noah soothed, wrapping his arm around her shoulder. He stood perfectly still, hoping his eyes would adjust to the darkness and he might be able to see something. It was pitch black, as if he were blindfolded.

He could hear Mallory making soft little hiccupping sobs. He could feel the presence of evil.

No, not Mattie. Not Mattie, he kept saying over and over in his head. But there was no way to deny it. Not now.

"Mattie," he called out, using an authoritative tone. "You need to let Mallory go. She's afraid." He slid his foot forward, bringing Rachel with him. The wall that enclosed the staircase would have blocked his vision, even if the light came back on. He had to get closer.

The sound of police sirens was growing louder; they could hear it even through the walls of the barn. He knew he only had a couple of minutes more, tops, before the cops would bust in. If he couldn't get Mattie to release Mallory and come to him, there was no telling what they might do.

"Mattie, please. We know you wouldn't hurt Mallory, but you have to let her go," Rachel begged.

"Come closer and she'll die," came a gravelly voice out of the darkness.

Noah froze, pulling Rachel to him. *Who is that? Is that Mattie talking? Mattie had never spoken a word in his thirty-eight years. It can't be.*

But Mallory had said he talked to her. . . .

"No, please. Don't hurt her," Noah said. "I'm standing still. I'm standing right here."

Rachel was holding on so tightly to Noah that her blunt fingernails bit into his arm. Every muscle in his body was tense, the hair on the back of his neck standing up on end.

Noah didn't know what to do. What to say. The voice was so . . . eerie. Almost inhuman. "Mattie? Is that you? I can't see you. Could you turn the flashlight on? So we can talk?" He slid the other foot forward, trying to see around the wall. The voice had come from the direction of Mattie's fort, built from his Bibles.

To Noah's surprise, the flashlight clicked on and dull light shone from around the corner.

"I just want to see you," Noah assured Mattie. "Don't be afraid. We just want to be sure Mallory's all right."

"Serves her right if she dies too," came the eerie voice.

Rachel gripped his arm, putting more of her weight against him, as if she was about to collapse.

He turned his head to brush his lips against her temple. "Trust me," he breathed. "I won't let anything happen to her. I would die for her."

"More sin. Nothing but sin around me. Sinners must be punished," the voice announced. "Child of sin."

"No, no, she isn't!" Rachel released Noah and stepped

around the corner. "She isn't a child of sin, do you hear me? I was married to her father when she was conceived!"

Noah felt as if someone had punched him in the stomach. He sucked in a breath of air, but he didn't feel as if he was getting any oxygen. Was it true? Was Mallory his daughter? Or had Rachel just lied to protect her child as any mother would have?

"Noah . . ." Rachel whispered as she reached behind her, took his hand, and pulled him forward, around the corner of the staircase.

He came into full view of the Bible fort, but he couldn't see anyone. Not at first, at least. The light was coming from behind it, limiting his vision. There he made out a form of someone hunched over, hiding, the flashlight held low so there was no direct light. Inside the fort, he could make out another dark form.

"She's Noah's child, Mattie," Rachel said loudly. "Conceived days before he went to prison." She clutched her hands together. "Let her go, Mattie."

"Yes, let her go, Mattie," the voice ordered.

Noah stared in confusion at the fort Mattie had built from his Bibles. It wasn't Mattie speaking.

Out of the corner of his eye, Noah caught a flash of movement behind the wall of Bibles. A little blond pigtail.

"Noah!" Mallory shrieked, leaping up and falling forward. The makeshift wall crashed to the floor, Bibles tumbling, sliding.

"Mallory!" Rachel lunged forward.

At the same moment, the form behind the far Bible wall rose up, bringing the flashlight with him, partially illuminating the room. Noah saw Mattie scramble after Mallory, reaching out with his big, meaty hands. Behind him, the form crashed through the rear wall.

Mallory tripped on the loose Bibles and fell. Mattie arched his back, reaching out for her, trying to cover her little body with his. The stranger dropped the flashlight, raising a long-bladed knife, poising it over Mattie's back. The man . . . No, it was a woman!

"Mattie, look out!" Noah threw himself headlong past Mattie. As he fell on top of the fallen Bibles, he grabbed the woman's thrashing legs. She screamed, a terrifying guttural sound sputtering from her mouth.

Noah wrapped his arms around her legs, bringing her down. "Get them out!" he hollered. "Run, Rachel!"

The woman fell so hard on top of Noah that she knocked the breath out of him. She wasn't tall, but she was heavy. Solid. She smelled of vanilla flavoring and rot.

The flashlight had hit the floor and rolled and was lost somewhere in the pile of Bibles, now emitting only a weak, yellow half moon of light.

Noah felt the blade sink into the back of his right thigh. It burned like fire.

Mallory was screaming. Mattie was making awful, animal-like grunts as Rachel tried to get him to his feet, out of the danger.

Noah flailed wildly, trying to reach the knife in his attacker's hand. He still couldn't see who it was. She was muttering under her breath. Chanting. He felt as if he was being crushed by evil.

The knife drove into his thigh, tore at his flesh like an animal's talon. He could feel his life's blood spilling out, running down his leg.

The woman's strength was inconceivable. Inhuman.

Something banged on the first floor above them. "Police!" a voice hollered.

"Help us! Help!" Rachel screamed.

Noah twisted beneath the weight of his attacker, and as they rolled, he caught a glimpse of her face in the flashlight beam.

It was impossible.

Then he saw the knife. She lifted it high and drew it downward.

It was only instinct, adrenalin, that drove him now. Noah raised his forearm, twisting until he thought his spine would snap. The knife sank into his arm, and blood seemed to fly from the wound. He was covered in blood; he could feel its warmth. Smell it.

Noah didn't want to die. For a long time he had wanted to die. Before prison. Certainly during his incarceration, even after he returned home. He thought he deserved to die for what he had done.

But he didn't want to die now. He wanted to live. He wanted to live to be a husband to Rachel, a father to Mallory, whether she was of his flesh or not.

Somehow, in an effort that seemed to defy the laws of physics, Noah managed to twist under her, rolling into a ball. He heaved his body against her, taking her by surprise. The knife fell from her hand, and his hand, covered in blood, found the hilt.

He raised it over her as she grunted and groaned beneath him, kicking at him wildly. Her sensible brown shoe caught him in the side. Her fist found his jaw. She grabbed a handful of his hair and pulled with all her might. She wasn't going to let him go. Not alive.

"Sinners must die. Sinners must die," she chanted in her unearthly voice.

Only seconds before, Noah had told Rachel he was willing to die for Mallory. He wondered now if he was willing to kill for her, for them?

Mallory had a right to a father. Rachel had a right to be loved. He wanted to love her.

God forgive me. Noah raised the knife and lowered it, tears filling his eyes as he watched it come down.

She grunted, convulsed as the blade sank into her side. At the same moment, she released his hair and he managed to throw himself backward. More Bibles tumbled. Hit him in the head.

"Police!" Footsteps pounded on the staircase.

Noah rolled onto his back and threw the knife as far as he could, into the darkness, out of his attacker's reach. "Here," he groaned, suddenly feeling light-headed. He meant to call out to the police, but bile rose in his throat and he thought he might be sick. The room seemed to be spinning around him.

Bright lights. Voices. A bath of warmth. At first, he thought he might be having a blackout, but this was different. More serene. More surreal.

"Noah? Noah!"

He heard Rachel's voice. He wanted to ask her if she was all right, if Mallory was all right, but the words wouldn't form on his tongue. He forced his heavy eyelids open and saw her face, backlit by brilliant white light. She was as lovely as any angel he had ever imagined.

"Oh my God. Oh my God, he's been stabbed," Rachel threw over her shoulder. "He's bleeding to death. Someone call an ambulance!"

She sounded so scared that he wanted to reach out, to take her in his arms and tell her everything was going to be all right. Even if he died now, he was going to be all right. They all were.

But his eyelids were too heavy. His arms wouldn't respond. He couldn't find his voice. The warmth was going out of the room. Cold . . . so cold. Slowly, Rachel's face faded until Noah fell into the darkness again.

"Get something to compress the wounds," Delilah told Rachel. "Anything."

Delilah fell to her knees to get a better look. Noah Gibson lay unconscious on the cellar floor in a pool of gore, surrounded by Bibles. There was a lot of blood, at least three stab wounds. It was hard to tell because he was covered in blood; the floor was covered in blood. She checked his pulse; he was still alive, but the beat was weak.

"Here." Rachel Gibson dropped to her knees beside Delilah,

amazingly calm considering the circumstances. "Will this work?" She offered a stack of clean sheets, and only then did Delilah realize Rachel's hands were shaking.

Delilah grabbed a sheet and laid it across the largest of his thigh wounds. His jeans were torn and the wound gaped open, blood still pouring from it. She was afraid his femoral artery had been hit; if it had, she doubted he'd make it to the hospital.

"I said, hands behind your back," one of the officers behind Delilah barked.

Delilah heard a scuffle.

"What are you doing?" Rachel cried over her shoulder. "What are you doing to him? Leave Mattie alone!" She grabbed Delilah's shoulder. "Please make them stop. It wasn't Mattie!"

Delilah looked over to see Ridgley and Cooper, the first backup unit, attempting to wrestle Mattie McConnell to his knees to handcuff him. The mentally handicapped man was resisting, making deep guttural cries of fear.

"Mommy!" little Mallory Gibson cried from Snowden's arms. "Mommy, help Mattie. They're hurting him."

"Someone get this little girl upstairs," Snowden ordered out of Delilah's line of sight.

Rachel squeezed Delilah's arm again. "Make them stop." Tears welled in her bright, frightened green eyes.

Both of them were now covered in Noah's blood.

"Didn't they hear what I said? It wasn't Mattie!" Rachel's voice choked with emotion. "It was someone else, someone trying to kill him. Mattie was trying to protect Mallory."

Delilah grabbed the sheets out of Rachel's arms, took her hand, and showed her how to apply pressure against Noah's thigh wound. No one had said they were looking for a third party. She had entered the cellar assuming Mattie McConnell had been Noah's attacker. It was an error she should not have made. "There was someone else?" She glanced around the cellar room, now illuminated by several high-powered police flashlights and lamps. "Who?"

"I don't know." Rachel used both hands to apply pressure on the wound. "But it was a woman, I'm sure of it. An older woman. Heavyset. I couldn't see her face in the dark," Rachel said. "But she's the one who stabbed Noah. She was trying to kill Mattie. She said she would kill Mallory too." Her voice became thin. "She kept saying something about sin. She sounded crazy. She's the killer, I know she is. The one who killed Judge Hearn and the others."

"How do you know that?" Delilah met her green-eyed gaze.

"This . . . it's going to sound crazy." Rachel looked down, then into Delilah's eyes. "But I could feel it. I could feel the evil in the room."

Delilah was quiet for a second. At face value, it *did* sound crazy, but she had once sat in on a pedophile interrogation and she knew exactly what Rachel meant by being able to feel the evil presence. It had been so strong back in that Atlanta interview room, it had chilled her to the bone.

"All right, we'll find her." Delilah touched Rachel's shoulder as she quickly got up. Her head was spinning with a thousand thoughts. A woman? Could their killer be a middle-aged, heavy woman? Was it Cora? Could that be possible? But she knew that in this crazy world, anything could be possible. "Keeping holding that against his leg."

"But there are more cuts." Rachel choked back a sob. "They're everywhere."

"I know. I'll send someone over to help you. The EMTs are on their way." She hurried over to Snowden, who was still holding Mallory Gibson. The little girl clung to him.

"I want my mommy. I want Noah," Mallory sobbed.

"In just a minute, sweetie," Snowden crooned. "One of my nice policemen is going to take you outside, and Mommy will come in a minute. She's taking care of Noah right now."

Seeing Snowden holding the girl so tenderly brought a lump up in Delilah's throat. She had never seen this side of him. She cleared her throat. "Mrs. Gibson says it wasn't Mattie. She says there was a woman here. Middle-aged. Heavyset. Says she stabbed Noah. Mattie seemed to be her target, but she threatened to kill the others too." She cut her eyes at Mallory. "Mrs. Gibson said she was talking about sin."

"You've got to be kidding me. There's no one else here." Snowden turned one way and then the other, looking around the room. "Someone checked the bathroom."

"Somewhere else in the cellar maybe?" she suggested. "That wall over there is just a partition. Apparently this is where Mattie slept until this week. Lopez found the Bible here."

He murmured under his breath, passing Mallory into her arms. "Get her upstairs; we'll search the building top to bottom. Cooper," he snapped to one of the officers. They had Mattie on his knees, but they still hadn't managed to get the handcuffs around his meaty wrists. "Go easy. No handcuffs. Mrs. Gibson says he's not our man. Get him upstairs. In a car, but no cuffs." He turned back to Delilah as he started for Noah and Rachel. "Get her upstairs. I don't know how this is going to go."

He glanced quickly in Noah's direction, and Delilah caught his meaning. Noah Gibson might not live to make it to the hospital. He might not live to get out of this barn.

It seemed a long walk to Snowden from the bottom of the staircase where he'd stood holding Mallory's small, trembling body to the pile of Bibles where Rachel knelt over Noah. He stooped down, took one of the sheets off the floor, and pressed it to Noah's arm.

"Rachel," he said softly. "You sure there was someone else?"

"Yes, I'm sure!" she flung at him. "A woman."

"Where is she?"

"I don't know." Rachel kept both hands pressed against the bloody sheet she held on Noah's leg. She was wearing shorts and a T-shirt; she was covered in her husband's blood. "It was dark. I was trying to get to Mallory. To get Mattie. Noah knocked the woman to the floor when she tried to stab Mattie in the back. She and Noah were rolling around. I saw the knife, but I didn't see her face. I . . . I think Noah might have stabbed her." She took a great shuddering breath. "Maybe she's lying somewhere here in the cellar. I don't know."

"Is there another exit, other than this staircase?"

"Where are the EMTs?" she asked him, seeming not to have heard his question. "He's bled so much. He's so pale."

"Rachel, listen to me." Snowden leaned closer to her, kneeling down on one knee, laying his arm on her shoulder. "I need to know if there's another way out of the barn from here."

She turned her head to look at him, her big green eyes filled with tears. She nodded. "There's a ladder in the back." She lifted her chin in the direction of the wall that was the partition. "It goes up to the main floor, then on to the loft on the upper floor. But we never use it. The rungs are rotting."

"But it's not boarded up?"

She shook her head.

"All right. You stay here. EMTs will be here any second."

"Where's Mallory?"

"Sergeant Swift took her outside. We'll have one of the EMTs have a look at her, but she's fine. Not a mark on her. Just scared."

"Mattie was protecting her. Do you know that? That must be why he escaped. Somehow he knew the killer was coming here. He must have come into the house, taken Mallory from her bed, and brought her here to protect her. He always felt safe in here. He'd built a fort with Bibles. I didn't really understand why before. It must have had something to do with the killer. He must have had some contact with her.

That has to be how you found the Bible with the verses cut out here."

"We'll sort it all out. We'll find her."

Snowden heard the familiar call of the EMT van's siren, a different tone than his police cars'. "They're here now. We'll get Noah to the hospital."

Snowden got to his feet and, out of habit, brushed his pant legs. When he felt something damp, he looked down. One knee was stained with blood. Noah's blood. He had falsely believed Noah was the killer, and his blood would be on Snowden's hands if Noah died.

More officers trooped down the stairs. Lopez must have called guys in from home, which had been good thinking. Especially if there would be a manhunt.

"Search the entire barn, all three floors," he ordered. "The suspect is still missing. We're looking for a middle-aged, heavyset woman, that's all we know. She could be wounded. Peterson, get your dog."

On the way up the cellar stairs, Snowden passed the EMTs. Everyone nodded. No one spoke.

Snowden prayed for the two men and the woman. Prayed for their healing hands. Prayed Noah would survive, so he could apologize.

Azrael stumbled through the darkness. No longer able to run. Lost. Scared. Abandoned.

Where was God now? Where was His commanding voice? But the holy presence was gone. Azrael had never felt so empty, so alone.

The Angel of Death had succeeded in all that God had asked until tonight. Was this it? Was that all there was? Was there no second chance?

Azrael would go back. Azrael would kill Mattie, kill him

for his mother's sin of adultery, just as Azrael had killed the father that day. Knocked him off his ladder.

God was all-powerful. God would not allow His Angel to fail.

Would he?

But God was not here in the dark woods and with each step, Azrael felt further and further removed from the Creator.

She pushed forward through the tangle of underbrush, briars scratching her face, her hands, and she fought a sob of despair. Her shoes were wet and uncomfortable. They rubbed on her corns.

Why have you forsaken me?

She had once been Azrael, but now she was just Alice again. Just plain, ugly, insignificant Alice Crupp. No, no it wasn't possible.

Alice stumbled to a walk, remembering the weight of the first brick in her hand before she had hurled it at Johnny Leager. She had not been afraid. God had told her that the sinner had deserved to die for his transgression of adultery. For committing carnal sin with the whore. Hadn't He?

She remembered the weight of the first brick and how it had made her feel powerful. The adulterer's first cry of pain, the first spatter of blood, it had made her heart pound in excitement, in a pleasure she had not known for a very long time.

The fear in Pam's eyes, like the other adulterer's, had electrified her. Never had Alice ever had such control over another human being, such utter authority. She was no longer the invisible, insignificant bread lady to be ignored. She was one of God's powerful angels, with the authority over life and death in her very hands.

Walking into Skeeter Newton's apartment that night, she had been glowing with authority. She had known, climbing those steps, carrying the machete she had found under Mattie's bed, that she was better than the thief. Killing the thief had been easier than she had anticipated, easier than the first adulterer, who had tried to defend himself with his arms, or the second, who had made little squeaking sounds as Alice had poured the gasoline over her, then flicked the lighter.

The thief had been high on marijuana or worse, crazed out of his mind. He had never even questioned Alice's presence. His hands had come off so neatly, with less force than she had anticipated. And the blood . . . the sweet smell of it.

Alice lifted her wet hand to her nostrils, inhaling deeply as she pressed forward, through the dark woods. It was the ex-priest's blood on her hands now. She liked the smell of blood and the power it gave her. The blood liked her.

She raised her head, thinking she saw a flash of light through the tree limbs. Headlights maybe?

She thought about the homosexual. The lesbian had, perhaps, been the easiest of all. Alice had felt bold that night. She had known what time the lesbian would walk her cute little dog. She had known that the lesbian wouldn't put up much of a struggle, not, at least, if Alice took her by surprise. The lesbian had known she had committed sin by lying with another woman. She had known, in her heart, that Alice had the right to judge her.

The crucifixion had not been planned. It had made Alice smile later when she was taking the little dog home, feeding it a treat and shutting it safely in the house until the police could find it. God had not planned for Alice to crucify the lesbian on the town's welcome sign. That had been Alice's idea. All her own. Clever. No one had known how clever Alice could be before, had they? Not even God.

Alice lifted her head, feeling stronger now. She spotted a clearing. She broke through the trees, pushing wet, hanging, tree branches aside, wading through the weeds.

So what if she had failed to kill Mattie? She would go back again. She would let the hullabaloo die down. Wait for the police to say their leads had gone cold, and then she would go back. She would kill the man who could not speak but could play the pipe organ like an angel.

Surely he was not an angel, but a work of the devil. He deserved to die as the spawn of the illicit affair all those years ago. Alice would kill Mattie and then she would kill the others; the ex-priest and his wife. He was a murderer. She was a liar.

The child had not been born of wedlock as she had said. It wasn't possible. If it had been possible, she would have known. God didn't have to tell Alice anything. Alice knew everything that happened in Stephen Kill. Anything she didn't learn on her own by sitting quietly, listening, those gossips Cora and Clara told her.

Yes, Alice would definitely kill the child born from un-lawful sex by the priest's wife. She deserved to die. They all deserved to die, to scream out in pain, to suffer, to die and rot in their graves.

Alice tripped on a fallen log and went down on one knee. She winced in pain as her hands hit the ground and she pushed herself upright on her knees. It was wet where she fell. She heard lapping water.

She looked up, both hands pressed into the wet grass and she thought she could make out the edges of a large pond. She could smell the familiar scent of rotting vegetation and hear the croak of bullfrogs.

A pond? It had to be Horsey Mill Pond. Alice had fished here as a child.

But that meant she was going the wrong way, that she was walking north instead of west. Home was west. In the dark, when she ran from the barn, she must have gotten her bear-ings confused. Her car was parked off County Road 307.

I'm going the wrong way, she thought, her heart tripping in her chest.

But this was all wrong. She felt the power, her confidence wane. She had to get home. Home into her nightgown, into her bed. They mustn't suspect. If they did, the punishments would end. The police wouldn't understand. They wouldn't let her feel the blood.

Somewhere in the darkness, in the direction she had come, Alice heard a dog bark and then howl. It was no stray, but a dog tracking something. There was no mistaking that sound. It was a dog tracking her . . .

Alice choked back a sob, genuinely afraid for the first time in months. She tried to stand, but she was too weak and she fell forward, her face slapping against the warm, slimy water of the mill pond. A twig snapped behind her, startling her and she rolled over, half sitting up.

"Who . . . who's there?" she called, her voice trembling. Despite the warm night air, she was cold now. Cold and light-headed. "Is someone there?"

With the passing of the storm, the sky had begun to clear and the moon had begun its ascent. Alice hadn't been able to see it in the woods, but its light now shone palely through the last of the dark clouds.

The outline of a tall figure materialized, illuminated by the moonlight, and for a moment, Alice feared it was the police. But it was not. The police would have identified themselves; they would have rushed toward her, not understanding what she had done or why.

The apparition moved calmly, slowly toward her.

"Who's there?" Alice repeated, squinting to see in the semidarkness. "Please . . ." Moonlight on a night like this could play tricks on you.

"Alice . . ."

It was a voice Alice did not recognize. Not the voice of God, but another voice. Was it heaven sent? "Yes?" Alice responded.

The figure did not speak again, but Alice watched as it drew closer, opening its arms, revealing gossamer wings.

"An angel," Alice breathed. "Oh, God, you have not forsaken me," she cried joyfully.

Still, the angel approached, and Alice stared in awe as it drew her into its wings and slowly lowered her backward. Alice was so surprised by the specter that she didn't struggle. She surrendered to the wings, gazing up in wonder.

But then the water began to seep into her nostrils.

"No," Alice murmured. She tried to sit up, but she couldn't. The angel . . . the creature was holding her down, pushing her head under the water.

Alice struggled in earnest.

"No, no," she cried as the back of her head sunk into the soft mud and the stinking, murky water poured into her mouth. Into her nose.

Alice choked. Gagged. She tried to hold her breath, but the water filled her mouth, her throat, her lungs. She attempted to suck in a breath of air when she could hold her breath no longer. Fire spread through her chest, filling her with agony.

She flailed, kicking her feet, trying to tear away the inhuman grip, the hands that held her under the water.

But Alice was no match for her attacker's strength. As her lungs caught fire and filled with water, she heard a voice in her head. At first it was just one, then many. She heard the adulterers scream in pain. Not just Johnny and Pam, but Jack, too. Then the thief. Then the homosexual.

She felt their anguish. It filled her, consumed her. And then, in the darkness of her own agony, she saw a light ahead, saw the fires of hell. She opened her mouth and screamed a silent scream that, at that moment, she realized would be eternal.

EPILOGUE

Five days later

Delilah sat beside Snowden in the cushy blue vinyl chair of the waiting room, pulling through a pile of paperwork in the plain manila folder on her lap. She was almost ready to submit her final report. She was waiting for the autopsy on Alice Crupp to come back, but it would be pretty cut and dry. The police dog had found her less than a mile from the Gibson home, already dead. She'd obviously fallen into the water, due to blood loss from the stab wound she'd incurred fighting Noah Gibson. She'd drowned in the mill pond, poor crazy old soul.

With the autopsy report expected by the end of the week, all Delilah had left to do was interview Noah Gibson, who had taken a turn for the good the day before and was now expected to live, despite how close he had come to death the night he was attacked. Later, over cups of coffee in the staff break room, the EMTs had related to Delilah that they had had to restart his heart twice before making it to Beebe Hospital.

Fortunately for Noah, a surgeon had been available, and after several blood transfusions, he was now expected to make a full recovery. Because of the depth of the thigh wound and the ligaments that were cut, he would need physical therapy and might walk with a limp for the rest of his life, but considering the circumstances, he was a lucky man to be alive. Some might even say it was a miracle.

"Snowden. Sergeant Swift."

Rachel Gibson approached them, smiling. Her face was pale and she appeared a little gaunt, but her smile lit up her face. "He's awake and he seems to think he can answer some of your questions."

"Please, call me Delilah." Delilah rose, tucking her folder under her arm. Rachel's smile was infectious. She was truly a beautiful woman, and she radiated happiness this afternoon. "How's he doing?"

"Doctors say great." Rachel opened her arms and brought her hands together. "The surgeon says there's really no other explanation for his survival except that Noah wouldn't stop fighting for his life. They estimate he lost almost two liters of blood before they could stop the bleeding. He should have been dead. Now they're talking about letting him out in the next two to three days."

"That's good news." Snowden smiled down on her.

"So you want to come in?" She opened a hand, leading the way.

Delilah followed Snowden and Rachel, but today, she felt no sense of competition with this woman. She was just happy Noah was going to live, happy no one else had died that night. Happy the killer had finally been found.

They walked into the private hospital room and were greeted by Noah Gibson, who was sitting up in bed, pillows piled behind him. He looked good for a man who had been so close to death. Looked good for any man, Delilah couldn't help thinking. Not only was he handsome with his classic bone structure and full head of hair, but there was something about his face that was different than it had been. Delilah had always thought he looked sad before. Now, like Rachel, he seemed to radiate light.

"Thanks for seeing us." Snowden shook Noah's hand and stepped back. "We won't stay long."

"Just a few things we want to go over with you." Delilah tugged a pen out of her breast pocket and opened up her folder to follow her notes.

"You want me to leave?" Rachel asked.

"Won't be necessary," Snowden said.

"Because we never got to interview Miss Crupp," Delilah started, "we'll never know exactly how this happened. We did discover from her medical records, however, that she was recently diagnosed with a possible psychological disorder."

"A psychological disorder?" Rachel asked. "What kind of psychological disorder?"

"I shouldn't even be telling you this." Delilah glanced at Snowden, then back at Rachel. "But you've been through so much. You deserve an explanation." She sighed. "Dr. Carson wasn't entirely sure what was wrong with Miss Crupp because she refused to seek further diagnostic treatment, but she claimed to be hearing voices, among other things."

Rachel and Noah exchanged glances.

"It's not a complete explanation, I know, but the woman was obviously very sick." Delilah glanced down at her folder. "Anyway, I understand your need to continue to keep private the information told to you while you were a priest, Noah, but—"

"I'll help you out as best I can," Noah said.

Delilah glanced at Snowden. "There's also some information the chief and I believe you and Mrs. Gibson need to have, concerning Mattie McConnell."

"Mattie? I thought he was absolved of any wrongdoing." Rachel turned to Snowden.

"Hon, let the officer speak." Noah took Rachel's hand and drew her toward him.

Rachel sat down on the edge of the bed.

Delilah started again. "After talking with Miss Cora Watkins and her sister, I discovered that Miss Crupp had left high school in the middle of her senior year, and rumor had been that she was pregnant. A Jack McConnell left town about the same time, but no one made any connection. Mr. McConnell returned, of course, but it was many years later before Miss Crupp moved back to Stephen Kill."

"OK," Noah said. "I vaguely remember hearing something like that."

"Well, I didn't. I questioned Miss Cora recently about Miss Crupp and why she had left town, and she never mentioned a possible pregnancy. I talked to Miss Cora again two days ago. Turned out she did know that Miss Crupp was sent away by her father to have her baby, and it was then put up for adoption. Cora was just trying to protect her friend—that was why she didn't tell me."

"I'll be damned," Noah muttered. "Cora with a conscience when it came to gossip? Who'd have believed it?"

Delilah gave a little smile. "Well, if she'd been a little more forthright, I might have looked more closely at Miss Crupp. Anyway, I did a little research, and it turns out Miss Crupp did become pregnant. One week after a Miss Alice Crupp gave birth in a Maryland hospital, a Jack McConnell took custody of a newborn male. The adoption was private so the records were sealed, but according to Cora Watkins, Jack McConnell is the father of Alice's baby."

"Mattie is Alice's son?" Rachel breathed, her eyes widening.

"We believe so. Apparently, instead of putting his grandchild up for adoption, Alice's father allowed the baby's father to take him. Maybe because of Mattie's handicap. Cora stayed in Maryland, got a job, tried to make a life for herself. I'm guessing she was never able to come to terms with the sin she saw herself as having committed. We found notebooks in her home filled with the ramblings of a mad woman.

All about sin. About God punishing sinners. About angels being sent to kill sinners. We also found a list of names written in blood. Johnny Leager's, Pam Rehak's, Newton's, and Hearn's names were all crossed out." She hesitated. "Yours was next on the list, Noah."

Rachel covered her mouth with her hand.

Delilah was surprised Noah didn't react in response to the idea that he was one of the killer's targets. Maybe the man had been through so much that it didn't matter, not now.

"So why was she after Mattie, then, if I was to be her next victim? We all know what sin I committed. But Mattie? What could he have possibly ever done wrong?"

"That I don't know," Delilah admitted. "From the footprints we found in your house that night, we think Miss Crupp entered your home, looking for you."

"Thinking Mattie was in jail," Rachel whispered.

"She went all the way up to your bedroom." Delilah rested her gaze on Noah's pale face. "But she couldn't find you."

"Because I'd blacked out in the nursery."

"At that point, we don't know what possessed her, but she left the house and entered the cellar where she apparently found Mattie and Mallory."

"And then she decided to kill Mattie?" Rachel questioned. "Why?"

"Guess we'll never know. Maybe it had something to do with her sins. Maybe she just got confused.

Noah exhaled. "So you think this was all just the result of a woman gone mad?"

"We suspect she had been stalking Mattie for some time. His name appears in the notebooks again and again even though he doesn't seem to have originally been a target. I haven't read through everything, but it appears that she came to your farm several times in June and July in the middle of the night to see him."

Rachel looked at Noah. "No wonder Mattie was so scared. It makes sense, doesn't it? Alice must have been coming to the house at night and that was why he started acting so strangely. Why he seemed so angry sometimes. Who knows what she was saying to him."

"But you never saw Miss Crupp at your place?"

Noah shook his head. "We never saw her."

"And you never spoke to Miss Crupp about any of your parishioners who might have previously sought counsel with you?"

Noah scowled. "Certainly not, Sergeant."

"So how did Alice know anything about Johnny Leager or Pam Rehak, or Skeeter or the judge?" Rachel rose from the bed. "She never worked at the church. She never had any access to any of Noah's files." She turned back to her ex-husband in the bed. "Cora," she said suddenly. "Cora told Alice."

"Exactly." Delilah exhaled. "I got a teary confession out of her. She said, over the years, she may have let some things *slip*. She said she never told anyone else, but she saw no harm in telling her sister and her best friend."

Noah hung his head. "That's awful." He looked up. "Does that make Cora an accessory?"

Delilah shook her head. "No. She had no idea her friend would go off the deep end. It was just more juicy gossip to share while they waited for the banana bread to bake." She looked to Noah. "But just to clarify, you never provided Miss Cora Watkins with any information regarding your parishioners either?"

"You know the answer to that, Sergeant."

Delilah looked down at her file; this was all really a formality. He was right. She knew the answers. But any job worth doing was worth doing right, her mama always said. Besides, she wanted Snowden to know she was thorough. She wanted him to know how seriously she took this job, how much it meant to her.

She pulled a notepad out of her pocket. "Now, if you could just go through the events of the other night, step by step, I'll get some notes and get out of here."

Noah related the events of that night, and in fifteen minutes Delilah and Snowden were saying their good-byes. Outside the hospital room, in the empty hall, Delilah stopped to put away her pen and notepad. She was relieved to have the case settled, but a part of her was sorry it would end here. With the case over, she doubted she and Snowden would be working together so closely again. Even if they couldn't have anything else, she wished she could keep working with him. They made good partners.

"You've done an excellent job with this case," Snowden told her. "I'm going to push the city council to let me hire our first detective, and I want it to be you."

She slid her pen into her breast pocket and looked up at him, surprised by the emotion she saw in his handsome face. "A promotion sounds great. Your approval means more."

His blue-eyed gaze met hers, and Delilah's breath caught in her throat as he shocked her by leaning down and covering her mouth with his.

"No one can know," he whispered against her lips. "I mean it. We would both lose our jobs."

Footsteps sounded in the hallway and a nurse appeared, pushing a cart. She didn't seem to notice them in the patient's door alcove.

Delilah took a step back, trying to catch her breath, her lips still tingling from his touch. "You go for a run tonight, you might find my front door open."

"I just might need that run," he said with a chuckle as he started for the elevator, his stride long and businesslike.

Delilah followed, trying not to grin like a fool, her handcuffs jingling as she hurried to catch up.

Noah watched Rachel for a moment in silence.

She stood at the window of his hospital room, looking out on the lawn below, bathed in sunlight. She was the most beautiful woman he had ever known.

"Hey," he said softly. "Want to join me?"

She turned, a smile on her face. "In your hospital bed? You're an injured man, you need your rest."

"Please?"

She glanced at the closed door. "Someone might come in."

He scooted over, trying not to wince. "Come on." He patted the bed beside him. "Best medicine I know."

Rachel only hesitated another moment, and then she kicked off her sandals and climbed into the bed. Noah wrapped his arm around her, and she stretched out beside him, her head on her chest. He smoothed her honey blond hair and kissed the top of her head. He was a lucky man. A blessed man. And he knew it. And he was going to remind himself of it every day for the rest of his life.

"Do you think it's true?" Rachel murmured.

"What?"

"That what Alice did was just the result of a madness?"

"What else could it be?"

She shrugged and then smoothed his hospital gown in a gentle caress. "I don't know. I just can't help thinking she didn't act alone."

"There's no evidence she had an accomplice."

"Sergeant Swift said she heard voices. Mallory said Mattie heard voices. I heard a voice in my nightmares. It was warning me, I think."

He was quiet.

"Noah, have you had a blackout since that night? In the hospital, I mean."

"No."

"And I haven't had one of my nightmares. I also haven't gotten that awful feeling, that feeling that's been haunting me for weeks, months. Not since she died, not once."

He rubbed her arm. "What are you suggesting?"

"Just that, maybe there was something evil in this town and maybe it wasn't Alice, maybe it was just something controlling Alice. Maybe your blackouts had something to do with it. Maybe whatever was making Alice do those things was trying to make you look guilty—to the police. To you."

"I doubt the police would go with that theory. Alice committed the murders. There's forensic proof. Her fingerprints were on that bloody machete."

"You and I know what we experienced. I know what it felt like in the cellar with her that night. I was definitely in the presence of evil. And how could Alice have had the strength to cut Skeeter's hands off? Something had to have given her that strength."

He sighed thoughtfully, not ready to go along with her theory, but not willing to totally dismiss it. "Guess we'll never know."

"Maybe not for sure." She smoothed his beard-stubbled cheek.

"What matters is that it's over." He took her hand and kissed it. "What matters is that I love you and I love Mallory and I love Mattie and I want us to be a family."

She lifted her head, pressing her chin to his chest. "You haven't asked me the question."

"What question?"

"You know what question. About Mallory. About what I said that night about you being her father."

He closed his eyes for a moment and then opened them to look into hers. "It doesn't matter to me if she's mine or not, I only—"

Rachel pressed her finger to his mouth. "She's yours, Noah."

Noah suddenly felt light-headed. "She's mine?" he whispered. "But she's so healthy. How is that possible? The boys—"

"The boys were born with the wrong combination of our genes and she wasn't. She got lucky—we got lucky. Mallory was born perfect. There's no further explanation."

"But she could carry the bad gene?"

"She could. She probably does, but what happened to us—with the boys—could only happen if she married a man who also carries the faulty gene."

"Not likely."

"No, not likely, but they can do so much now. Think where science will be when she's old enough to want a child. Genetic counseling . . . tests."

"Why did you take the chance when we'd decided it wasn't worth the risk?"

"I didn't mean to get pregnant. I actually had gone to the fertility clinic to talk with the doctors about a sperm donation."

"Then I went to jail."

"Then you went to jail, and I found out I was pregnant," she whispered. Her eyes glistened with tears. "I'm sorry I didn't tell you. I was just so angry with you."

"It's all right," he soothed, kissing her forehead, the tip of her nose. "It doesn't matter, nothing matters but us. Us, now." He brushed the hair from her cheek so that he could see her face. "So will you?"

"Will I what?"

"Marry me?"

She glanced down, suddenly looking guilty, then back up at him. "Actually, I didn't exactly tell you the truth there, either."

"What do you mean? I signed the divorce papers your lawyer brought me in prison."

She turned in the bed, lifting up so that she looked down into his eyes. "You signed them, but I didn't," she whispered.

Noah was so shocked for a moment that he didn't know what to say. Then he lowered his head to the white pillow and laughed. Laughed as he hadn't in many years.